House Justice

House Justice

A Joe DeMarco Thriller

MIKE LAWSON

Atlantic Monthly Press
New York

This is a work of fiction. Any resemblance to actual persons, living or dead, is purely coincidental.

Published simultaneously in Canada
Printed in the United States of America

FIRST EDITION

ISBN-13: 978-0-8021-1937-7

Atlantic Monthly Press
an imprint of Grove/Atlantic, Inc.
841 Broadway
New York, NY 10003

Distributed by Publishers Group West

www.groveatlantic.com

10 11 12 13 14   10 9 8 7 6 5 4 3 2 1

For my mother
Antoinette Nicholene Lawson
1921–2009

Acknowledgments

My thanks to Gail Lawson and Shawnessy McKelvey for reading drafts of the book and to my friend Frank Horton for his editing and his advice.

Bruce Farman for his help on the gun stuff. Any errors made on firearms, bullets, and such are mine, and mine alone.

To everyone at Grove/Atlantic—Eric Price, Deb Seager, Jodie Hockensmith, and Michael Hornburg. I'm particularly grateful to Morgan Entrekin for continuing to publish my novels, and my editor, Jamison Stoltz, for all the work he put into this book.

Lastly, to the dream team at the Gernert Company: David Gernert, Erika Storella, Will Roberts, Courtney Gatewood, and Rebecca Gardner.

Prologue

———————◆◆◆———————

The battery was dead.

For six years she had evaded discovery. For six years she had lived in their midst and endured everything she had to endure but now, after all her sacrifices—now, when it was time to go home and accept the medals no one would ever see—now, when she would be given a job where she wouldn't wake up shaking every night, terrified that the next day would be the day she'd be caught—now she was going to die because a car wouldn't start.

She overcame the urge to scream and pound the steering wheel in frustration. She needed to stay in control. She needed to think. But she couldn't stop the tears leaking from her eyes.

She couldn't understand why Carson had waited so long to tell her to flee. As soon as the story appeared in the newspaper she knew she was vulnerable but Carson had told her not to panic, that too many people had attended the meeting. Then, four days later, he sent the text message to her cell phone. Just a single word: eclipse!

Eclipse meant: run. Run for your life.

For the last two years she had been begging Carson to let her go home, and he kept saying that he would but he needed her to stay just a little bit longer. Just give me six more months, he said—and then it was six more after that, and six more after that. The manipulative bastard. If he had kept his word, she would have told her lover that she had to visit a fictitious dying aunt in Bandar-e Maqam and taken a routine, commercial flight to the coastal city, after which a navy SEAL team would have picked her up on the beach. But now she couldn't do that; there was no way she would be allowed to board a plane. So she had to use the backup escape plan, the plan they had never expected to use. And maybe that's why the battery was dead: because someone had forgotten to check on the car they'd parked in the garage so long ago. Or maybe, because Carson waited too long, no one had time to check.

She had fled from the ministry as soon as she received Carson's message and immediately called the four people in her network to alert them. None of them answered. That was bad. If they had been picked up they may have already talked. She knew they'd talk eventually because everybody talked in the end, no matter how strong they were. All she could do was hope they hadn't talked yet.

The backup plan had been for her to pick up a car hidden in a small, private garage two miles from the ministry and then drive to a house twenty miles east of the city. There she would be hidden, for weeks if necessary, until they could transport her safely across the border into either Afghanistan or Kuwait. When she left the ministry, she had wanted to sprint the entire distance to the garage but had been afraid that she would call attention to herself. So she had walked as fast as she could, knowing each minute she spent walking was one more minute for them to get the roadblocks in place.

But now the roadblocks didn't matter. Without a car she had no idea how she would get to the safe house. She couldn't take a bus: there were no bus routes that went near the house. And as for walking or taking a cab . . . the police, the military—and, of course, the brutes from the Ministry of Intelligence and Security—would all have her picture. They'd be showing it to cabdrivers and stopping every woman walking alone—and here, few women walked alone. And if she took a cab, and if the driver remembered her, not only would she die but so would the family who hid her at the safe house.

She forced herself to take a breath, to suppress the rising, screaming panic. Did she have any other options? Any? Yes, maybe one: the Swiss Embassy. The United States didn't have an embassy in Iran but the Swiss did. Moreover, the Swiss were designated as a "protecting power" for U.S. interests in Iran, meaning that if some visiting American got into trouble the Swiss would do their best to help him out. But what she wanted the Swiss to do went far beyond helping some tourist who had lost his passport.

The Swiss Embassy was close, less than a mile from where she was, and if she was careful—if she used the alleys and ducked through buildings—she might make it there and she might live. They would know if she entered the embassy, of course, and it would cause the Swiss enormous political problems, but maybe they would provide her sanctuary until her own people could get her out of the country through diplomatic channels. God knows what sort of trade they'd have to make for her and she couldn't even imagine the international uproar that would ensue, but she didn't care about any of that. She was too young to die.

The way she'd lived the last six years, she'd never had the chance to experience the joys of being young. Her youth had been stolen from her—so they owed her, and to hell with the political fallout that would occur if she ran to the Swiss. She had done her job—and now the diplomats and the damn politicians could do theirs.

Her mind made up, she exited the useless car, ran to the side door of the garage, and threw it open—and was immediately blinded by the headlights of two vehicles. Men armed with machine pistols closed in on her.

She just stood there, head bowed, shoulders slumped in defeat, unable to move. She could feel something draining from her body —and that something was *hope*. There were no options left. There was no place to run or hide. She wished, more than anything else, that she had a gun; if she had had one she would have killed herself.

It was over.

She knew what was going to happen next.

She knew how she was going to die.

Chapter 1

———◆◆◆———

Jacob LaFountaine, director of the Central Intelligence Agency, had
been a second-string middle linebacker at Notre Dame. At age fifty-
two, some of the muscle from his playing days had turned to fat, but
not that much. He was still a bull of a man: six foot two, broad shoulders, strong arms, a deep chest. His legs were thick through the thighs
but short in proportion to his upper body. He had dark hair, muddy
brown eyes set beneath the shelf of a heavy brow, and an aggressive
chin. He rarely smiled and he intimidated everyone who worked for
him.

He looked up in annoyance when Sinclair entered his office.
Sinclair was one of his deputies, a fussy nitpicker whom LaFountaine
didn't like but who was too good at his job to fire. He always looked
anxious when he talked to LaFountaine but today he looked more
than anxious—he looked ill, pale and waxen, as if he might be sick
to his stomach at any moment.

Sinclair held up a disc. "You need to see this," he said.

"What is it?" LaFountaine asked.

"A video that was delivered to the embassy in Kabul."

"I have a meeting in five minutes."

"You need to see this," Sinclair said, surprising LaFountaine with
his firmness.

LaFountaine made an impatient get-on-with-it gesture, and Sinclair put the disc into the DVD player.

"Brace yourself. It's bad," Sinclair said.

LaFountaine looked over at Sinclair, confused by the comment, but at that moment the video began. It showed the upper body of a woman wearing a typical Muslim robe and headdress. A veil covered her entire face, including her eyes. The camera pulled back and showed that the woman was kneeling, swaying slightly as if she was having a hard time maintaining her balance. Her hands were behind her back and LaFountaine thought they might be tied. The camera focused again on the woman's head and then a man's hand appeared and pulled the veil away from her face.

"Oh, Jesus," LaFountaine said.

The woman had been beaten so severely that it was impossible to tell who she was or what she had originally looked like. Her left eye was swollen completely shut, the eye socket obviously shattered. Her right eye was almost closed, and the part of the eye that was visible was filled with blood. Her lips were split, her jaw appeared to be broken, and her nose was a deformed lump.

"Is that . . ."

Before LaFountaine could complete the question, the man's hand appeared back in the picture, now holding a revolver, and the barrel of the weapon was placed against the woman's right temple. LaFountaine stood up but was unable to speak. The gun stayed against the woman's head for three seconds—three seconds that seemed like an eternity to LaFountaine—and during that time the woman did nothing. Because of the condition of her eyes, LaFountaine couldn't see the fear that must be in them, or maybe at this point, he thought, she was beyond fear. Maybe it was relief she was feeling. Then the gun was fired. There was no sound accompanying the video but LaFountaine could see the man's hand buck from the recoil of the weapon and watched in horror as blood and brain matter erupted out the left side of the woman's head. The camera pulled back again to show the woman lying on her side, blood forming a wet red halo around her head. And then the screen went black.

"Was that . . ."

"Yeah," Sinclair said, his voice hoarse. "It was Mahata."

"Aw, those bastards," LaFountaine said. "Those *motherfuckers!*" he screamed.

LaFountaine gripped the edge of his desk and the muscles in his upper arms flexed as he began to pick it up and flip it over. He wanted to unleash the rage he was feeling in a violent, destructive rampage. He wanted to smash every object in the room. He wanted to smash Sinclair. Then he closed his eyes and took a deep breath and walked over to a window so Sinclair couldn't see his face.

With his broad back to Sinclair, he said, "I've been praying for days that she made it out. When we didn't hear from her, I told myself it was because she was someplace where she couldn't send a message. But I knew in my heart . . ."

He stopped speaking; there wasn't anything else to say.

He stood looking out the window for another moment, then turned and faced Sinclair. "I want that bitch arrested," he said. His voice was a low, deep-throated growl, like the noise a dog might make before it attacks. "I want her phones tapped, I want her apartment searched, and I want someone to get into every computer system she uses."

"Jake, we can't . . ."

"I want her source, goddamnit! I also want every person in this agency who knew about Diller polygraphed before the day is over. That includes you."

"It wasn't one of our people."

"I want them all polygraphed. Today."

Chapter 2

———◆———

Sandra Whitmore knew she looked terrible.

The bastards had come to her house at two in the morning just like the fucking gestapo, and some lady cop had watched her get dressed—had even watched her pee—but they wouldn't let her put on any makeup or comb her hair. So now she stood in a jail jumpsuit, flip-flops on her feet, her face bloated and unadorned and looking all of its fifty-six years—and all her fellow journalists were watching. The courtroom was filled with journalists.

She hoped no one could see her feet; her toenails looked like talons.

The judge—some big-nosed, bald-headed bastard who thought he was God—was talking again. "Ms. Whitmore, you said in your story that your source was a CIA employee, and if what you said is true, the government needs to know this person's name. Your source divulged sensitive national security information, has caused the death of a CIA agent, and . . ."

Whitmore's lawyer rose to his feet. "Your honor, there is no proof that . . ."

"Don't you dare interrupt me," the judge snapped. "As I was saying, your source caused the death of a CIA agent, and this person could endanger other intelligence operations. In other words, your story was not only irresponsible but you are, right now, protecting a traitor. And contrary to what your attorney has argued, the identity of your source is not protected by the First Amendment or the press shield law. So if you don't name . . ."

Whitmore's lawyer—a pompous wimp in a three-piece suit—rose to his feet to argue with the judge again. Her lawyer. What a joke. He had made it clear that he worked for the *Daily News* and not for her, and if she didn't like that fact she could pay for her own attorney—knowing damn good and well that she couldn't afford one. But right now he was pretending that he cared about her welfare as he challenged the judge's last statement.

Whitmore didn't bother to listen to the legal wrangling; she already knew how this was going to end.

Her source. She couldn't believe it when he had called her. Why me? she'd asked. Why hadn't he called one of the heavy-hitters at the *New York Times* or the *Washington Post*? Or why not Sheila Cohen who worked for the *News* and had won a Pulitzer in 2007? The guy said he came to her because he didn't trust the flaming liberals at the *Times* or the *Post,* and he wasn't sure that Sheila had the balls for this kind of story. That had made her laugh; it also made her think that he didn't know Sheila Cohen very well.

Her source told her that a man named Conrad Diller—a junior VP at Taylor & Taylor, the company founded by playboy millionaire Marty Taylor—had met secretly with several high-ranking officials in Tehran. The purpose of the meeting had been to sell the Iranians equipment that would improve the guidance system for their Shahab-3 missile, the Iranian medium-range missile that could hit Tel Aviv. According to her source, the CIA was aware of the meeting but were doing nothing to stop Diller from completing the deal. He concluded that either someone at Langley was getting a kickback from Marty Taylor or, more likely, the agency was playing some sort of dangerous political game. Whatever the case, the sale had to be stopped and what Marty Taylor was doing had to be exposed.

The next question she'd asked had been: Why should I believe you? And that's when he had pulled out his CIA credentials. He also showed her proof that Diller had flown to Iran. Then she did what any good reporter would do: she confirmed the facts as best she could. She verified that Conrad Diller worked for Marty Taylor and verified, via an independent source, that he had taken a flight to Tehran from Cairo. She also called a guy at the *Wall Street Journal* that she'd had an affair with fifteen years ago and he confirmed that Taylor's company was in deep financial trouble. Whitmore figured that Marty Taylor had to be up to his pretty neck in red ink to be selling classified shit to Iran.

Lastly, she called the CIA and asked if the agency would care to comment on her story. They pulled the usual gambit of stalling until right before her deadline, and when they called back all they did was badger her for her source. When she refused to name him, they said that if she published, ongoing operations could be jeopardized. The CIA's lawyer then quoted some obscure federal code and said that if their operations were in any way compromised she could be subject to criminal charges. But that's all the arrogant bastards said, and they never said anything about some spy being in danger. And so she published—and now she was in a jail jumpsuit.

She remembered the shit storm that had erupted in 2003 when that CIA agent Valerie Plame had her cover blown by Scooter Libby—or whoever the hell it really was. A couple of reporters were jailed for contempt for refusing to reveal their sources and one, a gal named Judith Miller who worked for the *New York Times,* spent almost three months in jail for refusing to give up a source. Whitmore didn't know all the details regarding Plame, or what Miller had done; all she knew was that the leak investigation had gone on for months, had involved a gaggle of politicians and prominent journalists, and they came damn close to getting the vice president before it was all over.

And all that ruckus just for *naming* a spy—not for getting one killed.

She was in a world of trouble.

"Ms. Whitmore," the judge asked, "do you understand that I'm going to place you in jail for contempt and that you'll remain there until you agree to cooperate?"

Whitmore looked up at the judge's glowering face and then glanced over at a guy from the *LA Times* she knew. He didn't look the least bit sympathetic; he looked like he was having a ball. The little prick.

"Ms. Whitmore, do you understand me?" the judge repeated.

She looked back at the judge, directly into his beady eyes, and tilted her chin defiantly. "Yeah, I understand," she said. And then, for the benefit of all the media present, she added, "And you can lock me up forever. I'll never give up a source."

One of the journalists sitting behind her cheered, and she figured that whoever he was he had to be very young. The rest of the journalists all let out little groans as they wrote down the hackneyed, self-serving quote they would be forced to include in their stories.

Actually, she was petrified of going to jail. She had three addictions: nicotine, alcohol, and pain medication. She'd been taking painkillers ever since she sprained her back five years ago, and at work she went outside every half hour to smoke. And at night, *every* night, she drank half a bottle of cheap scotch. Jail was going to be a living hell—and the government was going to do everything it could to make it so.

But she would endure it, by God, she would.

This was the best thing that had happened to her in twenty years.

Chapter 3

When the story appeared in the paper, Conrad Diller knew he was going to be arrested, so he wasn't surprised when two FBI agents knocked on his door. He was only surprised that they had waited ten days. As they were placing the handcuffs on his wrists, he told his wife to call the lawyer.

He had spoken with the lawyer only once since the article appeared. The man had said, "When they come for you, they'll ask if you're Conrad Diller and you'll say 'yes.' Then they'll read you your rights and ask you if you understand them, and you'll say 'yes' again. After that, I don't want you to say another word. Do you understand?"

The lawyer had waited for Diller to say that he understood, but he didn't. What he had said instead was, "I'm not going to jail for this, and you damn well better make sure Marty Taylor understands that."

The federal prosecutor was a man named Barnes and he worked for the U.S. attorney responsible for the Southern District of California. He reminded Diller of his high school wrestling coach: five foot nine, a compact, muscular body, and gray hair cut so close you could see his red scalp through the bristles. And just like his old coach, Barnes wanted you to think that he was a tough little bastard and, in spite of his size, could kick the crap out of you. Diller had been afraid of the wrestling coach—and he was afraid of Barnes, too.

"Mr. Diller," Barnes said, "if you don't cooperate with us, you're going to spend at least ten years in a federal prison, a prison filled with violent, psychotic criminals. You will be beaten and gang raped and become the house pet of some demented sadist."

Diller's lawyer snorted—but it was an eloquent snort, a snort that implied that everything the prosecutor had just said was theatrical bullshit.

His lawyer was an overweight, badly dressed old man named Porter Henry. He was at least seventy, wore a wrinkled brown suit, a frayed white shirt, and a yellow bow tie speckled with little blue dots. When Diller was arrested, he had thought the law firm Marty Taylor used would defend him, but Taylor's lawyers refused, saying there could be a conflict of interest issue at some point in the future. They did recommend Porter Henry, though, and a little research on the Internet had shown that Henry won a lot more cases than he lost— but still, he would have liked it better if the guy had been someone more like himself, someone in his thirties who knew how to dress. He just couldn't relate to the old fart—and he didn't trust him either— but so far the guy had kept him out of jail.

"He's not going to do any time," Porter Henry said to the prosecutor. "Your entire case is based on the unsubstantiated testimony of a dead woman."

Now the prosecutor smiled—a thin, nasty little smile that didn't show his teeth. "Yeah, but she's one hell of a dead woman," he said. "A patriot who gave her life for her country, and her testimony is documented in reports she sent the CIA."

Henry snorted again. "Reports that we can't see in totality because they're classified."

"I'm not going to debate this with you, Mr. Henry," Barnes said. "Either your client admits he went to Iran on behalf of Martin Taylor or we go to trial. And I'll win in court."

When Porter Henry's only response was a negative shake of his head, the prosecutor looked at Conrad Diller and asked, "Are you in love with Marty Taylor, Mr. Diller? I'm trying to understand why you're willing to go to prison for a pampered millionaire who's disavowed any knowledge of your actions."

"This meeting is over," Porter Henry said.

"Then we'll see you in court," the prosecutor said.

Diller went back to Henry's office after the meeting with the prosecutor. The office was like its occupant: old-fashioned and musty. There was a massive desk stacked with correspondence and unanswered call slips; Audubon paintings of green-headed mallards hung on the walls; a scarred wooden table, one better suited for a farmhouse kitchen, was piled high with yellowing stacks of papers. Dusty law books were scattered *everywhere*—on shelves, on chairs, on the floor—and none of them looked as if they'd been opened in years.

Porter Henry plopped his wide ass into the swivel chair behind his desk and pointed Diller to the wooden chair in front of the desk. "Now, I know that guy scared you a bit, but . . ."

"I'm not going to jail," Diller said.

"Son, I want you to listen to me," Henry said.

Diller had noticed before that the old man had a fat, jovial face and was always smiling but the smile never reached his eyes—and he had really cold, dead eyes. Porter Henry was, upon reflection, a scary son of a bitch.

"All the government has," Henry said, "is some message—a message they can't admit into evidence in totality because it's classified. And this message was probably encrypted originally, which means somebody had to translate it from code into normal English. Or maybe it was passed to couriers, and God knows what the couriers did to the message. And the government is going to have to be able to prove that this woman was really at this meeting that you allegedly attended, and they can't do that."

"She was there," Diller said, "at least for some of it."

"But the government can't *prove* it," Porter Henry said, "unless they can get some Iranian to take the stand, and that's not going to happen." Then he smiled, exposing horsey, yellow teeth. "So relax. No jury is going to send you to jail when the government's entire case is based on the word of the CIA—the most unreliable, untrustworthy intelligence agency in this country's history."

"If they show the jury the video of that woman being killed, they'll fry me."

Henry shook his head. "They just showed you that video to scare you, Conrad, but the video is irrelevant and inadmissible. You're being accused of trying to sell classified technology, not for killing that agent. In addition, there's no proof that there's any connection between that young woman's death and you being in Iran, and the Iranian ambassador to the United Nations has denied that his government killed the woman. So don't worry about the video; a jury will never see it."

Before Diller could say anything else, Porter Henry continued, "I know you're worried but Mr. Taylor is paying you five million dollars for your troubles. I would think that would bolster your resolve. How old are you, Conrad?"

"Thirty-four."

"Thirty-four years old and five million dollars. Think about that. If you invest that money wisely, you can retire right now. You'll never have to work for the rest of your life. And all you have to do to earn the money is go to court and stick to your story: you were in Tehran as a tourist, you met with nobody, and the government can't prove otherwise. Young man, I wish I had had a retirement opportunity like yours when I was thirty-four." Porter Henry smiled when he said this, and again the smile didn't reach his eyes.

Conrad Diller didn't say anything for a minute. Then he said it again, "I'm not going to jail for Marty Taylor."

Porter Henry had no respect for men like Diller. When he was younger, much younger, he had defended thugs—bank robbers, dope addicts, muggers, car thieves. Those men had had no illusions about who they were or what they did, and they all knew that if they were caught they'd go to jail. They *expected* to go to jail.

But not Diller. He was one of those privileged young snots who had had every advantage. He had been raised by wealthy, doting parents, had gone to the right schools, and then had been lucky enough to get a job that paid extremely well. But he wasn't satisfied. He wanted a bigger house, a fancier car; he wanted to be a player. So he decided to do something that he knew was illegal—but when *he* was caught, he didn't expect to go to the can. No, not him. He expected his golden life would continue as it always had. Diller didn't just lack courage, he was one of those people who sincerely believed that he was above the herd and shouldn't be treated like the criminal he was.

Porter Henry picked up the phone on his desk. It had push buttons, of course, but he would have liked it better if it had had an old-fashioned dial. He liked the sound phones used to make when you dialed a number and the phone dial rotated back. Marty Taylor answered his call.

"I'm afraid young Mr. Diller lacks the necessary resolve," Porter Henry said. "He'll give you up if the case doesn't look like it's going his way."

"Aw, goddamnit. Why is it that everything I do these days turns to shit?"

Marty Taylor, Porter Henry thought, wasn't much different from Conrad Diller: he was another young snot who whined like a baby when things didn't go his way.

"So what do I do now?" Taylor asked.

"I would suggest that you talk to Yuri, Mr. Taylor. He'll know what to do."

Chapter 4

———◆———

Mavis looked up just as her boss walked through the door. He was a big man with a heavy gut, a broad back, and hair as white as snow. In spite of the weight he carried, he was still a handsome man, and when he smiled, and when those blue eyes twinkled, he could make her heart sing. But right now he wasn't smiling. He was moving toward his office like a man on a mission, and she knew what the mission was: he needed a drink. It was almost eleven a.m. and he hadn't had one all day—unless he had had one with his breakfast, which was possible.

She had worked for him for almost thirty years and she knew him as well as his wife did. Hell, she knew him better than his wife because she was sure that his wife didn't know half the things he'd done. He was an alcoholic and a womanizer and played outrageous games with the taxpayers' money, money that he treated as his own. He was lucky other people didn't know what she knew; if they did, he would probably be serving time in a federal prison.

She shook her head. Her boss: John Fitzpatrick Mahoney, Speaker of the United States House of Representatives—and God help the country.

He dropped a thick three-ring binder on her desk and said, "Have Perry read all that shit and tell me what it says," and then continued on toward his office.

He had just been in a meeting with some Treasury people, and she knew the notebook contained proposals for how to deal with a federal budget deficit that had reached an all-time high. She also knew he had sat through the meeting not paying attention to a single thing that had been said. Nothing bored him more than budget discussions. But Perry Wallace, his chief of staff, would stay that day until he had read every word in the binder. Then he would boil all the nonsense down to a single sheet of paper and Mahoney would most likely go along with whatever Perry recommended.

Mahoney was lazy, but he wasn't stupid. That's why he had a hard-working genius like Perry Wallace as his chief of staff—and her. She was just as indispensable to him as Perry, and he knew it, too.

He just didn't know that she loved him and always would.

———◆———

Mahoney loosened his tie, sat back in his chair, and put his big feet up on his desk. In his thick right paw he held a tumbler of bourbon. He took a sip and sighed. Nothing like the first one of the day. He looked around for the remote and fortunately it was sitting on his desk so he didn't have to get up and search the room for it. He turned on the television just as Jake LaFountaine was walking up to a podium to address a gaggle of reporters.

Mahoney knew LaFountaine had been director of the CIA an unprecedented eight years and had served under two presidents, one a Democrat, the other a Republican. He was a career spook. He had been in military intelligence when he was in the army, had worked at the NSA, been a deputy director at Langley, and prior to being appointed as director of the CIA had been the national security advisor. He had no known political aspirations and he tended to act like a man with no such aspirations. He had nothing but disdain for the media and this was evident every time he spoke to them—or about them. Even worse, LaFountaine wasn't the type to measure his words. So for him to be addressing the media instead of letting his PR guy do the job was very unusual, which was why Mahoney had decided to watch the news conference. He was sure LaFountaine had been given a carefully prepared script, but he also knew that he was likely to ignore it. He was like Mahoney in that respect.

LaFountaine stood for a moment, looking down at the podium, then gave the cameras the full force of his eyes. "As you all know," he said, "a CIA agent named Mahata Javadi was executed in Iran. The Iranian government has denied any responsibility for her death but I know they shot her, and before she died she was severely beaten, tortured, and most likely raped."

The journalists let out a collective gasp. The death of the spy had been reported—the way she had died had not.

"Mahata Javadi spent six years in Iran. Six horrible, stressful, perilous years. She was one of the bravest people I ever met, and she provided this country with vital intelligence on the most dangerous government on this planet. Our covert agents know, as I do, that they might pay the ultimate price if they are discovered and were it not for one thing I could accept Mahata's death. What I cannot accept is that she died because of a story published by an irresponsible journalist named Sandra Whitmore. Had it not been for Ms. Whitmore's story, Mahata would be alive today."

"Mr. LaFountaine," a reporter called out. "Can you tell us . . ."

"Shut up!" LaFountaine said.

Oh boy, Mahoney thought.

LaFountaine didn't say anything for a moment. He just stood there, head down, as he tried to regain his composure. Finally, he looked out at the reporters again and said, "The only reason I'm talking to you people today is because Ms. Whitmore claimed the source for her story was a member of the Central Intelligence Agency. I want you to know that every person at the CIA who had even the slightest knowledge of Mahata's mission or any knowledge of Mr. Diller's trip to Iran has been questioned, investigated, and polygraphed. No one— I repeat, *no one*—at the CIA was Ms. Whitmore's source. I will stake my job on that."

Now that's pretty gutsy, Mahoney thought.

LaFountaine paused. "But a week before Ms. Whitmore published her story I met with select members of the House and Senate to give them a routine update on intelligence matters."

"You son of a bitch!" Mahoney said, and he stood up, sloshing bourbon on his pants.

"During this meeting, I informed the committee that the CIA was aware that Diller had met with people in Iran. I told the committee we didn't want Diller arrested immediately because doing so could jeopardize an ongoing operation. I told them that we'd deal with Mr. Diller—and his boss, Martin Taylor—at some later date. So, contrary to what Ms. Whitmore implied in her story, the CIA was in no way covering up our knowledge of Diller's activities."

"Are you saying that someone in Congress was Whitmore's source?" a reporter asked.

LaFountaine just looked at the reporter for a moment, then walked away from the podium.

"You son of a bitch!" Mahoney screamed again.

Chapter 5

The florist locked the door of his small shop in Alexandria, put the CLOSED sign in the door, and lowered the Venetian blinds over the front window. He usually left the blinds open, even when the shop was closed. He liked people to be able to walk by and see the flowers— to see his work. He personally thought of the floral arrangements in his window as works of art, not advertising, and he had constructed most of the bouquets and wreaths himself. He had always been good with his hands but he was surprised to discover that the same hard hands that had been trained to maim and kill could fashion nature into beautiful, artistic displays.

He sat down on the high stool behind the sales counter and looked around his shop. He was going to miss it so much. He had never in his life known the tranquillity that he had found in this small, sweet-scented place; it was the only spot on the planet where the ghosts of his past didn't invade.

The florist had been told more than once that he didn't look like a man who sold flowers for a living. He was six foot three and had broad shoulders and very strong arms; his chest and forearms were matted with dark hair. And although his only regular exercise was walking the two miles from his home to his shop every day, he had good genes and his stomach was flat and he weighed the same as he had when he was thirty. He was fifty-three now.

He had a hard-looking face: dark, probing eyes, a prominent nose, and thin, cruel lips hidden by an impressive black mustache. He wore his hair cut close to his skull because he didn't like to fuss with it and because he had always worn it that way. There was a long scar on his left forearm, almost ten inches long, but it had faded to a thin white line that wouldn't have been noticeable if the color of the scar didn't contrast so starkly with his dark skin. When anyone asked him the cause of the scar he would laugh and tell them he'd tripped and fallen through a window when he was young. I was a clumsy boy, he'd say. He couldn't tell the truth: how the bomb fragments had magically flown past him on that horrible night leaving him with only one small reminder of how incredibly lucky he'd always been. As he sat there he thought it might be smart to let his hair grow out and, at some point, he'd have to shave his mustache, something he hated to do because he was vain about it.

He looked around the shop one more time, knowing he would most likely never see it again, and then called out to his assistant who was working in the back room. She was surprised when she saw the CLOSED sign on the door.

Marta Silverman was the same age as him. She was a plump, motherly woman, pleasant and reliable, and had been with him for nine years. He told her his brother was terminally ill and he was leaving that night to care for him. He said he might be gone for a long time, possibly several months, and that she should hire someone to help her while he was gone.

Naturally, she said how sorry she was. And naturally she said that she didn't know he had a brother as she'd never heard him speak of one before. And that was true. He never spoke of his brother because Mohsen had been dead for years.

He told Marta to take the rest of the day off, and after she left he walked back to the potting room. One table had bags of soil and fertilizer stacked on it and, without removing any of the heavy bags from the table, he pushed it to one side. The floor in the potting room was made of rough wooden planks, and using a screwdriver he pried up two of the planks that had been under the table. He reached down into the hole and pulled out a locked metal box he had hidden there sixteen years ago when he first opened the shop. His hope had always been that the box would remain hidden forever—but God had decided that was not to be.

He took out the pistols first: a Makarov 9 mm and a Colt .22 automatic equipped with a silencer. The weapons had been sealed in plastic bags and small packets of moisture-absorbing desiccant had been placed in the bags. He dry-fired the weapons a couple of times and they appeared to function properly. Later, he would disassemble and clean them thoroughly.

Remaining in the box was a switchblade knife and a pouch that contained two sets of false identification papers: passports, social security cards, and driver's licenses. The knife he would keep; the identity papers he would destroy. Being almost twenty years old, the documents were expired and he no longer looked like the young man in the pictures. Fortunately, the forger who had made the IDs was still alive and not in prison, and the florist had kept in touch with him. He would call the man today and get him started on manufacturing two new identities.

Lastly, he pulled out a prayer rug from a closet. He had never been a religious man, and he couldn't remember the last time he had prayed. He placed the rug on the floor, took off his shoes, then knelt and touched his head to the floor.

He asked God to assist him in his mission.

He prayed to God to grant him vengeance.

Chapter 6

"Honey, is that the bat phone ringing?" Betty Ann asked, calling out from the kitchen.

"Aw, crap, it sounds like it," Benny said, and with some effort he struggled out of the recliner's soft embrace.

They called it the bat phone because it came with a scrambler and was illegally connected to the telephone pole behind the next-door neighbor's house. Boy, had that been a bitch, hooking up that wire. He could still remember it: three in the morning, Betty Ann holding on to the base of the ladder so it wouldn't slip, her yammering at him to hurry up, him hissing at her to shut up, then dropping the pliers, almost hitting her head, and her shrieking loud enough to wake the dead. What a fun night that had been.

Benny Mark—not *Marks*—was fifty-six years old, five foot seven, and, depending on which weight-height chart you wanted to believe, he was either fifty or seventy pounds overweight. He had lost most of his hair when he was in his thirties and all he had now was a horse-shoe fringe of curly gray that ran around the base of his round skull. But neither his bald head nor his big, sloppy gut bothered Benny. Not much of anything bothered Benny. He was a content man, al-most always in a good mood, and this was reflected by his face: the laugh lines radiating from his small blue eyes, his lips perpetually turned up in a pleasant half-smile.

He walked slowly to his office. The bat phone was still ringing. There was no answering machine connected to it so it would ring until either the caller hung up or Benny answered.

"Hel-lo," Benny said cheerfully. The caller started talking immediately. Rude bastard. He didn't even ask how Benny and Betty Ann were doing, even though he'd known them both for years.

"Hang on a sec," Benny said. "Lemme get a pen." He opened the center drawer of his desk and looked into the little tray where the pens were supposed to be, but there weren't any. Goldang it, where were all the pens? It was like something ate them for snacks. He pulled the drawer all the way out. Ah, there was one, hiding all the way in the back.

"Okay, shoot," Benny said. He listened for about five minutes and took notes. He asked a couple of questions and concluded with, "Allrighty. I'll head out there tonight."

Benny got on the Internet, bought an airline ticket, made a reservation at a motel, and then walked into the kitchen to tell his wife he was going out of town. She was standing at the sink, washing the breakfast dishes, watching one of them dumb-ass morning talk shows, the one with the four broads all sitting around a table yapping.

He looked at his wife's ass and shook his head in dismay: she looked like a hay wagon from the rear. During their marriage the two of them had gained weight at about the same rate but fortunately Betty Ann still had her hair: a short perm she dyed dark red. And her face . . . he swore as they got older they had even started to look alike, both of them with broad noses, jowly cheeks, and double chins. The next thing you knew they'd be one of them dipshit couples walking along the street wearing identical hats and jackets, looking like fat ancient twins.

But she was a good ol' gal. No way would he trade her in for some young bimbo, not at his age, he wouldn't. She had a sense of humor, she didn't complain all that much, and when she was younger . . . oh, the jugs that woman had. He almost fainted the first time he touched them.

"That was Jimmy," Benny said.

"How's he doing?" Betty Ann asked.

"Who knows? The bastard, he's all business. He didn't even ask how we were. Anyway, I gotta leave tonight."

"Oh, no! Are you going to miss Dave's party?"

"When is it?"

"Friday."

"Yeah, I doubt I'll be back that soon. Make up some excuse."

"He'll be so disappointed. A sixtieth birthday's a big deal, you know."

"Yeah, it means you're one year closer to being dead," Benny said and cackled.

"Oh, you. Where are you going this time?"

"Myrtle Beach. I made a reservation at the Best Western on Ocean Boulevard. FedEx me a .32 there. And don't pack the gun in that Styrofoam bubble shit this time. That stuff gets all over the place. Just use newspaper or something."

Chapter 7

"I want everyone who attended that meeting polygraphed by one of my technicians," LaFountaine said.

He was speaking to John Mahoney and Clyde Rackman, and they were in Rackman's office. Rackman was the majority leader of the Senate, a tall, rail-thin man in his seventies with mournful eyes and wispy gray hair, and it seemed as if a strong wind might blow him away. His apparent frailty, however, was misleading. He worked fourteen-hour days, was as tough as any politician on Capitol Hill, and he could be downright vicious to any Democrat who didn't toe the party line.

"I don't think—" Rackman started to say but Mahoney interrupted.

"In your dreams. You're not hooking up wires to anybody here on the Hill, and you know it."

LaFountaine glared at Mahoney, and Mahoney glared back. Mahoney was older than LaFountaine by several years but both were big, bulky men and, except for their hair color, were actually quite similar in appearance. Glowering at each other across the conference table, they looked like two bulldogs ready to lunge at each other's throat.

"Somebody gave the story to that reporter, Mahoney," LaFountaine said, "and it wasn't one of my people. That means somebody that works in this building got my agent killed."

"Director LaFountaine," Rackman said, "I'd suggest that you be very careful about making accusations you can't prove."

"Fuck being careful, Senator. There are no cameras in this room. I want to know what you guys are going to do to get to the bottom of this."

"I'll speak to all the senators who attended your briefing," Rackman said. "And I'm sure John will talk to folks in the House."

"The staff weenies, too," LaFountaine said. "And there was some damn kid serving coffee, although I'm sure she wasn't in the room when I was talking."

"We'll talk to everybody," Rackman said, "but you made it clear the day you were over here that if anybody talked about Diller, one of your operations could be affected. I just can't believe that . . ."

"It wasn't just Mahata who was killed," LaFountaine said. "She had a network over there, four people who helped her. They're all missing and we're pretty sure they're dead, too. And we think they were all tortured before they were killed because one of them gave up Mahata's escape route."

Mahoney grimaced.

"I'm sorry," Rackman said, "but . . ."

"You guys have no idea how valuable that woman was to this country. We developed a perfect background for her, placed her in Iran, and basically told her to fuck her way into a position where she could obtain information. She was a beautiful woman, and as repulsive as it must have been for her, she did what we asked. It took her three years but she eventually became the mistress of a high-level guy in their defense department and landed a job as a translator. You can't even *imagine* the information she provided."

"Has the reporter said anything since they put her in jail?" Rackman asked.

Neither Rackman nor LaFountaine noticed but Mahoney glanced away when the reporter was mentioned.

"No," LaFountaine said. "That bitch hasn't had a story like this in twenty years. I heard they almost dumped her when the paper downsized last year, but they didn't want to get caught up in some feminist, EEO, lawsuit bullshit. And now she's a fucking star, sitting in that cell, playing the intrepid reporter."

LaFountaine smiled. It wasn't a pretty sight.

"But I found some things out about her. She's borderline claustrophobic so I got her put in the smallest cell they had. She's also addicted to painkillers, and I'm making sure she doesn't get her pills until she's almost out of her mind. I'm thinking about replacing the pills with placebos."

"Jesus," Rackman said. "Why in the hell would you tell me something like that? I can't know that you're . . ."

"Tough shit," LaFountaine said.

LaFountaine stood up. "I'm not screwing around here. One of your people leaked that story and if you don't find out who it was, I will. And when I find out, I'm not going to give a good goddamn about whatever political problems it'll cause you."

Rackman stood up, too. "I won't be spoken to in that manner and I don't like being threatened. I may have a talk with your boss." Rackman meant the president.

LaFountaine snorted. "Go ahead. If Whitmore doesn't give up her source pretty soon, I'm going to ask him to assign a special prosecutor and he'll question your folks under oath. And then I'll get whoever did this for perjury as well because I know the son of a bitch will lie."

After LaFountaine left, Rackman asked Mahoney, "Do you think he's right, John? Do you think somebody in Congress could have been Whitmore's source?"

"I dunno," Mahoney said.

Mahoney wasn't *exactly* lying. He wasn't positive that he knew who had leaked the story—but he had a pretty good idea who it might have been.

Chapter 8

————◆————

DeMarco was playing hooky.

What he was supposed to be doing was figuring out why a Republican congressman from Arkansas kept flying to Minnesota every weekend. Mahoney knew the guy was up to something, and he wanted to know what. If all the young congressman was doing was having an affair, then Mahoney—a man who had had many affairs—probably wouldn't do anything. But if the guy was up to something else, something illegal, well . . . DeMarco still had no idea what Mahoney might do. Turn the guy in? Maybe. Take him to the woodshed and make him see the error of his ways? Possibly. But more likely, unless the guy was a serial killer, Mahoney would just use the information to control his vote. With Mahoney, nothing was ever simple or certain.

But instead of rooting out mischief in politics, DeMarco was watching a baseball game. Curtis Jackson, the man who supervised the Capitol's janitors, had given DeMarco the ticket. A lobbyist had originally given the ticket to a congressman, and the congressman had passed it to Jackson, but because Jackson didn't want to burn up his vacation time, he had asked if DeMarco wanted to go to the game.

"On a Wednesday?" DeMarco had said. "Right in the middle of the workday? Hell, yeah, I wanna go."

And so there he sat, his seat right behind the Nationals' dugout. He couldn't remember the last time he had a seat this good. And he liked day games a lot better than night games, particularly when the weather was like it was today: a beautiful seventy degrees, not a cloud in the sky, the flags in the outfield barely moving. He took a sip of his beer and snuck another glance at the good-looking mommy sitting with the two little boys one row away. He noticed she didn't wear a wedding ring. Hmmm. Maybe he'd . . .

Shit! He could tell just by the sound the ball made coming off the bat that that baby was gone, outta the park, bye-bye baseball. The Mets now led four to zip, and it was only the second inning. But who cared? He had a beer, he had the sun on his face, there was a pretty woman to look at and hot dogs to eat—and he wasn't working.

The Nationals pitching coach and the catcher were out on the mound now. The shortstop was with them and DeMarco guessed he was there to translate, the pitcher being a Cuban defector who spoke only Spanish. DeMarco could imagine the conversation, the pitching coach saying to the shortstop, "Ask him why the fuck he keeps throwing fastballs belt-high, right over the plate?" The shortstop would then repeat the question in machine-gun-rapid Spanish, the translation probably beginning with, "This asshole wants to know why . . ."

Two minutes later the home-plate umpire broke up the bilingual conference, and just as the pitcher was fondling the rosin bag to delay his next pitch, DeMarco's cell phone rang. He looked at the caller ID. Crap. It was Mahoney.

"Where the hell are you?" Mahoney asked.

"Uh . . ."

Fortunately, before DeMarco had to invent a plausible lie, Mahoney said, "I don't care. Get over to Old Ebbitt's. I gotta meeting over at Treasury that begins in ten minutes. When it ends, I'll come over to the restaurant. I need you to . . ."

Crack! DeMarco looked up and saw the ball heading toward the right-field fence—and at the same time thirty-two thousand people at Nationals Park let out a massive groan.

"Where the hell are you?" Mahoney asked again.

The Old Ebbitt Grill was directly across the street from the massive structure that housed the U.S. Department of the Treasury. It had a mahogany-colored bar that seemed about a hundred yards long, a shiny brass foot rail that ran along the bottom of the bar, and behind the bar were about a thousand bottles of booze. He was served by a dignified bartender dressed in a white shirt and a black bow tie who spoke with an Irish brogue.

DeMarco approved of Old Ebbitt's bar.

He'd been relieved that he'd been able to get to the restaurant before his boss and he'd just taken a sip of his martini when Mahoney walked through the door. He stood on the landing in front of the hostess's lectern, his big white-haired head swiveling about as he looked for DeMarco. He finally saw him standing at the bar and made an irritated get-over-here gesture with his right arm.

DeMarco followed Mahoney to a table where Mahoney ignored him until his drink arrived—a double bourbon on the rocks. He opened his mouth to speak but then stopped and looked away, as if he was embarrassed about whatever it was that he was going to say. And this surprised DeMarco. Mahoney was a man who was rarely embarrassed by anything he did or said.

"Sometimes," Mahoney finally said, "a guy's dick can lead him into real trouble."

For a minute DeMarco wondered if Mahoney was talking about the congressman from Arkansas but swiftly concluded he wasn't. Mahoney was talking about himself.

"There's a reporter named Sandra Whitmore . . ."

"You mean the one . . ."

"Yeah. That one. When she was younger, she had a body that could stop traffic and I tossed her a story that almost won her a Pulitzer. She's never had a story as big as that since. Anyway, I got a letter from her yesterday saying that she's going to talk to her pals in the media about her love life if I don't help her."

"She's blackmailing you?"

Mahoney shrugged. "Go see her. See if something can be done to get her out of jail."

"From what I've read there's no way she's going to get out unless she gives up her source. I mean, what she did . . ."

"Yeah, well, go see if there's another option. She doesn't have the temperament to sit in a cell for very long."

"Okay," DeMarco said. He knew from past experience that arguing with Mahoney over the feasibility of an assignment was a waste of time.

"There's something else," Mahoney said. "LaFountaine's up to something."

"Like what?"

"I don't know. He came up to the Hill that day to give us an update on intelligence stuff, just like he told the press. But the thing is, he's always hated talking to us about what his guys are doing. We usually have to force his stubborn ass to brief us and then he'll tell us as little as he possibly can, and he'll make us just *drag* the information out of him. Well, that day he acted the way he always did, not saying shit about anything important, but right there at the end he tossed out that bit about Diller. He was casual about it, letting us know Marty Taylor was up to something illegal but that he wanted to hold off on arresting Diller and Taylor so it didn't screw up whatever operation he was running. And when he brought up the thing about Diller, the meeting was behind schedule, as usual, and so nobody even asked any questions."

"I don't understand," DeMarco said.

"What I'm saying is that LaFountaine telling the committee about Diller was completely out of character. So I think he's up to something but I can't figure out what."

"But what do you want me to do about it?" DeMarco asked. "I mean, he's the director of the CIA."

"Yeah, I know." Mahoney sat there brooding a moment, then said, "Ah, forget LaFountaine. You're right, there's probably nothing you can do. Maybe Emma could, but you . . ." Mahoney didn't complete the sentence but DeMarco knew what he meant. His friend Emma had once been a high-ranking member of Washington's intelligence community and she could do things in that arena that he couldn't even come close to doing—but even if that was the case, Mahoney's comment still stung, implying that DeMarco was, and always would be, lacking in so many ways.

DeMarco was a lawyer who had never practiced law, and if he continued to work for John Mahoney he never would. Mahoney had hired him only as a favor to an old friend, but because of the notoriety of DeMarco's father, Mahoney refused to give him a legitimate staff position. Instead, he buried DeMarco in a closet-sized office in the subbasement of the Capitol and made sure that no organizational chart connected him to the Speaker's realm.

DeMarco liked to think of himself as a political troubleshooter but that was a face-saving illusion. In reality, he was the guy Mahoney used whenever he wanted something done that he didn't want traced back to his office—like investigating congressmen taking mysterious weekend trips. He was Mahoney's voice when he wanted messages delivered to people he couldn't be seen talking to and, on more than one occasion, DeMarco had found himself in life-threatening circumstances when Mahoney had sent him down some dangerous political rat hole. He was also, to his great shame, Mahoney's occasional bagman, the one rich constituents passed the cash to when they wanted Mahoney's help navigating—or, more likely, circumventing—the legislative process. He should have quit working for the insensitive, conniving bastard years ago, but at this juncture of his life he couldn't afford to. He was neck-deep in debt and it was going to be impossible to find a better-paying job, particularly when he couldn't put down on his résumé most of the things that he had done for his last employer.

Mahoney drained the bourbon in his glass and said, "Just figure out how to get Sandy Whitmore out of jail before she turns me into a headline."

DeMarco was the man walking behind the elephant: the guy with the high boots, a shovel, and a big bucket.

34

Chapter 9

The bar was two blocks from the Metropolitan Correctional Center in Manhattan, almost the first drinking establishment you came to upon leaving the jail. It was a gloomy, depressing place, and its clientele—five men and one woman—uniformly ignored each other and the muted television behind the bar. These were people who were only interested in the glass in front of them as they sat there brooding about what life might have been.

The florist had gone to the jail that morning and asked to speak to someone about the procedure for visiting the prisoners. He was directed to a heavyset, red-faced guard with a small mustache who reminded him of an angry Oliver Hardy. When he spoke to the guard, he smelled tobacco, breath mints, and alcohol on his breath. It was no surprise that a bar was the guard's first stop after leaving work.

The florist watched as the guard ordered a second drink. He had finished the first one in a single swallow. He was drinking straight vodka, having waved off the ice and lemon slice offered by the bartender. He wanted cheap, high-octane alcohol and nothing else.

The florist took a seat on the stool next to him. Signaling the bartender, he said, "Another one for my friend."

"Who the hell are you?" the guard asked. Then he recognized the florist. "Hey, you were at the jail this morning. What do you want?"

"Wait until he brings your drink and I'll tell you."

The guard shrugged; he wasn't going to turn down a free drink.

The bartender placed the vodka in front of the guard, and the guard placed both hands around the glass as if he was afraid the florist might snatch the drink away. "Okay, so now tell me why you're buying me drinks."

The florist took out his wallet and spread five one-hundred-dollar bills on the bar.

"Jesus!" the guard said, and his head spun around to see if anyone else had seen the money. "You shouldn't go flashin' money around in a place like this."

"No one's watching," the florist said. "Pick it up. It's yours."

The guard didn't reach for the money—but he did place his forearm over the bills so they were partially hidden.

"What do you want?" the guard asked again.

"I'm a journalist," the florist said, "and I want you to call me every time Sandra Whitmore—"

"That reporter broad? The one who got that spy killed?"

"Yes, that one. Tomorrow, I want you to look at your records and tell me the names of everyone who's visited her since she was jailed. And starting tomorrow, whenever she receives a visitor, I want you to call me immediately. If her visitors represent an organization, like a law firm or another paper, I want to know that as well."

The guard looked down at the money peeking out from under his sleeve. "Naw, no way. I could get fired. I hate that fuckin' job but it's better than being unemployed."

"How would anyone know if you called me?" the florist asked. "And you're not doing anything illegal. Your visitors log is a matter of public record and I could obtain a copy by filing a FOIA request." The florist actually had no idea if that was true.

"Foyya?" the guard said.

"Freedom of Information Act. But if I have to file a FOIA request it'll take me weeks to get what I want—and you won't make any money."

The guard didn't say anything. He did sneak another look at the five bills under his forearm. He finished his third drink and called out to the bartender, "Tommy, another one, but give me an Absolut and not that rotgut you've been pouring."

◆◆◆

Mahoney had said that when Sandy Whitmore was young she had a body that could stop traffic, and DeMarco concluded that her body could still perform that function: Whitmore was substantial enough to make a formidable barrier.

She was a stout five foot four and her once trim calves now resembled those of a small sumo wrestler's. Her face was bloated, her nose was a porcine snout, and she had the complexion of a drinker— little broken blood vessels all over her cheeks that would have been more noticeable if her complexion wasn't already an unhealthy, near-stroke shade of red. Her hair was also red, or had been at one time. It was now badly dyed, streaked with gray, and brittle-looking.

DeMarco was thinking that there were probably a lot of married men like John Mahoney walking around: men who had affairs when they were young and would now be embarrassed to be seen with some of the women they once found so desirable. Mahoney's wife, Mary Pat, was, and probably always had been, ten times better looking than Sandra Whitmore.

"Who the hell are you?" Whitmore asked as soon as she entered the room.

"Mahoney sent me," DeMarco said.

Whitmore smiled—or *gloated,* to be accurate. "So, he got my letter."

"Yeah, he got your letter."

Whitmore heard the disdain in DeMarco's voice and said, "Hey, fuck him and fuck you. I need some help here. They've got me locked up in a windowless box and they're keeping my pain medication from me until I'm practically coming out of my skin. They're basically *torturing* me to get me to talk."

37

"Mahoney can't get you sprung from jail," DeMarco said. "You must know that."

"Bullshit. He's the Speaker of the House. He has influence. I want him to use it."

DeMarco just shook his head. "The only one that can get you out of here is the judge who put you here, and he's not going to do that unless you give up your source. Your story got a spy killed, and right now nobody has a lot of sympathy for you."

"Hey! It wasn't my fault that woman died and I'm sick and tired of people saying it was. If the CIA had been straight with me that never would have happened. And I'm not giving up my source. This is the best story I've had in years and there's no way I'm gonna ruin things by selling out."

"So you wanna be a martyr but you're not willing to burn at the stake."

"I don't like your damn attitude, buster, and I don't have to stand for it. Now what's Mahoney gonna do for me?"

DeMarco had told Mahoney that there wasn't any way he could get Whitmore out of jail but he actually had thought of a way. "You can't give up your source," he said, "but someone else can."

"What are you talking about?" Whitmore said.

"Let's say that someone saw you and your source talking, and this person was to tell the CIA. LaFountaine wants your source so badly that he'd waterboard the guy to get him to admit that he leaked the story to you. So give me the guy's name and where you met, and I'll try to find some way to connect him to you so the CIA or the judge or somebody can drag the truth out of him, but no one will be able to accuse you of giving him up."

Whitmore lit a cigarette and her eyes narrowed as the smoke drifted upward. She studied DeMarco for a minute, thinking about what he'd just said, then looked around the small room. "Couldn't you have asked for a room with a damn window in it?" she muttered. "I can't remember the last time I saw the sky."

DeMarco didn't respond; he'd been with her less than five minutes and was already tired of her company.

"Okay," she said. "His name is Derek Crosby and he works for the
CIA, just like I said in my story. And if you tell anyone I told you
that, I'll crucify Mahoney, I swear to Christ I will. I'll make him sound
like the biggest pervert since Hugh Hefner."

DeMarco ignored the threat. "How do you know Crosby's CIA?"
he asked.

"Do I look stupid to you?" Whitmore said. "He showed me his
credentials. And I called the CIA from a pay phone so there wouldn't
be any record of the call and asked to speak to him. When they rang
me through to his desk, I hung up before he answered because I was
worried they might monitor phone calls, but I know he works there."

"What does he look like?"

"Big, tall guy. Late fifties, early sixties. Curly, ginger-colored hair.
A bit of a potbelly but otherwise not in bad shape. And tan, like he
spends a lot of time outdoors."

"Any distinguishing characteristics? A scar, a tattoo, a limp, anything like that?"

"No. But he lisps."

"Lisps?"

"Yeah."

"Where'd you meet him?" DeMarco asked.

"The Hyatt by Grand Central Station."

"Did you meet him in his room or the bar or did you leave the
hotel?"

"The bar."

"Did you sit at the bar or at a table?"

"At a table."

"And do you know if Crosby registered under his own name?"

"Yeah. When I got there I used the house phone to let him know
I was there. I had to give his name to the reservation desk so they
could ring his room."

"This is good," DeMarco said. "I may be able to find someone on the hotel staff who saw you together."

"Or," Whitmore said with a smile DeMarco found obscene, "you could *pay* somebody to say they saw us together whether they did or not."

It didn't take long for ol' Sandy to get into the spirit of things.

"Wouldn't Crosby have known that your story would put this agent in jeopardy?" DeMarco asked.

"How would I know?" Whitmore said. "But from what I've read, LaFountaine's polygraphed everyone at Langley that knew about the spy and it wasn't very many people. So maybe Crosby was in the loop about Diller's trip to Tehran but he didn't know about the spy. Or maybe he never thought exposing Diller would hurt the spy. I don't know. All I know is it wasn't *my* fault that woman was killed."

DeMarco wanted to say, *Yeah it was, you remorseless bitch*—but he didn't.

Chapter 10

———◆———

Marty Taylor sat on a rock fifty yards from the Pacific Ocean.

He had just come from a board meeting and was wearing an Armani suit, a Dolce and Gabbana dress shirt, and black lace-up shoes that had cost eight hundred dollars. It was a gray, blustery day—so windy that when the surf crashed onto the beach he was drenched with spray—but he didn't care. He didn't care that the back of his pants was filthy from the sandy rock and his expensive clothes were soaked with saltwater.

Naturally, the board meeting had been devoted to what Conrad Diller was accused of doing, and trying to assess what impact his arrest would have on the company. The stock price had been headed toward the basement before this happened; tomorrow it was expected to reach an all-time low. And the Pentagon was threatening to send out a team to do a security review to make sure there weren't any more Dillers in the company. Every board member was absolutely dumbfounded that Diller, a young professional who made a good salary, would do such a thing. Well, everyone wasn't shocked—but Marty and the company's CEO, Andy Bollinger, had pretended to be shocked.

So now he sat alone on that wet, sandy rock and pondered the train wreck that his life had become. He was thinking the smart thing to do would be to walk into the ocean—and just keep walking until he disappeared. And for what must have been the millionth time he asked himself the question *How could this have possibly happened?* How could he have gone from the golden boy he'd once been to being the target of a federal espionage investigation?

Marty Taylor didn't look like a computer geek. He looked like a surfer, a Viking surfer. He was thirty-five years old, had long blond hair, blue-green eyes, and a dimpled Kirk Douglas chin. His stomach was flat and his arms and chest were well muscled because these days he spent more time exercising than he did working. When he was twenty-two, there was a picture of him on the cover of *Rolling Stone* playing beach volleyball. At the time, he'd already been getting a hundred marriage proposals a week, but after *Rolling Stone* put him on the cover in nothing but swim trunks and sunglasses, the number tripled.

He and his cousin Gene started Taylor & Taylor in Gene's basement. They worked twenty-hour days, took speed to keep going, and pot to come back down. Their initial interest was in games and they thought they might be the next Nintendo or Atari, but somehow they vectored from the games themselves into gaming peripherals—mouses, joysticks, virtual-reality gaming gloves—all those computer control devices that let you maneuver the gun-toting, bloodthirsty, animated maniacs in the games. The funny thing was, the military actually approached *them*; it had never occurred to him and Gene that there could be a military application for their work.

The modern soldier was raised playing computer games, and the technologies they were developing could be used for controlling things like Predator drones, mine-detection robots, and the navy's unmanned, deep-dive recovery vessels. And somehow they beat out the giants like Northrop Grumman and Raytheon and got a lock on a megabucks Pentagon contract, and when they expanded into missile guidance systems they got an even bigger chunk of the military market. They'd been magic back then, and when they took the company public they made a ton of money—an *obscene* amount of money.

They set up Taylor & Taylor similar to Microsoft and the other big outfits, although they were nowhere as big as Microsoft. A board of directors was formed with a bunch of wise old heads, guys who'd retired from Intel, the military, JPMorgan Chase, places like that. Gene became chairman of the board and CEO of the company. Marty's title was chief technical officer, which really meant that he could continue to do what he'd always done—dink around with the geeks and develop new gadgets—and he really didn't have anything to do with running the business.

Things went great for almost ten years—and then Gene goes and kills himself in a freak scuba-diving accident. Following his cousin's death, Marty, being one of the company's founders and its largest shareholder, became chairman of the board—a job he knew he was in no way equipped to handle. He didn't have Gene's business skills and the last thing he wanted to do was worry about the financial shit, which he didn't understand and which bored him to tears. So the board hired a CEO away from Coca-Cola, a guy that was a hot-shit in the business world—but the soda guy turned out to be a disaster. He was a control freak who couldn't relate to the geeks and the free-for-all attitude that existed in cutting-edge technical companies and he drove off half the talent. When the company's stock started to fall like a wingless jet, the board fired the soda guy and got another CEO: Andrew Bollinger. Bollinger was supposed to be a wizard when it came to breathing life into dying companies—but the wizard turned out to be the worst thing that ever happened to Marty Taylor.

Bollinger was a good manager—or at least in the beginning he was—but Marty could never relate to him on a personal level. He was a big, overweight, bald man almost twice Marty's age, and there was something soft and effeminate about him; he fit Marty's image of what a court eunuch would look like. He was a bachelor and he claimed his hobbies were cooking, gardening, and collecting antique Chinese art but it turned out Bollinger's real hobby was little boys. The guy was a flaming pedophile and it was Bollinger's "hobby" that opened the door to hell—and in through that door walked the Russian.

Yuri Markelov was a small-time crime boss involved in drugs, pornography, stolen auto parts, and transporting illegal aliens into the country. And though he may have been small-time, he was bright, very ambitious, and extremely ruthless. He got his hooks into Bollinger when Bollinger took a trip to Mexico City and spent a weekend with a ten-year-old boy—a poor slum kid provided by Yuri's organization. Yuri found out Bollinger was a wealthy man, videotaped his disgusting activities, and then used the video to blackmail him. But it didn't end there. Yuri then got the idea to use Bollinger to steal money directly from Taylor & Taylor.

Without Bollinger's expertise it could never have happened. In a six-month period, Bollinger replaced the company's chief financial officer with a man who wouldn't question his decisions and changed accounting programs to limit access. Then he set up a small, phantom R&D division that an outside auditor—such as those periodically hired by the board—would never notice just by looking at the company's books.

A company like Taylor & Taylor was always forming small teams to develop new products so Bollinger created such a team—on paper. And from an accounting standpoint, the nonexistent team looked no different than the company's other legitimate business divisions. That is, it appeared that money was being spent to pay for salaries, research costs, prototype development, computer equipment, consulting fees, et cetera, when the money was actually going to Yuri's bank account. And the amount of money that went to Yuri was minuscule in comparison to the total operating costs of Taylor & Taylor—not even half a percent of the company's total expenses—but it amounted to a few hundred thousand a month.

But Yuri wanted more; Yuri always wanted more. He decided he wanted to mail stolen auto parts overseas in boxes that bore Taylor & Taylor's logo and claimed to contain the company's products. He also wanted a place to stash illegal immigrants when he first brought them across the Mexican border. And Bollinger, capitulating to Yuri's every demand, turned one of the company's warehouses over to Yuri and even hired one of Yuri's guys into T&T's shipping division.

The day Marty's whole world came crashing down he was on a private beach in Sumatra with his latest girlfriend, a Brazilian swim-suit model with emerald green eyes. She was topless, lying next to him on the sand, and he was thinking he didn't care if her tits were fake, when his cell phone rang. The caller was an accountant who had worked closely with Gene before his death.

"I was gonna call the cops," the accountant said, "but I decided to call you first. I figured I owed you that."

"The cops! What the hell are you talking about?"

Marty's girlfriend looked over at him and let out a tortured sigh to let him know he was talking too loud and disturbing her karma.

The accountant explained. He had been looking for a place to store a bunch of old paper files and he found a warehouse in Chula Vista that the company leased but didn't appear to be using. He visited the warehouse and instead of finding it abandoned as he had expected, he found two company vans parked outside the place and four guys playing cards inside. The card players told the accountant in heavily accented English that the warehouse was being used for a special project—and to beat it and not come back.

Being a curious guy, the accountant started pulling the string. He discovered shipments leaving the warehouse and going to places like Latvia, the Ukraine, and Albania—countries where the company had no business. Then he started looking at the financials and he was sharp enough to determine that in an eighteen-month period more than two million dollars had been siphoned from the company and the money had disappeared into a Mexican bank account.

"A Mexican bank account!" Marty shrieked.

"Marty!" the girlfriend said.

"Bollinger," the accountant said, "is stealing money from your company and he's hooked in with some people that are doing things that are probably illegal."

45

"What in the fuck are you talking about!" Marty screamed, still unable to believe what he was hearing.

The girlfriend got up and flounced away.

"I like you, Marty," the accountant said. "I always have. And you're a genius when it comes to writing code. But since Gene died you've become a complete fuckup and you have no idea what's happening inside your own company. Gene would have been ashamed of you. So I'd suggest you drop whatever you're doing—or whoever you're screwing—and get back here before you end up in jail."

And Marty did. He flew home that very day. He called Bollinger when his plane landed in San Diego, told him what the accountant had said, and insisted that he wanted Bollinger's fat ass parked in his office in an hour. But Bollinger refused to see him until the next day and told Marty to meet him at the same warehouse in Chula Vista that the accountant had visited. Then he hung up before Marty could object. Marty drove from the airport to Bollinger's office, cursing the whole way, but when he arrived he was informed that Bollinger had left for the day and when Marty called him he wouldn't answer his cell phone.

When Marty walked into the warehouse the following day, Bollinger was there but three guys were with him. Two of them looked like thugs: stocky, hard-looking men wearing cheap leather jackets and pointy shoes. One of the thugs had a tattoo of a snake winding around his neck.

The third guy was different. In fact, he looked a lot like Marty Taylor: tall, good-looking, well built, with longish blond hair, and wearing a beautifully tailored English suit. Marty opened his mouth to ask Bollinger who the hell these guys were but then heard a sound off to his right—like someone trying to scream through a towel—and when he turned toward the noise, he saw the accountant who had called him in Sumatra. The guy was tied to a chair, gagged, and his face had been pounded into hamburger. Then Marty noticed the accountant's fingers were bleeding—and he almost puked when he saw that three of his fingernails had been yanked out.

"What . . . what the hell's going on?" he asked Bollinger, unable to keep the fear out of his voice.

The guy in the suit stepped forward and said, quite pleasantly, "Marty, my name is Yuri Markelov. I'm your new business partner."

The man spoke English well but he had an accent of some sort—Marty later learned it was Russian.

"You're what?" Marty said, still overwhelmed by the sight of the bleeding accountant. He looked over his shoulder at the door he had come through and saw the guy with the snake tattoo standing in front of it.

"I said . . ."

But the accountant distracted Yuri; he was making more strangled noises through his gag and bouncing his chair up and down. "Excuse me," Yuri said, and pulled a gun out of a shoulder holster that had been hidden by his beautiful suit, walked over to the accountant, and shot him in the head.

"Jesus Christ!" Marty yelled. He turned, intending to run out of the warehouse—he was going to run right over the guy with the snake tattoo—and then saw the guy was also holding a gun, and it was pointed at his chest.

"Now, as I was saying," Yuri said, reholstering his weapon in the same nonchalant way a carpenter would put a hammer back into his tool belt, "I'm your new business partner."

Yuri then explained to a wide-eyed Marty Taylor what Bollinger was doing—giving Yuri a small portion of the company's money—and why Bollinger was doing this. He also explained, quite calmly, how the company was being used to aid Yuri's other business interests. He actually said "business interests," like he was Warren Buffett and not a gangster who had just blown a man's brains out right in front of Marty's eyes.

"I know you're in a state of shock right now," Yuri said, "but later—assuming there is a later for you—you'll start thinking about going to the police. But let me tell you what will happen if you do that and if I'm arrested. First, Mr. Bollinger won't testify against me because he knows if he does, I'll kill him. And he doesn't want the world to know about his, ah, proclivities. Is that how you pronounce it?

Proclivities? Yes, I think so. At any rate, Mr. Bollinger will say it was you, Mr. Chairman of the Board, who ordered him to cooperate with me. He'll explain how your company has been doing so poorly that you decided to explore other markets. Do you understand what I'm saying, Marty? Bollinger will testify against you and make you my accomplice. So, if I go down, you go down.

"But that's not all. If I go to jail, my associates"—he nodded toward the thugs—"will kill your sister in Palo Alto. And they'll all rape her before they kill her. And your niece, that lovely ten-year-old girl who attends the Bowman School, will disappear and be sold to a man I know that likes to use young girls in his films. And you, of course, will be killed in as painful a way as I can devise—and I have a good imagination when it comes to things like that. So, before you run to the police, I'd suggest you think about everything I've said."

After that day in the warehouse, nothing was the same. Marty rubber-stamped every decision Bollinger made with regard to Yuri. Yuri began to "ask" Marty for small favors: the use of one of his houses and several of his cars, loans he had no intention of repaying. And Yuri ensured that Marty was directly implicated in his activities. For example, Yuri decided to start making his own porno films rather than selling those made by others. He obtained a Hollywood "director" and had Marty sign a company check for forty thousand dollars to allow the director to procure the cameras and other equipment he needed. The forty thousand showed up on T&T's books as marketing expenses.

One day, Marty drove up to LA and met with a guy he'd gone to Stanford with, a lawyer who now worked for the Los Angeles district attorney. They met at a restaurant and Marty told his friend what Yuri was doing and asked if he could be held criminally liable for Yuri's illegal activities. The short answer was: maybe. The problem, the lawyer explained, was that Marty had failed to act immediately when he witnessed Yuri murder the accountant. And although Yuri may have threatened Marty's family, Marty continued to do nothing while Bollinger was stealing money from the company and giving it to Yuri.

And because the company was publicly held, that had even more onerous implications. So maybe Marty would get immunity if he testified against Yuri but his failure to act in a timely manner was bound to have some negative repercussions.

Marty swore his lawyer friend to silence until he could decide what to do but when he returned to San Diego, Yuri and two of his goons were waiting inside his house. Yuri informed him that since that day at the warehouse, his people had been following him and he was aware that he'd spoken to the lawyer. Yuri then took off his suit coat, rolled up the sleeves of his silk dress shirt, and beat the hell out of him—he beat him until Marty told him what he had discussed with the lawyer. Then, as he lay on the floor bleeding from his nose and his mouth and wondering how many of his ribs were cracked, Yuri told him if he tried something like that again, both his kneecaps would be smashed and surfing would become a thing of the past. The next day, he read in the paper the lawyer had fallen down a flight of steps and broken his neck.

Marty thought about witness protection and if it had just been him he might have done it. But since Yuri had threatened his entire family that meant his parents, his sister, her husband, and his niece would all have to go into witness protection as well and he couldn't imagine destroying their lives that way. He even thought about hiring someone to kill Yuri but he had no idea how to procure that sort of service.

In his dreams, he killed Yuri himself. He killed him every night.

As bad as everything was, though, this thing with Iran was so much worse. It was one thing to sell ripped-off Mercedes parts to some guy in Latvia; it was a whole different ball game to start selling missile technology to the Iranians. But Yuri, because of an association he had with a Russian ex-patriot who now worked with the Iranian government, had seen an opportunity and forced Marty to send Conrad Diller to Iran. It had never occurred to them that a CIA spy would attend the meeting.

So now Marty was in even bigger trouble than he had been in before, if that was possible. If Conrad Diller admitted that Marty had sent him to Iran . . . well, hello Lompoc—unless, of course, Yuri killed him first. For the time being, Diller was sticking to the story that he'd been on vacation in Tehran and had done nothing wrong, and the old lawyer, Porter Henry, continued to think he might beat the government in court. Additionally, per Yuri's instructions, Marty had offered Diller five million dollars to be a stand-up guy, although Marty suspected Diller would never see the money.

But then Porter Henry called and said Diller wasn't a stand-up guy.

Not a problem, Yuri said.

Chapter 11

The florist was eating a late breakfast when he received a call from the guard at the Metropolitan Correctional Center he had bribed to keep him informed of Sandra Whitmore's visitors.

"She's being visited by a man named Joseph, uh, DeMarco," the guard informed him. "He went in to see her about five minutes ago."

"Spell the name," the florist said, and the guard did. "So who is he? And why is he visiting her?"

"I don't know why he's visiting her, but he said he was a lawyer. He showed me a District of Columbia driver's license for ID."

The florist hesitated a moment, then said, "Describe him."

"About six foot, dark hair. He's wearing a black suit, white shirt, and a red tie, or maybe it's maroon."

"I want you to call me when he's leaving."

The florist rushed out of the diner and caught a cab to the prison. His primary reason for coming to New York had been to wait until Whitmore was released from prison and when she was he would deal with her. And, just like the government, he wanted to know the name of her source. He had bribed the guard to keep him informed of her visitors hoping that maybe one of them would lead him to her source, although he doubted he would get that lucky.

But this DeMarco intrigued him. He knew from reading the papers that Whitmore had a New York lawyer, a man who also represented the *Daily News*. And until today, all the people who had visited her were local: her lawyer, her editor at the *News,* another female reporter from the *News,* and one woman who lived in her apartment building. So why was she being visited by this lawyer from Washington? He didn't know, but he doubted that DeMarco was her source. He couldn't imagine her source taking the risk of visiting her. Whatever the case, he wanted to know more about Mr. DeMarco.

The guard called back twenty minutes later and said DeMarco was just leaving the prison. When DeMarco caught a cab, the florist told his cabdriver to follow.

DeMarco entered the lobby of the Hyatt and looked for the concierge's desk.

In any prison movie—*The Great Escape, The Longest Yard, The Shawshank Redemption*—there's always an inmate known as "the scrounger." The scrounger was the guy who could get you anything, and DeMarco figured all the good prison scroungers had been New York hotel concierges before they got sent up the river.

You want tickets to a show, no sweat. Seats behind home plate at Yankee Stadium, piece of cake. A girl, well . . . *I don't know nothin' about no girls, pal, but for fifty bucks I'll bet a blonde named Tiffany comes knockin' on your door at ten.*

The concierge's name tag said he was Tony, and he looked like a lot of the Tonys that DeMarco had known: curly black hair, longish nose, hirsute as a small ape. DeMarco put five one-hundred-dollar bills on the countertop that served as Tony's desk. The concierge looked down at the money, then smiled at DeMarco. Tony had never worn braces.

"Yes, *sir,*" he said. "And what can I do for you?"

DeMarco gave Tony the date Derek Crosby had met with Sandy Whitmore, and said he wanted all the information on Crosby stored in the hotel's computers: Crosby's address, phone number, the license plate number for his car if he had parked at the hotel, and his credit card number. He particularly wanted the credit card number because

Crosby's credit card statement would prove that Crosby had stayed at the hotel, and DeMarco knew a way to get Crosby's statement. He was afraid Tony might balk when he asked for the credit card number —but he didn't. Apparently, five hundred bucks was more than sufficient to purchase Tony's conscience.

DeMarco then showed Tony a picture of Sandra Whitmore, not the picture in the papers the day she was jailed for contempt, but one taken off the *Daily News*'s Web site in which she looked a little less like the unkept creature she currently was. "The main thing I want," DeMarco said, "is the name of a person who can testify that this woman, Sandra Whitmore, was in the hotel the same day Crosby was here. Even better would be someone who can say they saw Crosby and the woman together. I know they had a drink in the bar, so start there."

"You got a picture of this guy Crosby?" Tony asked.

"Not yet," DeMarco said. He gave Tony the description of Crosby that Whitmore had given him.

"And if you can find somebody who can positively say Whitmore was in the hotel while Crosby stayed here," DeMarco said, "that's worth five hundred more to you and five hundred to whoever saw her."

Tony studied Whitmore's picture. "She looks familiar."

"Familiar's not good enough," DeMarco said. "I need a *witness*— a go-to-court, swear-on-a-Bible witness. But what I don't want is somebody willing to commit perjury."

"Okay," Tony said.

DeMarco could have simply placed an anonymous call to Langley and told the CIA that Crosby was Whitmore's source and that Crosby had been in New York shortly before the story was published. But he figured it would be better if he could find someone who had actually seen Whitmore with Crosby because that way Crosby couldn't deny having met the woman. But just placing Whitmore in the hotel on the same day Crosby was there might be good enough; that would at least give the CIA a starting point for breaking down whatever lies Crosby might tell his employer.

DeMarco looked down and saw a Manhattan magic trick had been performed: the five bills he had placed on the concierge's lectern had disappeared and he had never seen Tony's hands move.

"Give me until five," Tony whispered out the side of his mouth. "That way, I'll be able to talk to people on both this shift and the next one."

The florist wondered why DeMarco had given the concierge money. DeMarco could be a guest at the hotel and he might be trying to get tickets for a show or reservations at a restaurant, but since he had gone directly from the jail to the hotel, it was possible that his business with the concierge had to do with Whitmore. While DeMarco was talking to the concierge, the florist used one of the hotel's house phones, called the front desk, and asked if a Mr. DeMarco was registered at the hotel. The lady said no.

When DeMarco left the Hyatt, the florist followed. When DeMarco caught a cab, the florist caught one, too.

DeMarco ended up at a house in Queens that he entered without knocking. As the florist didn't know how long DeMarco would remain at the house, he paid the cabdriver an outrageous amount of money to sit there as long as necessary. While he waited, he called the man who was making his new identity. The man wasn't a hacker but he and the people that worked for him—all of them relatives—could use the Internet in the normal way to get information. He gave the ID maker the address in Queens and DeMarco's name and twenty minutes later the man called him back. The house belonged to a Gino and Maureen DeMarco. Gino was deceased. The DeMarcos had one son named Joseph.

So DeMarco was visiting his mother.

"One other thing," the forger said. "This man Gino DeMarco worked for the Italian mafia. He's dead because they killed him."

Now that was interesting: DeMarco had a blood link to a criminal, but he couldn't imagine a connection between Whitmore's story and organized crime. The more he learned about DeMarco, the more the man intrigued him.

As the florist sat there, he reflected again on what he was doing. Unlike his late brother, he wasn't an intellectual or a philosophical man; he couldn't articulate the correctness of the course of action he had chosen. All he knew was that his values—the values of his culture, the values of his family—demanded he act no matter the cost. It was the way it had always been and the way it always would be. They had selfishly and uncaringly destroyed someone he loved and he was the only one left to provide justice. And vengeance was justice.

He could have waited to see if the American legal system would punish the guilty but he had no faith in the courts, particularly not in a matter as complicated as this, one involving the press, the government, and wealthy people like Martin Taylor. He came to the United States twenty years ago because he figured the land of his country's greatest enemy was the safest place for him to hide. At the time of his arrival, he'd been prepared to hate America but over time he began to love his adopted home: its freedoms, its opportunities, even its people. But what he never grew to appreciate was the American legal system. It operated too slowly and it bent over backward to favor the guilty. He had witnessed too often—although it was no different in other countries—the way rich, powerful people evaded punishment for their crimes.

So he would provide the punishment—and he would leave it to people smarter than him to debate the morality of his actions.

At four thirty, DeMarco left the house in Queens and took a cab back to the Hyatt. The florist watched as he spoke to the concierge again, and saw the concierge hand him a piece of paper. DeMarco then looked at his watch, rushed from the hotel, and caught the next passing cab. The florist had driven his own car to New York so he could bring his weapons with him but it was parked in a garage several blocks away. He looked frantically for another cab and saw half a dozen coming down Forty-second Street toward him but they all had passengers. It was rush hour and every cab he could see was occupied, and he realized that DeMarco had been very lucky to get one. He watched helplessly as DeMarco's taxi disappeared from view.

He stood on the street for a moment pondering his next move, then looked back into the Hyatt.

The concierge was still at his post.

———◆———

DeMarco told the cabbie to take him to JFK. There wasn't anything else for him to do in New York and if the traffic wasn't too bad, he might be able to catch the next shuttle to D.C.

Tony had struck out finding anyone who remembered seeing Sandra Whitmore at the Hyatt. He did, however, give DeMarco all the information the hotel had on Crosby. Tony said he'd keep looking for somebody who had seen Whitmore, but told DeMarco not to get his hopes up.

DeMarco's parting words to the concierge had been, "No witness, no five-hundred-buck bonus. Keep looking." Tony assured him he would, but DeMarco had a feeling that he just might have to make that anonymous phone call to the CIA and inform them that one of their employees had been in New York just before Whitmore's article appeared—and let the boys from Langley take it from there.

He cursed when he saw the traffic jammed up in the Midtown Tunnel; he wasn't going to make the next shuttle. He wondered how many poor slobs had died in this city because they had the misfortune to have a heart attack during rush hour—which these days lasted from two until seven. Having nothing better to do, he pulled out his cell phone and called a sly fellow he knew named Neil.

Neil called himself an "information broker." What this meant was that he had a vast array of contacts in places that warehoused information on American citizens: Google, credit card companies, the IRS, et cetera—and if his paid informants couldn't tell him what he wanted to know, Neil had a small staff with the talent to hack into computers or simply spy on people if that's what a paying client required.

The most terrifying thing about Neil was that while half his clients were people in the private sector—often lobbyists—the other half were folk in the American government, people who were disinclined to get the necessary warrants or just wanted a leg up on the competition. Washington was a very scary place, and Neil was one of its dark denizens.

DeMarco gave Neil the information he had on Derek Crosby, told Neil what he wanted to know, and an hour later—just as DeMarco was trying to get his shoes back on after passing through security at the airport—Neil called him back. Neil confirmed that Mr. Crosby of Fairfax, Virginia, per his tax returns, was indeed an employee of the Central Intelligence Agency, a lowly GS-12, meaning that he was not a power player. He had used his Visa card to pay for a round-trip flight from D.C. to New York and for a one-night stay at the Hyatt. He had also charged a staggering bar bill to his card on the date Whitmore said she met with Crosby, and his beverages were purchased in the Hyatt's bar. Great. That was all DeMarco needed to know.

He thanked Neil and promised he would mail his fee to him tomorrow.

Mail cash, Neil said.

DeMarco checked his watch; his plane didn't board for half an hour. He decided he wanted to know one more thing about Mr. Crosby: he wanted to know exactly what he did at the CIA. Since LaFountaine had polygraphed everyone at Langley who knew about Diller's trip to Iran, how did he miss Crosby? He could have asked Neil to find out Crosby's job at the agency but he knew another person who could get what he needed to know and do so without hacking into a classified computer network.

Emma had worked for the DIA, the Defense Intelligence Agency, a group of Pentagon spies. Although she was now retired—or so she claimed—she knew a lot of people who worked at the CIA. She helped DeMarco occasionally on his cases because he'd once saved her life—a deed that occurred more by accident than an act of bravery on his part. She was older than he was, considerably smarter, and her attitude toward him was usually that of an impatient, somewhat intolerant big sister. She despised John Mahoney.

Asking for her help, however, was going to be different than dealing with Neil. Neil had helped because DeMarco—or, to be accurate, the U.S. Treasury—paid for his services. Emma was different. She wouldn't take money but she would demand to know why she should help DeMarco and, in particular, she would want to know why Whitmore would give DeMarco—a complete stranger—the name of her source. So he told her the truth, that Whitmore was blackmailing Mahoney, and that he was trying to identify her source in an under-the-table way so Whitmore could get out of jail.

"I'm not going to help you get her out of jail," Emma said. "That woman should be shot."

"This isn't about getting her out of jail," DeMarco said. "It's about exposing the rat in the CIA who gave her the information in the first place."

Emma didn't respond.

"Look, all I want you to do is find out what Crosby's job is at Langley. I'm just curious about the guy and it won't kill you to make a phone call."

"One phone call," Emma said. But he could tell that at this point she was curious about Mr. Crosby herself.

He gave her Crosby's description in case more than one Derek Crosby worked at Langley.

Tony walked out of the Hyatt, singing Dean Martin's "That's Amore" to himself.

It had been a *damn* fine day—he had almost two thousand bucks in his wallet. Five hundred from that guy DeMarco, one fifty from a man who said his wife was gonna divorce him if he didn't get tickets to *The Lion King,* over a hundred from out-of-town schmucks who just wanted to know where to go for this and that—and the real prize: a grand from a private dick who needed access to a room registered to Mr. and Mrs. Smith. Tony didn't know what the detective did in the room—he suspected he might have installed a video camera—and he didn't really care. It wasn't his problem that people named Smith kept screwing people they weren't married to.

So what should he do with the money? His old lady had been bitching because the TV was on the fritz, and his girlfriend was bitching because he wouldn't take her to Atlantic City. With the money in his wallet, he figured he might be able to make them both happy for a change. Yeah right, like *that* was possible. But he knew a guy who could get him a fell-off-the-truck deal on a Sony, and if he could get a cheap room in A.C., then maybe . . .

"That's a gun pressed against your spine. It has a silencer on it. If it doesn't kill you, you'll be in a wheelchair for the rest of your life. Now walk down the alley."

Oh, fuck me. Why today of all days? Why did this have to happen when I've got so damn much money on me?

"Hey, look," Tony said, "my money's in my wallet. Come on. Just take it. Don't hurt me."

The guy prodded him in the back and Tony started down the alley. He didn't want to go into that damn alley.

"Please. My wallet's in my back pocket, the left-hand side. Just pull it out right now."

The guy didn't say anything. He just kept pushing Tony along. He hadn't seen the guy's face but he sounded big—and foreign. He had some kind of accent.

They reached a Dumpster that had three big black garbage bags on top, and the man pushed Tony behind the Dumpster so they were hidden by the bags. Tony was facing a brick wall and he was eye level with a line of graffiti that read: *Jesus Loves You.* His first thought was, *If He loves me so much, why is there a gun stuck in my back?* But his next thought was that he hadn't been to confession in years and the last time he'd been to Mass was his nephew's wedding. He was going straight to hell if this guy killed him.

"You talked to a man named DeMarco today. At five, you gave him a piece of paper. I want to know what you talked about and what was on the paper."

Maybe Jesus did love him. The guy wasn't a mugger.

Tony told him everything he wanted to know: that DeMarco was trying to find a witness who could place a man named Derek Crosby in the hotel with a reporter named Sandra Whitmore on a particular day. He couldn't remember Crosby's credit card number, only that it was Visa, but he remembered the address in Fairfax. Thank God he had a good memory for numbers.

"And that's all we talked about and that's all I know," Tony said. "I swear to God. Please, just take my money and let me go."

"How were you supposed to get ahold of DeMarco? Was he planning on coming back to the hotel?"

"He gave me his cell phone number. He told me to call him if I found anything else out."

"Give me the number."

Tony reached into his shirt pocket and handed the guy the yellow Post-it that he'd written DeMarco's number on.

"That's it," Tony said. "That's everything."

The man didn't say anything for what seemed an eternity, and Tony wondered if the guy was thinking about whacking him.

"I want you to stand here for two minutes," he finally said. "Count to a hundred and twenty. Slowly. If you turn around or come out of the alley in less than two minutes, I'll kill you. And if you call DeMarco and tell him we talked, I'll also kill you. I know where you work."

"I won't call him," Tony said. And he wouldn't. No fuckin' way was he going to get in the middle of whatever the hell was going on.

Tony heard the guy walk away. He didn't bother counting. He wasn't leaving the alley for at least five minutes. As he stood there, he stared at *Jesus Loves You* and wondered if maybe he should give up his girlfriend. He figured adultery was the biggest sin he was currently committing. Plus, the girlfriend was becoming more of a wife than a girlfriend the way she nagged his ass, and even the sex had gotten kinda stale. Yeah, it was time to fly straight.

After he figured five minutes had passed, he headed toward the mouth of the alley, reaching for his cell phone as he walked. He was going to call his girlfriend and say he couldn't see her tonight.

Right now, he just wanted to go home and hug his kids.

——————◆——————

The florist walked two blocks from the alley and stepped into a bar. He didn't drink alcohol—he never had—but he needed to sit down for a minute and think, and he wanted to be someplace off the street.

He ordered an orange juice from the bartender and then his hand moved toward his breast pocket to pull out a cigarette and he almost laughed out loud. He hadn't smoked in years. It seemed as if doing the sort of work he used to do—following people, intimidating and threatening them—was doing more than just bringing back memories he wanted to forget. He was turning back into the man he had wanted to forget.

Now what? DeMarco had told the concierge he wanted proof that Sandra Whitmore had met with a man named Derek Crosby who lived in Fairfax, Virginia. *But why? Why would this Washington lawyer want to do that?* It was possible DeMarco's interest in Crosby had nothing to do with Mahata's death or the reason why Whitmore was in jail. Yes, that was possible, but seemed highly unlikely.

So. He had three options. He could do nothing, just sit in New York and wait for Whitmore to be released from jail, but that could be weeks or maybe even months. The second option was to find DeMarco and talk to him, and since he had the man's phone number and knew he lived in Washington, that shouldn't be too hard to do. Or he could question this man Crosby in Fairfax, Virginia.

He decided to talk to DeMarco, although he knew doing so could cause him significant problems. It was one thing to question the concierge, a man who had no vested interest in whatever was happening and who was afraid the florist might kill him. DeMarco could be a different matter. If he had to persuade DeMarco to talk—and he suspected he would—DeMarco would most likely call the authorities. Unless he killed him.

Well, he would decide when the time came; all he knew was that he couldn't stop now.

"Do you want another orange juice?" the bartender asked. "Maybe a shot of vodka in it this time?"

"No, but could I possibly purchase a cigarette from you?" the florist said. "Just one."

As DeMarco was walking down the Jetway at Reagan National, he turned his cell phone back on and saw he'd missed a call from Emma. He went to the nearest bar, ordered a beer, and called her.

"Derek Crosby works at the CIA," Emma said, "just as Neil told you."

"Yeah, I know, but what does he do there? Anything related to Iran?"

"I didn't finish," Emma said. "Derek Crosby is five foot seven, bald, and wears glasses so thick he should be able to see the canals on Mars. And he's the only Derek Crosby at the agency."

"Uh-oh," DeMarco said.

"Yeah, uh-oh. And he has nothing to do with Iran. He's an analyst in the Cuban section, which means he probably monitors the cigar and sugar markets, Cuba being the big military threat that it is."

"Aw, shit," DeMarco said.

Chapter 12

———————◆◆◆———————

When Yuri called, Ivan Dyachenko was in Escondido, a suburb of San Diego, eating breakfast with his Mexican mistress and their two children. He would eat dinner that night with his Russian wife and his other three children.

Ivan loved children.

Yuri told him what he wanted him to do and exactly how he wanted the job done. When he finished, Ivan tried to tell him that he could use a little extra cash because his wife's car had broken down and one of the kids needed . . . but Yuri hung up. The man was a heartless bastard.

Ivan returned to the kitchen, almost tripping over a pudgy baby boy clad only in a diaper, crawling around on the floor. He picked the child up and bussed him on his bare stomach, which was not easy considering the smell coming from the little tyke's diaper. His mistress asked if he wanted more huevos rancheros, more sausage, more juice, anything at all. When he said no, she got a look of concern on her pretty, plump face, as if worried that he might waste away if he stopped eating after his second helping.

People often asked Ivan if he'd been a weight lifter when he was younger and he understood why: he was a colossus with a head the size of a basketball and, like all the great Russian lifters, he had a big hard gut and massive arms and thighs. He wore a goatee, which he thought made his face look slimmer, but his Russian friends still told

him that he was the spitting image of Andrey Chemerkin, who had
won the weight-lifting gold at the Atlanta games in '96. But Ivan had
never lifted weights. In fact, the heaviest thing he could recall ever
lifting was a Ukrainian who couldn't have weighed more than seventy kilos.

Ivan had thrown him off a roof.

———◆———

Conrad Diller's place in Del Mar was a gorgeous white stucco house
with an ocean view and a Spanish tile roof. It had a three-car garage,
the lawn was professionally manicured, and there were majestic palm
trees on the grounds. Ivan just shook his head. He knew he would
never own a home like this one.

Ivan rented the crummy two-bedroom apartment for his mistress
in Escondido, the appliances so old they barely worked. He had to
set off bug bombs every month to kill the roaches, something he hated
to do because he was afraid the insect killer could affect the children.
He and his wife lived in an equally dismal place in a run-down building near the Gaslamp district in San Diego, although he paid no rent
for it because Yuri had an arrangement with the man who owned the
building. But that was the only perk his job provided. He owned no
real estate, had no pension plan or health insurance, and his income
was unpredictable. He was supposed to receive a percentage of whatever the organization made but his salary was inconsistent and seemed
to vary with Yuri's moods. It had occurred to him more than once
that he would have been better off driving a truck or working on the
docks as a stevedore but how could he get such a job? What would he
put down on a résumé? Education: none. Skills: strangulation. Ref-
erences: only Yuri, who could attest to his loyalty and his ability to
kill.

He looked up at Diller's house again. He could see lights on inside and had seen Diller and his wife walk past the windows several
times. Had Yuri just wanted Diller dead, it would have been easy.
He would have walked up to the door, knocked, and forced his way

into the house. Then he would have strangled Diller, raped and strangled his wife, and stolen a few things to make it look like a home invasion that had gone very, very bad. Yes, that would have been easy.

But that's not what Yuri wanted. Yuri wanted Diller disappeared. And not only that, he wanted his car left at an airport so it would look as if he had fled the country. So now he would have to snatch the man and his car, then take him someplace where he could bury a body, which was gonna be a real pain in the *zhopa*. He'd have to drive for miles to find a suitable place to dispose of a corpse.

Diller's neighborhood, he quickly decided, was not a good place for a kidnapping. Too many houses, too close together. Too many people out jogging or walking their silly dogs. The streetlights lit up the block like a football stadium and cops drove by periodically to protect these wealthy people. To do what Yuri wanted he'd have to wait for Diller to go someplace like an underground parking garage where he would be alone—assuming the guy ever left his house.

Why couldn't these things ever be simple?

Since he wasn't sure what to do next, he called his wife, then his mistress. He didn't talk to either woman for very long but he talked to all the kids who were old enough to talk. He talked the longest to little Elena, his oldest child with his wife. She was seven now and smart as a whip, and she told him about a boy at school she wanted to kiss. She cracked him up—but it gave him a funny feeling in his stomach to think about boys kissing his little girl.

Finally, he called Yuri. "Is there any way," he asked, "that you can get this guy to go someplace outside the city? You know, tell him you need to talk to him and he should meet you someplace where there are not a lot of people around?"

Yuri cursed as if Ivan had asked him to dig a ditch with his bare hands but said that what Ivan wanted could be arranged.

"Oh," Ivan added. "And can I get reimbursed for the money I have to spend on gas? I mean, I don't know if you've noticed, but the price of gas . . ."

Yuri hung up.

Chapter 13

———◆———

DeMarco took a seat next to Mahoney on the rough-cut wooden bleachers, hoping splinters wouldn't snag his pants.

"This thing with Sandra Whitmore is getting weird, boss," he said.

Mahoney ignored him and watched the pitcher throw a thirty-mile-per-hour fastball. The batter, who was about four foot three, smacked it good but right to the shortstop, and the shortstop scooped it up like a midget Derek Jeter and sidearmed the ball to first.

"Good glove," Mahoney yelled. "Good glove."

Every once in a while, and DeMarco had no idea why, Mahoney would leave his office, cab over to a ball field in southeast D.C. and, depending on the season, watch the kids play baseball or football. Almost all the kids were black, as were the spectators, and Mahoney would usually be the only white man there. After watching the boys play for a while, he'd head back to the Capitol, rejuvenated by the experience.

One time when DeMarco had met him at the field, Mahoney had been behind home plate wearing a too small chest protector and a mask. DeMarco assumed the regular ump hadn't shown up, that they had needed a volunteer, and Mahoney had raised his paw. Mahoney was having a blast that day, yelling "Stee-rike" at the top of his lungs and lumbering into the middle of the diamond to make calls at the bases. DeMarco had to sit through four innings and when the game was over Mahoney had an absolute glow in his eyes.

John Mahoney was a hard man to categorize.

"So, what's going on?" Mahoney finally asked as he continued to watch the game.

"Whitmore was set up by somebody, but I don't know why."

"Set up?" Mahoney said. Then he yelled out to the batter, "Good eye, son, good eye. Stay away from those high ones."

"The guy that leaked the story to her isn't who he said he was," DeMarco explained. Then he told Mahoney how Whitmore's source had used the identity of a real CIA employee. "So, I don't know if the guy who talked to Whitmore is really CIA or not, but whoever he is, he's not Derek Crosby."

Mahoney started to say something—probably to tell DeMarco that he didn't want to hear about what he *didn't* know—but just then a kid tried to steal third and the home-plate umpire, the only umpire in the game, called him out. Mahoney, who was closer to third base than the ump, leaped out of his seat and yelled, "He was safe! Safe!" One of the mothers sitting a few feet from Mahoney then called out, "Yeah, Lionel, that boy's foot hit the bag about an *hour* before he tagged him."

Lionel turned and glared at Mahoney—and DeMarco didn't blame him. The poor guy volunteered his time to ump these games and the last thing he needed was some big mouth stirring up the mothers and turning them into a screeching mob. Lionel also knew, whether Mahoney was right or wrong, that if he changed his call they'd yell about every call he made for the rest of the game. He looked directly at Mahoney and said, "Runner at third is out. Batter up." Then he slammed his mask down over his scowling face and took up his position behind the plate.

"Can you believe that guy?" Mahoney said to the mother on his right.

This was hopeless, DeMarco thought; he'd just have to wait until the game was over.

Twenty minutes later it was, and DeMarco and Mahoney started walking in the direction of the Capitol, looking for a cab. Mahoney's security guys would be having heart attacks if they knew where he was.

"Anyway," DeMarco said, "the guy who leaked the story to Whitmore may or may not be CIA, and right now I don't have any idea how to find him."

"Supposedly," Mahoney said, "there were only two groups of people who knew about Diller attending that meeting in Tehran. Select members of the House and Senate intelligence committees and people at the CIA."

"And LaFountaine said all his people were polygraphed," DeMarco added.

"Yeah, I know what he said."

"What? You don't believe him?"

"I'm not saying I don't believe him. I'm saying I don't trust him."

DeMarco wasn't sure what to say next, but before he could say anything Mahoney said, "I know LaFountaine's up to something but I think he's telling the truth about his guys not having leaked the story. He said he'd resign if one of them had, and he wouldn't have said that if he was lying. So he's probably right; somebody in Congress leaked this thing, and the guy who impersonated Crosby probably isn't CIA."

"Do you have any idea who in Congress could have leaked the story?" DeMarco said.

Instead of answering his question, Mahoney asked, "What did you find out about this fake CIA guy?"

"All I've got so far is a description. He's in his early sixties, tall, tanned, good shape, ginger-colored hair."

"Ginger?" Mahoney said. "What the hell's *ginger*?"

"You know, kind of a reddish-brown color."

"Well, shit. No wonder nobody could connect him to Whitmore. They probably didn't know what ginger was. What a stupid fuckin' description."

Sheesh. "And the guy had a lisp," DeMarco added.

"A lisp?"

"Yeah, you know, when he says . . ."

"I know what a lisp is," Mahoney said.

He and DeMarco walked in silence for half a block before Mahoney said, "You know about Gordon Liddy and Charles Colson?"

"Watergate?"

"Yeah. Well, Dick Nixon wasn't the only guy who employed people like Liddy. Almost every guy who's been in the White House has had a few people like him, goddamn commando zealots willing to do anything."

"What's this got to do with . . ."

"There was a guy like Liddy who worked for ___."

And Mahoney told DeMarco the name of the president.

"You're kidding!" DeMarco said. "I never would have thought . . ."

"Yeah, I know. Now he goes around building houses for the homeless and wouldn't say shit if he had a mouthful. Anyway, he had a young guy that would leak stuff he wanted leaked, and lean on people he wanted leaned on. The guy's name was Acosta, and I remember him because of the lisp. It's hard to act tough when you're lisping, and one time he tried to get tough with me."

Mahoney laughed at the memory.

"It would be a hell of a coincidence if this Acosta character was the one that talked to Whitmore," DeMarco said.

"Yeah, but there's something else that makes me think it could be him," Mahoney said. "Eight, ten years ago, Acosta was working for a lobbyist, and he and the lobbyist almost landed in jail for lying to a grand jury."

"What does this have to do with—"

"This particular lobbyist is very close to one of my, uh, friends."

"You mean one of the congressmen who attended LaFountaine's briefing?" DeMarco said.

Mahoney didn't answer.

"Well, which congressman is it?" DeMarco persisted. "I mean, if you know who started this whole thing, you oughta tell me. The name might help me identify Whitmore's source."

"Never mind that for now," Mahoney said. "Just look up Acosta. He could be dead for all I know, but he fits the description. And he's the kind of guy that would do something like this if the money was right. His first name is Dan or Dave, something like that, and he had kinda reddish hair—what I guess you'd call ginger."

The target's name was Dale Acosta.

Benny Mark was sitting in his rented Taurus in the lot where Acosta most likely parked his car. He had been sitting there for two days and his back was killing him.

When he had arrived at his motel in Myrtle Beach, there'd been an envelope waiting for him. Inside the envelope was Acosta's address, the make and license-plate number for his car, and Acosta's DMV photo. Benny always insisted on a photo.

One time he'd been hired to take out a snitch named Bob Reynolds. He'd been given Reynolds's address, which turned out to be an apartment in a housing project in St. Louis. So Benny popped Bob Reynolds —then found out the next day that he'd popped the *wrong* Bob Reynolds. Two Bob Reynoldses had lived in the same damn building. Boy, had he felt like a horse's patootie on that one—and from then on, he always got a photo.

Acosta lived in a short block of town houses on the sixth fairway of a golf course. The parking lot for the town houses was on the east end of the block and if Benny parked at the front of the lot, close to the fairway, he could see the front porch of Acosta's place from where he sat. But Acosta's car wasn't in the lot and Benny had never seen a light go on in Acosta's town house the whole time he'd been watching. The guy was obviously out of town or staying with a girlfriend or some damn thing.

He had called Jimmy yesterday and asked him if he had any idea where Acosta might be. Jimmy said he didn't know; he'd been told that Acosta was retired and he figured the guy would be at home. Well, he's not, Benny had said, and I'm goin' outta my mind, sittin' here on my ass all day. Do you think maybe you could find out where he is? But Jimmy hadn't gotten back to him, so Benny was still sitting.

The setup for the hit wasn't ideal. If the guy had parked in a garage it would have been better, but the lot where he parked was right out in the open and you could see it from the fairway and from the street, and there were cars driving by all the time. If Acosta went to his car at night, *late* at night, that might work, but the lot was pretty well lit.

So Benny came up with a plan.

The first day, he walked around in the rough near the fairway until he found a golf ball. Then, last night, when it was dark and nobody was playing, he walked to the front of Acosta's town house, which faced the golf course, and threw the golf ball at a window—and the ball bounced off the window. He went back to his car, got the tire iron, and jabbed the window with the pointy end and, fortunately, the window didn't shatter—which made him wonder what kind of glass it was made of. He then shoved the golf ball he'd found through the hole made by the tire iron. Perfect.

If Acosta ever came home, Benny was gonna put on a hat and sunglasses and knock on his door. He'd say, "Hey, sorry about that ball I put through your window, that fuckin' slice I got. I just came to settle up with you." If the guy didn't let Benny into his house, he'd show him the .32 and force his way in.

Benny always used little .32 caliber automatics when he worked. The gun was the quietest one he could find, and if he wrapped a towel around the barrel or shot through a pillow, you could barely hear it. After the job, he'd toss the gun—the cost of the gun was included in the cost of the job—and buy another one.

Yeah, he loved those little .32s. They were easy to conceal and quieter than a popcorn fart. They weren't the least bit accurate, of course, but that didn't matter because Benny couldn't shoot for shit and he'd never shot anybody from more than three feet away.

He always got a kick out of those professional killers they showed in the movies, those slick, evil-looking guys that used silenced weapons or could hit somebody with a rifle from three hundred yards or blow up cars with cell-phone bombs. Benny had no idea how to build a bomb and he had never used a rifle in his life. He wasn't a hunter and had never been in the military. And as for silencers—where the hell did you buy 'em? He didn't know. And if you bought one, then you had to machine the gun to fit the silencer and he didn't know how to do that, either. Benny assumed that there were professional killers out there like you saw in the movies but he suspected most of the real ones were guys like him: guys that just walked up behind people and shot 'em in the head.

Benny had never planned on being a professional killer but he'd been in Chicago working for a guy in the rackets there, and one day his boss said he needed somebody whacked. The boss had just been bitching about how this guy was a problem; he hadn't really been asking Benny to do the hit. But Benny and Betty Ann had been living in a shit hole at the time and they needed the money, so Benny had said that for five grand he'd do the job. The boss had stared at him like he was nuts, not ever thinking a guy who looked like Benny would do something like that. And that's when Benny said, "He'll never see me coming."

The next time it happened, he and the boss were having drinks with the big boss, and the big boss said *he* needed someone taken care of. And Benny's boss glanced over at Benny and said, "I know a guy who can do the job." And that's how Benny the professional killer was born.

Killing people wasn't, however, a full-time occupation. There just weren't that many guys who wanted people dead or were willing to pay someone to do the job. So he and Betty Ann saved up their dough and bought a bar in Tacoma, Washington, near the port there. He made maybe sixty grand a year after taxes, which was enough for him and Betty Ann to get by on, but he could always use the extra money. So when Jimmy had a job for him, he'd take it as long as it wasn't anything too tricky—and this thing with Acosta wasn't tricky at all.

The United States House of Representatives has its own historian and
DeMarco had always thought this position had been created so there
would be at least one version of history that put Congress in a positive light—or at least more positive than if the tale was told by someone not on their payroll.

Dr. Donald Finemore worked in Cannon House Office Building.
He was a shaggy-haired six footer in his forties who weighed maybe
a hundred and thirty pounds. The absence of body fat could have
been due to a tapeworm but was more likely explained by the racing
bike propped up against one wall. When DeMarco entered his office, Finemore was using a magnifying glass to study a small book
that looked as if it might fall apart if he turned a page too fast.

DeMarco said, "Dr. Finemore, I was wondering if . . ."

"Do you know what this is?" Finemore said, pointing at the book.

"Uh, no, sir," DeMarco said.

"It's a diary written by an African American who worked as a steward in the Capitol about 1900. One of his descendants found it in a
trunk in her attic and fortunately she brought it to me instead of trying to sell it on eBay."

"Well, that's, uh, really interesting," DeMarco said, "but I was
wondering . . ."

"It says here that Mr. Washington, the man who wrote this,
caught David Henderson having sex with the daughter of a senator. Henderson was the Speaker of the House during McKinley's
administration."

DeMarco almost said, *Well, I guess that proves the morals of House
Speakers haven't changed much in the last hundred years,* but he didn't.
Instead, he said, "Wow. That's really something." Finemore, unfor-
tunately, thought he was being sincere.

"Not only that," Finemore went on, so excited he was almost stam-
mering, "it says that this woman, the senator's daughter . . ."

Fifteen minutes passed before DeMarco was finally able to ask
his question, after having learned more about the sexual escapades

of politicians during the McKinley years than he ever wanted to know.

"This guy Acosta," DeMarco said, "worked for ____."

And he told Finemore the ex-president's name.

"Oh," Finemore said, sounding disappointed, as if anything that had happened in the last fifty years was way too recent to be of any interest to him.

"Anyway," DeMarco continued, "Acosta had some kind of job at the White House but not a bigwig position. He wasn't the chief of staff or the press secretary or anything like that. So I was wondering if you had anything around here with a list of staff members from that administration. I need his first name, but what I really need is a picture of him."

"Come with me," Finemore said. He didn't bother to ask why DeMarco wanted the information; he just wanted to get back to the steward's diary to see who else Speaker Henderson might have screwed. He led DeMarco to a room a few feet down the hall from his office, picked three books off one shelf, two off another, and dumped them on a table. When he dropped the books, a small mushroom cloud of dust rose into the air and DeMarco sneezed.

"You might find what you need in one of those," Finemore said. "If you don't, contact the White House historian and she might be able to help you."

It took DeMarco twenty minutes to find it: a thirty-year-old picture of *Dale* Acosta, not Dan or Dave as Mahoney had told him. Acosta was standing with the vice president and two other men at a charity golf event; Acosta's name was mentioned only because he was with the VP. And the young Dale Acosta in the picture was pretty much as Sandra Whitmore had described him: tall, well built, with ginger-colored hair. Regarding what functions Acosta had performed at the White House, the book said nothing and DeMarco wasn't surprised by this.

DeMarco thanked Finemore for his help and headed back to his office in the subbasement of the Capitol. From there he called Neil and an hour later Neil e-mailed him Dale Acosta's current DMV photo, one that was only two years old. Neil further informed him that Acosta lived in Myrtle Beach, South Carolina, and gave him an address. Per Acosta's tax returns he was retired, living on social security and investments from his 401(k). He was now single after two failed marriages.

———◆◆◆———

The florist was frustrated.

He had left New York that morning and driven to D.C. to find DeMarco. He didn't know if DeMarco was still in New York or not, but he figured the man would have to return home to Washington eventually. His plan was to wait outside DeMarco's house and question him when he came back.

The problem was, he couldn't get DeMarco's address.

He did the simple things first and checked the white pages directory on the Internet for the District of Columbia—but DeMarco didn't have a listed phone number. He then did a reverse lookup using the cell phone number DeMarco had given the concierge but all that told him was the number was for a cell phone and also unlisted.

Before he came to this country, if he had wanted to know where someone lived it wouldn't have mattered if the number was unlisted. He would have snapped his fingers—literally—and within an hour he would have had not only an address but a complete dossier on the man. But that sort of power was no longer his.

Finally, unable to think of anything else, the florist called the man who was making his new identity papers and asked him to see if he could get Mr. DeMarco's address. The ID maker had a relative at the Virginia DMV who helped him obtain the materials he needed to make fake driver's licenses, and this relative knew people who worked in the licensing departments in other states. So the florist knew the forger could get him the information he needed but he hated to let him know anything about his business. But in for a penny, in for a pound, as the saying went. So he asked the forger to get whatever information he could on Derek Crosby as well.

All the florist could do now was wait. Wait for Whitmore to get out of jail. Wait to see if the forger could get him an address for DeMarco. Wait until nightfall to visit either DeMarco or Crosby.

Chapter 14

———◆———

What DeMarco needed to do next was show Dale Acosta's picture to Sandra Whitmore to determine if Acosta really was her source—but that meant he'd have to make another trip to New York, which he wasn't anxious to do. Flying was just too painful these days, so to postpone the trip he decided to go see Emma.

He wanted to talk to her about Mahoney's comment about LaFountaine, that Mahoney suspected LaFountaine was up to something more than trying to figure out who was responsible for killing his agent. If there was anyone who would be able to guess what sort of games America's head spy might be playing, Emma, being a retired spy herself, was the one.

He arrived at her place in McLean and, as always, was envious she owned such a magnificent home. The place wasn't exactly a mansion but it was large and beautifully designed, both inside and out, and the grounds surrounding the house looked as if they could have been part of the national arboretum. DeMarco knew she paid professional gardeners a small fortune to care for her lawn and plants but he had no idea how a retired civil servant could afford to do this—and he knew Emma would never tell him. She was, without a doubt, the most enigmatic person he'd ever encountered.

The door was answered by Emma's lover. Christine was in her thirties—blue-eyed, blonde, slim, and lovely.

"Emma's not here," she said before DeMarco could even ask.

Christine was holding a cello bow in her hand. She played in the National Symphony, and she must have been practicing when DeMarco rang the bell. She seemed irritated to see him but he didn't know if that was because he'd interrupted her playing or if it was because he was the one standing there. The only thing they had in common was Emma, and Christine always acted as if DeMarco was an unwanted intrusion into their lives, which, if he was honest about it, he usually was.

"Shit," DeMarco muttered. "When is she coming back?"

"In a couple days, maybe three. She wasn't sure."

"Where'd she go?"

Christine hesitated and DeMarco thought for a minute she wasn't going to tell him. "New York," she finally said. "She left this morning."

Ah, this could be good, DeMarco thought. "Do you have any idea how I can get ahold of her?"

He knew Emma's cell phone number but he also knew that she rarely turned on her phone. For Emma, a cell phone was primarily a one-way communication device.

"Yes," Christine said—but that's all she said, and it looked as if that was all she intended to say.

DeMarco, naturally, began to feel a wee bit irritated. He'd known Emma longer than Christine, and it wasn't like he was some salesman who wanted to pitch her life insurance. On the other hand, he could understand why she wasn't immediately forthcoming. One time, when Emma had helped him with one of his cases, she'd been kidnapped, tortured, and almost killed by a Chinese spy. Yeah, that could explain Christine's reluctance. But still . . .

"Look," DeMarco said, "all I'm gonna do is e-mail her a guy's picture. I just want her to look at it."

That was a lie, but who cared? Christine was being a brat.

As Christine continued to ponder his request, she looked into his eyes trying to measure his capacity for deceit, and DeMarco did his best to look open and honest. This wasn't easy. As she stared, she tapped the cello bow against the palm of her left hand—which made him instantly envision the bow as a riding crop and Christine dressed in a leather bustier and thigh-high leather boots.

Finally, she said, "She's staying at Edith Baxter's in Manhattan. Edith invited her up there for a dinner party."

Edith Baxter was a prominent business woman whose son had been killed when terrorists bombed the trains in Madrid, and Emma had intervened when it appeared Edith was on the verge of suicide. If Edith was holding dinner parties it appeared that she was on the road to recovery, and that was good.

"The phone number's in the kitchen," Christine said. "I'll go get it."

She turned and walked down the hallway toward the kitchen, tapping the bow of the cello against her lower leg. As DeMarco watched her butt move beneath the lightweight cotton pants she was wearing, his S and M fantasy blossomed again.

He was sick. He needed help. Or maybe he just needed to get laid more often.

———◆◆◆———

DeMarco got lucky: Emma was at Edith Baxter's when he called. He quickly told her what had transpired with Sandra Whitmore since he had last spoken to her, concluding with, "So this guy Acosta might have been the one who impersonated Derek Crosby. It's a long shot, but I want to send you his picture and since you're up there already, maybe you could show it to Whitmore and see if Acosta's the guy."

Emma didn't answer.

He could envision her sitting there as she pondered his request. She was tall and always slim because she ran marathons. Her short, silver-blonde hair was perfectly and expensively styled. She had a patrician profile, and because the topic was Sandra Whitmore, her thin lips were probably turned downward in disgust and her blue eyes would appear to be glazed with frost.

"Emma," DeMarco said, "please. I really need to identify the person who leaked the story to her."

"So give everything you have to the FBI right now and let *them* investigate."

"Mahoney doesn't want to do that. At least not yet. And anyway, until Whitmore confirms that Acosta's her source, I really don't have anything to give the FBI."

Once again, Emma went silent and DeMarco could tell that she was really reluctant to get involved in this thing.

"Come on," DeMarco whined. "You're up there already. Save me a trip."

"I despise that woman," Emma said. "If I'm alone in a room with her, I just might snap her neck."

And Emma could.

"Don't snap her neck. Just show her the picture. If Whitmore confirms Acosta was the one who fed her the story, then I'll pass that on to the CIA."

He didn't bother to add, *if Mahoney will let me.*

"All right," Emma said. "How will you get the photo to me?"

"I'll e-mail it. Neil e-mailed it to me, so I'll forward it to you."

"Okay," Emma said. She paused, then added, "Joe, you better watch what you're doing."

"What do you mean?"

"I mean a CIA agent has been killed and Jake LaFountaine and all the people who work for him take that very seriously. More seriously than you could possibly imagine, since you've never been in the intelligence business. So I don't know exactly what your devious boss is having you do, but I'd suggest you not get cross-wired with LaFountaine, not over something as important as this."

Chapter 15

The Metropolitan Correctional Center is in lower Manhattan, half a block from Foley Square, tucked in behind the U.S. Courthouse. It's an unremarkable ten-story structure that looks like an apartment building whose architect had a penchant for long, narrow windows. A closer look at the windows reveals bars behind glass that has a somewhat yellowish tint. More obvious evidence of the building's function is the concertina wire enclosing the balconies.

Emma took a slow walk around the facility noting the placement of security cameras. In the alley between the courthouse and the prison, she saw two television crews standing around smoking and drinking coffee. Also in the alley were two gleaming black limousines and standing next to the limos were four men in dark suits who had the attitude of bodyguards rather than chauffeurs. She wondered if some Madoff-like swindler was appearing in court that day.

She was dressed in casual clothes: jeans and a T-shirt. On her head was a long-billed baseball cap and covering her eyes and a good part of her face were oversized sunglasses. She didn't want to be involved in this Sandra Whitmore mess and wished now that she had refused DeMarco's request. One thing she was definitely not going to do was be identified as one of Whitmore's visitors.

She approached the guard shack outside the facility. Keeping her head lowered so the camera behind the guard wouldn't get a clear view of her face, she informed the guard she was a messenger hired by Whitmore's lawyer to deliver a legal document she was required to place directly into Whitmore's hands. She showed the guard a New York state driver's license that identified her as Maxine Turner; the license was one of several she possessed from her days at the DIA, where she had sometimes needed alternate identities. She also showed the guard a corporate identification card that identified her as an employee of Elite Courier Services, a legitimate Manhattan messenger service. She had manufactured the ID that morning on Edith Baxter's computer and had laminated it at a local Kinko's. When the guard asked to see inside the envelope, Emma pulled out a six-page document she had downloaded from a Web site containing information in dense legal language about New York's press-shield law. She didn't show the guard the photograph that was also in the envelope. The guard directed her to a waiting room where she was patted down for weapons and contraband, then directed her to go through a metal detector, after which she was told that she would have to wait approximately forty-five minutes before she'd be allowed to see Whitmore.

Emma spent the time cursing DeMarco as she kept her face hidden by a magazine she found on one of the chairs in the room.

***

Sandra Whitmore sat across the table from Emma, sullen and suspicious. Her face was bloated, her eyes were puffy, and her hair was plastered to her skull as if it hadn't been washed in days. She reeked of cigarette smoke. There was no reason for letting herself go like this, Emma thought. She wasn't being held in a dungeon in Calcutta.

"Is that your source?" Emma asked, placing Dale Acosta's photograph on the table.

Whitmore looked at the photo as if Emma had just turned over the river card in a game of Texas hold 'em: her face gave away nothing. "I want to know who you are," she said to Emma for the second time.

"I told you who I am: I'm the person Joe DeMarco sent to show you that picture. That's all you need to know."

"But why should I believe you? How do I know this isn't some kind of trick?"

"Listen to me," Emma said. "I don't *like* you. I don't care if you sit in a jail cell until the day you die. The only reason I'm here is because I'm doing DeMarco a favor. Now if you don't want to confirm that's your source, I'll leave and you can stay here until you rot."

When Whitmore just stared at her, obviously trying to make up her mind, Emma rose to leave. She was halfway to the door before Whitmore said, "Yeah, that's him. That's Derek Crosby."

Emma turned around, shook her head slowly, and then smiled. She smiled because she knew how Whitmore would react to what she was about to say. "No," she said, "that's not Derek Crosby."

"What?" Whitmore said, confused by Emma's response.

"Derek Crosby works for the CIA. The man in that photo does not. He assumed Crosby's identity so he could feed you the story. In other words, he tricked you and he used you."

"What!" This time Whitmore shrieked the word. "Well, who the hell is he?"

Emma started to tell her Acosta's name but then decided not to. She didn't want Whitmore to know anything else because she was likely to publish whatever she knew and she was too selfish to care if that would hurt the government's case against Acosta. The other reason she didn't tell her was because she despised Whitmore and knew that not telling her would drive her crazy.

"Well?" Whitmore said. "Who is he?"

"Ask DeMarco," Emma said, and then turned away from Whitmore and rapped on the door to tell the guard waiting outside that she was ready to leave.

Whitmore stood up and screamed, "Goddamnit, tell me who he is! I have a right to know."

"Mahata Javadi had the right to live," Emma said. "You don't have a right to anything."

Whitmore's cell mate was lying on her bunk, reading a magazine. She looked up as Whitmore entered the cell and gave her a nod but didn't speak.

Whitmore's first two days in jail, she had had the cell to herself. She figured the folks who ran the place didn't want to put her in a cage with some violent psycho because if something happened to her, the *Daily News* would raise a front-page ruckus. But then they put another woman in with her, a petite black gal named LaTisha who wore her hair in cornrows. And it turned out that LaTisha was the perfect roommate: she didn't talk much, she'd been in prison before, and she seemed to know how the system worked. Most important, she'd been able to keep Whitmore supplied with cigarettes—although she was charging her fifteen bucks a pack.

Whitmore had told LaTisha her story the first day they met, how she'd been unjustly jailed because she wouldn't reveal a source. "Good for you, girl," LaTisha had said. "Nobody likes a snitch."

Whitmore didn't bother to explain that there was a big difference between a reporter not revealing a source and someone testifying against a criminal, but she didn't think LaTisha would appreciate the distinction. LaTisha seemed bright enough but she was pure ghetto.

LaTisha tossed the magazine she was reading onto the floor—one of those black fashion magazines where the models all looked like aliens to Whitmore with their flawless, metallic complexions, nonexistent waists, and arms and legs that were impossibly long and thin. "So how's it goin'?" she asked.

"Not good," Whitmore answered. "There's this asshole that's supposed to be helping me, but he's jerking me around."

"Oh, yeah," LaTisha said.

Whitmore could tell that LaTisha was expecting her to say more but she didn't. She liked LaTisha but that didn't mean she trusted her.

Whitmore lit a cigarette and flopped down on her bunk. It was a no-smoking facility but everybody smoked. What were the guards gonna do? Put 'em in jail? As she smoked, she thought that she didn't really need to know the name of her source to get released. If she told the judge a man impersonating a CIA agent had duped her, that would probably be good enough—good enough to get out of jail, that is. It would not be good enough, however, to keep her from looking like a complete idiot.

No, she needed to know the guy's name and why he had given her the story. Maybe if she had that information she'd be able to put the right spin on things. Maybe. With a grunt she got to her feet and went to the bars.

"Hey! Hey! I need to use the phone. Hey, is anybody out there?"

After a couple more minutes of yelling, a female guard waddled down the walkway and said, "What are you goin' on about?"

"I need to use the phone."

"Tough shit," the guard said. "We're busy right now. I'll take you to a phone later, unless you piss me off."

"Well, when will that be?" Whitmore asked.

"Now you're starting to piss me off," the guard said and walked away.

Whitmore cursed and slammed her right hand against the bars hard enough to bruise her palm.

"That's one mean, ugly bitch," LaTisha said.

Whitmore didn't say anything; she just stood there with her head pressed against the bars.

"How bad do you need to use a phone?" LaTisha asked her.

"Bad. I need to call a guy. He's got the info I need to get out of here."

"Is that right?" LaTisha said. "Is it worth a hundred bucks to you if I can get you a cell phone to use?"

"You can do that?"

"Girl, I told you. I know how things work around here."

"Fine. A hundred."

"You sure you're good for it? You owe me sixty already."

Her lawyer, the jerk, had given her a hundred bucks in cash the day she was jailed for contempt, but she'd gone through that pretty quickly at the rate she smoked. Since then she'd been borrowing from LaTisha and LaTisha had been keeping a running tab of every dime she owed her—and charging her 5 percent interest. LaTisha probably hadn't graduated from high school but she could calculate the vig on a debt as well as any loan shark.

"I'm good for it," Whitmore said.

LaTisha gave her a hard stare, but then said, "Okay. You'll have to wait until we go to chow, then I'll get one."

"You can't do it any sooner?"

"Hey, what do I look like? That T-Mobile lady?"

◆

LaTisha winked at Whitmore, rose from the table where they were eating, and approached a guard standing near the entrance to the kitchen. She pulled a hundred-dollar bill out of her bra, made sure none of the other guards were paying any attention to her, and passed the bill to the guard.

"I need a little privacy," she said.

When LaTisha spoke to the guard, all the ghetto was gone from her voice. She sounded like a Princeton graduate—which she was.

She entered the kitchen and walked into a pantry where they kept the potatoes and flour. It was the only place in the kitchen where she could hear above the din of pots and pans banging and the cooks yelling at each other. She tugged up the right pant leg of her jumpsuit, pulled a cell phone out of the top of one of her socks, and punched in a number.

"Foley," she said, "this is Clark. Whitmore's going to make a call from my cell phone in fifteen minutes. She's going to talk to somebody who has information to get her out of jail. That's all I know."

Linda Clark listened for a moment and hung up—and became LaTisha again.

Chapter 16

———◆◆◆———

DeMarco called Mahoney and after being placed on hold for fifteen minutes—which was about the average wait time whenever he called his boss—Mahoney came on the line.

"You were right," DeMarco said. "Acosta was the one who fed Whitmore the story. I had Emma show her his picture."

"Aw, shit," Mahoney said. "Why the hell did you involve her in this?"

DeMarco told Mahoney he had used Emma because she was already in New York and it had saved time, and without her help he never would have determined that Acosta was impersonating Derek Crosby.

"And you know she won't talk to anybody about this," DeMarco added.

"Yeah, but goddamnit," Mahoney said, "you know how she is."

What Mahoney meant was that Emma couldn't be relied upon because she wouldn't do what Mahoney told her and because she had morals and a conscience—two elements seemingly absent in Mahoney's makeup.

"Did she tell Whitmore who Acosta was?" Mahoney asked.

"No. She just showed her the picture."

"Well, that's good at least. That'll give you some time to find out who Acosta's working for."

"How do you know he's working for somebody?"

"Because guys like him never have their own agenda. They always have a boss. Plus, I can't imagine what motive he'd personally have for feeding the story to Whitmore."

"Okay, but I'm eventually going to have to tell Whitmore his name," DeMarco said. "I mean, I thought the purpose of this whole thing was to get her out of jail so she wouldn't tell the press about you, and if I don't give her his name . . ."

"Yeah, yeah, but hold off on telling her for now." Mahoney was silent for a moment as he pondered something, then added, "Tell her tomorrow morning. Late tomorrow morning."

"Okay."

"What I want you to do next is talk to Acosta. See if you can make him tell you who put him up to this and why."

"Aw, come on," DeMarco said. "Why don't I just give him to the CIA? I don't have the clout to make him tell me anything, but LaFountaine will hook wires to his nuts to make him talk."

"I don't want to tell LaFountaine, either. Not yet. I need to confirm something first."

"What do you have to confirm?"

"Never mind that."

Goddamn Mahoney. There was always another game.

"You just go see Acosta. Go see him tonight."

"Tonight! He lives in Myrtle Beach."

"So what? If you can't get a direct flight, there's gotta be some flight you can catch that'll get you close enough so you can drive there."

"Okay," DeMarco said and hung up.

He had no intention of flying to Myrtle Beach that night; he had a date and he was going to keep it. He'd fly down first thing in the morning and Mahoney would never know the difference. Plus, what Mahoney wanted him to do was stupid. There was no way in hell Acosta was going to talk to him. Eventually, Mahoney was going to have to tell LaFountaine that Acosta was the guy, and let the CIA or the Justice Department or whoever take it from there.

DeMarco's plan was to go home, get an online airplane reservation, take a shower and shave, then pack a bag for Myrtle Beach. Then tomorrow, bright-eyed, bushy-tailed, and—hopefully—freshly laid, he'd go see Acosta.

Yep, that was his plan—and to hell with Mahoney.

After speaking with DeMarco, Mahoney returned three phone calls he couldn't ignore. One of the calls was from the president's chief of staff, a political hit man who would stab you in the back without hesitation if he thought stabbing you would advance his boss's agenda. Mahoney recorded every conversation he had with the guy because he figured he was being recorded, too.

Once the important calls were out of the way, he poured three fingers of Wild Turkey over a single ice cube then plopped down on the couch in his office. It was hard to drink lying on his back but his big gut made a perfect platform upon which to rest the glass.

He ignited a cigar. He tried to blow a smoke ring—he always tried when he was alone—but he never succeeded, and this always irritated him. He figured the problem was his tongue. He had tried blowing smoke rings while looking in the mirror, and he could see that his lips formed the necessary, perfect *O,* so his tongue must be shaped wrong or too fat or something. But still, he tried.

He didn't think DeMarco would get anything from Acosta but it didn't cost him anything to let DeMarco try. What he needed to do, though, was give DeMarco some time to get to Acosta, which meant he needed to keep Whitmore in jail a little longer—but not long enough to piss her off and cause her to do something rash. And it would be best if any delay in releasing her couldn't be attributed to him. He puffed on his cigar and thought about his problem, and when the atmosphere in his office resembled a fog bank off Nova Scotia, he got off the couch and called another guy at the White House, a guy that owed him.

"Tommy, me lad," he said, "I need a wee favor. I want you to call a judge in New York named Bryer and . . . Yeah, that guy. Anyway, I want you to fly him down to D.C. early tomorrow and keep him overnight. Tell him his good work has come to the president's attention, and since two of the guys on the Supreme Court are about a hundred years old and in failing health, the president's decided it's time to make up his short list."

Mahoney listened for a moment.

"I don't want you to promise him anything. Just butter him up. Get his opinion on a couple of recent decisions the Supremes have made and pretend you've never heard such fuckin' wisdom. Then take him out and wine and dine him. I'll pick up the tab. The main thing is, I want him out of New York early tomorrow morning."

That task completed, Mahoney poured another glass of bourbon and resumed his position on the couch.

Glenda Petty, Democrat, Vermont. Raymond Rudman, Democrat, California.

Of the six House members who had been present when LaFountaine had told them about Conrad Diller's visit to Iran, Petty and Rudman were at the top of Mahoney's list for leaking the story to the *News*. And, of course, they just had to belong to his party.

Glenda Petty *hated* the CIA. She was convinced—paranoid, liberal, whack job that she was—that the CIA was running some kind of shadow government and, given half a chance, would engineer a coup to overthrow the elected president. She had bullied her way onto the House Intelligence Committee and she twisted LaFountaine's nuts every chance she got.

Now any normal person would have thought that if LaFountaine had wanted to hide Diller's visit to Iran from Congress, he never would have said anything about Diller to the committee. But Glenda wasn't a normal person. She'd think LaFountaine had told them about Diller for some underhanded reason and, just as the *Daily News* had implied, that LaFountaine hadn't wanted Diller arrested immediately because doing so would interfere with some devious CIA scheme.

Mahoney had to admit even he was suspicious when LaFountaine told them about Diller, so he could imagine Glenda had been ten times as suspicious. So, to get to the truth, Crazy Glenda, who could be as crafty and underhanded as anyone Mahoney had ever met, could have hired Acosta to leak the information to Sandra Whitmore to force the truth out into the open.

Yeah, Mahoney thought, that was a possible scenario, but as crazy as Crazy Glenda was, that scenario just didn't feel right to him. The main reason it didn't feel right was because he couldn't figure out how Glenda would know Dale Acosta.

Which brought him to Congressman Raymond Rudman.

Ray Rudman's biggest financial backer was a man named Rulon Tully, an avaricious egomaniac who was richer than God and who also had a personal beef with Marty Taylor. Taylor—a handsome son of a bitch who could have any woman on the planet—had the opportunity to screw Tully's wife and the horny bastard took it. After Tully found out about the screwing—via a headline in a tabloid rag— he divorced his wife and the divorce cost him a staggering amount of money, but the worst thing was that Tully was publicly humiliated when the media wrote about the affair.

So leaking a story that would damage Taylor's company and possibly land Marty Taylor in a cell would certainly make Rulon Tully do cartwheels of sheer joy—and Congressman Ray Rudman would have known this. Furthermore, as he had told DeMarco, eight or ten years ago Acosta and a lobbyist had gotten in trouble for lying to a grand jury. What Mahoney hadn't told DeMarco was that the lobbyist was the primary one used by Rulon Tully.

Yeah, Mahoney liked that explanation a lot better than Crazy Glenda leaking the story. And if Rudman leaked it to Tully, Tully, from everything Mahoney had heard, *was* the kind of person who would hire someone to impersonate a CIA agent.

But what could Mahoney do to confirm his suspicions? He could play hardball: he could call the U.S. Capitol Police and have them start looking at phone records and e-mails and see if they could find anything linking Glenda or Ray to Whitmore and Acosta. And with his clout, he could probably get the cops to do what he wanted without opening an official investigation and getting a bunch of warrants and crap like that. The problem with going that route was the word was bound to get out that he was investigating his colleagues—which could cause him, Ray, and Glenda a whole bunch of problems if they were innocent—or, for that matter, if they were guilty.

Naw, he better not do that, or at least not yet. For now, he'd just call them into his office, look 'em in the eye, question them, and see how they reacted—even though he already knew how they'd react. Glenda would go berserk. She'd rant and scream and threaten to rip his balls off, which she just might be capable of doing. And if she had leaked the story, she would lie. Ray Rudman wouldn't go postal like Glenda. He would act shocked, hurt, and bewildered—and, of course, he'd lie, too.

That was the problem when working with politicians. They all lied.

———◆◆◆———

Mahoney asked Glenda Petty to come to his office, making sure it sounded like a request and not an order. No point getting her back up prematurely.

When he asked her, as diplomatically as he possibly could, if she was the one who had leaked the story, she responded just as he had expected: her bony ass shot up from the chair in which she was sitting; her thin, shrewish features contorted into something even more shrewish; and she splattered spit all over his desk as she screamed at him.

Ray Rudman showed more control.

Rudman was about sixty, a genial guy who always seemed eager to please. When Mahoney first met him, Rudman already weighed more than two hundred pounds—not a good weight for a man only five foot seven—but after three terms in the House, the congressman had added at least another seventy pounds to his short frame. He looked like a bowling ball with feet.

"John," Rudman said, shaking his head in dismay, "I don't know how you could even think that I would do something like that. I'm . . . I'm hurt. And I'm offended."

"I know how close you are to Rulon Tully, Ray. And I know Tully would be very happy to learn something that could hurt Marty Taylor. And I can understand, Tully being a big supporter of yours, how . . ."

"Mr. Speaker, there is no way I would ever do anything to compromise national security," Rudman said, now doing his best to bristle with the anger he claimed to be feeling.

"Well, I know you wouldn't *intentionally*," Mahoney said, still trying to give Rudman a way out, "but . . ."

Rudman didn't bite. He rose—doing his best to look simultaneously dignified, offended, and picked upon—and said, "I'm late for an appointment, Mr. Speaker. After this, I'm not sure that we'll be able to work together the way we have in the past, and I'm very sorry about that."

After Rudman left his office, Mahoney poured another stiff shot of bourbon and walked over to the picture of Tip O'Neill that hung on one wall. In the photo, Tip was shaking the hand of an impossibly young John Mahoney. In the years to come, as Mahoney's hair grew white and his belly expanded, many would comment on his resemblance to Tip, although Mahoney always considered himself much better-looking.

"Rudman did it, Tip," Mahoney said to the photo. "I know the son of a bitch did it."

Chapter 17

It was early evening when the florist knocked on the door of the forger's house. The man who answered was a short Asian in his sixties who wore owlish-looking glasses, a faded Washington Wizards T-shirt, baggy shorts, and flip-flops on his feet. His name was Nguyễn Văn Tâm, or at least that was the name he had invented for himself. Like the florist, Tâm's real name was a distant memory.

Tâm had been Viet Cong during the American war in Vietnam. The florist had no idea what lies he had told or who he had bribed to immigrate to the United States but he now owned a restaurant, a dry cleaners, and a limousine service, all of which were staffed by his large Vietnamese clan. Providing fake IDs was something he did rarely these days, and usually only to assist other Vietnamese immigrants and a few old clients. Because he didn't have the technical knowledge to manufacture modern identity documents, he had turned that enterprise over to a niece who attended George Washington University, and the florist had never met the woman.

The florist entered a home that smelled of whatever dinner was being prepared in the kitchen, and the smells made his stomach growl, reminding him that he needed to eat. Tâm didn't offer him tea or invite him to sit, which surprised him. The man had always been courteous in the past, almost courtly.

Tâm wordlessly handed him an envelope. Inside were two passports, two driver's licenses, two social security cards, and two AAA
cards. The documents looked perfect but the florist had no idea if
they would pass inspection, particularly the passports. He took out
his wallet and paid for the identities but didn't return the wallet to
his pocket.

"Did you get DeMarco's address?" he asked.

Tâm looked at him for a long time with his bottomless black eyes
and the florist wondered if there was something wrong. Finally, Tâm
passed him an index card with DeMarco's address and home phone
number.

Tâm spoke for the first time. "I also learned he works for
Congress."

"Congress? What does he do there? How did you find this out?"

"I don't know what he does. And how I found out isn't something
you need to know."

Still shocked by what he had just heard, the florist asked, "And
Crosby, did you learn anything about him?"

"Yes. I learned he works for the CIA. Don't come here or call me
again. Ever."

It was after seven when the florist reached DeMarco's house in Georgetown, and he didn't see any lights on inside the house. He called
DeMarco's home phone and no one answered. It was likely DeMarco
was still in New York and might not be returning to Washington
for some time. He would wait a few hours—until after midnight—
and if DeMarco hadn't returned by then, he would pay a visit to Derek
Crosby.

Sandra Whitmore snatched the cell phone out of LaTisha's hand as
soon as LaTisha showed it to her.

She punched in DeMarco's number and almost cried with relief when he answered. "DeMarco, you asshole, I want the name of the guy in that photo."

"Not yet, Sandy. All I can tell you is that he doesn't work for the CIA."

"I already know that! That snooty bitch who showed me his picture told me. But I need his name."

"I need to verify something before I give it to you."

"Goddamnit, DeMarco, don't you dare play games with me!"

"Just give me until tomorrow morning. You can stand it a few more hours."

"No, I can't!" Whitmore screamed.

"Well, you're gonna have to," DeMarco said and hung up.

"You son of a bitch!" Whitmore said. She pulled back her arm to throw the phone at the wall but LaTisha said, "Hey, don't break that phone."

Whitmore returned the cell phone to LaTisha, flopped down on her bunk, and put her forearm over her eyes. She was so damn tired, tired of everything: the failed marriages, the countless affairs that had never amounted to anything, her lousy job, never getting a break. When she'd been young—back when she had a waist and tits that stuck straight out—things had been good. She had used her looks to her advantage and hadn't felt bad about that at all. But she'd lost her looks years ago. She couldn't remember the last time she'd been laid. But now she had a chance, not for sex, but for a life—if that damn DeMarco didn't screw things up for her.

The story was golden: Marty Taylor, the CIA, and a dead spy. And the fact that she'd been tossed in jail made it even better because now she was part of the story. There was definitely a book in this, and maybe a job with some other paper, some place where she could start over, like Washington or LA. But what she couldn't do was come out of this looking like a moron, which right now she did. She obviously needed to know the name of the guy who had fed her the story and why he had done it, particularly now that she knew he wasn't CIA.

That damn DeMarco. If he didn't tell her what she wanted to know by tomorrow she was going to make good on her threat. She was going to call *People* magazine and tell them about John Mahoney and one drunken night at the U.S. Capitol. If they thought John Edwards cheating on his wife was a big deal, or that governor with the Argentinean mistress, wait until they heard about the Speaker of the House screwing reporters—especially *this* reporter. It wouldn't hurt her reputation—hell, it would probably help her reputation—but it would sure as hell hurt Mahoney.

Mahoney hadn't been the Speaker then, but somehow he'd gotten the keys to the Speaker's office and one night, after they'd polished off a bottle of bourbon, they went out onto the Speaker's balcony, which overlooked the National Mall. It was two in the morning but the balcony was lit up by floodlights and every once in a while a security guard would walk by on the terrace below them. If the guard had looked up at the right moment he would have seen her bare ass up on the balcony rail, her flaming red hair hanging down to the small of her back, and her legs wrapped around John Mahoney's big ears. She still got a little tingle in her groin thinking about that night but that wouldn't stop her from telling the whole world what the philandering bastard had done.

DeMarco closed his cell phone and looked across the table at his date.

Colleen Moran was in her late thirties, blonde, attractive, and very fit. She had a personal trainer. She was a partner in a firm that specialized in corporate tax law—or, to be accurate, in corporate tax evasion. She made more in a month than DeMarco made in a year. She'd been divorced twice and had an eleven-year-old son, but the boy lived with his father. DeMarco suspected that there were mama crocodiles more maternal than Colleen Moran.

She would call DeMarco periodically and invite him to dinner; he rarely called her, although he was always happy to see her. She was bright and witty, she gossiped about important people—excluding her clients—and she was good in bed. He was convinced, however, that for her sex was akin to exercise, something she felt the need to do periodically to maintain her mental and physical well-being, but she wasn't emotionally invested in the act. He never knew, nor did he care, if he was the first man she called when her libido tickled, or if he was further down on the list.

"Sorry about that," he said to her, "but I had to take that call."

"That's okay," she said, "as long as no one calls later and interrupts us doing something important."

DeMarco smiled, turned off his cell phone, and refilled her wineglass.

Chapter 18

At the time DeMarco was eating dinner in Washington, it was five p.m. in San Diego and Marty Taylor was sitting on the deck of his sailboat trying to hack into a bank's computer.

He had spent most of the day on the boat. He had wasted the morning cleaning things that didn't need to be cleaned and shining things that didn't need to be shined, and then spent the afternoon trying to figure out how to get the money he needed to escape from Yuri.

He had decided the best thing for him to do was simply disappear. If he stayed where he was, Yuri was going to bleed him dry and he'd most likely be implicated in Yuri's crimes. And although Yuri had said he'd kill Marty's family, he'd only do that if Marty did something to put Yuri in jail. But if Marty just walked away from everything—from the company, his family, and the cops— Yuri would have no reason to go after his family. And to make sure of this, he would send Yuri a note before he left telling him that if anything happened to the people he loved, he'd come back and do whatever was necessary to put Yuri behind bars.

But what he couldn't do—what he *wouldn't* do—was flee empty-handed.

He couldn't sell his stock because Yuri—via that pedophile Bollinger —would know if he tried and, as a major shareholder in the company, there were SEC controls that prevented him from simply calling up a broker and cashing out. And he didn't have much cash left in his bank accounts—just a few hundred thousand—because Yuri kept asking for "loans." But he had a lot of *stuff*: a yacht worth a couple of million; the sailboat, which was worth half a million; three houses (Yuri was currently living in one of them); five or six high-priced cars (two of which were now in Yuri's possession); some absurdly expensive pieces of art; and a ranch in Arizona that he'd never seen. He even had a racehorse. The horse, even though it had won only a couple of races, had turned out to be a pretty good investment because when they put the animal out to stud Marty had made more money selling the horse's semen than he ever made when the animal was racing.

If he waited too long to escape, Yuri would eventually take away everything he owned. In fact, he was surprised Yuri hadn't already begun to liquidate his assets. He assumed the only reason he hadn't was because Yuri was still making a ton of money off the company, but at some point, he'd go after the rest of Marty's things. The good news was that while Yuri knew about some of his possessions, there were others Marty was pretty sure he didn't know about, like the horse and the land in Arizona. He figured if he sold everything he owned, he could get twenty to thirty million without even haggling over prices; the houses alone would bring in ten or twelve million, even in the current market.

But he had to find a way to do it that Yuri wouldn't see. He couldn't have a real estate agent show up at the house that Yuri was currently occupying and start showing it to potential buyers. He knew a guy, though, a broker, and he was pretty sure the guy could sell his stuff in some under-the-radar way.

But say he sold everything and got the money. Then what? He couldn't just get on a plane and fly to Tahiti. Yuri might track him down, and when he found him, he'd make him suffer like God's worst enemy. So he needed a new identity—a passport, a driver's license, and credit cards made out in some other name—but he had no idea who to contact to get those things. And even a false ID might not be enough. He had a pretty famous face so he'd have to see a plastic surgeon. He knew one in Rio, one that a couple of his ex-girlfriends had used—but he really didn't want to do that. He liked the way he looked; women *loved* the way he looked.

After he spent a couple hours thinking about all that depressing shit, it felt like his head was just gonna explode—and that's when he took out the tequila and his laptop and tried to hack into a Wells Fargo computer. He wasn't planning to steal anything; hacking was just something he did to relax, to have a little fun—to make him feel like he did in the old days before Yuri had taken over his life.

And at that moment, as if the devil had been eavesdropping on his thoughts, he felt the sailboat move as someone climbed on board. He turned his head and saw Yuri walking toward him.

Yuri, as usual, was beautifully dressed: designer sunglasses, a light-weight linen suit, a silk T-shirt, and Italian loafers sans socks. Marty had no idea how much of *his* money Yuri spent on clothes. He reminded Marty, particularly when he wore sunglasses, of that actor Viggo Mortensen. Or maybe Yuri reminded him of Viggo only because Viggo had once played a Russian mobster in a movie.

Yuri ignored him. He walked over to the rail of the sailboat, lit a cigarette, and admired the harbor view for a moment. Finally, he turned and said, "I want you to call Diller. Use a public phone, not your cell phone. Tell him to meet you at the ranger station at the Cuyamaca Rancho State Park tonight at nine."

"Why do you want me to meet with Diller?" Taylor asked.

"I don't want you to meet him," Yuri said, and crushed his cigarette out on the deck Marty had just buffed.

──────◆◆◆──────

Conrad Diller looked at his watch again. It was nine thirty. Where the hell was Taylor? He was half an hour late, but then Marty was a flake and had never been known for being punctual. Diller decided he'd wait ten more minutes and then he'd leave.

He wasn't surprised Marty had wanted to meet him late at night and in an out-of-the-way place. The old lawyer, Porter Henry, had told them to avoid contact with each other prior to the trial so they couldn't be accused of collaborating on a story. He was guessing the reason Marty wanted to see him was that Marty was going to try to convince him to hang tough and not hand him over to the federal prosecutor for a get-out-of-jail deal. Well, good luck with that. He'd tell him the same thing he'd told the lawyer: he wasn't doing time for Marty Taylor.

What a debacle the Iranian thing had been. He'd been called to Marty's office one day, and with Marty was the CEO, Bollinger, and a guy he'd never met who was introduced only as John, a consultant who specialized in foreign business opportunities. Bollinger had told him that they wanted him to take a vacation to the Middle East and, for the most part, it *would* be a vacation. He could visit Jerusalem, Damascus, Cairo, and anyplace else in the region he wanted, and the company would pay for the trip. His last stop would be Tehran.

"Tehran?" he had said, having not a clue where this discussion was going.

"Yes," Bollinger had said. "We want you to explore the possibility of, uh, interfacing our control systems with the Shahab-3."

The Shahab-3 missile had been developed by the Iranians, most likely with some outside help, but everybody knew it was a piece of shit. Kids flinging stones with slingshots had a better chance hitting what they were aiming at.

Naturally, the first question he had asked was, "Isn't that illegal?"— knowing damn good and well it was.

To which Bollinger had responded, "If we actually sold them the technology, it would be. Today, that is. But we're not talking about an immediate sale. You see, things with Iran are starting to change a bit, not quickly, but gradually. Some folks I know back in Washington have said that maybe, some time in the future, we might actually be able to work with the Iranians. You know, if they back off on building nukes, we might be able to help them with conventional weapons designed only for defense of their homeland."

Diller knew this was all bullshit. He suspected that the company was in so much financial trouble they were actually thinking about making an under-the-table deal with Iran. But he'd been smart enough not to say anything; he had just sat there waiting for Bollinger to tell him why he, Conrad Diller, should put his young ass on the line in this way. But Bollinger wasn't through with his spiel.

"All we want you to do," Bollinger had said, "is sit down and talk with them. Talk to them about how we could improve the performance of the Shahab, and"—Bollinger meant tell 'em how T&T's technology would allow them to put one of their missiles right in the Israeli prime minister's back pocket, if that's what they wanted to do— "and get an idea of how much they'd be willing to pay. If they're interested, we'll work out the details later. You know, how to upgrade their systems, tech support, any issues we might have with U.S. export laws, stuff like that."

"I see," Dilller had said, still waiting to hear the magic words. And then they came.

"We were thinking," Bollinger had said, "that if you do this and you're successful, a bonus of two hundred thousand might be appropriate."

He had sat there for almost thirty seconds, until the silence in the room became strained, and he had noticed that John—the guy hadn't said a word during the meeting—was starting to look a little perturbed. Well, fuck John.

"I'm thinking half a million might be more realistic," he'd finally said, already envisioning himself sitting on the deck of a condo on Lake Tahoe that he and his wife had seen last year.

Then something odd had happened. Bollinger, instead of looking over at Marty Taylor to see if he wanted to meet his price, looked over at John, and John nodded his approval. His immediate thought had been, Who the hell *is* this guy? So he asked.

John explained, in an accent that sounded Eastern European, that his job was to put Diller in touch with the right people when he arrived in Tehran. And meet the right people he did—and then that article appeared in the *Daily News* and ten days later he was arrested. It had never occurred to anyone that a damn CIA agent would attend the meeting.

After he was arrested, Taylor upped his "bonus," saying he'd give him five million if he didn't implicate the company in his Iranian vacation. Well, he had decided that five million wasn't enough. After he met a third time with Porter Henry, he concluded the old lawyer was right: the government was going to have a tough time convicting him based on the word of a dead spy. So if the case went to trial he might win, but if he saw things weren't going his way, then he'd give the government Marty Taylor and Andy Bollinger—and that John guy, although he suspected John wasn't the man's real name.

The way he looked at it, he was currently making two hundred grand a year and if he worked twenty more years, and if the market performed the way it normally did, five million was about what he would have made during that period. But who said he was going to stay at the two hundred grand per year level? With his brains, he could eventually be the chief executive of some big company and in a twenty-year period could make tens of millions, maybe hundreds. Now, of course, with the Iran case hanging over his head, he wasn't going to be the chief of anything. So he figured, considering his lifetime earning potential, that five million wasn't anywhere near enough. He was thinking twenty million was a more reasonable number. Yeah, he was glad Marty Taylor had wanted a meeting—but he wished the guy would hurry up. It was getting cold, and it was sort of creepy in this place, too.

It was pitch black in the woods surrounding the ranger station and there were no streetlights around the gravel parking lot. The only light was a porch light near the ranger station door, and he had parked fifty yards away from the door. There was another car in the lot, which surprised him, considering the hour. When he had first arrived, he had thought it might be Marty's car, although it wasn't the sort of flashy thing that Taylor usually drove. Then he took a closer look at the parked car and noticed the driver's-side window was broken and some wires were hanging down near the steering column. It looked like the car might have been stolen and abandoned at the ranger station. Whatever.

"Mr. Diller," a cheerful voice called out, and he almost crapped his pants.

He spun around, the adrenaline surging through him, making his entire body tingle, and he saw a man—and the son of a bitch was *huge*. The guy looked like he could have been an offensive tackle for the Chargers but somehow, despite his size, he'd managed to get within three feet of him without making a sound.

"You are Mr. Diller, correct?" the man asked, moving even closer to him.

He had read somewhere that adrenaline was a hormone that preceded a "fight or flight" decision—and every instinct he had was *screaming* at him that this was a flight situation. He needed to get away from this monster.

"Uh, yeah. Did Marty Taylor send you?" Diller asked, but he was looking over at his car, wondering if he could get back inside it before the man could react. The problem with that bright idea was the big bastard was standing too close to him, and before he'd be able to open, close, and lock the car door, the man would certainly get him. No, his best bet would be to forget about getting back into his car and just run like hell. He was sure he could beat a guy this size in a flat-out foot race.

"Not exactly," the man said.

Fuck this, Diller thought, and he pivoted on his right foot to run, but when he did, the guy's hand shot out like a steam-driven piston and grabbed him by the throat. He tried to break the man's grip but he couldn't, even using both of his hands, and when he tried to kick him the man just squeezed harder and shook him like a doll.

Then the guy put his other hand around Diller's throat and really began to squeeze.

Chapter 19

At midnight, the florist finally gave up on DeMarco returning home that night and drove to Derek Crosby's house in Fairfax. The lights were off in Crosby's home and hopefully this meant that Crosby was in bed and asleep and not out of town.

He put on a black ski mask, exited his car, and took the silenced .22 out of the trunk. There was a small patio at the back of Crosby's house and the house could be entered from the patio through a sliding glass door. Using the butt of the .22 he broke the glass in the door, reached inside, and unlatched it. No alarm. He waited a moment to see if the sound of the glass breaking had awakened anyone. It apparently had not.

He didn't know if Crosby had a wife or children. If he did, that would complicate things but, since he was armed, the situation was manageable. Using a penlight, he walked quickly through the small house, through the kitchen, the living room, and a bedroom that had been converted to an office. The fact that the bedroom was used as an office was good; this made it seem unlikely that Crosby had children living with him. At the back of the house was a closed door that he assumed was Crosby's bedroom.

He opened the bedroom door, immediately switched on the overhead light, and was relieved to see a man lying in bed alone. The man woke up when the lights went on, and when he saw the florist standing in the doorway, he shrieked. Then, without considering the possibility that the florist might shoot him, he reached for his glasses on the nightstand and put them on. The lenses of the glasses were incredibly thick and they magnified the man's eyes, eyes which grew in size when he was able to see that the florist was masked and holding a gun.

"Are you Derek Crosby?"

"Yes. But what . . ."

"Get out of bed. We need to talk."

✦

"Take off your pajamas," the florist said. This was an old interrogator's ploy: a naked subject always felt more vulnerable.

"What?" Crosby said.

"Take off your clothes. If I have to tell you again I'll pistol-whip you."

Crosby was bald and short. His arms and legs were thin and his chest was hairless and narrow. Nude, he was almost child-like.

"Remove your glasses."

As blind as Crosby appeared to be, making him remove his glasses would increase his sense of helplessness. He didn't resist as the florist took him by the arm, walked him to the kitchen, and duct-taped him to a chair.

"You met with a reporter named Sandra Whitmore in New York. What did you tell the reporter?"

"I don't know what you're talking about," Crosby said. "I've never met with any reporter and I haven't been to New York in five years. I swear. I'm telling the truth."

The florist simply repeated the question, and again Crosby denied meeting with Whitmore.

"Okay," the florist said. He checked a few of the drawers in the kitchen, finally finding what he wanted in the cabinet under the sink: a box containing white, plastic garbage bags. He took one of the bags, placed it over Crosby's head, and sealed the bag tightly around Crosby's neck with duct tape. He watched as the plastic sucked up

107

against Crosby's mouth and nose, and then looked on dispassionately when Crosby began to thrash in the chair as the oxygen inside the bag was depleted. He had done this sort of thing before; he removed the bag just seconds before Crosby passed out.

"What did you tell the reporter?" the florist asked for the third time.

Crosby, now crying, snot running from his nose, swore again that he had never met with Whitmore. The little man's chest was heaving so much the florist was concerned he might have a heart attack—but that was a risk he was willing to take. He placed the bag over Crosby's head again.

As he was sealing the bag, Crosby screamed, "Stop! I'm telling you the truth."

"No," the florist said. "You're lying. I know you registered at the Hyatt in Manhattan; you charged the room to your credit card. I know you were there."

"The credit card!" Crosby yelled. "That's not my credit card! I called Visa and told them."

The florist removed the bag from Crosby's head. "What are you talking about?"

Crosby said that someone had taken out a credit card in his name and charged a trip to New York. The florist shook his head in disbelief.

"Look in my desk! Please. There's a file marked Visa. Look at it. You'll see I'm not lying."

The florist hesitated, then went to Crosby's den and found the file. Included with a copy of an e-mail that Crosby had sent to Visa was a signed statement from one of Crosby's coworkers who was willing to swear Crosby had been at Langley the two days he had supposedly been in New York.

The florist went back into the kitchen and stood there looking down at Derek Crosby.

"Did you find the file?" Crosby asked. The florist didn't answer.

Derek Crosby was not physically strong nor was he brave. But even brave men become terrified when men in ski masks wake them in the middle of the night, strip them naked, and torture them. It was still possible Crosby was lying about meeting Whitmore, and the Visa file was part of an elaborate cover-up, but he didn't think so. He could spend another hour suffocating Crosby repeatedly with the plastic bag and then he would be certain, but he was already convinced that Crosby was telling the truth.

He placed a strip of duct tape across Crosby's mouth. "I'll be back in a moment," he said.

He walked into Crosby's unlit living room and sat down in the dark to think. It had been a mistake coming to see Crosby. He should have waited until after he had questioned DeMarco. Impatience had always been his biggest weakness. Now, if he didn't kill Crosby, Crosby would report that someone had tortured him and asked questions about Sandra Whitmore. And he would not only tell the police, he would tell his employer, the CIA. Crosby hadn't seen his face but he would be able to say that the man who tortured him spoke with an accent. Crosby might even be able to identify from his accent that he was Iranian.

He should kill Crosby—that was the logical thing to do—but he couldn't. Crosby had not been one of those responsible for Mahata's death.

To delay Crosby from calling the police, he found the man's cell phone and removed the battery, then ripped the wires out of the phones in Crosby's house. He made sure the man was still taped securely to the chair and the tape over his mouth wasn't restricting his breathing, and left the house. Crosby would eventually free himself and by then the florist would be long gone—but the hunt for him would begin.

Chapter 20

DeMarco had set his watch alarm for five a.m., and he cursed Mahoney when the alarm sounded. He slipped from Colleen Moran's bed, dressed, left a note on the kitchen table saying that he'd had a wonderful time, and tiptoed from the house. He was going to have to hustle to make his flight to Myrtle Beach on time. Fortunately, his house was only a couple of miles away.

When he reached his place, he rushed in and grabbed the bag he'd packed the night before. He checked his watch. If he did it quickly, he'd have time to shower and wash the smell of sex from his skin. He stripped off his shirt as he hustled toward the bathroom.

When the prisoners were taken to breakfast in the morning, LaTisha nodded to a certain guard and the guard nodded back, and LaTisha walked into the kitchen as she had the night before and called her contact at Langley again. She didn't know how many people were working this op, but considering that everything they were doing was illegal—spying on Whitmore, monitoring calls without warrants—she sure as hell hoped it was a small number. Her contact was an agent she'd never met named Tom Foley, and although she'd only talked to him twice, he didn't exactly fill her with confidence.

"This is Clark," she said. "Did you intercept the call last night?"

"Yeah," Foley said. "She called a lawyer who works for Congress, some guy named DeMarco. He visited her the day before yesterday, and we were still doing background checks on him when she called last night. We don't know why he visited her and we couldn't make much sense out of the call. Whitmore said something about a woman showing her a picture of some guy, and DeMarco said the guy was *not* CIA, but he wouldn't give Whitmore the man's name. So we're not sure what the hell to make of it all."

Foley sounded like he was out of breath, like he was running while he was talking.

"Could DeMarco be Whitmore's source?" Clark asked.

"Maybe, but we don't think so."

"Well, shit," Clark said.

"And there's something else," Foley said, and he told her what had happened to Derek Crosby.

"Someone tortured him?" Clark said. "Why in the hell would—"

"Look, I don't have time to talk right now. I have to brief LaFountaine."

"Fine. But, Foley, we gotta wrap this up. If I have to spend any more time with that aggravating, chain-smoking bitch, I'm gonna kill her."

Tom Foley was limping down the hall toward LaFountaine's office as fast as he could, being careful his cane didn't slip on a floor that looked as if it had been recently waxed. He'd been using the cane for almost thirty years, and walking with it had become second nature to him—but he still wished they wouldn't wax these fucking floors so often.

When he first became a gimp, it had bothered him a lot. He was twenty-four at the time, and although he wasn't movie-star handsome, he'd been an athletic guy with a good body. He figured he'd never get laid again walking around with a third leg, but soon found out he was wrong about that. Women loved going to bed with a spy injured in the line of duty; the only thing that would have been better than a cane was a black eye patch.

The bullet that crippled him not only got him laid more than he deserved, it was also the best thing that ever happened to his career. An agent who had been out in the field trading bullets with the bad guys was given a lot of slack and he was, at least early on, advanced over people smarter than him because of his injury. And, of course, so they didn't forget, he constantly reminded folks of how he'd been crippled—or how he had supposedly been crippled.

It happened in Cairo. It had been his first overseas assignment, and being a newbie he was never given anything important to do. He was the one they sent out for food when the secretary wasn't there and the three months he spent in Egypt had been incredibly boring. Then, one night, his boss asked him to drive him to a meeting because the agent who was supposed to drive was having a recurring bout of malaria. The only reason Foley was picked was because he had just completed a course in Farsi. The guys they were meeting were two young Iranian dissidents who, for whatever reason, opposed the ayatollah. The Iranians spoke English but the boss wanted Foley along in case they started jabbering to each other in their own language. He was surprised when the boss told him to check out a weapon from the ordnance locker.

The meeting took place a couple of years after the shah, Mohammad Reza Pahlavi, had been overthrown. The Ayatollah Khomeini was in charge of Iran at the time and was rabidly anti-American—which was rather understandable as the Americans, and the CIA in particular, had done everything they could to keep the shah in power and were now doing everything they could to get the ayatollah out of power. The purpose of the meeting was to give the dissidents a briefcase full of money and instructions on how the money should be spent to cause the ayatollah as much grief as possible. At that point the CIA didn't have any expectation of unseating Khomeini but they still wanted a few folks stirring the pot.

The meeting was held in a house in Cairo the agency leased, and somehow it got compromised. A couple of heavyweights from Iranian intelligence had followed the dissidents to Cairo and they burst into the house and, without saying a word, started shooting people. One of the dissidents was killed immediately and Foley was shot in the right knee. After he was hit, he didn't do anything but scream and scramble behind a couch so he was out of the line of fire, and he had no idea what happened after that. When all the shooting stopped—there must have been a dozen shots fired in that room in about eight seconds—the shooters were dead and Foley's boss was on the floor, his gun in his hand, blood pouring out of his chest and stomach. Miraculously, the other dissident, who was also holding a gun, didn't have a scratch.

Foley told the unhurt Iranian to take the briefcase and get the hell out of there, then dragged himself over to a phone, called the duty officer at the embassy, and told him to send an ambulance and a clean-up crew—and to hurry because both he and the boss were badly wounded. His boss died while they were waiting for the medics to arrive.

Because of his injuries they didn't debrief him immediately. After he got out of surgery and while he was still groggy from the drugs he'd been given for pain, they asked him what had happened. He told the truth—with one small variation: he said that he *and* the boss had shot the bad guys. He shouldn't have lied but he didn't want to admit that he had been hiding behind a couch while his boss was getting killed. It occurred to him later that what he had done had been incredibly dumb because if they had checked his weapon they would have seen it hadn't been fired, but that never happened. No autopsies were performed and the Iranian bodies and the weapons were all disposed of—and Tom Foley the hero was born.

After he was discharged from the hospital in Germany, they sent him back to Langley, and when he walked into the office with his new cane—the same one he still used today—folks stood up and clapped for him, and for the rest of his career he milked his injury for all it was worth. The other thing that happened was that he was promoted into the Middle East section at Langley and tasked with analyzing intelligence data on Iran. Although he had rudimentary knowledge of Farsi and had spent three months in the country, he suspected the main reason

he got the assignment was because he had supposedly killed two Iranians. Be that as it may, after thirty years he was an armchair expert on
Iran and one of the few people in the Company who had known about
Mahata Javadi's assignment, which unfortunately now placed him in
a position where he didn't want to be: talking to Jake LaFountaine about
what they were doing to catch the people who had killed her.

"We still don't know who Whitmore's source is," Foley said, and
LaFountaine clenched his big jaw so tightly that Foley was surprised
he didn't crack a molar. "But last night a CIA analyst named Derek
Crosby who works the Cuba desk was tortured by somebody who
thought he had met with Whitmore in New York."

"What in the hell are you talking about?" LaFountaine said.

Foley, in all his years at Langley, had never briefed a sitting director
one-on-one. He was just too low on the totem pole to do that. Normally,
the DCI talked only to Foley's boss, but Foley's boss was in the hospital having his prostate removed, and consequently he had to talk to the
guy directly, which he didn't like doing at all. Jake LaFountaine just scared
the shit out of him—particularly after what had happened to Carson.

Foley explained how a man in a ski mask had broken into Crosby's
house and asked Crosby about meeting Whitmore in New York. He
also told LaFountaine how somebody had gotten a credit card in
Crosby's name and used the card to stay at a hotel in New York about
a week before Whitmore's story broke.

"Somebody impersonated Crosby," Foley said, "and it's possible
that whoever it was, was Whitmore's source. And that's not all. There's
a guy named DeMarco involved in this thing. He visited Whitmore
in jail the other day, and—"

"So who is he?"

"He's a lawyer who works for Congress."

"For Congress?"

"Yeah. And after he visited Whitmore, some woman visited Whitmore and showed her a picture of somebody. Whitmore told Clark—"

"Who the hell's Clark?" LaFountaine asked.

Foley felt a bead of sweat roll down his neck and into his collar. "The agent we put in Whitmore's cell."

"Oh, that's right. Go on."

"Well, Whitmore told Clark DeMarco had information that could get her out of jail, and after that we intercepted a call from Whitmore to DeMarco. Whitmore demanded the name of the guy in a picture she'd been shown, but DeMarco wouldn't give it to her."

As Foley talked, LaFountaine looked like he was about to explode— and Foley could understand why. He was doing a *horrible* job of briefing the man, tossing out all these different names, making things sound even more confusing than they really were. He just wanted this meeting to end.

"So who was the woman who visited Whitmore?" LaFountaine asked.

Aw, shit. "We're not sure."

"You're not sure? What the hell does that mean?"

"The woman identified herself as Maxine Turner, a courier for a messenger service. But when we contacted the messenger service, they said that no one named Turner worked for them. She had a New York state driver's license, and we've identified eight Maxine Turners in New York, but none of them match the woman's description. And we didn't get one clear picture of her off security cameras at MCC."

"Jesus," LaFountaine said. "So what else do you know about DeMarco, other than the fact that he works for Congress?"

"Well, we really don't know much else." Seeing the look on LaFountaine's face, he quickly added, "But you remember a few years ago, that Chinese spy who was trying to get nuclear secrets from a shipyard on the West Coast? And you remember the Speaker of the House was kidnapped at the same time?"

"Yeah," LaFountaine said, "but what does that have to do . . ."

"This DeMarco character was on the edges of that whole mess. We never were able to find out exactly how he was involved, or what his role was, but he was mixed up in it. Anyway, we think DeMarco may work for John Mahoney but there's nothing official that says he does."

Foley heard LaFountaine mutter something. He thought he heard him say, "That fuckin' Mahoney."

"Could DeMarco be the guy who tortured Crosby?" LaFountaine asked.

"We don't think so. DeMarco's five eleven. From what we got out of Crosby, the guy who tortured him was at least six three. Plus, he had some kind of foreign accent."

"What kind of accent?"

"Crosby wasn't sure."

LaFountaine shook his head. "Is that it?"

"Yeah, pretty much. We're still trying to get a handle on DeMarco and the woman who visited Whitmore at MCC, and we've got a tech at Crosby's house trying to find fingerprints."

"Where's DeMarco now?"

Aw, shit. "We don't know. He didn't go home last night and after he talked to Whitmore he turned off his phone, so we couldn't use that to find him. We'll pick him up today when he goes to work and stay on him after that."

LaFountaine shook his head and the expression on his face left no doubt about his opinion of Foley's competence. Finally, he said, "So. At this point, you have no idea who leaked the story to Whitmore, but you think it might have been someone impersonating a CIA analyst named Derek Crosby. Crosby was tortured to determine his connection to Whitmore, but you don't know who tortured him. You know a congressional lawyer talked to Whitmore, but you don't know what they talked about or why the lawyer is involved in this thing. You know a woman showed Whitmore a picture that got her all excited, but you don't know who the woman is or who was in the picture. And you've lost the lawyer. Now did I get all that right?"

"Uh, yes, sir," Foley said. "I'm sorry, but—"

"Get out of here," LaFountaine said, and Tom Foley limped toward the door as fast as he could.

It was time to retire, he thought, as he walked back toward his office. He was involved in an operation on American soil that was outside the CIA's charter and therefore illegal. But then what they were doing was illegal in so many other ways as well. They had infiltrated an agent into the prison where they were keeping Whitmore, they had broken into Whitmore's apartment looking for information on her source, they had hacked into computers at the *Daily News,* and they were monitoring phone calls without warrants. And those were just the crimes that Foley knew about. People were going to go to jail if what they were doing ever got out.

What happened to Mahata was terrible, and every person at Langley felt bad about it, especially people like Foley who had known her. But LaFountaine . . . he was allowing this thing to affect his judgment: losing his temper with the media, publicly accusing Congress of leaking classified dope, doing things that were going to get the whole Company in trouble.

Then there was what had happened to Carson. That had been unbelievable.

Carson had been Mahata's control, and as soon as LaFountaine found out that Mahata had been killed, he recalled Carson to Langley to find out what had gone wrong. He met with Carson privately so no one knew what was actually said during their meeting, but at one point LaFountaine's secretary heard LaFountaine screaming at Carson at the top of his lungs, then heard furniture being overturned, and when Carson came out of the meeting he looked like he'd been in a barroom brawl.

Carson resigned from the agency the following day. He was old enough to retire, and after what had happened to Mahata his career was finished anyway, but Foley heard through the grapevine that LaFountaine had wanted Carson officially fired so he wouldn't get a pension. Fortunately, the lawyers convinced LaFountaine that going after Carson's pension wouldn't be smart—not after he had beaten the hell out of the man.

Chapter 21

As the florist pulled up to DeMarco's place, he saw DeMarco rush out the front door with one of those travel bags on wheels. He cursed as DeMarco flung the bag into the trunk of his car and took off.

He followed DeMarco to Reagan National Airport and parked his car in the same lot where DeMarco parked. An airport wasn't good; it was going to be almost impossible to follow DeMarco to wherever he was going. As DeMarco was walking toward the terminal, the florist went to the trunk of his own car and placed the .22 he had used to threaten Derek Crosby inside the trunk—he couldn't take it with him into the airport—and removed the small duffel bag that he'd taken to New York. The clothes inside the duffel were dirty but that was the least of his problems.

He followed DeMarco into the terminal, and as DeMarco had never seen him, the florist stood in line behind him when DeMarco used one of the electronic check-in computers. But even as close as he was standing, practically breathing down DeMarco's neck, he couldn't see where the man was going. The florist wouldn't be able to follow him into the terminal and past security unless he had a ticket himself. He was going to lose him again.

And then God smiled on him, as He had so many times before.

DeMarco had some problem with the check-in procedure and he called an attendant over and the florist heard him say, "I've got a reservation on the next flight to Myrtle Beach but this fu . . . this computer won't give me a seat assignment for some reason."

The florist got lucky a second time when the flight to Myrtle Beach wasn't full, and DeMarco didn't even glance at him when he boarded the plane.

At the Myrtle Beach airport, DeMarco proceeded directly to the Hertz rental car counter and fortunately there were two men in line ahead of him. The florist went to Avis where there was no one waiting, and Avis—trying harder—processed him faster than DeMarco, and he was waiting on the airport exit road as DeMarco drove past. As he followed DeMarco, he wondered where he could get a gun. If he had the opportunity to talk to DeMarco in South Carolina, he might need one to control him or to convince him to talk.

DeMarco pulled into a strip mall a few miles from the airport and parked in front of a restaurant offering breakfast twenty-four hours a day—which reminded the florist that he was hungry, starving actually, as he hadn't eaten in the last twelve hours. The florist knew that he should get something to eat while DeMarco was eating because he might not get a chance later. He looked around the strip mall to see if there was another restaurant—and saw the pawnshop.

The pawnshop owner was a big-boned woman with short gray hair and wire-rimmed glasses. She was wearing a man's long-sleeved white shirt, blue jeans, and a wide hand-tooled belt with an enormous turquoise and brass buckle. Attached to the belt, on her right hip, was a holster containing a black automatic. She didn't say anything when the florist walked up to the counter and looked at the weapons she had in stock. There weren't any pistols but she had four shotguns and two rifles; not much of a selection but he didn't have time to go to another store. The shortest weapon she had, and therefore the easiest to conceal, was a .20-gauge, pump-action Mossberg Bantam.

"The Mossberg," the florist said. "How much?"

"Three hundred."

He had no idea if that was a fair price or not; he hadn't bought a weapon in twenty years.

"I'll take it."

"Cash," the woman said.

The florist nodded, and the woman unlocked the case and took out the shotgun.

"I'll need shells, too. I'd prefer deer slugs if you have them."

With a grunt she stooped down and pulled a box of ammunition from the shelf beneath the counter.

"Don't load that weapon in my store," the woman said, and patted the pistol on her hip.

"I won't," the florist said, suppressing a smile.

"Good. That'll be three thirty."

The florist counted out four one-hundred-dollar bills and fanned them out on the counter.

"I'll need to see your ID and . . ."

The florist put another hundred-dollar bill on the counter.

"Do you want a carrying case, too?" the woman asked.

DeMarco finished his breakfast, then checked his watch. It was half past ten.

Mahoney had told him to call Whitmore this morning and he figured now was as good a time as any. He knew Mahoney wanted him to check out Acosta before he called but he figured that even after he gave her Acosta's name it was still going to be several hours before she could get to the judge and get out of jail. And he knew Acosta wasn't going to tell him anything anyway.

Since he had no idea how to call an inmate at a federal prison, he called information, got a general number for the prison, got transferred until he reached someone in administration, said he was a lawyer from Congress, got transferred again, and then he was finally speaking with a slug named Riley.

DeMarco told Riley he needed to talk to Whitmore. Riley told him if he wanted to talk to a prisoner he could show up during scheduled visiting hours, the rules for which were posted on their Web site. This caused DeMarco to repeat the words "lawyer" and "Congress" several times. For good measure, he told Riley that his need to speak with Whitmore was related to national security. To this, Riley responded by saying, "Not my problem. Visiting hours are . . ."

Finally, DeMarco landed a solid uppercut to Riley's bureaucratic chin when he invoked the name of a liberal New York congressman. The congressman's daughter had recently spent two days at MCC after throwing rocks at a federal building during a protest and was apparently not treated like the princess her daddy thought she was, and the congressman was currently trying to get all the prison bosses fired. Riley told DeMarco that he'd have to wait until he could get Whitmore to a phone, which could take a while.

The guard that came to Whitmore's cell was white, but otherwise identical to the black guard she normally saw: big bust, big rump, big arms—and a permanently pissed-off temperament.

"You got a call," she said to Whitmore.

"Who is it?" Whitmore asked.

"How the hell would I know," the guard said.

As soon as Whitmore left the cell, LaTisha pulled her phone from her sock and called Tom Foley at Langley.

"They just took Whitmore out of the cell. They're taking her to a phone. She's getting a call from someone."

"Well, hell, Clark," Foley said. "We don't have every landline at that jail tapped, you know."

"Shit."

"Pump Whitmore about the phone call when she gets back."

"You just do your damn job, Foley. I'll take care of mine."

"The man who impersonated Derek Crosby is a guy named Dale Acosta," DeMarco said.

"Shit," Whitmore said. "So what do you know about Acosta?" She wondered if someone monitored the prison's phones.

"Sandy, I'm not your research assistant. All I know is that Acosta lives in Myrtle Beach, South Carolina, and he doesn't work for the CIA. I heard from a pretty good source that when he was younger he was a White House plumber type, but I don't know that for a fact."

"You mean like Gordon Liddy?"

"Maybe."

"But why would he—"

"Sandy, you got the name. Call the judge and give up Acosta and get out of jail. Or don't. I don't care. Just don't bug Mahoney again."

————◆◆◆————

The guard walked Whitmore back to her cell and as soon as she was inside LaTisha asked, "What's going on? You look upset."

"I'm fine."

"You don't look fine. It looks like whoever called you—"

"Quit buggin' me! I need to think."

"Hey!" LaTisha said. "Don't you start actin' the snippy bitch with me or there won't be no cell phone, no cigarettes, no nothin'. I'm just tryin' to be, you know, supportive and shit."

Whitmore didn't say anything. She flopped back down on her bunk and lit a cigarette.

How could she spin this? How could she come out of this thing without looking like a fool?

The first thing she had to make clear was that even though Acosta may have lied about being a CIA agent, he didn't lie about the fact that the CIA was covering up Diller's trip to Iran. Yeah, that was important. Her source may have lied about his identity but her story, every damn word of it, was still accurate. The next question would be: But *why* did he feed you the story? And to that she'd say: Because he obviously wanted the public to know that Marty Taylor's company was doing something illegal and the CIA wasn't doing anything about it. And he posed as a CIA agent because if he hadn't he wouldn't have been a credible source.

But then someone would ask the tough question: If your source didn't work for the CIA then how did he know about Diller's meeting in Iran? To that she'd have to say she didn't know but it was clear that Acosta is connected either to someone in Congress who had attended LaFountaine's briefing or to someone in the CIA. How else could he have gotten his hands on CIA credentials and borrowed the identity of an actual CIA employee? Yeah, that was good. She'd point at all the reporters and say, As good as these guys are—Acosta and whoever he works for—they would have conned you just as easily as they did me. So what we have here is an elaborate conspiracy most likely engineered by someone inside the federal government. They used me to expose a real CIA cover-up and, unfortunately, because the CIA wouldn't come clean with me when I asked them to comment on my story, that poor girl got killed. So when I found out that my source lied to me about working for the CIA, I no longer had an obligation to protect his identity and I gave the judge his name because I had to get out of jail to get to the bottom of this mess. But what would she say when someone asked her how she had found out that Acosta was a phony? That was easy. She'd give 'em a big wink and say, Now, boys, you know that I *never* give up a source, a legitimate one, that is.

Hmm. Not bad, but not great—but it was the best she could do. She was still going to look incompetent for not having figured out that Acosta wasn't really CIA, but being the victim of a government conspiracy would make her look a little less stupid and would put the blame on the government instead of her. And whether she looked stupid or not, she had to get out of this cell. If she had to stay here another day she was going to slash her wrists.

"Can I use your cell phone again?" she asked LaTisha.

LaTisha ignored her.

"Hey, I'm sorry," Whitmore said, trying to sound contrite. "That call I got just rattled me. But now I can get out of here, which means I can get you your money."

"So you're gonna snitch out your source."

"I'm not snitching. I'm . . . look, never mind. Can I use your phone? Please."

"Two hundred bucks."

"Two! Last time it was one."

"That was before you got snippy."

LaTisha handed her the phone and added Whitmore's most recent charge to the running tab she was keeping. At this point, Whitmore had no idea how much money she owed LaTisha; she'd stopped keeping track days ago. And it really didn't matter. She had no intention of paying her, anyway.

Whitmore punched in the number and said, "This is Sandra Whitmore. Is my so-called lawyer there?" A moment later, the lawyer picked up and she said, "Tell the judge I'm ready to talk."

There was a long silence on the other end of the phone. "Ms. Whitmore," her lawyer said, "I need to know who your source is before you talk to the judge and I need to know why you've suddenly decided to reveal his name. And then I need to discuss all this with management at the paper, to make sure what you're doing is in the paper's best interest."

"Listen to me," Whitmore said. "If your bony ass isn't down here in half an hour to get me out, I'll get a public defender. I don't need you at this point."

It felt good saying that but she wondered if she'd have a job when this was all over. Probably not, considering how she'd been duped by her source. She definitely needed a book deal.

Her pompous lawyer met her in a private interview room forty-five minutes later. The first thing he told her was that the judge was out of town, visiting someone in Washington, D.C., and wouldn't be back until tomorrow.

Sandra Whitmore screamed so loudly one of the guards burst into the interview room to see if she was okay.

Chapter 22

Benny couldn't believe it: Acosta was finally home.

His car was in the parking lot, the windshield and bumper all bug-splattered like the man had driven a fair distance. Benny had no idea where Acosta had been, but he must have gotten back late last night after Benny had returned to his motel.

Benny was thinking he should wait until nightfall to take care of Acosta but then he noticed that there wasn't anybody playing on the fairway. The weather was good and it was midday, the middle of the week; there should be a foursome of old farts out on the course slicing their balls into the rough. He got out of his car and looked up and down the fairway: nobody as far as he could see. Huh? He wondered if they were doing some work on the course or if a water main had broken or something.

He looked down the block of town houses. None of Acosta's neighbors were outside. The town houses didn't have front yards—the fairway was their front yard—but behind each town house was a small, fenced-in backyard. If one of Acosta's neighbors decided to go outside to barbecue his lunch or plant petunias, they'd be in the backyard and wouldn't see Benny unless they looked out their front windows. And if they did look out the window, the only thing they'd be able to tell the cops was that they saw a fat guy wearing a ball cap and sunglasses walking by.

Yeah, it was time to get this thing done.

He walked down the cart path to Acosta's town house, knocked, and a tall guy opened the door. Benny had looked at Acosta's photo before he left his car and the guy standing in front of him was definitely Acosta.

"Yes?" he asked when he saw Benny.

Benny smiled. He knew how he looked when he smiled: short, fat, friendly—and harmless.

———————◆◆◆———————

DeMarco knew Acosta lived someplace on the Glendon Hills Golf Course, but the address system was totally confusing. He went to the pro shop to get directions and the guy there told him that Acosta's place was on the sixth fairway, and showed him how to find the street on a little map. As he was walking out of the shop he saw they had some clubs on sale and he picked up a pitching wedge. He couldn't pitch for shit and he liked to think it was because he didn't have the right club. The one he picked up had a nice feel to it: the weight was good, the length was right, and he liked the grip. Then he looked at the price tag.

———————◆◆◆———————

"Hey, sorry to bother you," Benny said, "but I'm the guy who broke your window."

"My window?" Acosta said. Then he looked at the floor near the picture window and saw the glass. "Shit," he said, but he didn't sound too upset. "I was in Atlanta visiting my sister and I didn't even look at that window when I got home last night."

"I just moved in here, over on the third fairway," Benny said, jerking his head in that direction. "I didn't think it would be good to start off busting a neighbor's window and not making things right."

Now Benny figured if Acosta was an honest man, he'd say his insurance would cover the window. He couldn't imagine someone living on a golf course and not having insurance for this sort of thing.

But Benny was guessing that Acosta was like most people: he'd try to make an extra buck whether he needed it or not, and if he could screw the insurance company while he was at it, that'd just be the icing on the cake. And sure enough . . .

"Hey, that's decent of you," Acosta said. "Most people would never have said anything. Come on in."

Benny followed Acosta into the town house, and since Acosta's back was to him, he pulled the little .32 out of one pocket and a towel he'd taken from his motel out of another pocket.

Acosta was saying, "The last time I had to replace that window, it cost five fifty. I know that sounds high but that's double-pane glass and . . ."

Benny placed the towel over the barrel of the .32 and shot Acosta in the back of the head. He barely heard the shot himself; no way anyone outside the town house would have heard it. He looked down at Acosta. He wasn't moving—not even a twitch—and Benny didn't see any blood pumping out of his head, so he figured the guy was probably dead. He knew he should check Acosta's pulse but that would mean kneeling down, which wasn't easy for a guy his size. So because the towel he'd used now had a bullet hole in it, he tossed it aside, picked up one of those stupid little throw pillows from Acosta's couch, placed the pillow over the .32, and shot Acosta in the head again.

"That oughta do it," he said to the dead man.

He stood there for a minute, thinking. He hadn't touched anything but the pillow, and it was made from some nappy corduroy stuff, and they wouldn't be able to get prints off that. The towel he'd used was a plain white one, didn't have the motel's name on it, and they couldn't get prints off that, either.

Everything looked copacetic. Time to go.

———◆———

DeMarco found the block where Acosta's house should be and pulled into a parking lot at the east end of the street as the guy in the pro shop had told him. There were about ten cars in the lot, but it was only half full. He didn't see names or numbers on any of the parking spaces so he figured it was okay to park there and his rental car wouldn't get towed.

He saw all the houses on the block were these cute, narrow, two-story town houses, and he wondered how much they cost. The cart path for the golf course served as a sidewalk for the town houses, and the address on the first door he passed led him to conclude that Acosta's place was at the far end of the block. He started down the cart path, expecting at any moment to get beaned by a golf ball, and then noticed no one was playing on the course, which was odd considering the time of day.

As he walked, he admired the fairway. The grass was a lush, well-tended green, and across the way was a good-sized pond with a big weeping willow on one bank, its branches dipping down into the water. Ducks were skimming across the pond and it was a cloudless, windless, perfect day.

DeMarco could imagine himself living someplace like this when he retired. Each morning he'd rise at nine or ten, play eighteen holes, then spend his afternoons in the clubhouse drinking vodka and playing gin. DeMarco realized his dreams had shrunken over time. He'd gladly settle for the life Dale Acosta appeared to be living.

Looking back down the cart path, he noticed a chubby guy coming out of a town house about where he figured Acosta's place would be. Probably one of Acosta's neighbors. The man was dressed like a golfer—blue Windbreaker, a loose-fitting bright yellow polo shirt, Bermuda shorts that came past his chunky knees, a ball cap, and sunglasses. DeMarco figured the guy was off to play his daily game. As he passed DeMarco, the guy smiled and nodded to him, and he reminded DeMarco of that actor on *Cheers,* the one who played Norm, which made DeMarco wonder whatever had happened to Norm. He probably owned his own golf course with all the money he was making from reruns.

Benny wondered if the guy coming down the cart path had seen him leave Acosta's place. Maybe—and that wasn't good.

As Benny got closer to him, he recalled a job he had done for some Italians in Kansas City, a little turf war where the wops didn't want to use one of their own shooters, so they had called Jimmy, and Jimmy had sent Benny. The guy that had been the target in KC looked a lot like the guy walking toward him right now: he had goombah leg-breaker written all over him.

As Benny passed the goombah, he smiled, wanting to see how the guy would react, if he acted suspicious in any way. If he acted the least bit funny, Benny was going to walk past him then spin around and shoot him in the back. But he just nodded at Benny; he didn't seem worried about a thing. Maybe the guy hadn't seen him leave Acosta's place after all.

———◆———

DeMarco knocked on Acosta's door. No one answered. He knocked again. Shit. He hoped he wouldn't have to sit around for hours until Acosta finally showed up. He turned to go back to his car and noticed a hole in Acosta's front window, the picture window that faced the fairway. That would be one drawback to living on a golf course: having to replace your windows a couple times a year or else having to cover them with wire mesh. Then he saw the man lying on the floor.

DeMarco went back to the door and turned the doorknob, expecting it to be locked, but it wasn't.

———◆———

Benny walked past the last town house on the block and turned the corner, but then stuck his head out and looked back down the cart path. Aw, shit. The goombah was knocking on Acosta's door; he had been going to see Acosta. Of all the rotten, doggone luck. He thought the guy might leave when Acosta didn't answer, and it looked like he was about to, but he stopped and looked in through the window—and then he entered Acosta's town house. Son of a gun.

DeMarco could see that it was Dale Acosta on the floor. He could also see the man had been shot in the back of the head two or three times. Being careful not to step in the blood, he bent down and felt for a pulse in Acosta's right wrist. There wasn't one.

He reached for his cell phone to call the cops but the phone wasn't on his belt where it was supposed to be. Then he remembered: the seat-belt buckle in the rental car had been digging into his side, right where his phone was clipped to his belt, and he'd taken the phone off and put it in one of the cup holders. He could use the phone in Acosta's house, but he didn't want to screw up the crime scene. Plus, he wanted to get out of the house.

He left Acosta's place and started jogging back to his car. As he jogged, he thought about the guy he had passed on the cart path. He thought he had been one of Acosta's neighbors, but maybe he wasn't. Maybe he'd been coming out of Acosta's town house like he'd originally thought.

He wondered if Norm had killed Dale Acosta.

Now what? Benny figured if the goombah was straight, he'd call the cops right away. And he'd seen Benny clear as a bell; he'd looked right into his eyes when they passed on the cart path. It was time to boogie. But wait a minute. The guy had just come back out of Acosta's town house and was now running down the cart path. It looked like he *hadn't* called the cops; he hadn't been inside Acosta's place long enough to do that. But why was he running?

Whatever the reason—too bad for you, goombah.

The florist had no idea why DeMarco had traveled to Myrtle Beach, nor did he know if his trip was connected in any way to Sandra Whitmore, so when DeMarco turned his car into the main entrance of the golf course and went into the pro shop, the florist became really confused. Could the man have flown to South Carolina just to play golf? DeMarco was wearing a suit, so he didn't think so, but why had he come here? A few minutes later, DeMarco came out of the pro shop and the florist followed as DeMarco wound his way through the streets near the golf course and finally parked in a lot adjacent to a short block of town houses.

The florist waited until DeMarco parked and exited his car, and then he drove into the parking lot. He watched from his car as DeMarco walked down the cart path; it appeared that he was visiting someone who lived in one of the town houses. He had no idea what was going on but when DeMarco came back to his car he was going to find out. He would use his new shotgun to persuade Mr. DeMarco to go for a ride with him.

He looked down the cart path again. A short, heavyset man was walking toward DeMarco. DeMarco and the fat man passed each other, and the fat man continued up the cart path toward the parking lot. The florist watched as DeMarco knocked on the door of one of the town houses, then knocked again. It appeared that whoever DeMarco was visiting wasn't home and DeMarco started to leave, but then he stopped and entered the town house. Then something odd happened.

The fat man who had passed DeMarco on the cart path had reached the end of the block. The florist had expected that he would go to one of the cars in the parking lot but instead of doing that he stopped and poked his head back around the corner of the last town house. For some reason he was watching DeMarco and didn't want to be seen.

Now DeMarco was visible again. He had entered the town house but had rushed back out and was now running down the cart path. Why was he running? The florist switched his gaze back to the fat man. Oh, no! The fat man had a gun in his right hand. It appeared that he was going to wait for DeMarco to run past him—and then shoot him.

The florist couldn't let that happen. He needed to know what DeMarco was doing and now he needed to know what the fat man's role in this game was. He was afraid, however, that he wasn't going to be able to get to the shotgun in the trunk fast enough to save DeMarco. He exited his car, staying low so he was hidden by the body of the car, and removed the Mossberg from the trunk.

DeMarco burst into the parking lot and ran for his rental car, which was only a couple of spaces away from the last town house on the block. As he ran, he punched the button on the remote to unlock his car and when he did this he heard a little *crack*. He was momentarily confused, wondering what the connection was between him punching the remote and the cracking sound, but then there was another *crack* and the passenger-side window of his car shattered. What the hell?

He looked over his shoulder and saw a guy pointing a gun at him. It was Norm—and he was shooting at him! DeMarco immediately dove behind a car, the car parked next to his in the lot. An instant later, a bullet zinged off the asphalt almost hitting his head. What the fuck was going on?

"Doggone it," Benny muttered.

The goombah had run past the end of the building faster than he'd expected and he missed with his first shot, firing right behind the guy. He fired a second time but missed again and hit the window of a car. It was hard to hit a moving target with any pistol, but with the little .32 it was even harder. The gun—or maybe it was him—wasn't the least bit accurate if the target was more than a few yards away. But still, how the hell had he missed twice?

Now the damn guy had dropped to the ground and a car was shielding him, so Benny fired low, hoping to get lucky and hit him, but his real objective at this point was just to keep him pinned down behind the car. If the goombah was armed—and based on the way he looked, he might be—then Benny was in trouble. But Benny didn't think he was armed; if he'd been packing heat, he would have returned fire by now. Benny was going to run right up to him and plug him in the face from two feet away. Even *he* couldn't miss from that distance.

DeMarco knew he couldn't stay where he was. Pretty soon, Norm would figure out that he wasn't armed and would run up and kill him. But where the hell could he go? In one direction was the golf course, and if he went that way he'd be right out in the open, on the fairway. In the other direction, he'd have to cross twenty feet of open ground to the next row of cars, and once again he'd be exposed. Whatever the case, he couldn't stay where he was. He was going to have to get up and run like hell, zigzagging the whole way, and hope the guy didn't shoot him in the back. He started to get to his feet, but before he could he heard a horrific *boom* and what sounded like a car window just exploding. It sounded like someone *behind* him was firing a big gun. Jesus, there were two of them! He was dead.

It was almost comical watching the fat man run for his car.

The fat man had been running toward DeMarco when the florist fired his first shot. He intentionally missed and blew out the window of a nearby car to startle him, and when he did, the fat man skidded to a stop, almost falling on his backside. The fat man snapped off one shot at the florist with the small-caliber gun he was using, and the florist immediately returned fire, blowing out the window of another car—and that's when the fat man ran to his car, jumped in, and drove out of the parking lot.

The florist looked over to where DeMarco was hiding; he couldn't see him. He was still on the ground behind his car. To keep DeMarco's head down, he fired at DeMarco's car, blowing out the driver's-side window, then got into his car and followed the fat man out of the parking lot.

He knew he had to leave the area—someone would call the police if they hadn't already—but he had a choice to make: should he go somewhere nearby and wait for DeMarco or should he follow the fat man? He decided to follow the fat man; it would be too dangerous to remain near the golf course with the police on their way.

DeMarco had no idea what was going on but he was going to die if he didn't do something. Norm had fired three or four shots at him, and then someone with a much louder weapon had fired twice, and he heard car windows all over the parking lot being shattered. He couldn't tell if both guys were shooting at him or if the other guy was shooting at Norm. He was about to get up and take off running when he saw Norm's chunky legs from beneath the car. Norm wasn't running *at* him; he was running away. A moment later he heard a car squeal out of the parking lot.

DeMarco figured this was the best chance he was going to get. With Norm gone, he was going to run down the cart path, away from the shooter behind him, but just as he started to get to his feet the driver's-side window of his rental car exploded, and he threw himself back down on the ground. He started belly crawling, having no idea where he was going, just wanting to be on the move, but then he heard another car leave the lot. Now it was completely quiet and he could sense that he was alone in the parking lot. He lay there, breathing heavily, and then cautiously got to his feet and looked over the hood of his car. The shooters were gone.

He saw a couple of elderly men standing on the cart path looking at him. He figured the old guys lived on the block and must have heard all the shooting and windows breaking. DeMarco yelled at them, "I'm calling the cops." He reached inside his rental car, grabbed his cell phone from the cup holder, and called 911—and got a busy signal. How the fuck can you get a busy signal on a 911 call! DeMarco called again and this time a woman answered.

"911 operator. What is the nature of your emergency?"

"Someone tried to kill me!" DeMarco yelled.

"Sir, please calm down and tell me where you are."

"I'm in the parking lot on the sixth fairway at the Glendon Hills Golf Course and two guys were shooting at me. And there's a dead guy in one of the houses here."

"Sir, could you please speak slower."

———◆◆◆———

Benny was sweating like he was sitting in a sauna. It had been a long time since he'd run that fast and been that scared. And he'd never been in a gunfight in his life. But who the hell was the guy with the shotgun? All he'd seen was a big, dark-haired guy with a mustache. Maybe he was the goombah's buddy. Goombahs liked to travel in pairs. Whatever the case, it was time to get the hell out of Dodge.

He realized he was driving too fast, took a breath, and tapped on the brake. The last thing he needed was a cop stopping him right now.

———◆◆◆———

The florist could see the fat man's car two blocks ahead of him. He had driven like a maniac out of the golf course housing development and the florist thought for sure that he was going to lose him. Then, fortunately, the fat man slowed down and a block later he was stopped by a red light.

As the florist followed the fat man, he tried to sort out what had happened. DeMarco, for reasons he didn't understand, had made a trip to Myrtle Beach apparently to see someone who lived in one of the town houses at the golf course. He had seen the fat man pass DeMarco on the cart path but DeMarco didn't speak to him, so it appeared that DeMarco didn't know the fat man. Then the fat man, for some reason, tried to kill DeMarco. None of this was making sense. He needed to take DeMarco and the fat man. He needed to take them someplace where he could question them without being interrupted.

The fat man eventually turned into a motel parking lot, got out of his car, looked around cautiously, then took the stairs to a unit on the second floor. The florist was betting that he would want to get out of town as soon as possible and was probably packing his bags right now.

He could go to the fat man's room and take him there, but that was problematic. He would be on edge, and if the florist knocked on his door, it was unlikely he would open it, or if he did he'd be ready to kill. He would wait until the fat man left his room.

The florist exited his car and, holding the Mossberg down by the side of his leg, took up a position near the staircase the fat man had used to reach the second story of the motel. He would wait there, out of sight, and when the fat man came down the stairs he would take him.

Chapter 23

———◆———

Whoever said it got it right: No good deed goes unpunished.

DeMarco had behaved like a law-abiding citizen—so now he was sitting in a jail cell.

After he called 911, four cop cars had arrived at the parking lot simultaneously, light bars flashing, sirens screaming, and six cops got out of the four cars, all of them with weapons in their hands. DeMarco could tell they were really keyed up, so he needed to be careful or he might get shot. He had been standing in the parking lot when they arrived, and as soon as the cops exited their vehicles, he showed them that his hands were empty. He didn't raise his hands over his head— he didn't want to come off as some sort of suspect—but he held them up, chest high, palms turned outward, to show he was unarmed.

"I'm the guy who called 911," he yelled. "The shooters are gone."

One of the cops said, "Sir, stand right where you are and put your hands behind your head."

Great.

Five of the cops fanned out to search the area but the one who had spoken to him came over to him, frisked him, then asked what had happened. And Citizen DeMarco told him: He'd come to visit Dale Acosta, found the man dead, returned to his car to call the police, and then all hell broke loose. He told the cop about Norm, the short, heavyset guy he saw leave Acosta's town house. He said Norm had taken a couple of shots at him, and then someone else had started shooting at him—or maybe at Norm—but he never saw the second shooter.

The cop then asked him why he was visiting Acosta and that's when DeMarco, being very polite and respectful, said he couldn't tell him. He said he was a lawyer and mumbled something about lawyer-client privilege, which, he was pretty sure, didn't apply to the situation at all. Still being courteous, he said that maybe after he made a phone call to his boss he could say more. The cop told him not to move, walked a few feet away, and made his own phone call. As soon as he finished his call, he spun DeMarco around, put handcuffs on his wrists, and read him his Miranda rights.

No good deed goes unpunished.

At the police station DeMarco was handed off to a tall, lanky detective who had a toothpick stuck in the corner of his mouth. The guy had redneck lawman written all over him. DeMarco told the detective the same story he'd told the uniformed cop in the parking lot, including that he couldn't say why he was visiting Dale Acosta until after he talked to his boss.

"You sure you wanna hold out on me?" the detective asked. The toothpick bobbed up and down as he spoke. "I mean after you just admitted you were in the same room as the dead man?"

But DeMarco, good soldier that he was, stuck to his guns.

He was taken to a cell where he met his cell mate, a man who smelled as if he had bathed in Jack Daniel's. "My name's Rudy," the man said. DeMarco responded by nodding his head and saying, "I'm Joe." Then Rudy, a good-sized guy who had biceps the size of grapefruits, stood there swaying as if he might collapse any minute and said, "I don't like the way you're lookin' at me." *Oh, shit,* DeMarco thought, but then Rudy flopped down on his bunk, passed out, and began to snore.

———◆———

Two hours later, Rudy was still snoring and DeMarco was giving serious consideration to smothering him. Rudy was spared by the arrival of the toothpick-gnawing detective.

"You feel like talking yet?" the detective asked.

"No," DeMarco said, "and you assholes can't hold me unless you're going to charge me with something."

"I'd suggest you watch your language," the detective said. "And we *are* charging you."

"With what?" DeMarco screamed. "Calling 911?"

"Vandalism."

"What!"

"Yeah, there were a lot of broken windows in that parking lot and we think maybe you're the one who broke 'em."

"That's bullshit and you know it. Those windows were *shot* out and you know I didn't have a gun on me."

"Maybe you threw it away."

"This is bullshit!"

"Language," the detective said.

"And if you're charging me, you have to arraign me so I can get bail and you have to let me see a lawyer and you have to let me make a phone call."

"Now that's all true," the detective said. "The problem is, we're pretty busy today and the court's got quite a back log and we got guys like Rudy over there who are in line ahead of you. Might be a while before the judge gets around to hearin' your case."

"You . . ." No, no, calling the guy a cocksucker would not be smart. Instead DeMarco said, "Look, all I'm asking is for you to let me call my boss and tell him what's going on. After I've talked to him, I might be able to tell you why I was going to see Acosta. I've already told you everything else I know."

"Who's your boss?" the detective asked.

"A guy you really don't wanna piss off," DeMarco said.

"Is that a fact?" the detective said, a little smile tugging at his lips. Then he looked at his watch. "Damn, it's way past my lunch time. You hungry?" he asked DeMarco.

DeMarco realized that he was. "Yeah," he said.

"Well, that's too bad," the detective said and walked away.

Ten minutes later, Rudy woke up. He sat on the edge of his bunk for a while, head in his hands, and DeMarco figured the guy was hungover so badly it felt like his skull was going to explode. Finally, Rudy trained his bloodshot eyes on DeMarco.

"My name's Rudy," he said.

DeMarco assumed Rudy had no recollection that he'd already introduced himself. This was good. "I'm Joe," DeMarco said. Then he waited for Rudy to tell him a second time that he didn't like the way DeMarco was looking at him.

But he didn't. Instead, Rudy said, "I sure hope I didn't do nothin' mean to you."

"Uh, no," DeMarco answered.

"That's good." Rudy shook his head sadly and said, "Sometimes when things ain't goin' so good down at the mill, I go over to Seth's and get drunk. And then I get mean. I don't know why, but I do. At first I feel good, and I like everybody, but the next thing I know people start pissin' me off. And then ol' Seth, he calls the cops and I wake up here. Man, I hope I didn't go whuppin' on nobody."

"Yeah, me, too," DeMarco said.

"Well, I suppose I better call my wife and tell her where I am. She's gonna give me the dickens."

Then Rudy took a cell phone out of his back pocket.

"They let you in here with a phone?" DeMarco said.

"Huh?" Rudy said. "Oh, yeah. They know me. I do this a couple times a year, so they just chuck me in here until I sober up, then I plead guilty and Judge Sims makes me go pick trash on the highway."

The wheels of justice.

"Uh, Rudy, do you think I could use your phone after you're finished? I'll pay for the call."

DeMarco told Mahoney he was incarcerated in South Carolina and that the police were being mean to him, then told him what had happened.

"Someone killed Acosta?" Mahoney said.

"Yeah."

"Huh," Mahoney said, like he was thinking about Acosta's death but he didn't seem particularly concerned that his faithful employee had almost been killed.

"So, can I tell 'em why I was visiting Acosta?"

"Hell, no! Don't tell 'em shit. I gotta figure out how I want to play this."

"But these rednecks aren't going to let me out of here if I don't tell them something!"

"Don't worry about it," Mahoney said. "I know a guy down there."

DeMarco was willing to bet that if he'd told Mahoney he was in jail in Bangladesh, Mahoney would have said "he knew a guy down there." He just hoped that whoever the guy was he could get him out of jail.

Chapter 24

Mahoney called a man named Scott Hayden, whose ancestors had ruled South Carolina when it was still a colony. Hayden had never held a political office but he had so much money that he had more influence than any elected official in the state. He had served with John Mahoney in Vietnam.

They didn't talk about the shared experience of combat, though. Instead, they reminisced about a weekend they had spent in Las Vegas prior to being sent overseas. Thinking they both might return home in government-issued coffins, Hayden took a few thousand out of his bank account—even at the age of eighteen he was obscenely rich—and treated his friend Mahoney to a smorgasbord of gambling, booze, food, and girls. Neither man had a clear recollection of their long weekend in Vegas because 90 percent of it had been spent in an alcoholic haze, but they figured they must have had a good time—a belief reinforced by the fact that they both came down with a case of the clap a week later.

After the past had been recalled and thoroughly embellished, Mahoney asked Hayden to get DeMarco sprung from jail. He then sat sipping bourbon and looking out the window at the National Mall while he swirled the whole Whitmore mess around inside his head. He finally decided since Whitmore could now get out of jail and wasn't likely to tell stories about his sex life, he might as well be up front with LaFountaine. He wasn't sure that was a smart thing to do because he didn't trust LaFountaine, but the thing with this dead spy was just too big a deal not to play it straight.

He called LaFountaine and told him what DeMarco had learned: that an ex–White House operator named Dale Acosta had leaked the story to Sandra Whitmore posing as a CIA agent, and Acosta had been killed. He said he figured Acosta was working for somebody but he didn't know who, and he said he didn't know who had leaked the story to Acosta's boss.

Which was sorta true. Mahoney was pretty sure Ray Rudman had leaked the information to Rulon Tully and that Tully had hired Acosta, but he wasn't positive, so he didn't *exactly* lie to LaFountaine.

LaFoutaine's response to Mahoney being so open and honest was, of course, to get pissed. He was pissed that Mahoney had been doing his own investigation and had been withholding information from him. He was also pissed that one of his employees had been attacked and tortured in his own home, and he figured Mahoney was some-how responsible for that, too.

At that point, and as was usually the case whenever Mahoney and LaFountaine talked to each other, both men started screaming into their respective phones, swearing, and not listening to a word the other man was saying. They were just too much alike.

Finally, they calmed down, or maybe they just ran out of things to say. LaFountaine broke the silence, saying they needed to get together and talk face-to-face, and Mahoney agreed. Then they both said they were sorry for losing their tempers, though neither man was.

———————◆◆◆———————

Benny changed out of his sweat-soaked clothes, packed his suitcase, and left his motel room. He stood outside the door for a moment, looked down into the parking lot, and didn't see anyone. Good. The .32 was tucked into the waistband of his pants, concealed by his shirt, and he kept his hand near the gun as he walked down the stairs.

Moving quickly toward his car, he opened the trunk with the remote and tossed his bag inside. As he closed the trunk lid, an object that felt like a gun barrel was pressed against his back.

He held up his hands and turned his head slowly. It was the guy from the parking lot, the big guy with the mustache, and he was holding a shotgun. Benny thought about pulling out the .32 and spinning around and shooting the guy—and quickly concluded that would be just about the dumbest thing he could do.

"Give me your gun."

Benny pulled out the little .32 and the man took it from him.

"Now get in the car. You're going to drive."

Benny noticed the guy had some sort of accent. He didn't think he was a cop—if he had been, he would have said so—but he didn't look or sound like a wop, either, so Benny didn't think he was the goombah's partner. But if he wasn't the goombah's partner then who the hell was he?

Benny got into the car. The gunman opened the rear passenger-side door, tossed the shotgun onto the backseat, then pointed the .32 at Benny's face while he opened the passenger-side door and entered the car.

"What's your name?"

"Benny."

"Okay, Benny. Buckle your seat belt and start the car. I'll tell you where to go."

What kind of fuckin' mess had Jimmy gotten him into?

———◆———

An hour after DeMarco talked to Mahoney, a uniformed cop came to the cell and opened the door.

"You can both go now," the cop said.

"Did I hurt anybody, Kenny?" Rudy asked the cop.

"No, but you kicked over some guy's Harley and really fucked up the chrome. That's gonna cost you."

"Dang," Rudy said.

DeMarco was given back his belt, wallet, watch, and cell phone, and then taken to an office occupied by a big, gray-haired guy in a suit. Also present in the office was the detective who had originally questioned DeMarco.

"Mr. DeMarco," the man in the suit said, "my name's Frank McDaniel. I'm the chief of police. I want to, uh, apologize. It seems that maybe things got a little out of hand, that maybe we were a little, uh, overzealous, but a murder like this, well . . . Anyway, I'm sorry you were detained. We've got your statement and your description of the suspect but I hope it'll be okay for us to call you if we need anything else. And I hope there're no hard feelings."

"Yeah," the detective said, "I screwed up, and I hope there's no hard feelings."

DeMarco could tell that neither McDaniel nor his detective were the sort who apologized for much of anything, so he figured whoever Mahoney had called had landed on the chief like a ton of bricks.

"Sure," DeMarco said. "And when I file a lawsuit against you clowns for unlawful arrest and mental anguish and violating my civil rights and any other fuckin' thing I can think of, I hope you won't have any hard feelings, either."

"Now look," McDaniel started to say, but DeMarco interrupted him.

"I'm kidding. Can somebody, please, just give me a ride back to my car?"

———◆◆◆———

They drove west out of Myrtle Beach until they came to a two-lane dirt road that looked promising, and the florist told Benny to turn onto the road. Twenty minutes later, he told Benny to stop when he saw a grove of trees on the right-hand side of the road that would shield them from passing cars.

"Get out of the car," he said.

Benny hesitated; he didn't want to go into the trees.

"Benny, if I wanted you dead I would have killed you back at the motel. Now get out."

He nudged Benny into the trees, prodding him in the back with the .32. To his credit, Benny didn't start blubbering or beg the florist not to kill him. Benny, it seemed, was a fatalist, and a tough one, too.

"Okay, stop," the florist said when they were no longer visible from the road. "Now listen to me, Benny. I'm not a policeman. I'm not bound by any rules. If you don't tell me what I want to know, I'm going to hurt you. Badly. Do you understand?"

Benny nodded.

"Now tell me why you tried to kill DeMarco."

"Who?" Benny said. He must have seen the impatience flare in the florist's eyes because he added rapidly, "No. Wait, wait. I'm telling the truth. I don't know anyone named DeMarco."

"DeMarco was the man you tried to kill in the parking lot at the golf course. Why did you shoot at him?"

"Oh, the goombah," Benny said. "He saw me."

"I still don't understand. What did he see you doing?"

Benny hesitated. "How do I know you're not a cop?"

"Benny, would a cop have brought you out here? Would a cop have come to your motel by himself, without a bunch of other cops? No, a cop would have brought a SWAT team with him and arrested you. I'm not a cop, Benny, but I'll say it again: I will hurt you if you don't start talking."

"Okay," Benny said. "I don't know what's going on. I was hired to kill this guy Acosta and I killed him, and DeMarco saw my face after I did the job. I figured he was going to call the cops, so I tried to kill him, too. But I'm just hired help. I don't know what's going on."

"Who's Acosta and why were you hired to kill him?"

"I don't know. He was just the mark. That's all I was told."

"So who hired you?"

"I don't know. I never know. I get a call, I'm given a name, and I do the job."

"Then who called you?"

Benny hesitated. "Look, I can't tell you that, I mean if I did . . ."

The florist shot Benny in the left foot.

Benny fell to the ground, clutched his bleeding foot, and began to whimper—and the florist could understand why. There are many delicate bones in the foot and the bullet had probably broken several of them.

"Benny," the florist prompted.

"Jimmy called me," Benny said through clenched teeth. "He's the middleman, the one the customers call."

"Tell me Jimmy's last name and where he lives."

"Man, if I do that . . ."

"Benny, do you want me to shoot you in the same foot or the other foot? I'll let you choose."

"Jimmy Franco. Not James. He lives in LA. He owns a pawnshop there."

The florist thought Benny was telling the truth.

"What are you going to do now?" Benny asked.

"Don't talk, Benny. That's what I'm trying to decide." After a moment he said, "Give me your wallet."

"Hell, yeah. Take the money," Benny said, and with some effort he extracted his wallet from his back pocket and tossed it to the florist.

The florist opened it and saw that Benny had two driver's licenses, one in the name of Benjamin Mark and one in the name of Benton Mandak. Clever—with either ID he could answer to the name Ben and not get confused.

"So who are you Benny, Benjamin Mark or Benton Mandak?"

"Mandak."

The florist shook his head. "I don't think I believe you, Benny. What will it be? The same foot or the other foot?"

"Okay, okay. I'm Benny Mark. I use the Mandak ID to travel when I'm working."

"I don't know, Benny. You're such a liar."

"I'm Benny Mark, I swear to God."

The florist laughed. They all swore to God. "But how can I be sure you're telling the truth?"

"I don't . . . wait a minute. Look at the other stuff in my wallet. I got an AARP card there, an Allstate card, an HMO card. They all say Benny Mark. You don't need to shoot me again."

"Okay, Benny, I believe you. Now you're probably thinking that you'll call Mr. Jimmy Franco if I let you go. But if you do, and if Franco isn't there when I get to LA, or if he looks like he's expecting me, then I'm going to come to your house in"—he looked at the Benny Mark ID—"in Tacoma and kill you. Do you understand?"

"Yeah, I understand."

"Okay. Good-bye, Benny."

The cops dropped DeMarco off at the golf course and he was pleased to see his rental car was still in the lot. But two windows had been broken and there was glass all over the inside of the car and he wondered what kind of hassle he was going to have when he returned it to Hertz.

He brushed the glass off the seat and started the car, then just sat there trying to figure out what he should do next. He finally decided to go back to D.C. Dale Acosta was dead, so he wasn't going to learn anything from him, and Sandra Whitmore could now get out of jail without telling the media nasty things about his nasty boss.

So, as that famous banner on that aircraft carrier had said, Mission Accomplished.

The florist returned to Benny's motel, dropped off Benny's car, and got into his own rental.

Now what?

He knew a man named Jimmy Franco had hired Benny to kill Acosta, but he didn't know why. He knew DeMarco had been going to visit Acosta, but he didn't know why he was doing that, either. He had two choices. Talk to DeMarco or fly to LA and talk to Jimmy Franco. The answer was obvious: he needed to talk to DeMarco. DeMarco was the key to all of this.

He drove back to the golf course, the last place he'd seen DeMarco, but DeMarco's car was no longer there. So where had DeMarco gone? Was he still in Myrtle Beach, had he returned to Washington, or had he flown back to New York to see Whitmore again? When DeMarco had gotten on the plane he had an overnight bag so maybe he was still in Myrtle Beach. Maybe. Too many maybes.

Then he remembered that DeMarco had rented a car from Hertz. If he had left Myrtle Beach he would have returned his rental car. He called Hertz, told the lady who answered that he was a policeman and needed to know if a Mr. DeMarco had returned his rental car. He said the car had been involved in a crime and some of the windows had been shot out. The Hertz lady said if he came to her office and showed her his identification, she'd be happy to cooperate with him, but without seeing his ID she couldn't give out any information about a customer. She was very polite—but very firm. The florist figured that his accent—not an accent similar to those who reside in the southern United States—didn't work in his favor.

He was tired. He had been on the move for days and he needed to sleep. He also needed to wash his clothes; they smelled. He dropped his clothes off at a dry cleaners that advertised four-hour service, then checked into a motel, took a shower, and slept for a couple of hours. Then he called every motel and hotel in Myrtle Beach listed in the yellow pages to see if DeMarco had checked into any of them. He had not.

Tomorrow he would fly back to Washington, wait until DeMarco returned to his house, and make him talk.

———◆◆◆———

Benny had thought for sure that he was gonna die; he couldn't believe that the big bastard hadn't killed him. But still, he was screwed. His foot was bleeding and it felt like every bone in it was broken. It hurt like a son of a bitch. And he was out in the boondocks, miles from Myrtle Beach, and the guy had taken his cell phone and driven off in his rental car. It was like the man didn't want to kill him, but didn't care if he bled to death.

He took off his shoe and saw that his sock was saturated with blood. He carefully peeled off the sock and saw one little hole in the top of his foot and a slightly bigger one in the bottom. There was also a hole in the bottom of his shoe, which was the least of his problems. He ripped a piece of cloth from his shirt and used it to make a bandage, but the bandage didn't stop the bleeding. He wondered if you could bleed to death from a couple little holes in your foot and figured you probably could, so he took off his belt and cinched it around his calf. The only thing he knew about applying a tourniquet was that it had to be really tight but if he left it on too long his foot would rot off. But what choice did he have?

He crawled around the grove of trees until he found a fallen branch that would support his weight and then started limping down the road. His belt/tourniquet kept slipping down around his ankle so finally he just took it off and hoped for the best. Then he got lucky: he fell, and when he fell, a colored guy in an old pickup saw him and stopped to see if he was okay.

Benny couldn't believe it: an honest-to-God Good Samaritan.

He told the colored guy his car had broken down and he'd been walking to find a phone and call a tow truck, but then he had stepped on this huge goddamn nail that was sticking up through a board lying in the road.

The man asked him not to swear, please, and not to use the Lord's name in vain.

"You betcha," Benny said. "Sorry about that. But could you please give me a ride back to my motel in Myrtle Beach?"

The man did—he was a saint—and when they arrived there, Benny thanked the man profusely and was delighted to see his rental car was back in the parking lot and that the keys were in it. He hadn't checked out, so he went back to his room and the first thing he did was wash off his foot in the bathtub. It was a mess. The bullet holes were still bleeding, though not as bad as before, but the pain was a lot worse, like there was a buffalo standing on his instep. The only good news was that the bullet wasn't in his foot.

He knew he should go to a doctor but he couldn't do that. The doctor might recognize that Benny had been shot and then he'd call the cops, and the cops might be able to figure out that he was the guy who had killed Acosta. So going to a doctor in Myrtle Beach was out of the question. He was just going to have to live with the foot until he got back home.

He called the front desk, told the hayseed clerk his stepping-on-a-nail story, and said that unless they wanted blood all over the carpet, he needed to bring him some big bandages, cotton balls, and tape. Oh, and a bottle of aspirin or Motrin or Advil or something. The clerk took his time but finally brought the stuff Benny needed. He washed his foot again, stuffed cotton balls in the holes, and bandaged it all up.

After he had swallowed six aspirin, he lay down on the bed and asked himself the question he'd been thinking about ever since he got shot: Should he, or should he not, call Jimmy Franco and warn him that one mean son of a bitch might be coming his way?

If he called Jimmy and told him he had admitted to the big guy that Jimmy had set up the hit on Acosta, Jimmy would most likely send someone to Tacoma to kill him. Jimmy—because he was a merciless, paranoid shit of a human being—would be afraid that because the big guy knew about the hit Benny might eventually be arrested and, if he was, he might testify against Jimmy for a better deal—which, of course, he would do if it ever came to that. On the other hand, if the big guy got to Jimmy in LA and didn't kill Jimmy, then Jimmy would also know that Benny had given him up and then Jimmy would *definitely* send somebody to Tacoma to kill him.

But there was something the big guy didn't know: Jimmy, because of the shit he was into and because of the shit he'd pulled in the past, had a lot of protection. He *surrounded* himself with bodyguards. So the big guy was going to have a tough time getting to Jimmy, and if he tried, there was a very good chance Jimmy's men would kill him before he ever talked to Jimmy. But then that presented another problem. When the big guy saw all the protection around Jimmy, he might figure the protection was there because Benny had warned Jimmy, and then he might come to Tacoma and kill Benny like he'd promised.

Benny groaned. This was just too fucking complicated—there were just too many different ways things could play out—and he was having a hard time thinking with the way his foot was hurting. He finally decided that no matter what he did, somebody was likely to try and kill him, and most likely it would be Jimmy, so therefore screw Jimmy. He would call Betty Ann, tell her to turn the bar over to her idiot brother, and meet him in Canada. There was a cheap resort on Vancouver Island in a town called Ucluelet. He'd gone there salmon fishing with some guys once, and the place was super remote. Nobody would ever think of looking for him there. Yeah, he and Betty Ann would hide out in Canada and fish for salmon until this whole thing was finished.

Chapter 25

"Good morning, Ms. Whitmore," the judge said. "I understand you're now willing to identify your source."

"Yeah," Whitmore said.

They were in the judge's chambers. The only people present were his honor, the federal prosecutor, a court stenographer, Whitmore, and her stick-up-his-butt lawyer—which was fine by her. The press would find out within the hour that she'd given up her source but this way she'd be able to leave the courthouse without having to fight her way through a gauntlet of reporters. She didn't want to deal with the media until she had a chance to change her clothes and fix her hair—and get a drink.

"I would have told you yesterday," she said to the judge, "but you weren't here."

"Sorry about that," he said, "but I had to make a little trip to Washington."

She noticed he smiled slightly when he said this, like he was tickled pink about something. In fact, the man seemed to be in a pretty good mood in general and not the crabby asshole he'd been in open court. Whatever.

"So, if you're ready, Ms. Whitmore," the judge said, nodding to the stenographer.

"My source was a man named Dale Acosta who lives in Myrtle Beach, South Carolina."

"And who is Mr. Acosta?"

Whitmore looked over at her lawyer and then said, "I don't think I have to tell you anything more. You wanted the name of my source and you got it."

She saw the judge's lips compress, his good humor instantly evaporating—but then he relaxed. It was as though he didn't feel like letting Whitmore spoil his good mood.

"Very well," he said. "Now that the court has the man's name I'm sure the government will learn whatever they need to know about Mr. Acosta. Pay your fine and you can leave."

"Fine? What fine?"

"Ten thousand dollars, Ms. Whitmore. If you'd been paying attention the day I held you in contempt, you would have heard me say that."

"I don't have ten thousand on me. Hell, I don't have ten thousand in my bank account."

The judge gave her a little not-my-problem shrug.

She turned to her lawyer, who had yet to open his mouth, and said, "Well? Are you gonna help me out here?"

Her lawyer cleared his throat and said, "The *Daily News* will pay the fine, Your Honor."

The judge made an I-could-care-less face.

———◆———

After they left the judge's chambers, her lawyer had wanted to talk to her about her source and what she planned to do next, but Whitmore told him to take a hike. She went to her apartment and the first thing she did was go to the cupboard where she kept the scotch and found out she had no scotch, which meant she had finished the bottle the last night she was home. She thought she should take a bath and change clothes before going out for a drink, but decided to hell with that. She had never needed a drink so bad in her life. She grabbed her purse and her cell phone and practically sprinted to the nearest bar.

She slammed down the first drink and immediately ordered another one. The bartender gave her a funny look and she figured it probably had to do with the way she looked, her hair all wild, no makeup on her face. And she sorta stank, too—but she didn't care. She was going to have at least one more drink, and then she'd go home and take a bath.

As she was sipping the second drink—cheap scotch had *never* tasted so good—she thought, *Now what?* What was her next step?

She took out her cell phone and was pleased to see the battery wasn't dead. It was her lucky day. It got even luckier when DeMarco answered on the second ring.

"DeMarco, I'm outta jail," she said. "So, thanks," she added, although she didn't feel particularly grateful to the hard-nosed bastard. "But now I need to know more about Acosta, who he's working for and all that."

"Sandy," DeMarco said, "I don't work for you. My job was to get you out of jail, and you're out. We're done."

"Well, maybe I'm not done with Mahoney," Whitmore said.

"Threatening Mahoney is not a good idea. He helped you out on this one but if he thinks you're going to blackmail him for the rest of his life . . . Sandy, John Mahoney is not a nice man."

Whitmore snorted. "You think I don't know that?"

"I'm just telling you that you don't want to push him into a corner. People have tried to do that before and it's turned out badly for them."

Before Whitmore could say anything else, DeMarco added, "Anyway, Dale Acosta's dead."

"What?" she shrieked. "How did he die?"

"He was shot at his home in Myrtle Beach."

"Jesus. Well, who killed him?"

"I don't know. I don't know who he was working for and I don't know who killed him. Direct any other questions you have to the cops in Myrtle Beach."

"I will, but—"

"Good-bye, Sandy," DeMarco said and hung up.

———◆◆◆———

Dead? Acosta was dead? What the hell was going on?

Maybe the guy who had paid Acosta to impersonate a CIA agent had killed him so he wouldn't talk. Or maybe his murder had nothing to do with the story.

Whitmore took another sip of her scotch. *God,* that tasted good.

She realized then that it didn't really matter who had killed Acosta or who he had been working for. Once his name came out, there were going to be a million reporters pursuing the story. There was no way she could have this thing to herself anymore. No, her job was no longer the story—her job was making a buck off this whole thing. In fact, the more she thought about it, Acosta getting killed was *great* news. It showed that the conspiracy in which she'd been ensnared was not just complex—it was deadly.

Oh, what a story. A dead spy. A dead source. The CIA. Marty Taylor.

Book deal. No doubt about it.

———◆◆◆———

Halfway through her third drink, she thought that she should hold a press conference right away. By now the media had to know she'd given up her source and had been released from jail, so she needed to talk to her brother reporters soon to make sure they got the story straight. In particular, she needed to make sure the headlines in tomorrow's papers didn't imply that she'd caved in.

To get the most exposure, she should call up the TV guys. But she didn't want to appear on camera the way she looked right now—and particularly after she had had a couple of drinks. No, that wouldn't be smart. Plus, if she held a televised press conference, she'd have to write up a statement to read and then deal with a bunch of reporters screaming questions at her, and she didn't feel like doing that right now. Tomorrow she'd go on some show—*Good Morning America* or the *Today* show, one of them. They'd be dying to have her on and they wouldn't throw a bunch of hardball questions at her. But she couldn't wait until tomorrow to tell her side of the story.

Then she thought, *Why not hold a small press conference right in the bar with just a few newspaper guys?* She really should go home and wash her hair before she met with them, but decided to hell with that. She didn't want to stop drinking and she didn't want to move, and regarding her appearance . . . well, she'd just point out to them that this is what you ended up looking like when the government tosses you in jail and tortures you. And she'd definitely been tortured, the way they'd held back her pain medication.

She got a phone book from the palooka behind the bar and called reporters she knew at the *New York Times* and the *Wall Street Journal*, and the New York stringers for the *Washington Post* and the *LA Times*. She told them where she was and to be here in half an hour if they wanted the story. She said if anyone brought a camera she'd call the whole thing off. After she had called all the other papers, she called the *Daily News*. No way was she giving the *News* an exclusive. The *News* was not her ally. For that matter, the *News* might not even be her employer at this point.

She was on her fourth drink when all the reporters assembled around her table and she was feeling about as mellow as she ever felt.

"Yeah," she said, spreading her arms wide, "I'm out of jail. I gave up my source."

The reporters smirked, which was just what she'd expected. Then she told them what had happened: how a man posing as a CIA agent had been her source and that the guy was now dead.

"Whoa!" they all said.

"Yeah," she said. "Somebody, maybe somebody inside the government, engineered this whole thing. They fed me the story—which, by the way, was accurate—but as soon as I figured out who my source really was . . ."

"But how'd you figure out that Acosta was the guy?" the *New York Times* reporter asked.

Now it was her turn to smirk. "Just because I was in jail didn't mean I stopped working the story. Anyway, whoever was behind this—maybe somebody in Congress, maybe somebody at the CIA—popped Acosta because they knew I was on to him. So, since my source lied to me about his identity, I gave him up to the judge."

"But why would—" the *Journal* reporter started to ask.

"That's all, boys. I'm still on this story so that's all you're getting. But I just wanted to make sure you heard it directly from me, that I may have been tricked by Acosta but he would have tricked any one of you, too."

"I don't know about *that*," the reporter from the *Washington Post* said, a smug smart-ass who parted his long hair in the middle like a girl.

All the reporters left soon after that except her colleague from the *Daily News*. He stuck around to say, "You're in the shits, big time, Sandy. I hope you know that. No matter how you try to spin this, Acosta snookered you. But as bad as that is, there's no way you should have talked to the other papers before you talked to us." The reporter shook his head, pretending he felt badly for her. "I just hope you have another job lined up."

Whitmore smiled. "I'm not sure I need to have another job lined up, Bobby. I'm thinkin' book deal here. And before you got here, I called a producer at *Good Morning America,* and they're gonna have me on tomorrow."

She sat back in the booth and started in on the scotch the guy from the *LA Times* had bought for her, the only one decent enough to spring for a drink. She felt so good right now that she didn't feel like ever leaving the bar. Yeah, she was going to stay right where she was in this nice, soft booth until they had to pour her into a cab. And while she was sitting, she'd think about how she was going to handle all the interviews coming up—and how she was going to spend the money she was going to make. She almost forgot that the *Daily News* reporter was still there.

"Bobby," she said, "I don't know how things are gonna end up, but you got a dead spy, a dead guy who was pretending to be a spy, and a valiant reporter—namely, *moi*—who was maybe set up by the fucking CIA. Oh, yeah, Bobby, I'm thinkin' *major* book deal. Movie rights, too."

"Who's gonna play you in the movie, Sandy. Miss Piggy?"

"Oh, screw you, Bobby. Now quit being a prick and buy me a drink."

Chapter 26

The florist awoke feeling refreshed but more frustrated than ever. All he had learned in Myrtle Beach was that DeMarco had been planning to visit a man named Acosta but Acosta was killed before DeMarco could talk to him. And he didn't understand why Benny Mark had been hired by a pawnshop owner in LA named Jimmy Franco to kill Acosta. He needed to relocate DeMarco to find out what was going on, and the best chance for doing so was in D.C.

Before going to the airport, he stopped at a drugstore and bought materials for mailing a package, then drove to a post office and mailed the gun he had taken from Benny Mark to general delivery in Los Angeles. If he had to go to LA to talk to Franco he was sure he would need a weapon and he didn't want to go through the hassle of trying to buy one in California. He also disposed of the Mossberg shotgun. He tossed it into a Dumpster, but before he did he disassembled it and smashed the barrel on the ground a few times to render it useless. He didn't want some kid finding the weapon and shooting himself.

At the airport, he purchased a ticket for Washington and had just passed through security when he looked up at one of the television monitors in the terminal. A female newscaster was saying Sandra Whitmore had been released from prison and that she had given up her source—a man named Dale Acosta who had impersonated a CIA agent named Derek Crosby. Acosta, the newscaster added with a wide-eyed look, had been found dead in his home yesterday in Myrtle Beach, South Carolina. The woman then began to rehash the entire Whitmore saga but the florist was no longer listening. He just stood there, thinking, as the other passengers in the terminal swirled by him. He at last understood the connection between Acosta and Crosby—Acosta had impersonated the little man that he had tortured. He headed back to the ticket counter to exchange his D.C. ticket for one to New York.

Sandra Whitmore's time had come.

Mahoney had arranged to meet LaFountaine at an IHOP in Clarendon. They picked the restaurant because it wasn't a place where they were likely to encounter other politicians or spies—and because Mahoney felt like having a waffle for breakfast. Waffles were a treat.

LaFountaine was already there when Mahoney arrived. Mahoney ordered coffee; he wanted to add a shot of bourbon from his flask but decided he'd wait until LaFountaine left before doing that. As soon as the waitress walked away from their table, LaFountaine said, "So, what was this guy, DeMarco, doing talking to Whitmore?"

"No, no," Mahoney said. "Let's start with you telling me why you ever told us about Diller visiting Iran in the first place. If it was so important to keep that information secret, why did you say anything at all?"

"I told you because I have a legal obligation to keep Congress informed."

"Jake, it's too early for bullshit. Give me a straight answer or I'm walking."

LaFountaine stared at Mahoney for a moment, then finally said, "I told you because of Jean Negroni."

Jean Negroni was the secretary of Homeland Security, but Mahoney didn't understand what she had to do with Diller's trip to Iran. LaFountaine explained.

"It shouldn't come as any surprise to you that Homeland pays attention to folks who fly out of places like Iran and end up in America.

And when an American citizen visits Iran, that also makes Homeland wonder why. At any rate, Negroni's guys knew Diller had flown to both Damascus and Tehran and I found out that she was thinking about picking him up and questioning him, and I didn't want her doing that."

"Why not?" Mahoney asked.

To delay answering, LaFountaine sipped his coffee, then dabbed his lips with a napkin. He lowered his voice and said, "Do you know what Marty Taylor's company makes?"

"Yeah, something to do with missiles."

"Right. He manufactures control systems for missiles and a bunch of other military hardware. And, well, we had an idea."

"We who?"

"My guys. The CIA. We wondered if there was a way we could modify Taylor's equipment without the Iranians knowing about it and then if they ever tried to shoot one of their missiles in the wrong direction, maybe we could control the missile."

"You gotta be shittin' me," Mahoney said.

"No. It was a good idea. We weren't sure it could be done—the Iranians aren't fools—but I wanted to explore the idea. And if we could have found a way to make it work, we would have used Diller to sell the modified hardware to the Iranians. So that's why I didn't want Diller arrested right away and why I didn't want Negroni's people tipping him off that we knew he'd been in Tehran. But then Diller's trip was front-page news before we could even start to study the concept."

Hmm, Mahoney thought. That would have been pretty slick if LaFountaine had been able to do what he'd just said. He could just see the Iranians firing some rocket and a technician sitting in a spy ship parked in the Persian Gulf turning a joystick and making the rocket land right in the grand ayatollah's hot tub. But LaFountaine still hadn't told him what he wanted to know.

"You didn't answer my question, Jake. Why did you tell the committee about Diller?"

"Negroni insisted. She told me she wouldn't pick Diller up and interfere with my plan but only if I told the president and the intelligence committee the reason why. She wanted to make sure the president understood that if it had been up to her, she would have arrested Diller immediately but she held off because I asked her to. She also didn't like being the only person outside the CIA knowing what we were planning about the Iranian missiles because if something went wrong somebody might blame her in some way. In other words, she wanted her ass covered."

"Yeah, but you didn't really tell us what you had in mind. You didn't say anything about giving the Iranians some tricked-out control system."

LaFountaine shrugged. "I told the president everything and I told you guys as much as you needed to know. And I didn't lie to you when I said that arresting Diller would affect an ongoing operation. But I didn't see the point of letting people like Glenda Petty piss all over my idea until we had completed the research."

There you go, Mahoney thought, that was the Jake LaFountaine he'd always known and loved. Then he had another thought, "Well, hell," he said. "For all you know, Negroni was the original source of the leak. Maybe one of her people paid Acosta to talk to that reporter."

"It wasn't Negroni. She wouldn't do that and you know it. It was one of your guys, John, and that brings us back to the question of why DeMarco was visiting Sandra Whitmore."

Mahoney lied, of course. "I sent him to see her because of you. At your press conference you basically accused Congress of divulging national security information, so I wanted to see if there was any truth to that. Then one thing just led to another."

LaFountaine's dark eyes flashed and it looked like he was going to lose his temper, but he didn't. Instead, he closed his eyes for a moment and when he opened them he said, very softly, "Let me tell you about Mahata. I went to Georgetown University one day and gave a speech to an auditorium full of kids. We were having a hard time recruiting the right kind of people, and I figured I needed to get out there and tell folks that we were the good guys and not the evil fuckups the press always makes us sound like. Anyway, I gave the standard spiel about the CIA's role in the war on terror and, as usual, there were a couple of hecklers in the audience. The speech ended with the campus cops dragging one kid out by his hair and me getting pissed and telling those brats they were nothing but a bunch of dilettantes."

Mahoney smiled. He could see LaFountaine losing his temper with the college kids. He would have done the same thing.

"After the speech, I was walking back to my car and this girl comes up to me. She was beautiful. She had eyes so big you could fall into them and disappear. I thought she had followed me out to give me a ration of shit, but the first thing she said was that she was born in Iran, that the Iranian government had killed her entire family, and she spoke four languages. And she wanted to work for the CIA.

"I brought her into the agency, John. Me. Personally. She was only twenty years old at the time, twenty-two when she finished her training and we inserted her into Iran. She was an incredible woman. Brave, smart, resourceful." LaFountaine hesitated a beat, then added, "I loved that girl."

Mahoney nodded his head but he was thinking that LaFountaine was being literal when he said he had loved Mahata. He didn't know if LaFountaine had had an affair with her—maybe he did, maybe he didn't—but he definitely felt about her in a way that went beyond a boss caring for one of his employees.

"So I want whoever killed her," LaFountaine said. "I want them all. Somebody paid Acosta to impersonate one of my people and give the story to Whitmore. But now Acosta's dead and the only lead we have to follow is that half-ass description of the killer that DeMarco gave the Myrtle Beach cops. And you may not have heard this yet, but Conrad Diller is missing. They found his car at LAX but nobody can find him."

"He skipped the country?"

"Maybe, but he never entered the airport; if he had, one of the security cameras would have picked him up and none of them did.

The FBI's got two dozen agents trying to find him, but one possibility is that Diller's dead, and without his testimony we won't be able to get Marty Taylor.

"I don't know where this is going next, but there's one thing I do know: I'm not going to sit around and wait for the FBI or the Department of Justice or the goddamn sheriffs in Myrtle Beach to do something. I'm going after these people myself."

"Okay," Mahoney said. "So what do you want from me?"

"I *know* one of your guys leaked what I told you at that briefing, and I think it was Ray Rudman. Rudman's biggest backer is Rulon Tully and Tully benefits if something bad happens to Marty Taylor. And I know something else. Tully got a call from the Rayburn Building an hour after that committee meeting ended."

"From Rudman's office?"

"No. From Diane Frazer's office."

Frazer was a congresswoman from Utah.

"Frazer? She wasn't at the meeting."

"No, but her office is two doors down the hall from Rudman's, and we found out from Frazer's secretary that Rudman popped in unannounced to visit Frazer after the meeting. The secretary had an errand to run, so she didn't see Rudman leave Frazer's office, but the call to Tully was made from Frazer's conference room. We think Rudman used the phone in the conference room after he talked to Frazer, and he used it because he didn't want the call traced back to his office."

"Did you have warrants to look at these phone records," Mahoney asked.

"What do you think?" LaFountaine said. "But even if I could prove Rudman called Tully, I can't prove that they talked about Diller's meeting in Iran. Rudman will just . . ."

"Well, at least it's good to know you're not bugging every phone on Capitol Hill."

LaFountaine ignored the jibe. "Rudman will just say that Tully is a big supporter and they talked about some bill going through the House. But I know Rudman talked to Tully about Diller."

"Let's say you're right," Mahoney said. "So what?"

"Tell me the truth, John. Do you want Rudman in Congress? Do you want a guy in *your* House who will pass classified dope to a constituent just to keep his seat?"

"No."

"Then help me get him. Him and everybody else involved in this."

"But how can I help?"

"You got this guy DeMarco, and—"

"DeMarco's not *my* guy. He doesn't work for me, at least not directly. He's just sort of an odd-jobs guy the members use sometimes."

"Fine," LaFountaine said. "But I got a feeling he'll do what you tell him, and I want you to tell him to help."

"Why do you need him?"

"I don't *need* him—I mean, I could live without him if I had to—but I want to minimize the number of people involved in this thing. And DeMarco's already in it."

"You mean you want to limit the number of CIA agents involved because you know if one of them gets caught, you'll have a major problem."

LaFountaine shrugged.

Mahoney didn't say anything for a moment, but he was thinking, *Never try to bullshit a bullshitter*—and he knew LaFountaine was bullshitting him. He was lying about why he wanted DeMarco and Mahoney knew why he was lying.

"Okay," Mahoney said. "You can have DeMarco but only on one condition: I don't want it getting out that Rudman leaked the story. I want to find some other reason for getting him out of the House."

"So you know Rudman did it."

"I know it but, just like you, I can't prove it. But what I don't need is another congressional scandal. Our approval rating is already a negative number, so I don't need the whole world knowing a guy in my own party can't keep a secret."

"Okay, I'll agree to that condition."

That was too easy, Mahoney thought.

"You have a plan of some kind?" Mahoney asked.

"Not really. Since there's no way to prove Rudman talked to Tully about Diller, Rudman's not going to jail for that unless he confesses. But maybe we can put him in jail for something else he's done. Or maybe we can prove Tully was behind Acosta's murder. Or maybe we can get Rudman and Tully to turn on each other for something not related to Mahata. I don't know—and that's why I want DeMarco. We've done a little research on him and we know he's a tricky bastard. Maybe he can help us come up with something."

LaFountaine left a few minutes later and Mahoney took out his flask, added a shot of bourbon to his coffee, and ordered a waffle from the waitress. And because the waitress was a good-looking gal in her forties, he spent a little time flirting with her.

While he was waiting for his breakfast, he sipped his laced coffee and tried to figure out exactly how many lies LaFountaine had told him.

He didn't mind lending DeMarco to LaFountaine because he really did want Rudman out of Congress. But he knew that LaFountaine had lied to him about the reason why he wanted DeMarco. LaFountaine didn't want DeMarco because he wanted to minimize the number of CIA agents involved, nor did he want DeMarco because DeMarco was a devious guy that could help him. LaFountaine employed several thousand devious people, and most of them were smarter than DeMarco. No, LaFountaine wanted DeMarco for a completely different reason: LaFountaine wanted a fall guy—a scapegoat to pin things on if something went wrong—and he wanted a fall guy who didn't work for the CIA. But even though he realized what LaFountaine was doing, Mahoney had decided to let DeMarco get involved for one simple reason: he wanted DeMarco inside the CIA's tent so he could keep Mahoney informed about what LaFountaine was doing. DeMarco was *his* spy—and Mahoney was going to use him to spy on the spies.

He figured that LaFountaine had also lied about not having some plan for getting Ray Rudman. LaFountaine wasn't the type of guy who wouldn't have a plan—and he sure as hell wouldn't be relying on DeMarco to develop one. LaFountaine had also agreed too easily about not exposing Ray Rudman as the source of the leak. LaFountaine wouldn't give a rat's ass about whatever political problems he might cause Mahoney if Rudman's part in Mahata's death was revealed. But since LaFountaine couldn't prove that Rudman was the leak, maybe that's why he had agreed. Hmmm.

He also thought some more about LaFountaine's plan for using Taylor's equipment to control Iran's missiles. He had no idea if such a thing was technically feasible. What he did know was that kind of tricky James Bond crap always seemed to backfire on the CIA. But had LaFountaine really wanted to delay arresting Diller until he had studied the concept? Maybe. His gut told him LaFountaine wasn't lying about that. What he was less sure of was the part about LaFountaine telling Congress about Diller because Jean Negroni had made him.

He didn't know Jean Negroni very well but there was one thing he did know: unlike John Mahoney and Jake LaFountaine, she was an absolute straight arrow. In fact, Mahoney had always thought she was *too* straight for the job she had. So Mahoney could see her insisting that LaFountaine tell Congress and the president about Diller but the big question was this: Did Negroni *really* know about Diller's trip to Iran and did she *really* make LaFountaine inform Congress? All Mahoney had to do to determine this was call Negroni and ask her—but LaFountaine would have known that. So the bottom line was he believed LaFountaine not because he trusted LaFountaine, but because he didn't believe LaFountaine would lie to him about something he could so easily verify.

Sheesh, things got complicated when you were dealing with a sneaky son of a bitch like Jake LaFountaine—and that's why he knew he had made the right decision to keep DeMarco in the game.

"Here's your waffle, sir," the waitress said, sliding the plate onto the table.

Mahoney looked at the woman's face—then at her chest—then into her eyes. "It's just so unfair," he said, shaking his head in mock dismay.

"I'm sorry," she said, not understanding. "What's unfair?"

"So many pretty women—so little time."

Chapter 27

———◆———

DeMarco spent the day after he returned from Myrtle Beach loafing around his house, washing clothes, and paying a few bills. He even vacuumed and dusted, things he did about once a month whether the place needed it or not. By five p.m. he was hungry and, deciding he was too lazy to cook for himself, walked over to M Street in Georgetown for dinner.

He ended up at The Guards restaurant. He liked The Guards because it was usually quiet and not packed with a herd of drunken college kids like every other establishment on the M Street strip. He took a seat at the bar.

There were four other guys sitting at the bar, all wearing suits, all in their forties or fifties. They didn't look alike, but there was a sameness to them: they all seemed tired and a little depressed, staring down into their drinks at the end of a long day, ignoring everyone else around them. And DeMarco had this feeling that they were all lonely, that they had no wives to go home to, or wives they didn't want to go home to, and they were all in dead-end jobs they didn't like. In other words, guys just like him. And now he was starting to get depressed.

And then *she* entered the bar.

She had long, dark hair framing a narrow face. A perfect nose, full lips, big dark eyes. She had an hourglass figure encased in a black suit, the hem of the skirt stopping just above her knees. On her feet were four-inch stiletto heels.

She was every man's fantasy, and every guy in the bar was thinking the same thing, *Please, please, Lord, let this woman sit down next to me.*

She stood in the doorway for a moment—and then walked straight to DeMarco.

"Joe," she said, "why don't we go sit in a booth where we can talk?"

"Do I know you?" he asked, knowing he didn't, knowing there was no way that if he had ever met this woman he would have forgotten.

"No," she confirmed.

"Then how do you know me?" he asked.

"Let's get a booth," she said and walked away, certain that he would follow.

"Hey, you wanna drink?" he called out to her.

"Diet Coke."

As he was waiting for her drink he couldn't help but look over at the guy sitting closest to him. The guy had a *Why you?* look on his face and DeMarco just gave him a small, smug smile, as if beautiful women picked him up in bars all the time.

Her Diet Coke and his martini in hand, he sat down across from her.

"How do you know me?"

She took a leather case out of her purse and flipped it open. "Angela DeCapria. CIA."

"CIA?"

"Yeah."

He figured the CIA had found out that he had met with Whitmore, was perturbed because he had, and now wanted to know what Whitmore had told him. All he knew for sure was just looking at Angela DeCapria was worth whatever aggravation she might cause him.

"So what can I do for you?" he asked.

"My boss and your boss have agreed that we're going to work together."

"My boss?" DeMarco said.

"Mahoney. The Speaker."

"I don't work for Mahoney," DeMarco said.

"Yeah, whatever," Angela said, and when she said it she reminded him of all those girls in Queens he'd known growing up. "All I know is that Speaker Mahoney and Director LaFountaine have decided we're working together. You can call Mahoney later to confirm this."

"What are we working together on?" DeMarco asked, but he was thinking that spending time with this woman would be better than any job Mahoney could possibly give him. And then she pulled the maraschino cherry from her drink and sucked the fruit off the stem— and DeMarco fell in love.

"We're going to destroy the lives of all the people who were involved in getting Mahata Javadi killed."

DeMarco shook his head. He imagined it was 1960, and sitting in a bar in Miami is a CIA agent and a Cuban, and the agent is telling the Cuban how the CIA is going to help him and his friends take down Castro. Later, the Cuban would be lying on the beach at the Bay of Pigs watching his friends die. There was no way DeMarco was going to get involved in some illegal, half-baked CIA scheme that could land him in jail—or maybe get him killed like Dale Acosta.

"I don't think so," he said. "But can I buy you dinner?"

"Joe, just so we don't waste a lotta time here, go call this guy that you don't work for right now. Then, after he tells you that you're my new partner, we'll have some dinner and talk. And dinner's on the agency. We're loaded."

———◆◆◆———

When DeMarco came back to the table and she saw the look on his face, she said, "Okay. I'm glad we got that settled."

They ordered dinner—steak and a baked potato for DeMarco, a Cobb salad for her—then she said, "So, let's start by talking about what you know about Sandra Whitmore and Dale Acosta."

"How 'bout we get acquainted first," DeMarco said.

Angela shrugged. "I'm already acquainted with you. I know where you went to grade school, who your mother is, who your father was—which, by the way, blew me away when I found *that* out. I know you were married and your wife left you to marry your cousin, a guy who's a fence for Tony Benedetto up in New York. And I know, no matter what the goddamn paperwork says, that you work for John Mahoney. So, like I said, I'm pretty well acquainted with you."

"Yeah, but I don't know you," DeMarco said.

"What's to know? I was raised in an ugly little town in Pennsylvania. My granddad worked at a steel mill and my dad worked there, too, until we started buying all our steel from China. Now my dad's a drunk who works at Wal-Mart. My mother's a saint and my sister is Goody Two-shoes, married to an accountant, and she has two kids that are cuter than kittens and I love 'em both."

"How'd you end up with the CIA?"

"I wanted to be a cop. I got a degree in criminal justice, became a cop, and about the time I got tired of being treated like a meter maid, 9/11 happened and the CIA was hiring. End of story."

"You married?"

Angela hesitated and for the first time DeMarco saw some of her glibness disappear.

"Yeah, I'm married."

"You're not wearing a wedding ring."

"I don't wear a ring, Sherlock, because I'm left-handed and the ring screws me up if I have to shoot my gun."

"Is DeCapria your husband's name?"

"My maiden name."

"What's your husband think about you—"

"Hey, enough. Now we're acquainted. Let's get to work."

During dinner, DeMarco told her everything he knew and everything he had done, with one exception: he didn't tell her why Mahoney had sent him to help Sandra Whitmore in the first place. Angela nodded her head while he talked, as if he was confirming things she already knew. He concluded by saying, "But I don't know who started this whole thing. I mean, I know someone leaked the information about Diller's trip to Iran, and after that Dale Acosta was hired to tell Whitmore, and Whitmore published the story, but I don't know who the original leaker was."

"We think it was Congressman Ray Rudman," Angela said.

"Why?"

"Because Rudman's biggest supporter is Rulon Tully and Tully hates Martin Taylor, and leaking the story hurts Taylor."

"But that doesn't prove . . ."

"And because your boss agrees with us that Rudman was the original source."

It would have been nice if Mahoney had told him about Rudman, but now DeMarco could understand why Mahoney was going along with this thing: he wanted Rudman out of Congress but he didn't want to deal with the political fallout of publicly exposing him.

"Is that it, DeMarco? You're not holding anything back?"

"No," DeMarco lied.

"Okay. So this is what we have. We suspect Rudman told Rulon Tully about Diller's meeting in Tehran. Tully, probably through a middle man, hires Dale Acosta. Acosta impersonates a CIA analyst named Derek Crosby and feeds the story to Whitmore. Then it gets interesting. Somebody kills Acosta. But who, and why? The logical answer is that Tully had Acosta killed because when Mahata died Tully realized it was a whole new ball game and he couldn't take the chance that Acosta might give him up. Does that sound right to you?"

"That sounds logical but we don't have any proof."

"We don't need no stinking proof," she said, making DeMarco smile. "And then we've got the mystery man."

"What mystery man?"

"The guy in the ski mask who tortured Derek Crosby."

"Tortured Crosby? What are you talking about?" DeMarco asked and she proceeded to tell him how a man had broken into Crosby's house and smothered him with a plastic bag to get Crosby to confess to meeting with Whitmore, which Crosby never did. While DeMarco was still trying to digest this latest piece of information, Angela continued.

"And the guy who tortured Crosby may be the same guy that saved your life in Myrtle Beach."

"I'm not sure the other shooter was trying to save my life. I couldn't tell if he was shooting at me or at Norm."

"Norm?"

"Sorry," DeMarco said, and he explained how the fat guy who killed Dale Acosta looked like the actor who played Norm on *Cheers*.

"I *loved* that guy," Angela said. "But to get back to the issue of who was shooting at whom, we took a peek at the crime-scene report and, based on statements you gave them about the relative position of the shooters and damage done to cars in the parking lot, it looks like the mystery man was shooting at Norm. Or at least most of his shots were aimed at Norm. So we think the mystery man saved your life."

"But do you know for sure that the shooter in the parking lot was the same one who questioned Crosby?"

"Not for sure, but it makes sense that it was him. We think he's been following you."

"Nobody's been following me."

Angela snorted. So far that was the least attractive thing that DeMarco had seen her do. "Like you'd ever know," she said. "I followed you from your house to this restaurant. Did you see me?"

"No."

"So, as I was saying, we think the mystery man started following you when you went to see Whitmore in New York. You get a lead on Crosby and this guy breaks into Crosby's house and questions him. You get a lead on Acosta and you go to see Acosta, and he's with you again. And maybe that's why he saved your life—because you keep leading him to all the people involved in this."

DeMarco, because his pride was wounded, still wanted to deny being followed but didn't see the point.

"But how did he know that I visited Whitmore in the first place?" he asked.

"We're not sure," Angela said. "But maybe he did the same thing we did and bribed someone at the jail to keep him informed of Whitmore's visitors."

"Huh. So, now what?"

"Now it's time for you to do some homework. In my car, I have all the information we have on Ray Rudman and Rulon Tully. We're still researching Marty Taylor. And, being the CIA, we have a *lot* of information. You need to study it tonight and see if anything in the files gives you any bright ideas for how we can get these guys."

"And if I don't get any bright ideas?"

"Then I guess we'll have to go with one of *my* bright ideas," she said. "But right now what we have to do is check into a hotel."

"A hotel?"

And a fantasy erupted full-blown in DeMarco's head: Angela DeCapria found him so handsome, so irresistible, that she had to take him someplace and . . .

"Since we don't know who the mystery man is but we think he's following you, we need to make sure you're someplace where he can't get to you. When we leave here, we're gonna go back to your place— I already have people watching your house—and you're going to pack a bag, and then we're going to drive around for a bit. While we're driving, some of my friends will be looking for anybody following us, and if somebody is we'll get the guy. If nobody is, we'll check into a hotel."

So much for fantasies.

Chapter 28

The florist wasn't following DeMarco.

He was standing in an unlit doorway near the Patterson Houses, a massive public housing project in the Bronx. For the last hour he had been watching a small crew of teenagers selling drugs to other teenagers and people of indeterminate age who looked barely human, their bodies so wasted from the substances they took.

The florist wanted a gun but because he'd flown to New York, he hadn't been able to take any of his weapons with him. He was certain, however, that some of the young drug dealers he was watching were armed and that one of them would provide what he needed.

A new man joined the crew. He was taller and older than the teenagers, in his midtwenties. He spoke to the group for a moment, struck one of the teenagers in the face, knocking him to the ground, then jabbed his index finger sharply into the chest of another young man. The florist assumed he was the boss and was unhappy about some issue related to either security or profitability.

The florist smiled slightly. All these young men probably thought they were very tough and he was sure they frightened the law-abiding citizens in the neighborhood, but the florist, with his background, was unimpressed and certainly unafraid.

The boss finished berating his crew and walked away in long, confident strides—directly toward the doorway where the florist was

standing. When the man passed the doorway, the florist stepped out
of the shadows, startling him, and the man reached behind his back.
The florist figured this was where he carried his weapon—in the back
waistband of his jeans—and this theory was pretty much confirmed
when the man said, "You could get your ass blown away, you old fool,
jumpin' out at a man like that."

The florist apologized and pretended to be appropriately cowed,
and the man turned and continued walking. The florist followed. As
they walked, the man turned his head a couple of times and scowled,
not liking the florist behind him. The florist waited until they turned
a corner and were no longer visible to the man's crew, then rapidly
closed the distance between them.

The man turned and said, "What the fuck do you think you're
doin'?"

The florist punched him in the face, spun him around, pulled a
9 mm Glock from the waistband of the guy's pants, and hit him in
the head with it.

Now he had a gun.

The first day the florist had arrived in New York, while Sandra Whitmore was still in jail, he had identified that she lived in an apartment
building in Tribeca. All he had to do was call directory assistance to
get her phone number and address.

The building didn't have a doorman—it was not an upscale
residence—but all the exterior doors were kept locked. He punched
the buzzer corresponding to Whitmore's apartment number; no one
answered. He then punched several more buzzers and finally a woman
who sounded very old responded. "UPS," he said. "What?" the old
lady said, and he said, "Delivery. UPS." She buzzed him into the
building.

He took the stairs up to Whitmore's fourth-floor apartment and
knocked on her door. No one answered. He looked at his watch—
nine p.m. Where could she be? One of the newspapers he had read

said she was appearing on several radio and television talk shows; another said she was talking with two publishing companies about writing a book. It appeared that Whitmore had become a minor celebrity and was cashing in on Mahata's death—which made him even angrier—and he wondered if that was the reason why she wasn't home, because she was off promoting herself. Whatever the case, all he could do was wait for her to return.

He knew he couldn't remain standing in the hallway; some other tenant might see him and call the police. From the stairwell, however, he could see her apartment door, so he took up a position there, leaving the stairwell door cracked open so he could look down the hallway.

At ten thirty he heard the elevator ding. He peeked down the hall and saw Whitmore staggering toward her door. She appeared to be drunk. Very drunk. Making no attempt to be stealthy, he left the stairwell and walked down the hall directly toward her. Whitmore reached her apartment, took her keys from her purse, and, with some difficulty, inserted a key into the keyhole. She saw the florist walking toward her and she scowled at him but didn't say anything. The florist paced himself perfectly and just as Whitmore unlocked her door he was standing next to her, and as the door swung open he grabbed her by the nape of the neck and shoved her into her apartment.

Whitmore let out a shriek as he propelled her through the door, and she stumbled and landed hard on the floor. The florist shut the door, stepped over to her, and pressed the drug dealer's Glock against her forehead. "Be quiet," he said.

The woman was repulsive. She reeked of alcohol and tobacco. Her jowly face was red and bloated and particularly hideous contorted as it was with fear and anger.

"Get up," the florist said. "Sit on the couch."

The apartment was a mess. Overflowing ashtrays and lipstick-smeared glasses sat on every flat surface; clothes, fast-food cartons, and newspapers were scattered about on chairs and on the floor. The aroma of old cigarette butts and something rotting in the kitchen was overpowering.

"Who are you?" Whitmore asked.

The florist kicked her wide ass. "Get up. If I have to tell you again, I'll drag you by your hair."

The woman heaved herself to her feet and staggered toward the couch. Her words slurred by alcohol, she mumbled, "I don't have any money."

The florist walked over to another chair, tilted it so that the pizza carton sitting on it fell to the floor, then sat down and pointed the Glock at her face.

"Why did you print the story?" he asked.

That was really the only question he had for her. He knew Acosta had given the story to her. He didn't know why Acosta had done so—maybe he'd find out after he talked to the man in Los Angeles—but all he wanted to know from this woman was *why*.

"What?" she said. "What are you talking about?"

"Your story on Conrad Diller, the story that got Mahata Javadi killed. Why did you publish it? I know, from everything I've read and heard on television, that the CIA told you that publishing the story would compromise their operations, but you published anyway. I want to know why."

"Who are you? CIA?"

"No. I'm not from the government and I'm not a policeman. But I am a man that will hurt you very badly if you don't answer my questions."

The woman appeared to grow more confident now that she'd overcome her initial fear. Or maybe she was so drunk she didn't understand that she should be afraid. He imagined she'd always been an aggressive woman, used to getting her way, and she confirmed this when she said, "You're not going to use that gun. Somebody will hear it."

The florist had once been very good with a pistol—with any weapon, for that matter—but except for shooting Benny Mark in the foot, he hadn't fired a pistol in years. He hoped he hadn't lost all his skill. He pulled the trigger and the bullet passed so close to the left side of Whitmore's head that it actually tugged at her hair. He wasn't worried that her neighbors would react to the sound of a single gunshot.

Whitmore's eyes grew wide with shock and she clamped a hand over her mouth to keep from screaming.

"Why did you print the story?"

"Because, because . . . because it was news. Because an American company was trying to sell banned technology to Iran and the CIA wasn't doing anything about it."

"No, that's not what I mean. Why did you print the story after the CIA told you that doing so could harm their operations?"

"Because I didn't believe them. That's what the CIA always says when you ask them to comment on a story."

"But why would they lie to you?"

"Because they're the goddamn CIA! That's what they do, they lie."

The florist shook his head. "I don't believe you. I think you published the story to help your career and you didn't care what the consequences might be."

Sandy Whitmore opened her mouth to argue, but then stopped. She didn't have an argument.

"Who are you?" she asked again.

This time he told her.

"Oh, Jesus," she said.

He shot her. He shot her in the center of the forehead, right above the bridge of her nose. He was still very good with a pistol.

Looking at her sitting there on the couch—her thick legs splayed wide, her gross features slack in death, the ugly red-black hole in her forehead—he noticed he didn't really feel anything, that there was simply an emptiness in his chest. He certainly felt no remorse for killing her, but at the same time he didn't feel the satisfaction he thought he would feel for avenging Mahata. If he felt anything, he felt diminished by what he had done, the same way he had felt when he was forced to torture that little man Crosby.

There was an old Chinese saying he recalled: Before you embark on a journey of revenge, dig two graves—meaning one for your enemy and one for yourself.

Be that as it may, and regardless of how he might feel, before this was all over more than two graves would be needed.

Chapter 29

Two hours after having dinner with Angela—an hour of which was spent driving around to confirm that no one was following DeMarco —they checked into adjoining rooms at the Sheraton in Crystal City. Considering the CIA's budget, DeMarco said he'd been expecting a suite at the Four Seasons in Georgetown; this comment caused Angela to make that unattractive snorting sound she made whenever he said something stupid. When they reached their rooms, she handed him the CIA's files on Rulon Tully and Ray Rudman and, in a you-better-do-it tone of voice, told him to read the files before falling asleep.

The file on Rudman was so boring it was almost impossible to keep his eyes open. It contained Rudman's biography from the time he left high school to the present, noting that he'd been married for twenty-five years to the same woman and had two children and two grandchildren. He'd been a semi-successful real estate agent before vectoring off into politics, and was a one-term mayor of Anaheim before being elected to Congress.

Rudman's personal and campaign finances were analyzed in detail. The conclusion in both cases was that Rudman didn't appear to be doing anything either illegal or immoral. There was no evidence he had ever broken his marriage vows; he didn't gamble online or spend hours on the Internet looking at porn; he didn't purchase silky underwear for himself at Victoria's Secret. He had taken a couple of congressional junkets paid for by lobbyists, and the trips appeared to be complete boondoggles, but Rudman had been operating in compliance with those weak laws that governed the relationship between lawmakers and lobbyists.

The report noted that Rulon Tully and the people he employed were Rudman's biggest financial backers. Rudman represented the Forty-seventh Congressional District, which included Santa Ana and parts of Fullerton and Anaheim. The author of the report concluded that Tully's reasons for supporting Rudman mostly likely had little to do with the fact that Rudman was a Democrat or the geographic area he represented. Rudman had seats on three congressional committees: the House Committee on Appropriations, the Subcommittee on Defense, and the Select Intelligence Oversight Panel—and two of these committees, Defense and Appropriations—could steer business Tully's way and initiate legislation favorable to Tully's concerns. It appeared, however, that all of Tully's contributions to Rudman—the documented ones, that is—were legal.

There was one innocuous-sounding sentence in the report that provided an indication as to how far the CIA had gone in its research. The sentence read: "Medical records reviewed; nothing found worth pursuing."

Rulon Tully's file was ten times bigger than Rudman's, as befitted a man worth several billion dollars. Half the report was taken directly from articles written by the mainstream media and all these articles documented Tully's genius or his ruthlessness or both. Tully had graduated from MIT at the age of twenty-two with double degrees in electrical engineering and business and by the time he was twenty-four he had patents on two devices, both worth millions. The irony was that both devices had medical applications; this was ironic because nothing DeMarco had read about Rulon Tully suggested that Tully cared in any way about the health or welfare of his fellow man.

Tully started his own company at the age of twenty-eight and immediately thereafter began gobbling up other companies like some sort of financial Godzilla. His attitude toward his competitors—and the world in general—was: take no prisoners. He had allegedly used industrial spies to best rival companies and been accused of patent infringement and stock price manipulation. He'd been sued numerous times for his tactics but won in court almost every time, and when he didn't win, the appeals would stretch out for years because he could afford the stretching. Employees who had been fired and who had the courage to talk to the press made it sound as if Bangkok sweatshops had better working conditions than Tully's companies.

The one-night affair that Tully's wife had had with Marty Taylor was also documented extensively. From what had been written, it appeared as if Taylor was the kind of man who would screw any woman that was convenient and appealing, and he didn't bed Tully's wife because he was trying to hurt Tully or because he had been deeply in love with the woman. Taylor just had an opportunity to lay her, and lay her he did, apparently never thinking that fucking the wife of one of the wealthiest men in the Western hemisphere might not be a wise thing to do. DeMarco was also surprised by the appearance of Tully's ex-wife: she was cute but she wasn't the knock-your-socks-off trophy wife you might expect to find on the arm of a multibillionaire. Regarding the appearance of the billionaire himself, DeMarco could not recall seeing a more homely individual. In fact, to call Rulon Tully homely was being charitable.

However, and just as it had been with Ray Rudman, the CIA's researchers had not been able to prove that Tully was doing anything illegal, which didn't surprise DeMarco, because the Department of Justice, the SEC, the IRS, and numerous private law firms had never had any luck in this same regard.

There was one document in Tully's file that stood out, and it was a copy of a police report related to the death of a prostitute in Ventura. The prostitute had been beaten to death in a motel room. According to the report, the clerk at the motel had seen a man who resembled Rulon Tully going into the room with the prostitute—and very few people bore a resemblance to Tully. Later, the clerk recanted his story and the prostitute's pimp was eventually convicted of murdering her.

It was clear, however, that the cop who wrote the report was convinced Tully had been with the prostitute prior to her death.

It was after two a.m. when DeMarco fell asleep.

***

The sound of a hard, insistent little fist beating on his door awakened him. Thinking it must be some sort of emergency, like maybe the hotel was on fire, DeMarco jumped out of bed, tripped over one of his shoes, and stumbled to the door. He struggled to undo the security gizmo that wouldn't allow the door to open completely, and when he finally opened it he saw it was Angela who had awakened him.

"Sandra Whitmore's been killed," she said.

"What?"

"I said, Sandra Whitmore's been killed."

"What?" he said again.

"Wake up! Get dressed and meet me down in the restaurant."

"What time is it?"

"Six thirty. Now get moving."

He noticed then that she was wearing a sweat-soaked T-shirt, shorts, and running shoes. She must have been exercising or jogging and this was the first time he realized that she wasn't perfect. Nobody who wakes up at dawn to exercise is perfect—they're nuts. He also noticed she had fantastic legs and, when she spun around after flinging orders at him, he also concluded she had a marvelous, trim little butt as well. Which made him wonder what she thought about how he looked in his ratty old Redskins T-shirt and boxer shorts, his face unshaven, his hair all matted down on one side from the pillow. He was guessing she wasn't fantasizing about him like he was about her.

But six thirty? She was out of her mind. He closed the door, stumbled three steps to the bed, and collapsed back onto it.

***

"Who killed her?" DeMarco asked.

"We don't know," Angela said. "It could have been a burglar.

Nothing appeared to have been taken from her apartment but maybe she walked in on a robber and he panicked and killed her, and then took off before he stole anything."

"Do you think that's what happened?"

"No. We think—and so do the cops—that she was killed for some reason related to the story she published. Maybe some superpatriot whacked her because he held her responsible for Mahata's death. Or maybe the same guy who killed Acosta killed her, although we can't think of any reason why he'd do that."

"I can think of somebody who might have killed her."

"Oh, yeah. Who's that?"

"You guys. The CIA."

"That's not funny, DeMarco."

"I wasn't trying to be funny. Who had a better motive for killing her than the agency?"

"The CIA did *not* kill her."

"Okay," he said but his tone implied that he wasn't totally convinced. "Did Mahata have any relatives, somebody who would want revenge?"

"No. Her family was killed in Iran when she was four, after which she was adopted by an American-Iranian couple and brought to the States. The details are skimpy but her biological father was an academic involved with some group that opposed the government's policies, and in Iran political opposition often means death. At any rate, Mahata didn't have any living biological relatives, the couple who adopted her was killed in an automobile accident four years ago, and because she'd been in Iran for the last six years she didn't have any close friends here, either. So we don't know who killed Whitmore or why, but it wasn't the CIA, and it wasn't someone related to Mahata. The agency will keep the heat on the NYPD to find Whitmore's killer but right now our priority, yours and mine, is getting Rudman to admit that he leaked the story."

"Why do we have to get him to admit it?"

"Right now we're pretty sure Rudman did it—my boss is sure and so is Mahoney—but before we destroy Rudman's life we need to be more than *pretty* sure. We need to be *positive*. So if we can't prove he leaked the story in some other way, we need a confession."

"And how do we make him confess?"

"I'm thinking we just Taser the shit out of him."

DeMarco raised an eyebrow in surprise and she said, "I'm joking." But DeMarco wasn't too sure about that.

"You looked at Rudman's file," she said. "Did you see anything in it we could use to pressure him?"

"No, but I have to tell you, that file's kinda skimpy. Most of what's in there is a matter of public record. But I know a guy. He calls himself an information broker but he's really a hacker, and he can get stuff your guys might not be able to get."

Angela laughed. "DeMarco, who do you think you're talking to here? What's in those files you read is what we learned; you have no idea what we did. We have hackers that can run circles around your hacker."

"I wouldn't bet on that," DeMarco said. He couldn't believe he was actually defending Neil, one of the most arrogant, obnoxious people he knew.

"Well, I would. Anyway, since we didn't get anything looking at records, right now we have two guys following Rudman. Maybe they'll come up with something."

"You have CIA agents tailing a United States congressman?"

"No. We have two private detectives tailing him."

"Jesus. You guys, you're . . ."

"Hey!" Angela said. "One of our people was killed. She was tortured and raped and killed. So we're not screwing around here, and you better get used to it."

"I know but . . ."

DeMarco didn't exactly know how to say what he was trying to say. He wasn't a man that normally occupied the moral high ground—in fact, he wasn't sure he had *ever* occupied the moral high ground—and yet here he was, standing on that high hill all by himself. He tried again.

"Look, I know you want payback for what happened to Mahata, but you're part of the United States government—a government that supposedly believes in the law and due process and . . . and whatever. You don't get to act like some street gang that does a drive-by shooting when another guy in the gang gets killed."

Angela just looked at him for a moment, then said, "I think you need to see something."

They went to Angela's room. She booted up her laptop, made DeMarco take a seat in front of the computer, and put in a CD.

When Mahata's executioner pulled back the veil exposing her face, DeMarco had to stand up and walk away. Angela waited until he came back to the chair and made him watch the whole thing again, from beginning to end. After he saw Mahata fall to the floor, the blood pooling about her head, he just sat there, numb, unable to express all the emotions he was feeling. All he knew for sure was that nobody deserved to die like that.

"Now do you get it, DeMarco? So, yeah, you're right, this is about revenge—but I don't want to hear any more street gang bullshit from you. We send our people into places you can't even imagine, to keep nuts with suitcase nukes from blowing up that building where you work. And our agents know if they're caught, they'll suffer the same fate as Mahata and there won't be any due process involved. So every agent we have needs to know that if they're killed, we're going to get the people who killed them. We *owe* them that. And if you don't understand that, it's because you've never had your ass on the line, not the way our people put their asses on the line."

She waited for DeMarco to say something but he didn't have anything to say because she was right: he had never risked his life the way Mahata had and he probably never would.

"We gotta go," she said. "We need to meet a guy."

As they entered the McDonald's at Sixth and Independence, Angela looked around but didn't see whoever she was looking for and took a seat. DeMarco ordered a Big Mac, a large bag of fries, and Diet Cokes for him and Angela. When he had asked if she wanted anything to eat, her nose had crinkled up as if eating McDonald's greasy fare would be like dining on something plucked from a Dumpster.

Five minutes later, Angela pointed toward the doorway with her chin and said, "There he is."

"Him?" DeMarco said. "You've got to be kidding."

The man who had just walked through the door of Mickey D's had to be over seventy. He was maybe five foot six—if you allowed for the curvature in his spine—and had wispy gray hair and a body that seemed to be wasting away from something like TB. He took little short, shuffling steps, and DeMarco figured it was going to take him an hour to cross the thirty feet from the door to the table where he and Angela were seated.

While DeMarco was taking a physical inventory of the man they had come to meet, Angela said, "That guy could follow you across a desert in broad daylight and you wouldn't see him."

"Maybe so," DeMarco said, "but I'll bet if I started running, he'd have a hard time keeping up."

The man finally reached their table. Angela introduced him as Morrie, no last name. He was one of the two private detectives the CIA had hired to follow Ray Rudman, although DeMarco was pretty sure that Morrie didn't know he was working for the CIA.

"So, Morrie," Angela said, "what'd you get?"

"Nothing, sweetheart, but it's only been two days. The guy just acts like your basic politician, spends most of the day in his office at the Rayburn Building or over at the Capitol. After work the first night, he attended some function, the second night he worked until six, went to a restaurant, ate like a pig, then went straight home to that condo of his on Capitol Hill. We went into the condo yesterday but—"

"You broke into Rudman's house?" DeMarco said.

Morrie looked over at DeMarco, his expression making it clear that he didn't appreciate being interrupted, then slowly swiveled his turtle head back to Angela. "But we didn't find anything. No kiddy porn or anything like that under his bed. No weird sex toys. No evidence he's stepping out on the missus with either girls or boys. The only vice this guy has is food. You shoulda seen the stuff in his refrigerator."

DeMarco had about six fries remaining in his paper french fry bag, and when Morrie finished talking he reached across the table and, without asking DeMarco, pulled the bag toward himself. DeMarco gave him a what-the-hell-are-you-doing look but Morrie ignored him.

"Does he have a safe inside his condo, someplace secure for hiding things?" Angela asked.

"Where's the ketchup?" Morrie said.

DeMarco wordlessly handed him a ketchup packet and Morrie ripped it open with his false teeth and squeezed the entire packet over DeMarco's fries.

"Morrie, does he have a safe?"

"Nope," Morrie said. "If he had one, I would have told you what's in it."

Maybe DeMarco had underestimated Morrie's talents.

Morrie took the six french fries remaining in the bag into his hand, the ketchup staining his fingers red, and shoved them all into his mouth at once. He chewed maybe twice then swallowed and DeMarco watched his throat swell momentarily like a snake swallowing a frog.

"Well, stick with him for a couple more days," Angela said. "Call me immediately if you get something."

"Hey, if that's what you want, sweetheart," Morrie said, and then he rose to his feet and shuffled toward the door.

"He ate my french fries," DeMarco said.

"Let's get out of here," Angela said.

———— ◆◆◆ ————

They left the McDonald's and walked down to the National Mall. Angela said she needed some air and some exercise so they took a stroll like a pair tourists—tourists who were trying to figure out a way to coerce a confession out of a United States congressman.

"We're getting nowhere," Angela said, after a while. "We need to do something."

DeMarco didn't say anything. He couldn't get the image of Mahata's face out of his head. And her face was the only part of her that could be seen in the video; who knew what her interrogators had done to the rest of her body. And then there was the horror of being raped, probably several times by several men. He figured her captors had probably gotten everything they needed to know from her in the first few hours; after that they weren't questioning her—they were torturing her. They were punishing her for having duped the Iranian government for so many years.

"Are you sure Mahata doesn't have any relatives who are still alive?" DeMarco asked.

"We're as sure as we can be," Angela said. "Although she was a U.S. citizen when she joined the Company, she was born in Iran and so were the people who adopted her. So before she was given a security clearance, we investigated her background as thoroughly as we've ever investigated any employee, including multiple polygraph tests. The bottom line is we believe what she told us: that her biological parents and all the rest of her family were killed when she was four. There were no records we could get to in Iran to confirm this but we talked to a guy over there who knew her father and he told us the same thing."

"Does anyone else know that her whole family's dead? I mean other than the CIA?"

"I'm sure some people must know. Friends she had in school, friends of her adopted parents. But it's not public knowledge. And when she was killed, we didn't give the media any information about her family. That's agency policy. Why are you asking all these questions?"

DeMarco didn't answer for a minute, not at all sure if he wanted to do what he was about to propose. "We think Ray Rudman told Rulon Tully about Diller," he said, "but we can't prove it, and you said you needed a confession. And it doesn't look like your pal Morrie is going to be able to get anything you can use to squeeze a confession out of the man."

"Yeah, but what do Mahata's relatives have to do with that?"

"What if someone close to Mahata wanted to avenge her death and that person held a gun to Ray Rudman's head and asked him if he had leaked the information to Tully."

"What do you mean?"

"I mean, what if someone held a gun to Rudman's head?"

"Are you serious?"

"Yeah, I'm serious."

She stopped walking and looked at him. "Are you saying you'd be willing to do that?"

"Yeah," DeMarco said.

DeMarco's close association with John Mahoney had made him particularly cynical when it came to the goodness of politicians. And it seemed like about once a month there was a story in the papers about some legislator getting caught taking bribes. The most recent case was a congressman nabbed by the FBI with ninety grand inside his fridge, the money being payment for political services rendered. He didn't think all politicians traded their votes directly for cash but he did believe that the environment in which they worked was morally corrosive. In 2005, the *Washington Post* had reported that there were more than thirty-four thousand registered lobbyists in Washington, which meant that there were approximately sixty lobbyists for every member of the House and Senate. And corporations paid for this army of manipulators—and paid them extremely well—because experience had shown that they were very effective when it came to bending the hearts and minds of our elected officials. But what Rudman had done had gone far beyond the typical sins that politicians committed to remain in power. DeMarco had seen Mahata's face—and he was now willing to do whatever it took to get the man out of office.

"But I need to be someone who has a plausible motive," DeMarco said. "And the only people I can think of with such a motive would be a relative or the CIA. And I'm guessing you wouldn't want me posing as a CIA agent."

"You got that right."

Angela pondered DeMarco's proposal for one long block as they continued down the mall in the direction of the Lincoln Memorial. As they were looking into the sculpture garden in front of the Hirshhorn Museum, at a statue by Rodin called *Crouching Woman,* she said, "Okay. I'll check with LaFountaine, but I don't think he'll object."

"You don't want to do that," DeMarco said.

"Why not?"

"Because your boss—if he's anything like my boss—will not want to be put in the position of knowing what we're about to do."

"Yeah, maybe you're right."

"But you need to call Morrie and tell him and his partner to take the night off. I don't want them following Rudman to a meeting with me. And you need to call Rudman to set up the meeting. If he thinks he's meeting a woman, I think he'll be more likely to come."

"Okay."

"There's still a problem. I've never met Rudman, but because my office is in the Capitol he might recognize me."

"That's not a problem," Angela said.

They drove to a small house in College Park, Maryland, that belonged to a lady named Marge, a middle-aged woman with unruly gray hair, a good-natured face, and wide hips. She sat DeMarco down in front of a big mirror, hauled out a steamer trunk filled with cosmetics, and went to work.

While she was spreading goop on his face, she told him that she had worked in LA as a makeup gal for a film company but had to come back to Maryland to take care of her mother. She had been in town only a couple of months when she was approached by a man—

a man who never said what organization he represented—and after that she had a job altering the appearance of federal agents who wanted to talk to various violent lunatics without being recognized. She said the work wasn't as challenging as turning men into aliens from another planet but it helped pay the bills.

It took her just an hour to change DeMarco into the Incredible Iranian Hulk.

His skin was a shade darker than normal, his nose was a bit longer and a bit wider at the base, his jaw thrust out a few millimeters farther, and the cleft in his chin had disappeared. The changes weren't significant but he was pretty sure his own mother wouldn't recognize him. The other thing about the makeup job, and he couldn't quite put his finger on why, was that he looked extraordinarily brutal and he was a pretty hard-looking guy to begin with.

"Wow," he said.

"That's great, Marge," Angela said. "All he needs now are brown eyes."

"I've never worn contacts," DeMarco said.

"Yeah," Angela continued, as if DeMarco wasn't in the room, "give him brown eyes, and then I think we're done here."

"But do I look Iranian?" DeMarco asked.

"Iranians are technically Indo-Europeans, and their skin color varies from white to dark brown. They're Persians, not Arabs. She only made your skin darker to make you less recognizable—and because most Americans think Iranians are Arabs."

"I wonder if I should use an Iranian accent."

"Mahata didn't have an accent. Anyway, do you know how to do an Iranian accent?"

"No."

"Well, I guess that answers your question."

The woman who called had a very seductive voice.

She said that she represented Mr. Tully and they needed to meet that night. She wouldn't say *why* they had to meet, however, just that it was per Mr. Tully's orders and it was related to recent events surrounding the late Sandra Whitmore. Rudman didn't agree immediately; Tully was his most powerful supporter but he didn't work for the man and, goddamnit, he resented Tully thinking that he'd just drop whatever he was doing. But then, being a politician and a pragmatic man, he decided he couldn't risk angering Tully, so he swallowed his pride and agreed to meet her.

Rudman sat at his desk a few minutes more, stewing, then called the lobbyist he had planned to dine with that evening—which made him even more annoyed at Rulon Tully. The lobbyist had made reservations at the best French restaurant in the District, a place where wine and dinner for two would cost at least four hundred dollars—and the lobbyist would have picked up the tab.

All he could do at this point was hope that the woman looked as sexy as she had sounded on the phone.

She had told him to meet her at a tavern near Middleburg, which was an hour's drive from D.C. She said the tavern would be closed but the door would be unlocked. He hadn't wanted to drive that far but he didn't complain. He wasn't a well-known public figure but it was probably still prudent to meet someplace outside the District where there was less chance that somebody might recognize him.

The tavern was located at an unlit crossroad. There were no other businesses nearby, and the closest house he had passed was two miles away. He never would have found the place without the GPS navigator in his car. And now he understood why the woman had said the place would be closed even though it was only eight p.m.: it had plywood over the windows, graffiti on the concrete walls, and looked as if it had gone out of business months ago. He didn't get out of his car immediately; he felt uncomfortable meeting in an abandoned building in such an isolated spot. His instincts told him to drive away, but then he'd have to face Rulon Tully's ire, which could be considerable—and possibly career-ending.

He pushed tentatively on the tavern door and it swung inward on squeaky hinges. Because the front windows were covered with plywood he had thought it would be completely dark inside the place, but it wasn't. The plywood had been ripped off one window on the west side of the building, and the main room was dimly illuminated by the weak evening light coming through the opening.

He looked around. He was standing on a scarred linoleum floor and there was a long bar on one side of the room. Behind the bar were a broken mirror and empty shelves. There were no chairs or tables in the room. On the ceiling was an unmoving, two-blade fan. Even though he didn't expect an answer, he called out, "Hello. Is anybody here?"

"Yes," a voice said.

Rudman let out a yelp, his heart hammering, and spun around—and saw a man standing there, a broad-shouldered, dark-complexioned, cruel-looking man holding a pistol. The pistol was pointed at his chest. Rudman backed up, holding his hands out in front of him, and said, "Please. Don't shoot me."

———◆◆◆———

"What do you want?" Rudman asked. "Money? I have three hundred dollars in my wallet, credit cards, too."

DeMarco didn't say anything; he just continued to point the gun at Rudman's chest. The video of Mahata dying flashed in his mind and he had an overwhelming urge to pistol whip the man.

He didn't have to act like he hated Ray Rudman.

"Do you know who I am?" Rudman said. "I'm a United States congressman. If you kill me, the FBI will come after you."

When DeMarco still didn't say anything, Rudman added, "Is Tully afraid I'm going to talk? Is that why you're doing this?"

Finally, DeMarco spoke. "Mahata Javadi was my sister."

"Oh, God," Rudman said. "Look, you have to believe me. I had nothing to do with her—"

"Turn around," DeMarco said. When Rudman didn't move, DeMarco grabbed him roughly by the arm and spun him around. Rudman let out a girlish shriek when DeMarco touched him.

"Get down on your knees—the way she was when they shot her."

"No, you can't . . ."

DeMarco kicked Rudman hard in the back of his right knee and the congressman fell to the floor. He reached down, took Rudman by the hair, and pulled him to a kneeling position. Then DeMarco pressed the barrel of the gun against the back of Rudman's head. The gun belonged to Angela and it was unloaded because DeMarco had no intention of shooting Rudman accidentally or on purpose. But Ray Rudman didn't know that—and he pissed his pants in fear when the barrel touched his head.

"I know you told Rulon Tully about Diller's trip to Iran," DeMarco said. "I want to know why."

"But I didn't. I swear. I never—"

"Do you know how my sister died? They beat her face to a pulp before they shot her. They tortured her for days. So answer my question. Why did you tell Tully about Diller after Mr. LaFountaine told you that disclosure of that information could jeopardize a CIA operation? Why did you do it?"

When Rudman didn't respond immediately, DeMarco jabbed him hard in the back of the head with the gun barrel. "I'm not going to ask you again," he said.

"Because he hates Marty Taylor! I just figured Tully would like to hear that Taylor was doing something illegal and later on he'd get in trouble for it. I never thought he'd leak the story to the press."

"You're a liar," DeMarco said. "I think you're the one who suggested he tell the media. Did you arrange for Dale Acosta to impersonate a CIA agent?"

"No. I swear. I never met Acosta. I didn't know anything about him until I read in the papers that he was dead. Look, you have to believe me. I had no idea . . ."

"I'm not going to kill you today," DeMarco said, "but if you don't resign from Congress by the end of the week, I will. And before I kill you, I'm going to beat you half to death, the way they beat Mahata. You'll die as hard as she did."

DeMarco backed up to the door of the tavern, opened it, and stepped into the twilight. As the door swung shut, he could hear Rudman retching.

———————◆◆◆———————

"Rudman did it," DeMarco said.

"Goddamnit," Mahoney muttered. "Sometimes it's a bitch to be right."

DeMarco had wanted to show up at Mahoney's condo in the Watergate complex in his Iranian-killer disguise and scare the hell out of Mahoney, but he realized that would be rather childish. Instead, he went back to the Sheraton where he and Angela were still staying and spent an hour scrubbing his face with soap and hot water until he was his handsome Italian self again.

By the time he arrived at Mahoney's it was almost midnight but his boss was still awake and waiting for him. Mahoney's wife, Mary Pat, was a sane person who valued her health and was already in bed. And unlike her husband, she didn't ingest half a bottle of bourbon before going to bed, so the next morning she would wake up looking daisy-fresh, as opposed to Mahoney who would look like a day-old corpse.

After he finished telling Mahoney about his encounter with Rudman in Middleburg, DeMarco asked, "What are you going to do if he doesn't resign?"

Mahoney pondered the question for a moment. "My gut says ol' Ray ain't gonna resign. He can't tell anyone he was threatened by

Mahata's brother because that would lead to speculation that he leaked the story. But what he'll probably do tomorrow, after he stops shaking and throwing up, is go to the Capitol police and tell 'em a tale about someone threatening him, and the cops will provide round-the-clock protection for a while."

"So, like I said, what are you going to do if he doesn't resign?"

Mahoney shrugged. "The party will support some other Democrat when his term's up. And since every district adjacent to his in Orange County is held by a Republican, there's a good chance he'll be replaced by one—but I can live with a Republican more than I can live with Rudman."

"I recorded what he said. I could send the tape to the media."

"No way. I'd end up with a fuckin' circus on the Hill. Rudman will say that he confessed only because you held a gun to his head, and he's not going to get expelled, much less convicted, based on a forced confession. But the media won't believe Rudman and they'll punch me silly, saying that Congress can't be trusted with a secret, and every spook outfit in town will have a permanent excuse for not telling us what they're doing. So I don't want anyone hearing that tape, but tell your little CIA buddy that I'll make sure Rudman doesn't serve another term. That's the best I can do."

"Yeah, well, my little CIA buddy and her boss have another idea. Unless you stop them, they're going to send the recording to Rulon Tully."

Mahoney tilted his head and made an I-hadn't-thought-about-that face. Then he nodded, as if, after thinking about it, that didn't sound like a bad idea.

"Did you hear what I said? If they send the recording to Tully, there's a good chance he'll have Rudman killed, and that's not what I had in mind when I made him admit that he talked to Tully. I mean, I know if Rudman's exposed that'll be embarrassing to you and the party, but do you want—"

Mahoney interrupted him and made one of the longest speeches DeMarco had ever heard him make. "Did it ever occur to you," he said, "that this isn't about me being *embarrassed*? I've served this country my whole life. I've fought for it. I've been wounded fighting for it. And in spite of some of the things I do, I've never betrayed my country, and I despise the people that do. And you know that old cliché about how you can be shot for treason? Well, it's bullshit. When was the last time somebody in this country was executed for treason? If they catch somebody giving away secrets to the Chinese or the Russians, they send 'em to jail, but that's all that happens. And when it comes to rich bastards like Marty Taylor and Rulon Tully . . . well, you can forget about them even doing time. But these people betrayed their country and they got an agent killed. And this agent, like LaFountaine said, was providing us intelligence on a regime that wants to give nuclear bombs to terrorists. So, Joe, if these guys kill each other, do you really think I give a shit?"

Mahoney jerked his big chin at the door and said, "Keep me posted."

Chapter 30

———◆———

"Why did you do it? I'm not going to ask you again."

"Because he hates Marty Taylor! I just figured Tully would like to hear that Taylor was doing something illegal and later on he'd get in trouble for it. I never thought he'd leak the story to the press."

Xavier Quinn hit the stop button on the recorder. "What would you like me to do?" he asked.

Quinn said these words without the slightest trace of emotion—and this, as usual, annoyed Rulon Tully. It annoyed the shit out of him. It would be nice if just once Quinn could at least *pretend* to care about his employer's welfare. He despised Xavier Quinn.

But he despised everyone.

It was a case of which came first, the chicken or the egg. As a boy, Rulon Tully was shorter than most other kids his age and had a head that was incredibly large in proportion to his narrow-shouldered, scrawny body. He had rubbery lips that were the color of earthworms, protruding eyes, and a small, red lump for a nose that provided an unsightly perch for his glasses. At the same time, he was smarter than *everyone*—including his parents and his teachers. He had an incredible memory—not quite photographic, but almost—and a facility for math and science that was preternatural. By the time he was twelve, he was doing differential equations while the rest of the morons in his class were struggling with elementary algebra. The end result of all this was that he was disdainful of his peers because they were stupid—and they made fun of him because of the way he looked. He hated them when they wouldn't accept him—and they hated him because he was unattractive, smart, and obnoxious. But which came first? Did the other children turn Rulon Tully into a misanthrope or was he a misanthrope the day he emerged from his mother's womb?

And he *was* a misanthrope. He knew this because a very expensive psychiatrist had told him so. He had seen the psychiatrist three times a week for a six-month period when he was in his thirties, each hourly session costing him nine hundred dollars. At the end of six months he had learned the clinical name for his condition but he learned nothing to change his view of his fellow man. He simply added the psychiatrist to the long list of people he hated.

Xavier Quinn, on the other hand, wasn't misanthropic. He was simply disinterested in anything not directly related to his job and he didn't sympathize or empathize with anyone—not even his employer. He also rarely showed joy or anger. Rulon Tully's expensive ex-psychiatrist probably had a name for Quinn's condition, too, but Tully didn't care. He wanted his head of security to be competent, brutal, and loyal—and Quinn met all those criteria.

But Rulon Tully still despised him.

"I suppose Rudman could die," Tully said, "but at this point that would be too risky."

Quinn just stood there; his employer had neither posed a question nor given him a task.

"And you still don't have any idea who killed the reporter?" Tully said.

"No," Quinn answered.

Just "no"—the word uttered with no indication that Quinn was sorry he was unable to answer Tully's question—and Tully wanted to scream at the man. He knew from past experience, however, if he started screaming Quinn would just stand there, his face completely impassive, as Tully ranted.

Quinn was ex-military, and maybe that was why he was impervious to Tully's rages. He had short, dark hair; was good-looking in an unremarkable way; and had a compact, muscular body—a body he maintained in the million-dollar gym that Tully had built for his ex-wife, that adulterous bitch.

"And you have no idea who made this recording?" Tully asked.

"No. But there are other things we do know. We know that Mahata Javadi didn't have a brother—I still have a few contacts at Langley—so whoever talked to Tully was lying. We also know this person didn't send the recording to the press or the Bureau—they just sent it to you—which leads me to believe that whoever is behind this doesn't want to publicly expose Rudman. Finally, we know that the recording can't be used to convict Rudman of a crime because it was a co-erced confession, so convicting Rudman isn't what they want."

Tully spun his stool around. He liked the drafting stool for that reason: he could spin it all the way around and if no one else was in the room, he liked to see how many revolutions he could make it spin with a single push. He even oiled the mechanism to make it spin faster. His record was four and a half spins, although no one knew that but him.

"So why do you think they sent the tape?" Tully asked, although he already knew the answer to this question.

"I think," Quinn said, "that the person who sent this recording has deduced that you had Acosta killed and would like for you to kill Congressman Rudman."

"I agree," Tully said. "And I think that tells us who sent us the recording."

"Who?"

"The CIA. They want somebody to pay for the death of their spy." Tully spun the chair around again, then continued. "And you know what *that* means?"

"No," Quinn said.

"It means they'll be coming after me next."

"So what are you going to do?"

Tully smiled. "I'm not going to do anything. Rudman may have confessed with a gun to his head but he's not going to testify in court.

He's not going to implicate himself and he's too afraid to implicate me. And the cops can't prove I had Acosta killed. So I'm not going to do a damn thing."

—◆◆◆—

After Quinn left, Tully's anger—which was always smoldering at some level—swelled to the point where he felt like breaking every object in the room. This whole mess had started because of Marty Taylor and now, because of what he had done to destroy Taylor, he was being targeted by that vengeful prick who ran the CIA. He shoved off as hard as he could with his short right leg and his small right foot, and did a three-turn spin on his drafting stool. He spun around and around and around—hating Marty Taylor.

The drafting table and stool were well-publicized affectations. He had used a drafting table for a brief period when he obtained his first patent and he told reporters that he still used the table because it helped him think, because it reminded him of his roots. That was all bullshit, of course. A PR gal he had hired said he needed a few quirky things to set him apart, to make him *colorful*—as if his appearance wasn't enough. The drafting table had been one of those quirky things. His Japanese garden planted with exotic bonsai plants, the ponds surrounding his house filled with butterfly koi, his position on the board of the children's cancer foundation—those were all part of his manufactured image, too.

He didn't give a damn about the koi, the dwarf plants, or the bald-headed kids.

He didn't even care about making money anymore. He had more money than he could possibly spend and it had been a long time since simply buying something—a piece of art, a mansion, the most ex-pensive car in the world—thrilled him in any significant way. What he really cared about, what he really loved, was power.

He had discussed this with his psychiatrist when they explored the subject of what made him happy and why he was so unhappy. It was then that he realized the thing that made him happiest was knowing thousands of people worked for him and he could, any time he desired, disrupt and even destroy their lives by firing them. He loved that the arrogant, high-powered executives he employed cowered around him, like obsequious priests kissing the cardinal's ring. It thrilled him that powerful politicians danced to his whimsical tune, terrified if they offended him he would use his wealth to run them out of office. And there was absolutely nothing he liked better than swooping down on a company and taking it over, knowing everybody in the company was just *sick* with anticipation, realizing that their fate was in his hands.

His therapist couldn't cure him and had shown him that he would never be truly content, not the way normal people were. But were it not for one thing, he could have been *almost* content, or at least as content as it was possible for a man like him to be. He had wealth, he had fame, and, most important, he had the power of a wrathful god over a large segment of the population on several continents. The one thing that prevented him from reaching his own distorted version of bliss was Marty Taylor.

What he felt for Taylor was something *beyond* hate. Hate, he reserved for the human race. His feelings for Taylor went so far beyond hate that there wasn't even a word for it, at least not one he knew. He could have had Taylor killed, and had thought many times about doing just that, but killing him wasn't enough. Killing him, no matter how slowly and painfully it was done, was just too quick. It would be over too soon. He didn't want Taylor to die; he wanted him to *suffer,* and suffer for years, and not just physically. He wanted to humiliate him and strip him of his wealth and put him in a cage. Yes, he loved that image: some tattooed skinhead making pretty Marty Taylor his prison bitch—over and over and over again.

Rulon Tully was in his forties when he married for the first and only time. Prior to that time, he had had many, many women. He paid a good number of those women to sleep with him, but there were others, beautiful women, who gave themselves to him even as stunted and ugly as he was. The problem was he knew that these women didn't love him and only wanted him because of the lifestyle he could give them, and he never allowed himself to be seduced by some grasping gold digger with an angel's face and a perfectly sculpted body. Being a misanthropic genius, he was incapable of deluding himself into thinking that any of those women really loved him or wanted him for who he was.

And then along came Shelly. She had been his masseuse. Because of the body that God had so cruelly given him, he needed daily massages to loosen knotty muscles, to relieve the pain of aching joints, and to make bearable a spinal column that felt like a bony snake gnawing at the flesh surrounding it. And that had been Shelly's job, to use her wonderful, strong hands to treat all those ailments, and she'd been good at it.

Shelly was pretty but she wasn't beautiful. She was short and somewhat stocky; she reminded him, physically, of the gymnast Mary Lou Retton. "Cute" was the word most often used to describe her. Right from the beginning, he sensed that she wasn't repulsed by his looks. She was a simple person with a good heart and he could tell she genuinely enjoyed his company. The fact was, though, and he was objective enough to realize this, she enjoyed *everyone's* company; she was just one of those perpetually optimistic, good-natured souls who liked 99 percent of the people they met. So, the fact that she liked him wasn't unusual, but what was unusual was that she was the only person he'd ever met who liked him for who he was and not for what he owned. She didn't laugh at his jokes because she wanted a bigger tip; she didn't flatter him outrageously to pump up his ego; she even kidded him for being just as short as she was, and nobody—absolutely *nobody*—dared to make jokes about his size.

Five months after he met her, he convinced himself he loved her— although it's hard to be sure you're in love when you're a misanthrope— and he asked her to marry him. And for a brief time, for almost two years, it was as if his misanthropy went into remission, as if he were afflicted with a cancer rather than a mental illness.

Then handsome Marty Taylor stepped in and destroyed his life.

He and Shelly had attended the film festival in Cannes that year, and Marty was there. He didn't like Marty Taylor, of course, but he'd met him on several occasions and had to admit that the man was as charming as anyone he'd ever known. Shelly, of course, thought he was delightful. Then, as luck would have it, he had to return unexpectedly to California because of some business disaster, one that could have cost him millions had he not reacted, but Shelly wanted to stay in Cannes. She loved seeing all those movie stars. Before he left, he made the mistake of asking Marty to make sure his wife had a good time while he was gone—and Marty made sure that she had a *very* good time. And as bad as her unfaithfulness was, he learned of the affair via a front-page picture in a tabloid newspaper. So not only did he have to suffer her betrayal and the agony he felt when he lost the one person in the world that he thought had genuinely loved him, but he also had to endure the humiliation of the entire world knowing he was a cuckold.

There was just no word to describe how much he hated Marty Taylor.

———◆◆◆———

Rulon Tully considered himself to be a ruthless man, but he was hardly the most ruthless man that Xavier Quinn had known. Quinn was a West Point graduate and he had the military skills to be a good officer but not the political ones. Realizing this, he resigned his commission in his early thirties and became a military consultant—a mercenary, in other words—to some men who were *truly* ruthless: African dictators and Russian oilmen.

At the age of forty-two, Quinn looked at his bank account and the scars on various parts of his anatomy, and accepted a job as Tully's head of security. And although Tully had never resorted to mass murder as some of Quinn's previous employers had done, he had asked Quinn to do a number of illegal things on his behalf. Quinn had blackmailed Tully's competitors. He had stolen industrial secrets.

He had bribed politicians and IRS investigators and, if bribes didn't work, he blackmailed them, too. But the things he did for Tully were not as risky as what he had done in the past, and the benefits were enormous.

He had started out at a salary of two hundred thousand a year and, thanks to Tully's advice, invested his money wisely. And because he lived with Tully, he paid nothing for food, had no home, and didn't own a car. The only things he spent money on were health insurance and clothes, and he was frugal when it came to his wardrobe. He had decided, arbitrarily, that he would retire when his savings reached two million but now, because of this thing with the CIA spy, he was thinking that retiring short of his goal would be prudent.

Reflecting back on it, he should have retired after Tully killed the whore.

Tully had been impossible to be around after his wife slept with Marty Taylor. He fired people left and right and verbally abused anyone who came near him. He had temper tantrums like a four-year-old. One night, possibly to lessen his torment but more likely because he wanted to inflict his pain on someone else, he sought out a prostitute. Before his marriage he had used prostitutes frequently, usually preferring small Asian women who were as short as he was.

That night Tully, a man who had little control over his emotions at the best of times, unleashed all the rage and shame he was feeling on an eighteen-year-old Filipino hooker. Quinn had no idea what caused him to snap, but Tully beat her to death. He hit her with his tiny fists until he broke a bone in one of his hands, then pounded her face with a lamp. Afterward, when he came to his senses—when he saw the red-splattered walls and the mangled body on the blood-soaked sheets—he called Quinn. Quinn cleaned up the crime scene as best he could but he knew that if the police pursued the case with any diligence they'd arrest his employer. Fortunately, the victim was a prostitute and the detective in charge of the case was a flexible person. In the end, the crime was pinned on the prostitute's pimp and the detective took an early retirement to fish on his new boat.

It was after that that Tully began to resort to murder when no other solution presented itself. It was as if the death of the prostitute had completely loosened those weak moral shackles that had previously constrained him, if only marginally. He took any loss in an intensely personal way—as if he was still that odd-looking little kid in school and the butt of every joke—and his ego demanded that he win every time. And if he couldn't win honestly, or if his lawyers and paid politicians couldn't win for him dishonestly, then he'd do whatever needed to be done: blackmail, bribery, and, following the whore's death, murder.

The second killing had been an SEC investigator who just wouldn't go away. It was possible that the SEC man could have put Tully in jail after years and years of legal wrangling, but if Tully had gone to jail it would have been a Martha Stewart experience. And Quinn pointed this out to Tully—that if the SEC succeeded, the worst thing that would happen to him was a few months in a country-club prison and possibly some community service. It may have been the remark about community service—the degrading image of having to wear a reflective vest while picking up trash on the highway—that pushed Tully over the edge.

So he told Quinn to take care of the SEC investigator, and Quinn did, using Jimmy Franco as the mechanism for disposing of the man. And then came Acosta.

In the case of Acosta, Quinn could somewhat understand why Tully had Acosta murdered, because the death of the CIA spy had raised the consequences of leaking the story to a whole new level. But still . . .

It was time to quit working for Rulon Tully.

Chapter 31

The taking of Jimmy Franco went badly.

On his first day in LA, the florist picked up the gun that he had mailed to general delivery, bought ammunition and two extra magazines, then spent the remainder of the day researching Franco. Using a computer at a public library, he found an Internet site that, for forty-five dollars, would provide available public records for any U.S. citizen. It amazed him how little privacy people had these days. He learned that Franco, in addition to owning a pawnshop as Benny Mark had told him, had other business licenses. He owned a used-car dealership, a strip club—called a "gentlemen's club"—and an apartment building. He had also been arrested twice. The first arrest was for allegedly prostituting the strippers in his club and the second time was for hiring men to assault a tenant in his apartment building who had refused to be evicted. He wasn't convicted in either case. He also found a photo of Franco on the Internet; in the photo Franco was posing with a girls' softball team and the girls wore T-shirts that advertised his pawnshop.

His second day in LA, the florist decided to visit the pawnshop and question Franco if he was there. He knew he was taking a risk by doing this because Benny Mark could have called Franco and warned him that the florist might be coming his way. He wasn't too concerned, however; he expected that Franco would either be alone in his shop or, at most, have a single employee helping him. He could handle two men by himself.

As soon as he entered the pawnshop, he realized he had made a mistake. There were five young Hispanic men in the shop, loitering in battered chairs. All were well muscled and heavily decorated with body art. As soon as the florist stepped through the door, they all looked at him, tensed up, and two of the men put a hand behind their back—the florist assumed that they were reaching for weapons. For an instant he considered turning right around and leaving but changed his mind. He pretended to ignore the young men and walked directly up to the sales counter where Franco was standing.

Franco was about the florist's height—six foot three—slender and gray-haired. He wore wire-rimmed glasses that had bifocal lenses, and he was dressed casually in a polo shirt and jeans. He didn't seem alarmed or guarded or suspicious in any way when the florist approached the sales counter. All he said was, "What can I do for you?"

The florist asked to see a Martin guitar hanging on the wall behind the sales counter. He strummed it a couple of times like he was trying to judge the quality of the instrument, asked Franco the price, shook his head as if it was more than he could afford, and left the shop.

It had never occurred to him that Franco would surround himself with so much protection. He knew Franco was a criminal—a middle man for hiring contract killers—but why all the muscle? Then, thinking about Franco's arrest record, it occurred to him that the man was most likely the kingpin of a small criminal enterprise—the strip club that was actually a brothel, the used-car dealership that would be ideal for moving stolen cars and purloined auto parts, the pawnshop that could be used for fencing stolen merchandise. It was also possible that in the course of his business, Franco had offended gangs in the area or other criminals, and that's why he employed all the bodyguards. Whatever the case, taking him wasn't going to be as easy as the florist had thought.

He watched Franco leave work that evening. Two black Honda SUVs with tinted windows pulled up in front of the pawnshop and double-parked on the street. Then three of the five young men he had seen earlier left the pawnshop, but not Franco. The men stood outside on the street, hands beneath their shirttails or inside the deep pockets of their shorts or baggy jeans, and observed the surrounding area for a couple of minutes. Satisfied it was safe, one of the men nodded toward the pawnshop door and Franco exited the shop and quickly but calmly entered the lead SUV. Franco's departure from his place of business reminded the florist of video footage he had seen of the Secret Service escorting the president into a limousine, except none of the Secret Service agents had spiderwebs tattooed on their necks.

Franco's two-car motorcade drove to a high-rise five miles away and entered an underground parking garage. The florist figured that Franco had selected the apartment building for his living quarters because it would be easier to defend than a house. He probably lived on one of the upper flowers—a place immune to drive-by shootings— and he imagined that some of his bodyguards lived in nearby units and continuously watched the lobby, garage, and elevators.

This was not going to be easy.

On his fourth day in LA, the florist got the opportunity he'd been looking for. Franco left his pawnshop at seven p.m. and the florist noticed he was dressed more formally than the first time he had seen him—he was wearing a black suit with a dark blue shirt, but no tie. Once again he left the shop in a two-car convoy with his five body-guards, but instead of heading to his own apartment, they drove to a small apartment complex in West Hollywood. While two of his guards went into the building with Franco, the other three remained in the parking lot, standing outside their vehicles and surveying the sur-rounding buildings as if they were looking for snipers. Franco reap-peared ten minutes later and with him was a beautiful young Latina who was at least thirty years his junior.

Franco's next stop was a restaurant, and judging by the type of cars the valets were parking and the attire of the people entering the restaurant—the florist thought one of those people might have been Tom Hanks—the florist concluded that the place was expensive and exclusive and probably required a reservation made weeks in advance. It wasn't the sort of place the florist was going to be able to walk into and pose as a diner, not dressed as he was in black jeans and a black T-shirt. He was dressed for kidnapping people, not for a night out on the town. The good news was that this was not an establishment that would permit Franco's bodyguards—young men that looked like gangbangers—to loiter at the bar.

As soon as Franco and his date entered the restaurant, the car containing three of his bodyguards drove off, and the florist wondered if they were headed to some less exclusive place where they could eat while their boss was dining. The other two bodyguards remained in their car, smoking and watching people enter the restaurant. They never saw the florist, who was parked fifty yards behind them.

The florist decided that this might be the only chance he was going to get. He drove into the alley that provided access to the rear of the restaurant. Dumpsters and garbage cans ran along the back wall of the restaurant, but fortunately it was a fairly wide alley and if he parked close to the wall of the building opposite the restaurant other cars could still get past him. This was good; he didn't know how long it would take to do what he planned and he didn't want his car towed.

What he needed was for a busboy, cook, or waiter to come outside for a smoke. And he needed the person to be approximately his size. Fifteen minutes later, a man came out, a busboy judging by his clothes. He was wearing a white jacket, a white shirt, and a clip-on black bow tie. His pants were black—similar to the florist's. He wasn't as tall as the florist, but he was overweight and his jacket and shirt would probably fit.

The busboy stepped a few feet away from the restaurant's back door, lit a cigarette, then pulled a cell phone from a pocket and began to talk. As he spoke, he walked up the alley in the florist's direction, gesturing wildly with his free hand. The florist got out of his car, verified that there was no one else in the alley, and walked toward the busboy. As he passed the busboy, he nodded to him in a friendly way—and as soon as he was past him, he spun around and hit him with the butt of Benny Mark's .32. The busboy collapsed to the ground, his cell phone still in his hand, and the florist could hear the voice of a woman talking angrily in Spanish until he closed the phone.

He dragged the busboy to his car, dumped him into the trunk, and then drove to another alley and quickly removed the unconscious man's clothes. After he was dressed in the busboy's shirt, jacket, and bow tie, he gagged him, bound his hands and feet with duct tape, and placed him back into the trunk of the car.

The florist entered the kitchen of the restaurant and it was bedlam: cooks yelling at cooks, cooks yelling at waiters, waiters yelling at busboys, everybody yelling in Spanish. He grabbed a tray to partially hide his face and walked rapidly through the kitchen, into the dining room, and directly toward the sign for the restrooms. He spotted Franco and his companion as he walked; they were drinking wine but not eating. The florist guessed that they had ordered but that their meals hadn't arrived.

Fortunately, the restroom didn't have a distinguished-looking old man passing out hand towels. The florist entered one of the stalls, leaving the door cracked open so he could see who entered the room. Now it was up to fate—and Jimmy Franco's bladder. All he could do was hope that Franco would use the restroom before he left the restaurant and, when he did, that there wouldn't be too many other customers in it.

It was forty-five minutes before Franco entered the restroom, and the florist watched as he used the urinal. He stepped out of the stall as Franco was washing his hands. No one else was in the room. He pressed the .32 against Franco's back.

"What the fu—"

"Shut up," the florist said. "If I wanted to kill you, you'd be dead right now. All I want to do is talk. But if you do anything to attract attention, if you resist in any way, then I will kill you. I'll have no choice. Now walk ahead of me. We're going out through the kitchen."

The florist placed the barrel of his gun against the small of Franco's back and pushed him toward the restroom door. He used a hand towel from the restroom to obscure his weapon. When they entered the dining area, the florist maneuvered Franco quickly through the tables, prodding him continually with the gun. They were halfway to the kitchen when Franco tried to get away. He spun toward the woman he'd been dining with and screamed, "Dolores! I'm being kidnapped! Get Cholo. Get Cholo!"

Customers stopped eating and everybody was now looking at Franco. Then a woman yelled, "He's got a gun!"

Now the florist *wanted* chaos. He fired his weapon twice at the ceiling, and the customers started screaming and he could hear chairs being knocked over and people running. He grabbed Franco by the neck—he had large hands and they were strong—and he shoved him toward the kitchen. He slammed Franco into the swinging door that separated the kitchen from the dining area and continued to propel him forward, and as he did he aimed his gun at the cooks so they'd get out of his way. Finally, he reached the back door of the restaurant.

With his hand still on Franco's neck, he pushed Franco toward his car. When they were a couple feet away, he hit Franco in the head with the .32, then hit him again when he saw that the first blow hadn't rendered him unconscious. With the adrenaline flooding through his system the way it was, he hit Franco harder than he had intended and he prayed that he hadn't put the man into a coma.

He was just shoving Franco onto the backseat of his car when he heard a gunshot and felt something burn across his upper left arm. Then two more shots were fired, one ricocheting off a nearby wall. He pulled the .32 from his waistband and spun toward whoever was shooting at him. It was Franco's lovely date, Dolores. The damn woman, instead of getting Franco's bodyguards as she'd been told and as he had expected, had followed him outside the restaurant and was now shooting at him with the small-caliber gun that she must have had in her handbag. Only in LA.

The florist didn't want to kill the woman. He fired a shot at her and it zinged loudly off a garbage can near her, and she dove back inside the restaurant. He fired two more times to encourage her to stay in the restaurant, then got into his car and began to drive.

Now all he had to worry about was being stopped by the LAPD or Franco's men, and Franco's men were the bigger concern. Although people had seen him in the restaurant, they had seen him only briefly and they had probably been too frightened to make good witnesses. And if the police could find a witness who could actually describe him, the witness would most likely tell the police that he was Hispanic, and the cops would turn their attention toward any Hispanic enemies Franco had. Dolores, Franco's girlfriend, had seen his car but he was pretty sure she'd been too busy dodging bullets to get a license-plate number.

At least he hoped so; he didn't want to have to kill a cop.

He drove into a parking garage and removed the busboy from the trunk. He noticed when he did so that one of Dolores's bullets had punctured the trunk and he was relieved to find the busboy unhurt. The man was conscious by then, his eyes huge with fear. The florist lifted him out of the trunk, which wasn't easy considering the man's weight, and placed him on the ground. He then duct-taped Jimmy Franco's hands and feet, gagged him, and placed him in the trunk. Before driving away, he told the busboy, "I'm sorry I had to do this to you but if you talk to the police I'll have to kill you. Remember, I know where you work."

The florist cruised the streets of LA looking for a place where he would be able to question Franco without being disturbed, finally selecting an industrial complex where warehouses the size of airplane hangars surrounded an empty parking lot. He circled the parking lot

twice, looking for cameras and security guards, and when he didn't
see any he stopped the car.

He opened the trunk. Franco was still unconscious. He pulled
Franco from the trunk and propped him up against the side of the
car, then took off the busboy's shirt and examined the wound to his
shoulder. The bullet had just grazed his left bicep; the wound stung,
and it was bleeding, but not badly. He was, as he'd always been, a
lucky man. He tore a strip of cloth from the busboy's shirt and bandaged the wound, then changed back into his own clothes.

Franco was still unconscious and this wasn't good. He had hit him
too hard. He ripped the duct tape off Franco's mouth but the man
didn't stir. He slapped his face lightly and Franco groaned. Thank
God. He slapped him again, a little harder, and Franco slowly opened
his eyes.

"Wha . . ." Franco said, confused, trying to remember what had
happened, focusing finally on the florist's face.

The florist pressed the barrel of his gun against Franco's forehead.
"Listen to me," he said. "You hired a man named Benny Mark to kill
a man in Myrtle Beach, South Carolina, named Acosta. I *know* you
were the middle man. I want to know who hired you and I will do
whatever I have to to make you talk. I will cause you great pain. I will
torture you. Do you understand?"

"Who are you?" Franco asked. His voice was raspy but the florist
could see that Franco's mind was functioning once again—and he
could see that he wasn't appropriately afraid.

"Did you hear what I said?" the florist demanded, but Franco's only
response was to glare at him. "Tell me who paid you to hire Benny Mark."

"If you don't let me go, right now, you'll never get out of LA alive,"
Franco said.

The florist didn't want to hit Franco in the face, afraid the man
might already have a concussion and that hitting him in the head
would just slow things down. He placed duct tape once again over
Franco's mouth, ripped open Franco's shirt to expose his chest, and
then reached into the car and pressed down on the cigarette lighter.

When the lighter popped, he showed the glowing tip to Franco and saw the man's eyes widen. Franco probably expected that he would remove the tape over his mouth and question him some more, but the florist didn't. He didn't have time for that.

He pressed the cigarette lighter against Jimmy Franco's chest.

———◆———

As he looked at the six blistered, circular, red burn marks on Franco's gray-haired chest, he recalled once in Iran when he had done something similar to an Iranian businessman who traded with the West. The businessman had flouted one of the ayatollah's many rules, but even worse, he was an arrogant man who thought his wealth would protect him. It had been the florist's job to make the man see the error of his ways, and he had used a soldering iron on his feet. He remembered that the stench of burning flesh had almost made him vomit.

He had burned Franco three times with the lighter *before* he removed the tape on his mouth, convinced that Franco would tell him nothing until he saw exactly what the florist was willing to do and how far he was willing to go. After he removed the tape, Franco gave him a name: Xavier Quinn.

The problem he now had was that he couldn't be sure that Franco was telling the truth. With Benny Mark, he had had no doubt. Benny was not a man who was willing to suffer for the sake of honor, or for any other reason. Franco was different; he'd lie to protect a client but he'd also lie to protect his own reputation. He wasn't surprised Franco gave him a name—anyone would have—but how could he be sure the man was telling the truth? That was the problem with this sort of hasty, brutal interrogation: it often produced false results. If he had had the time and the facilities, he would have imprisoned Franco and researched Xavier Quinn to see if Franco's answer was logical, and then he would have tortured Franco some more. Since he couldn't do that, he told Franco that he knew he was lying and burned him three more times. Franco stuck to his story.

Now what? If he let Franco go, Franco would immediately call the person who had hired him, whether that person was Quinn or someone else. And Franco wouldn't be worried about the florist coming for him again because now that Franco knew about him, he would be ready. Moreover, Franco and his ragtag army of tattooed thugs would hunt for him if he let Franco go, and if he had to remain in LA there was the possibility they might find him. If he killed Franco, that would solve all these problems, but if he did, and if Franco had lied to him about Quinn, then he would have destroyed the only lead he had. He mulled all this over and finally made the only decision he could make.

The florist could rationalize what he was about to do. He could tell himself that Jimmy Franco was a criminal and an accomplice to the murder of Dale Acosta, and he therefore deserved to die. But that still didn't make killing him right; unlike Sandra Whitmore, Jimmy Franco was not one of those responsible for Mahata's death.

Unfortunately, to complete his mission, he had no choice.

He shot Jimmy Franco, placed the body in a Dumpster, and covered it with cardboard.

He said a prayer for the man's soul as he drove away.

Chapter 32

———◆———

Nothing was happening—nada, zip, not a thing—and this didn't bother DeMarco at all.

It had been four days since the CIA had sent the Rudman recording to Rulon Tully, and so far Tully had done nothing. Nor did Ray Rudman resign from Congress. He did, as Mahoney had predicted, get protection from the Capitol police. Rudman was probably wondering when the other shoe was going to drop—when his name would be mentioned in the press as the source of the leak—and he was probably sweating bullets while he prepared the denials he would make to the media. But getting Rudman out of Congress wasn't DeMarco's problem—unless, of course, Mahoney made it his problem.

The cops had made no progress in figuring out who had killed Sandra Whitmore or Dale Acosta, and the media were in a feeding frenzy. Whitmore, alive, had never been popular and her fellow reporters had treated her with disdain when they found out that she'd been duped by Acosta. But now she was dead—the martyr she had never intended to be—and the reporters were screaming for answers. Two tabloids had suggested the CIA was behind her murder; the more respectable papers weren't brazen enough to make that claim directly but they, too, hinted at dark conspiracies and were demanding that the cops find the killer of their fallen comrade.

As for the man who had kept DeMarco from being killed in Myrtle Beach, neither the police nor the CIA had any idea who he was. No one had gotten a clear look at him in South Carolina and he had left no useful evidence in the golf course parking lot. What was even more puzzling was that no one could understand what connection he might have to Mahata Javadi. And since the mystery man was still unidentified and on the loose, DeMarco, at Angela's insistence, continued to reside at the Crystal City Sheraton.

Since DeMarco had nothing better to do, he pursued the assignment Mahoney had given him several days ago: finding out why the Republican congressman from Arkansas kept flying to Minnesota. He had been planning to follow the guy but couldn't do that now because the CIA wanted him on a short leash. So he did something he didn't normally do, and contacted a private detective with a proven reputation for discretion and had him bird-dog the congressman.

DeMarco had no idea how the detective managed to get the information—he was very good at his job—but he determined the congressman was HIV positive, had been so for a number of years, and the drugs he had been taking were no longer working. He was seeing a specialist at the Mayo Clinic trying to find an effective treatment.

"So, now that you know, what are you going to do?" DeMarco asked Mahoney.

"What am I gonna do? I'm going to say a prayer for the guy. And you tell this detective you hired that if this ever gets out I'll run him out of town on a rail."

Angela called and told him to meet her outside the main entrance to Georgetown University Hospital but her voice sounded odd when she talked to him—less confident, less in control.

"You okay?" he asked.

"I'm fine. I'll see you at ten."

DeMarco was waiting outside the hospital at ten but Angela didn't show up until ten twenty. When he saw her, she was leaving the hospital with a tall, well-built man. He was strikingly handsome and his blond hair was perfectly combed like that anchorman on the news, that Brian Williams guy. DeMarco knew immediately the man was Angela's husband, a hunch that was confirmed when he gave her a little peck on the lips before he sauntered away. And he did *saunter*; he walked like he held the world in the palm of his hand—and maybe he did. He had Angela.

DeMarco waited until her husband was out of sight before approaching her.

"I'm sorry I'm late," she said.

He knew if she was late it was her husband's fault.

"Is everything okay with you?" he asked.

"Yeah, I'm fine. Let's get going."

He could tell she wasn't fine but whatever was bothering her, he knew she wasn't going to share it with him.

"So what's going on?" he asked. "Did something happen with Rudman or Tully?"

"No. And I can tell you that my boss isn't too happy about that."

DeMarco almost said, Well, making your boss happy ain't my problem—but he didn't.

"We're still waiting for Tully to do something about Rudman," Angela said, "but in the meantime, we're gonna go talk to an FBI agent. He's been checking out Marty Taylor and learned something he thinks we'd like to know."

"Why would the FBI tell the CIA anything about Taylor?" DeMarco knew that interagency cooperation, particularly between the CIA and the Bureau, was rarer than flying pigs.

"We have an arrangement with this particular agent," Angela said.

DeMarco assumed this meant that the FBI agent was some sort of CIA mole in the Hoover Building.

"I'm going to tell him you're CIA," Angela said, "because I'm pretty sure he wouldn't like talking to someone from Congress. Let's hope he doesn't ask to see your ID."

"And if he does?"

"Tell him to go piss up a rope. That's the way a real CIA agent would treat an FBI dweeb."

<hr/>

They met the FBI agent at a bistro on K Street and, fortunately, no rope pissing was required. His name was Ryan Schommer and DeMarco thought he looked like a weasel with a bad comb-over: he had shifty eyes, a pointy nose, a weak chin, and a dozen greasy strands of dark hair fanned across the top of his head. Or maybe he just looked like a weasel because DeMarco knew he was double-timing his employer.

After everybody had coffee cups in front of them, Angela said, "So, Ryan, what did you find out about Marty Taylor?"

"We never had any reason to look at him or his company until Diller met with the Iranians," Schommer said. "And if you just look at public records, all you see is a company that's not doing too well, which isn't too surprising since Taylor seems to spend more time these days surfing and dating models than he does running his business.

"But then this thing happens with Diller. Taylor's lawyers, of course, have said that Taylor had no idea Diller was visiting Iran, and so far we haven't been able to crack that story. And then Diller goes and disappears."

"You don't have any leads on him yet?" Angela asked.

"Nope, and we have a platoon of guys looking for him. We found his car at LAX, but he never boarded a flight, not in LA or any other airport in the area. We're sure of that. And because of what else we found, we think he may be dead."

"So what else did you find?" Angela said, and DeMarco could tell that she was beginning to get a wee bit impatient with Mr. Schommer.

"The thing with Diller, it never made sense. Why would a guy like Marty Taylor ever try selling stuff to Iran? Even if his company's headed for Chapter Eleven, why would he *personally* take that kind of risk?"

"You said Taylor wasn't spending a lot of time watching the store, so maybe someone else at his company was the one working with Diller," DeMarco said.

Schommer smiled at DeMarco—a weasel beaming. "That was our thinking, too. So we started looking hard at who else is involved in Taylor's company."

"Ryan, quit teasin' me here," Angela said. "What did you find?"

"Russian mafia. Maybe."

"Connected to Taylor?" Angela said. "You gotta be kidding."

"No. We got a warrant to look at Diller's phone records and there was a phone call to an auto-body shop in Chula Vista just before he left for Iran. In that same phone bill were two calls to a BMW dealership in Del Mar. We do a little snooping and find out Diller and his wife both drive BMWs, they bought the cars from the dealer in Del Mar, and they were having the fifty-thousand-mile service done on one of the cars. So we wondered, Why the hell is Diller calling a body shop in Chula Vista? A yuppie like him wouldn't even know how to find Chula Vista. So we pull the string and find out the shop is owned by one Jorge Rivera . . ."

"Who's Jorge . . ."

"Probably an honest citizen. But Jorge's business partner is a man named Yuri Markelov, and the San Diego PD suspects the place is a chop shop but has never been able to prove it. Hmmm, we said, and we pulled the string some more, which leads us eventually to the NYPD's organized crime guys, which then leads us to a guy named Lev Nikolai Girenko."

"Who is—" Angela started to say, but Schommer held up a hand, silencing her.

"Lev Girenko immigrated to this country twelve years ago and became a citizen at lightning speed. Your average Mexican, it takes him about ten years to get his papers if he's lucky, but Lev was reciting the Pledge of Allegiance in eighteen months, which means somebody got heavily greased. Anyway, not long after Lev gets here, he's got eight or ten guys working for him, mostly people he brought over from Russia. Lev and his crew operated in Brooklyn for about four years, then they all disappeared. Here one day and gone the next. NYPD had no idea where they went, and since they were out of the Big Apple, they didn't care. They suspected that Lev found the competition too hot in Brooklyn or, for all they knew, somebody had buried him and his whole crew in a landfill. Yuri Markelov was Lev's right-hand man in New York."

"But what's the connection between these Russians and Marty Taylor?" Angela asked, her exasperation growing. "I mean, other than one phone call to a body shop, which, for all you know, could be a wrong number."

"It could have been a wrong number," Schommer said, "but we didn't think so. We got another warrant and looked at the body shop's phone records and, lo and behold, a call was made from the shop to Iran at the same time Diller was in Iran. Now we have no idea who made the call, if it was Markelov or somebody else, and we don't know who they called in Iran—all we could find out is that the call went to a cell phone. We've asked those sneaky fucks over at the NSA to see if they intercepted the call and they claim they didn't, but who knows with those guys."

"Are you saying that Diller was working for Yuri Markelov when he went to Iran?"

Schommer shrugged. "Again, we don't know. But here's one other little tidbit for you to think about. Right now, Markelov is living in a home that's owned by Marty Taylor. That is, the deed to the house is still in Taylor's name, but maybe Markelov is renting from Taylor or maybe he just bought the house and the paperwork hasn't caught up with the sale. Whatever the case, Mr. Markelov's current place of residence struck us as intriguing. But as far as Yuri or Lev being involved in Taylor's company . . . well, that's about ten levels above the way guys like them operate. What I'm saying is, when they were in New York, they would force their way into legitimate businesses, but *little* businesses. Beauty parlors, dry cleaners, restaurants. Body shops, like the one in Chula Vista. They'd get their hooks into the owners through gambling or sex or flat-out intimidation, and they'd extort protection money from them, steal their profits, and eventually sell off the business's assets. Then they'd move on to something else and do it all over again. But Taylor & Taylor isn't a mom-and-pop operation, so it's hard to imagine how they could be involved in a business that complex."

"Why aren't these guys in jail?" DeMarco asked.

Schommer shrugged. "They were never a priority for the Bureau or the NYPD. I said they were Russia mafia but that makes them sound, I don't know, *grander* than they really are. Lev's crew is a small gang of thugs; they ain't the Gambino crime syndicate. The other thing is the cops couldn't get anybody to testify against them. Lev had a reputation for dealing with problems in a way that made it difficult to find stand-up witnesses. So when Lev and his boys left New York, NYPD said good riddance and didn't waste any more time on them."

"What about the cops in San Diego," Angela asked. "Have they got anything on them?"

"Other than their suspicion that the shop in Chula Vista is being used to move hot car parts, no."

Schommer finished his coffee and said, "So, my friends, we're missing a whole bunch of pieces here. We don't know where Lev is. We don't know if Yuri is still working for him or if he's out on his own. We don't know why Yuri is living in one of Marty Taylor's houses. We don't know why Diller was calling a suspected chop shop or why a call was made from the shop to Iran. But there is one thing we *do* know. We know that you don't want to see the words Russian mob, Iran, and weapons technology in the same sentence, and we're gonna get to the bottom of this."

———◆———

"This is good," DeMarco said after Schommer left.

"Why's that?" Angela asked.

"Because now you can let the FBI go after Taylor and you don't have to do anything."

Angela shook her head. "The FBI may get Marty Taylor but they'll never get Rulon Tully. Even if Tully kills Rudman, they'll never trace the killing back to him. And if Rudman was to come forward tomorrow and admit that he gave classified information to Tully—which he'll never do—we still wouldn't be able to get Tully."

"Why not?"

"DeMarco, Rulon Tully isn't a guy that has an attorney—he's a guy that has his own *law firm*. With his money, we'll both be in our graves before Tully sees the inside of a jail cell."

"So what are we . . ."

Angela's cell phone rang. She answered it, listened for about five seconds, said "Yes, sir," and hung up.

"That was LaFountaine. He wants to see us."

"Are we going to Langley?"

DeMarco had never been to the CIA's headquarters; a tour would be cool. He particularly wanted to see the inscription he'd always heard about, the one at the entrance to the main building that said: And ye shall know the truth and the truth shall set you free.

But killjoy Angela burst his bubble. "DeMarco," she said, "do you think Mr. LaFountaine wants it on the record that you visited him at his office? You keep forgetting. This is like that old *Mission Impossible* show: if we get caught, the agency will disavow any knowledge of our actions. So, no, we're not going to Langley. We're meeting him at a marina near the Pentagon on a boat that belongs to an old friend of his, a former vice president of the United States."

———◆———

The yacht LaFountaine had borrowed for the meeting was one of those magnificent old wooden boats built in the forties or fifties; it was all gleaming hardwood and shiny brass rails and fittings. DeMarco imagined it had huge Rolls-Royce engines, a wet bar stocked with expensive cognac, and a master bedroom fit for a king. He would have gladly moved out of his Georgetown home to live on the yacht, and the fact that he didn't know how to operate any boat bigger than a canoe wouldn't be a drawback. He'd buy one of those white yachting caps with scrambled egg on the brim, sit on the bow, drink martinis, and watch the sunset—and if the boat never left the pier that'd be fine with him.

Angela must have been having similar thoughts because as soon as she saw it, she said, "Oh, man, will you look at this boat." But then she added, "Can you imagine what it must cost to maintain this thing?"

Women—always able to ruin a perfectly decent fantasy with some completely unnecessary, practical observation.

When DeMarco and Angela stepped on board the yacht, a deep voice called out from below, "I'm down in the galley."

DeMarco had seen LaFountaine only on television, and the impression he had always had was that LaFountaine was an arrogant prick, but a really smart prick and not a guy you'd want to cross. He had the same impression when he met him in person.

LaFountaine was dressed in a dark suit—no yachting cap for him— and sitting on one side of a built-in dining table, so DeMarco and Angela sat on the other side, next to each other. After they were seated, LaFountaine asked, "Well?"

Angela gave a succinct report of their activities. DeMarco could see she was nervous, like a fourth grader reading a book report to the class, and it irritated him that LaFountaine could make her feel that way.

When she finished, LaFountaine said, "So we've got two dead people, Whitmore and Acosta, and we don't know who killed them. And Diller, the one guy that can testify against Marty Taylor, is missing and may be dead. Ray Rudman is still a United States congressman and he's now being protected by the Capitol police, and Rulon Tully is apparently ignoring the recording we sent him. And now the FBI tells us some Russian gangsters may be behind Diller's trip to

Iran, but the FBI has no proof, and the way they work it's going to take them months to do anything about Taylor. Is that about right?"

"Yes, sir," Angela replied.

"You got anything to add, DeMarco?"

"No," DeMarco said. He didn't bother to add "sir." He didn't work for the guy.

DeMarco expected LaFountaine to blow up at them at this point and tell them what a lousy job they were doing—that's what Mahoney would have done—but he didn't. He just sat there spinning his wedding ring on his finger and staring at the space between their heads.

"Actually," he said, "this isn't going too badly. Two of the people responsible for Mahata's death are dead, and now I know for sure that Rudman was the leak. I'll figure out some way to deal with that bastard later. But I want Tully."

"Sir, I'm not sure how we can get him," Angela said. "What I'm saying is, I doubt we're going to be able to find any evidence that he had anything to do with leaking the information to Sandra Whitmore or killing Dale Acosta, so there's no way we'll be able to convict him of a crime."

LaFountaine sat there brooding in silence for a moment, thinking about what Angela had just told him, and DeMarco could almost see the wheels spinning inside the man's big Machiavellian brain.

"Do you think this Russian gangster is really behind Diller's trip to Iran?" LaFountaine asked.

Angela shrugged. "I don't know, but it makes a lot more sense that he'd do this than Marty Taylor."

"And there's something you don't know," LaFountaine said. "When Mahata told us about Diller meeting the Iranians, she said one of the people who attended the meeting was an ex–Russian army officer. She had never seen the Russian before and he didn't say anything during the meeting but he came with Diller. Or, to be accurate, she said that he came into the meeting room at the same time as Diller."

"Do you think this Russian army officer might have known Yuri Markelov before he came to the United States?"

LaFountaine shrugged, and DeMarco wondered what it would be like to have a job that dealt with so much ambiguity.

LaFountaine got up and poured a cup of coffee, then just stood for a long time next to the galley stove. Finally, he said, "I want you to give Tully to the Russians." Then he sat back down and told them what he meant.

DeMarco spoke for the second time during the meeting. "People could get killed if we do that."

LaFountaine looked at DeMarco and said, very softly, "I don't care."

"Yeah, well, I do," DeMarco responded. "And I don't work for you."

LaFountaine smiled. "No, but you work for John Mahoney, and right now Mahoney and I have an agreement. I've agreed not to tell the media that a man who belongs to his party shot off his mouth and got my agent killed. But if you don't do what I want, I no longer have any reason to honor my deal with your boss, and I think you know how he'd feel about that."

LaFountaine rose from the table. "Angela, turn off the coffeepot and lock up the boat when you leave. There's a padlock on the deck near the hatch."

DeMarco and Angela just sat there, not speaking, as they listened to LaFountaine's slow, heavy footsteps on the deck above them as he departed.

DeMarco moved to the other side of the table, to where LaFountaine had been sitting, so he could face Angela. "You don't think he's going too far?" he said.

She didn't respond. She was a loyal company gal, and whatever she might really be feeling, she wasn't going to disagree with her boss to an outsider. But she surprised him.

"He feels guilty," she said. "If he hadn't said anything to that committee about Diller, Mahata would still be alive and he knows it."

"So what? Just because he feels guilty doesn't mean he gets to play high executioner."

Angela turned away and gazed out the porthole, irritated by either DeMarco or the box that LaFountaine had put her in. She was probably wishing she was on a cruise ship instead of sitting on a boat in the Potomac, being used as LaFountaine's pawn. Or maybe not.

She rose to her feet and said, "You can do what you want, DeMarco, but I've got a job to do."

Chapter 33

———◆———

"We may have a problem," Quinn said.

Rulon Tully made no attempt to hide his irritation; he was in a good mood and he could tell Xavier Quinn was about to ruin it.

Tully had spent the morning dealing with various corporate problems by yelling at his overpriced executives via video conferences. He loved video conferences. He set them up so he could see the executives but they couldn't see him. And when he screamed at them, he knew they felt like they were talking to an invisible, angry god—a god who would rain down fire and brimstone upon them if they didn't keep him happy. But now here was stone-faced Quinn, and the feeling of satisfaction he had gotten from ranting at his executives was already beginning to fade.

"What sort of problem?" Tully asked.

"I'm not sure," Quinn replied.

"Well, goddamnit, then why . . ."

"Jimmy Franco is missing."

"Who's Franco?" Rulon asked.

"Franco hired the man who killed Dale Acosta."

"Why the hell did you tell me that?" Tully muttered.

"Because you asked," Quinn said. "Anyway, Franco is missing."

"How is his being missing connected to me?"

"It appears that someone has followed the trail from Whitmore to Acosta to Franco. And the next step on that trail is me—then you."

"But you don't know for sure that Franco's disappearance is connected to us."

"No."

"Will Franco talk?" Tully asked.

"Not to the police," Quinn said. "But it may not be the police who talk to him. It could be the CIA. You suspected that they were the ones who coerced Rudman to confess and sent you that recording. So, maybe, although I don't know how, they connected Franco to Acosta's murder. And if the CIA has Franco, they'll make him talk."

"Do you think the CIA would actually kidnap and torture an American citizen?"

"They've done it before."

The liberal media had accused the CIA of detaining terrorist suspects, some of them American citizens, and shipping them off to prisons in foreign countries for interrogations. Tully had always thought the stories were most likely fabrications but Quinn had a military background and had worked in some rather unorthodox jobs, so it was possible that he knew what he was talking about.

"And there are two new players in all this," Quinn said.

"Who?"

"One is a man named Joseph DeMarco. He's a lawyer and he visited Whitmore in prison, and right after he did, Whitmore gave up Acosta as her source. And then the day Acosta died, DeMarco was in Myrtle Beach and he was involved in a shoot-out with Acosta's killer and an unidentified man."

"A shoot-out? Goddamnit, what in the hell are you talking about?"

Quinn explained that the day Acosta was killed, DeMarco was the one who found Acosta's body. And when he left Acosta's place to call the police, the man Jimmy Franco had contracted to kill Acosta tried to kill DeMarco, but then another man intervened and drove off Acosta's killer. But neither DeMarco nor the Myrtle Beach police knew who either of the shooters were.

"You got all this from the Myrtle Beach police?" Tully asked.

"Yes, and from an administrator at the prison where Whitmore was being held."

"Have you talked to the killer Franco hired?"

"I don't know who he is. That's the way these things work. I hire Franco and he hires the killer, but the killer doesn't know me and I don't know him. It's safer for everybody that way."

Tully didn't like anything he was hearing. He particularly didn't like the fact that Quinn was giving him supposition instead of facts. He couldn't make decisions based on Quinn's guesses.

"What do you suggest, Xavier? I hope the purpose of this meeting isn't just to give me things to worry about."

"I would suggest, sir, that until I can sort this all out you stay here on the estate where I can protect you best."

Chapter 34

The florist sat back and rubbed his tired eyes. After six hours of research, he had finally found what he needed.

Because he didn't think it would be safe to stay in LA after killing Franco, he had driven to Fresno and then spent the day sitting in front of a library computer trying to locate Xavier Quinn. When he had interrogated Franco, he didn't ask how Quinn and Franco knew each other. He didn't have time for that. He had wanted only two things: Quinn's name and his location. But Franco said he didn't know Quinn's address, he hadn't seen the man in years, and Quinn had contacted him by phone and he couldn't remember the phone number.

Fortunately, Xavier was not a common name. A "people search" site on the Internet identified only seven Xavier Quinns in the United States. Two of these Xavier Quinns were almost eighty and one was in his early twenties, so he crossed them off his list. The fourth Quinn lived in Alaska, and he arbitrarily crossed that one off his list as well. Alaska was just too . . . too far out of the mainstream, too remote.

That left three Quinns: one in Boston, one in New York, and one in California. Only the Quinn in New York had a listed phone number, so he called the number and a woman answered.

"St. James rectory," she said, "may I help you?"

"Uh, yes," the florist said, "may I speak to Xavier Quinn."

"I'm sorry, but Father Quinn is saying Mass right now. May I take a message?"

A priest. He crossed that Quinn off his list, although religious clerics of any kind—be they Christian, Jew, or Muslim—were never people he trusted.

He then plugged the name Xavier Quinn and various word combinations into Google—*"Xavier Quinn" Boston*; *"Xavier Quinn" CA*; *"Xavier Quinn" MA*—and patiently begin looking at the results. He discovered that the Xavier Quinn in Boston was Xavier Quinn, CPA, and was a partner in an accounting firm. An accountant? Could an accountant be involved in all this? Possibly, if there was some sort of money motive related to exposing Conrad Diller's trip to Iran. He found nothing on the Xavier Quinn who resided in California until he came across a newspaper photo of a Xavier Quinn getting into a limousine with a man named Rulon Tully. Quinn was identified as Tully's chief of security.

The florist had heard of Rulon Tully but didn't know much about him. All he knew was that the man was a billionaire. The photo he had found was connected to a story about Tully visiting a manufacturing plant in Ohio and the factory workers almost rioting when they heard Tully planned to shut down the plant. Quinn's name was mentioned in the article because he had Tasered one of the workers when the worker attacked Tully.

He next typed *Tully* *"Conrad Diller"* into the search engine but Mr. Google spit nothing back. Since he knew from the newspapers that Conrad Diller worked for Martin Taylor, he tried *"Martin Taylor"* *"Rulon Tully"*—and hit the jackpot. There was article after article about Martin Taylor having had an affair with Rulon Tully's wife, after which Tully divorced his wife. Tully definitely had a motive for wanting to hurt Taylor. But was the Xavier Quinn who was Tully's chief of security the man that had contracted Jimmy Franco to kill Dale Acosta? He couldn't be sure, but logic told him he was. This supposition was reinforced as he spent more time looking at other stories about Mr. Rulon Tully. From the articles, he learned that Tully

was a ruthless individual who would do anything to get his way—
the sort of man who wouldn't care if exposing Conrad Diller would
put a CIA spy in danger.

The florist needed to talk to Rulon Tully and the Xavier Quinn
who worked for him.

Chapter 35

After the meeting with LaFountaine, Angela had driven DeMarco back to the Sheraton in Crystal City. She was preoccupied during the drive, most likely thinking about how to accomplish the mission her boss had given her. DeMarco, on the other hand, spent no time at all thinking about how to execute LaFountaine's orders. What he was thinking about instead was that everyone involved in this thing—LaFountaine, Angela, and even Mahoney—was willing to do anything to avenge the death of this spy. And maybe that was the right thing to do, but neither LaFountaine nor Mahoney was taking the risks and breaking the laws. He and Angela were the ones at the pointy end of the spear and DeMarco knew if he was caught doing something illegal, Mahoney wasn't going to step forward and say DeMarco had been acting on his behalf. He wondered if Angela knew that her boss was the same kind of guy. He also knew screwing around with the Russian mob was a good way to get killed.

When they reached the hotel, Angela dropped him off at the entrance, said that she had phone calls to make and a meeting to go to, and told him to keep his cell phone on so she could reach him. She concluded with, "And pack your things. I have a feeling we'll be leaving for California tomorrow."

"To do what?" he asked.

She didn't answer him. She just drove away. If she wasn't so good looking, he would have found her extremely annoying.

But instead of packing as directed, he went to the Capitol and told Mahoney what LaFountaine had in mind regarding Rulon Tully and some Russian gangsters. Mahoney listened without any apparent reaction.

"This thing is getting out of hand," DeMarco said. "We ought to leak the recording I made of Rudman confessing and let the cops and the media take it from there."

Mahoney just sat there, staring off into the space above DeMarco's head. DeMarco guessed that he was most likely trying to figure out whether anything LaFountaine was doing could come back and bite him. He finished the bourbon remaining in his glass, rose from his chair, and said, "I gotta go vote on something."

At eleven o'clock the next morning, Angela called DeMarco and told him to meet her in the hotel bar and to bring his suitcase with him. She'd already checked them out of the hotel. They were catching a flight to San Diego in three hours but they had to talk to someone first.

DeMarco found her at a table in the bar, staring down at the traffic on the Jeff Davis Highway. When he ordered a beer, she gave him a look that seemed to say, *Isn't it a bit early for that?* He ignored the look. She, as usual, was drinking a Diet Coke; so far that was the only thing he'd seen her drink, other than water.

They didn't speak to each other.

DeMarco was pissed. He had no idea what she'd been up to or what she was planning, and he was getting damn tired of being dragged along in her wake. He was about to tell her this when she waved to a man who had just entered the bar, a stocky guy in his fifties carrying a briefcase and walking with a cane.

The man sat down at their table and Angela introduced him as Tom Foley. Before she could introduce DeMarco to Foley, Foley smirked and said, "And I assume this is the magnificent Mr. DeMarco, our friend from Congress."

DeMarco decided right then that he didn't like the guy.

"So did you get what I needed?" Angela asked.

"In a way," Foley said. "Unfortunately I couldn't find anybody suitable for DeMarco to play, not in the time we had, so you're going to have to do this yourself, Angie."

"What in the hell are you talking about?" DeMarco said.

Foley winked at him and said, "You'll see."

DeMarco didn't like winkers. He definitely didn't like Foley.

To Angela, Foley said, "I found a gal over at Justice. She's perfect."

He opened his briefcase and took out a manila envelope. From the envelope, he pulled a Virginia state driver's license. The photo on the license showed a woman in her midthirties with long blonde hair. She had a thin face, close-set eyes, and pinched features, and seemed as if she might be perpetually annoyed. But since it was a DMV photo, the woman probably *had* been annoyed.

DeMarco wondered what Foley was doing with the woman's driver's license and then concluded that it was probably a duplicate of the woman's license. The CIA employed a bunch of sneaky shits.

"Her name's Pamela Walker," Foley said.

Angela was still looking at Pamela's picture. "Yeah, she'll do," Angela said. "What's her story?"

"She's a lawyer," Foley said, "and she had an affair with her boss. The guy dumped her about the same time a job that would have been a promotion for her opened up. She applied for the job, didn't get it, and went bananas. She filed an EEO complaint, claiming that she didn't get the job because *she* dumped her boss, who's married by the way. She also filed a sexual harassment complaint against the guy. She became, in other words, a gigantic pain in the butt for Justice but then, while all her complaints were going through the system, she fucked up a case they'd been working on for five years. Apparently, she's not just a bitch but an incompetent bitch, so Justice is now trying to fire her. Pamela, naturally, is suing Justice, saying that Justice is retaliating for all the complaints she's filed, and her lawyer is trying to take a great big bite out of Justice's ass."

"You're right," Angela said. "She's perfect."

Perfect for what?

"All the background on her complaints and one small newspaper article on the whole mess are in the envelope," Foley said. "As an added bonus, the newspaper article has a bad photo of her."

"Can you get her out of Washington for a while?"

"We think so. There's a lady in Miami. She used to be one of us but now she runs a law firm down there. She's gonna call Pamela, go all Gloria Steinem on her, and tell her how she's read what the male-dominated establishment at Justice is trying to do to her. She'll invite Walker down for a job interview, become her new best friend, and, as long as we're footing the bill, she'll keep Walker in Miami as long as she can."

"As long as she can may not be long enough," Angela said.

Foley shrugged. "We'll cross that bridge when we come to it."

DeMarco didn't know what they were talking about but he was willing to bet that that particular phrase—*we'll cross that bridge when we come to it*—was fairly common to CIA planning.

———◆———

After Foley gave Angela the package on Pamela Walker, he loosened his tie and ordered a Manhattan. DeMarco could tell that Angela was anxious to leave for the airport, but since they still had two and half hours before their flight left, and as the airport was only a five-minute cab ride from Crystal City, she decided to sit with Foley for a while.

Foley and Angela exchanged some office gossip, the usual water-cooler rumors about who was getting transferred, who was retiring, and who was getting divorced. Because DeMarco didn't know any of the people they were talking about, he began to get very bored.

Foley ordered a second Manhattan, oblivious to the look Angela gave him. Angela, she of the Diet Coke, didn't approve of people drinking on duty, let alone so early in the day. She had told DeMarco this when they first met, and he had informed her that he worked for Congress and drinking on duty was a job requirement.

Foley then began bitching about the new house his wife had made him buy, a four-thousand-square-foot monster in Springfield. He said his mortgage payments had doubled and so had his commute time. "There was absolutely nothing wrong with the place we had in Falls Church," he said. "And this new place, the size of it, my heating bill's tripled and it costs twice as much to water the damn lawn."

DeMarco looked at his watch and said, "Angela, I think we'd better get going." They had plenty of time but he was really tired of Foley.

"Yeah," Angela said. As she reached for her purse, she said, "And thanks, Tom. You did a good job on this."

Turning serious, Foley said, "You get these guys, Angie. Mahata was good people. She was the best." Then he shook his head and added, "LaFountaine should never have cut it so close."

"What?" Angela asked.

"I said . . ."

DeMarco had always thought that it was just an expression, a guy turning as "white as a sheet," but Foley actually did. His ruddy complexion, made even more ruddy by two drinks, blanched as the blood drained from his face.

"I didn't say that, Angie. Do you understand? I didn't say anything and you didn't hear anything. You gotta promise me. Please. I don't wanna lose this job. I'm too damn old to start over."

Foley suddenly got up, grabbed his briefcase and his cane, and limped away as fast as he could. He was moving so fast that at one point his cane slipped and he almost fell.

"What the hell was that all about?" DeMarco wondered out loud.

Angela was still watching Foley as he turned a corner and disappeared from view.

"I don't know," she said, "but I have to find out. Call the airport and get us on a later flight, sometime after five. I need to talk to someone."

Chapter 36

His condo was in a six-story building on Connecticut Avenue in the District, one of those stately places with elaborate cornices built after the Second World War. She imagined it was absurdly expensive and it surprised her that he lived there. He had spent almost his entire career working outside the country and she would have guessed that the time he had spent in the condo could be measured in months, not years. But he had never married and he had the money, so she assumed that when he was home for those brief periods he wanted a haven, and this place would certainly be one.

She flirted her way past the doorman, took the elevator up to his floor, and rang the bell. She didn't know if he was home. She could have called before she came, to verify he was there, but she hadn't wanted to give him the opportunity to tell her not to come. She exhaled in relief when he opened the door.

He didn't look like a legend. He was a tall, thin man with sparse gray hair. Reading glasses were perched on the end of a long, bony nose. He was wearing moccasin slippers, khaki pants, and a Cornell University sweatshirt that was so wash faded she wondered if he had actually purchased it when he was in college. He was holding a book in one hand and she was willing to bet that the book was about history or politics—or some politician's autobiography, which he would have said belonged in the genre of historical fiction.

He had a fading bruise on his right cheek and his left eye was slightly blackened. The injuries had been inflicted by Jake LaFountaine.

"Angela," he said. "I swear, you get more beautiful every day."

Bill Carson had a soft Southern accent that Angela loved. He'd been raised on a place in Kentucky where they bred derby winners; his family didn't own the thoroughbreds, they just trained them. And though he must have been surprised to see her, he didn't look or sound it. It was almost impossible to surprise Bill Carson.

Carson was the real thing—he was the one you read about in spy novels, except the job was a lot less glamorous and lot more danger-ous than the novelists imagined. He'd been out in the field since the hot days of the Cold War. He'd been in Russia and South America and Afghanistan, and almost every other place on the planet the CIA felt the need to go. He'd been wounded in the line of duty and al-most killed more than once. For the last five years he had been the primary controller for a string of agents in Iran, Afghanistan, and Pakistan. He'd been Mahata's control.

Angela didn't know what had happened with Mahata—but she did know that Bill Carson, after thirty years of service, should have been given a medal by the president and the accolades of everyone at Langley —and not sent out the door with a beating by LaFountaine.

Carson led her to his den and the room was just what she would have expected of a lifelong bachelor. There was a small fireplace with a marble hearth, dark leather chairs, and stained-glass lamps—and shelves and shelves of books. On the fireplace mantel was a model of a three-masted frigate—a replica of the USS *Constitution*—and she suspected he'd constructed the model himself. Carson had the pa-tience and mania for detail required for that sort of hobby—these also being character traits needed for a controller of spies.

"Would you like a cognac?" he asked her.

"Thank you," she said, although she knew she wouldn't drink it.

When he had opened the door, all she had seen were the fading bruises. Now she noticed how haggard his face looked and that he had lost weight since the last time she'd seen him. On his chin was a day's worth of unshaven gray stubble, which was unusual for a man as fastidious as him. And he looked bone tired, as if he hadn't slept in days, as if he'd spent his nights lying open-eyed in his bed, staring into the maw of hell. If it had been anyone other than him—anyone less strong than him—she would have wondered if what had happened to Mahata had made him suicidal.

He poured Courvoisier into two snifters, handed her one, took a seat, and waited for her to speak. He knew she hadn't dropped by just to tell him how sorry she was for the way he had been treated. She also knew it was unlikely that he would tell her what she wanted to know. They had worked together but only briefly, and although he liked her he didn't owe her in any way.

"Bill," Angela said, "LaFountaine has me going after the people who got Mahata killed. Bodies are dropping, and more are going to drop—and I'm fine with that. But I think LaFountaine is keeping things from me. He might even be playing me."

Carson smiled, but it wasn't because Angela had said something funny. It was a sad smile, a weary smile, a smile that seemed to say, *Does nothing ever change?*

"Why do you think that?" he asked.

Instead of answering his question, she said, "What happened, Bill? What did LaFountaine cut too close with Mahata?"

Carson took a sip of his cognac while looking at her over the top of the snifter. He gave no indication that he knew what she was talking about—she would never have played poker with him—but he didn't ask her to clarify her question and it didn't look as if he was going to. He may have been booted out of Langley—literally booted out—but that didn't mean he was going to divulge Langley's secrets. No matter how he felt about LaFountaine or what LaFountaine may have done, Carson would never betray the agency or its precepts, and one of those precepts was that you didn't share information with people who had no need to know. And Angela, technically, didn't have the need.

"Do you remember after 9/11," he said, "the so-called blue-ribbon commission they formed to look into what went wrong?"

"Yes, but what does that have to do with—"

"One of the committee's astute, armchair observations was that there was an overreliance on technology and an underreliance on HUMINT."

What he meant was that the 9/11 Commission had berated the intelligence community for relying too heavily on spy satellites, Predator drones, and electronic eavesdropping, and not having enough spies in the enemy's camp.

"But the problem with human beings is . . . well, they're human. They make mistakes. They misunderstand, they become confused. They forget things that need to be done. And when you're the one in the field directing these fallible people, you're often directing them remotely. Communications are terse and coded and sporadic. You can't ask all the questions you'd like to ask; you can't double-check their work. It's very . . . *imprecise* in the field, Angie."

She had the impression he was saying out loud all the things that he had been going over repeatedly in his own head in the sleepless nights since Mahata's death.

"Are you saying LaFountaine didn't give you the time to do the job right, Bill? Is that what was cut too close? Did he wait too long after the article appeared in the *News* to tell you to pull Mahata out?"

"I had all the time in the world. In Mahata's case, I had six years."

"Then what did LaFountaine cut too close?"

He shook his head. "Angie, I can't tell you what you want to know. I wish I could but it's need-to-know, and only LaFountaine can bring you into the circle."

"I understand," she said.

And she did. But, goddamnit, she was tired of it—tired of being kept in the dark, tired of being used, tired of being excluded. In spite of her aversion to drinking on duty, she drained the cognac snifter in one swallow, and after she did she had an urge to throw the beautiful glass into Carson's fireplace and watch it shatter. They did that in old movies and she always thought it looked silly and over the top and it offended her practical sensibilities—the thought of having to clean up all that broken glass—but now she felt like doing just that. She had an overwhelming desire to break something.

"Did you hear LaFountaine's press conference," Carson asked, "when he told the jackals about Mahata's death?"

"Yes," she said, "but—"

"Do you remember him saying how deeply embedded she was, what fine product she produced? Didn't that strike you as odd, Angie? The director of the Central Intelligence agency admitting, publicly, that we had inserted an agent right into one of the most sensitive ministries in Iran? Why would he do that?"

She couldn't tell if he was seriously puzzled by what LaFountaine had done or if he was trying to instruct her with his question. She suspected he was telling her something important, but she didn't know what.

"I don't know," she said. "But one thing I do know is that you didn't deserve to be treated the way he treated you."

Carson smiled again, but this time there was genuine mirth in it. "People assume that LaFountaine attacked me in his office that day. It's apparently never occurred to anyone, including you, that maybe *I* was the one who attacked *him* and he was simply defending himself."

"What are you saying, Bill? Was it his fault she died, or yours? Will you just give me a straight answer?"

"I'm saying it was complicated and you shouldn't judge LaFountaine —or me—too harshly. We're human, too."

Chapter 37

———❖———

They ended up taking the red-eye to San Diego because DeMarco couldn't get them on an earlier flight. Angela barely said a word to him while they were waiting to board the plane, and didn't say anything at all when they were in the air. She wouldn't tell him who she had gone to see—invoking the CIA mantra of *need to know*—and she refused to be drawn into a discussion about the dangerous assignment that LaFountaine had given her. So DeMarco had two drinks, put on headphones, and fell asleep.

They stepped off the plane in San Diego, stiff jointed, exhausted, and fuzzy headed—symptoms familiar to overnight, crosscontinental travelers. A young guy wearing jeans, a T-shirt, and a Padres ball cap met them at baggage claim. He looked like a college kid but, if he was one, DeMarco was pretty sure he wasn't a full-time student.

"Where's Markelov now?" Angela asked.

"At his place, probably sleeping," the kid said. "He was out late last night partying. The man's a party animal. Dave's watching him, and he'll call if Yuri takes off, but my guess is that he'll be at home until this evening. So, if you need to get some sleep, you probably have time."

"Is the FBI watching him?"

"Not yet. We couldn't spot any surveillance and we talked to your guy Schommer back in D.C. He said they were still looking at records, getting justification for warrants, all that legal nonsense." The kid laughed. "That's the problem with the Bureau; they hire too many lawyers and they think like lawyers."

———— ◆◆◆ ————

Getting some sleep had sounded like a great idea to DeMarco, but iron-woman DeCapria was still on the job.

"How do I look?" she asked.

They were in Angela's room at the Hilton on Harbor Island. She had on black-framed glasses and a blonde wig that fit so well and looked so real that DeMarco couldn't tell it was a wig. She was holding Pamela Walker's driver's license next to her face.

DeMarco liked her natural hair color better, but there was something sexy about the blonde wig. It made her look sorta tarty, and sometimes tarty was good. He wanted to say, *You look like every man's fantasy, you look so good that I want to . . .*

"You look good," he said.

"I mean, do I look like her?"

"She's not as pretty as you. Her lips are thinner and her nose . . . but yeah, if this guy Yuri gets a copy of her real driver's license, I think he'll think it's just a bad picture."

"Yeah, that's what I think, too," Angela agreed.

"I'm going with you," DeMarco said.

"No way. How do I explain you?"

"Tell him I'm muscle you hired for protection."

"No, I'll be all right. And I don't want him getting a look at you. We may need you later."

"Angela, the guy you're going to see is a gangster and I've got some experience with gangsters, a lot more than you have."

"You mean your father?" she asked.

DeMarco ignored the question. "You know, people see *The Godfather* and Marlon Brando scratching his cheek, acting all wise and thoughtful, and they get the wrong idea. Let me tell you something: mob guys aren't wise and thoughtful. They're a bunch of thugs that usually aren't very bright and their solution to almost every problem is violence. And if they think you're trying to set them up, they'll kill you."

Angela looked at him and nodded her head, but it wasn't because she appreciated the wisdom of his words.

"You're going to have to tell me about your dad sometime," was all she said.

———— ◆◆◆ ————

Angela rang the doorbell of Yuri Markelov's house, which, according to Ryan Schommer of the FBI, was really Marty Taylor's house. The house was in Coronado and overlooked San Diego Bay. She didn't know anything about the California real-estate market, but she was guessing the place would sell for several million. She would have given her eyeteeth to have a home like this.

The door was opened by an enormous man wearing a cheap brown suit and a white polo shirt. He was at least six six and so broad he completely filled the doorway. He had a shaved head, a goatee, and a neck that was about the same diameter as a fire hydrant. He was speaking on a cell phone and he raised a finger to her in a just-a-minute gesture. She heard him say, "Take him to the emergency room and don't worry about the insurance. They'll take care of him." He paused and said, "No. Take him now. Take a cab."

He closed the cell phone and muttered, "Stupid *suka*." Looking at Angela, concern still etched on his face, he said, "One of my sons. He's been coughing all night. That's not good, is it?"

"Uh, no," Angela said. "That doesn't sound good. Look, I'm here to see Yuri Markelov."

The giant smiled at her but shook his head. "I'm sorry, but you should have called first. He's already with a girl, and he won't want to be disturbed. But leave me your name and I'll tell him you came by. You're very pretty, I'm sure he'll want to see you again."

"I'm not one of Yuri's bimbos," she said. "Tell him I have information for him, important information related to Martin Taylor's company. He'll want to see me."

Now the man frowned; he wasn't sure what to do.

"Okay. I'll tell him you're here."

He started to close the door but before he did, he said, "If you've lied to me, I'm going to hurt you."

And Angela couldn't help but think about DeMarco's lecture on the fundamental nature of gangsters.

———————◆◆◆———————

Angela was escorted to a glass-walled sunroom that had white wicker furniture, a beautiful Spanish tile floor, and looked out on to a swimming pool and the San Diego Bay. Markelov was standing with his back to her, near a wet bar, pouring coffee from a carafe into a delft-blue China cup. He was wearing a bathrobe that reached almost to his ankles and there was a gold Chinese dragon embroidered on the back of the robe. When he turned around, she saw the robe was open and under it the only thing he wore was a black Speedo swimsuit; his long blond hair was wet as if he had just come from the pool. Angela had to admit that he was a good-looking man with a terrific body. Very few men his age looked good in a Speedo.

He smiled at her and said, "I don't understand why you're here. Ivan said something about Martin Taylor's company but I don't have anything to do with his company. I socialize with Marty occasionally, we tend to go to the same clubs, but we're not in business together."

"He must be a pretty good pal to let you live in his house."

Yuri shrugged. "I told Marty I was looking for a place to live while my house is being remodeled. He spends almost all his time at his beach place at Oceanside so he rented this house to me. I like it so much, I'm thinking about buying it."

"Would you like to show me the rental agreement?"

Yuri stopped smiling. "Who are you? And what do you want?"

"My name's Pamela Walker and I'm a lawyer at the Justice Department."

"You're a lovely woman, a very lovely woman, but I'm afraid you're going to have to leave. I don't talk to lawyers unless my own lawyer is with me."

"Why don't you hear what I have to say first? After you do, I think you're going to put me on your payroll."

"You're here to apply for a job?"

"You could say that."

Yuri started to say something else, but Angela said, "Why don't we start with Conrad Diller."

"Who's Conrad Diller?"

Angela nodded. "That's fine. Pretend you don't know him, but let's talk about him anyway. Conrad Diller was arrested for trying to sell U.S. missile technology to the Iranian government. It was suspected that he was doing this on Marty Taylor's behalf but before that could be proven, Diller disappeared. But you made a big mistake with Diller because—"

"I don't know any Diller," Yuri said, and this time there was an edge to his tone.

"—because now the FBI is looking very, very hard at Taylor's company. Until Diller was arrested, the FBI never had any reason to investigate Taylor but when a U.S. company attempts to sell dangerous things to our enemies, the Bureau tends to sit up and take notice. And you know what they noticed, Yuri? They noticed you."

"I don't know what you're talking about."

As if he hadn't spoken, Angela continued, "It all happened because of a phone call Diller made. I don't have all the details yet—I'll get them eventually—but because of this phone call they somehow linked you to Diller and Marty Taylor, and they found out that you used to work for, or maybe you *still* work for, an old Russian gangster named Lev Girenko."

"I don't work for anyone. I'm an independent businessman."

"And a darn good one, I'll bet. But as I was saying, until Diller was arrested, the FBI didn't care about you. They may have suspected that you were doing whatever it is that Russian mobsters do, but you just weren't at the top of their people-to-catch list. But now you are." Angela shook her head as if she felt very sorry for him. "You should never have tried dealing with the Iranians. Not in *this* day and age."

"You're mistaken. I don't have—"

"Please. Stop saying that. I didn't just pick your name out of the phone book. I came here because the FBI has already started to investigate you, and I know this because I work for the Justice Department. But you're lucky. Do you know why?"

Yuri shook his head slowly, his eyes now reptilian in their coldness. He was no longer in a flirtatious mood.

"You see, the thing about the FBI and the Justice Department is that they're competent and thorough and have enormous resources, but they tend to move slowly because they want an airtight case before they go to court. They don't like to lose and be embarrassed. And that's what's going on right now. The FBI juggernaut is just starting to move, and it will probably be several months, maybe even a year, before you're arrested, but eventually you will be. They'll start with surveillance, watching you, Taylor, and people in Taylor's company."

"Am I under surveillance now?"

"Not yet, and I wouldn't be here if you were. But you soon will be, and while they're watching you they'll start talking to people that have left Taylor's company. They'll eventually get justification for warrants to tap phones, and finally they'll get warrants to look at financial records, which is where they'll get you. The numbers always tell the story. And someplace along the way, they'll find people to testify against you to avoid being prosecuted. Maybe they'll turn Taylor himself. So, you have a few months, but in the end, if you don't do something to protect yourself, they'll get you. I guarantee it."

"What do you want?"

"Today, I want twenty-five thousand dollars."

"Today?"

"Yes. And then I want another ten thousand every time I provide you with more information on the FBI's investigation. Now, you have to understand that even with me helping you, you still may be arrested but if you have someone at Justice keeping tabs on things, your chances of staying out of jail will improve. For example, if I was able to tell you that the FBI is talking to certain people, maybe you could convince those people not to talk."

"I need to see if you're wearing any recording devices. Take off your clothes."

Angela laughed. "In your dreams," she said. "I'm not taking anything off. And you don't have to say anything. You just need to listen."

Yuri shook his head irritably. "Ivan!" he yelled.

The big guy with the goatee rushed into the room. His head almost touched the top of the doorway; he was a monster. Angela was going to kick him in the nuts if he tried to get her clothes off, but she had a feeling that wouldn't stop him for long. She started to stand up to defend herself but then Yuri said, "Get the . . . the device. See if she's wearing a wire."

Ivan came back into the room with a box the size of a digital camera that had a small antenna protruding from the top. He passed the bug detector over her body, including between her legs. He smiled apologetically when he pressed the device against her crotch. When he was finished, he looked at Yuri and shook his head.

"Her purse," Yuri said.

Ivan took her purse and dumped the contents on a coffee table and the first things that fell out were two identical cell phones.

"See if the cell phones are turned on," Yuri said, knowing that cell phones can be turned into recording devices.

"They're off," Ivan said.

Ivan uncertainly examined the rest of the things that had spilled from her purse: makeup, a brush, her wallet, and a thick envelope. The envelope wasn't sealed; he opened the flap, saw only paper, and set it aside. Ivan's brow was furrowed with concern. Angela suspected that he was just bright enough to realize he had no idea how the FBI might disguise a bug. He picked up a lipstick tube, took the top off it, then, seeing that it contained nothing but lipstick, put the tube down next to the other articles on the table and shook his head at Yuri. Yuri nodded and Ivan left the room.

Yuri studied Angela, apparently trying to decide what to do next. As he was looking, he closed the bathrobe and she was glad he did. The bulge in the Speedo was a distraction. While she waited for him to make up his mind, she began to put her things back into her purse. She left the envelope and one of the cell phones on the table.

"Do you want to know how Conrad Diller was caught?" she asked.

"I already know. A CIA spy saw him in Iran. It said so in the newspaper."

"That's not the whole story. The newspaper article was written by a woman named Sandra Whitmore, and she was the one who reported that Diller was in Iran. The spy was killed after Whitmore's story was released, and that's when Diller was arrested. But how did the reporter get the information in the first place?"

"I have no idea," Yuri said. He tried to make it sound as if he didn't care about Angela's answer but she could tell that he did. She had his complete attention at this point.

"Well, I do. And that's another reason why you're going to give me twenty-five grand. I'll give you the name of the person who's responsible for all the troubles you're about to have, and I'll also tell you how you can make some money off this person to compensate for what he's done."

"Tell me why you're doing this."

Angela handed Yuri the envelope. "I filed a lawsuit against Justice for sexual harassment and discrimination, and because of that Justice is trying to fire me, alleging I bungled a case."

"Sexual harassment?" Yuri said, and smiled slightly. She imagined sexual harassment was not a topic included in the Russian mob's training program.

"I'll win the lawsuit eventually and I'll keep my job, but my career is over. They'll give me shitty assignments, never promote me again, and destroy my reputation so that I'll never be able to get a decent job with a private law firm. So I'm rather annoyed at the Justice Department right now and I need money—a lot of money—since my career has gone down the toilet.

"And you're not the only guy I'm going to help. I've already contacted two other people being investigated by Justice, and I'm going to contact two more in addition to you and make them the same deal: that I'll keep them informed of progress on their cases in return for a fee."

Yuri arched an eyebrow as if he might be impressed by her initiative and the magnitude of her scheme, then took the papers out of the envelope. He looked around the room, searching for something, and finally spotted a pair of reading glasses sitting on a window ledge. He put on the glasses and was just starting to read the information on Pamela Walker when a voice said, "Hey, baby, who's this?"

Angela turned. Standing in the doorway was a young blonde—a *really* young blonde. The girl looked like she was eighteen or nineteen years old. She was wearing a cobalt blue bikini and was absolutely stunning. She made Angela feel like an over-the-hill crone.

"Ah, Heather, my love, you're up," Yuri said.

It was two o'clock in the afternoon.

"This is a business associate of mine," Yuri said to Heather, "and I need to talk to her privately for a few more minutes. Why don't you go have a little swim until I'm done?"

Heather looked at Angela as if she didn't like Yuri's business associates to have such good legs.

"Can I at least get a cup of coffee?" Heather asked. Heather was kind of whiny.

"There's coffee in the kitchen, darling," Yuri said. "Now run along, please. We'll have something to eat as soon as I'm finished here."

Heather flounced from the room, displaying her best asset: her perfect nineteen-year-old ass.

Yuri finished reading the papers Angela had given him.

"And how do I know that you're the Pamela Walker mentioned in these documents?"

Angela handed Yuri a driver's license and a Justice Department identification badge that had her picture on it but identified her as Pamela Walker. "And I'm sure you can find someone in Washington who can verify that I've told you the truth about my problems with the Justice Department," she said.

"I can do that, and I will," Yuri said. He paused a beat, then added, "Okay. Tell me what else you know."

"Twenty-five thousand," Angela said.

"You're just going to have to trust me on that," Yuri said. "If what you have to tell me is worth that amount, I'll give you half the money now and the other half after I've checked you out."

"Trust you? I don't think so."

"Pamela, please. If I am who you think I am, you know I could give you the money and then have Ivan take it away from you before you leave. Or, what I could do instead of giving you any money at all is have Ivan persuade you to talk to me. Ivan isn't a naturally cruel man but he can be quite brutal if necessary. So please. Just talk. And if what you tell me is worth what you're asking, I'll pay you. I have that amount of cash here in the house."

Angela pretended to think this over and finally nodded her head. "Okay. The man who started this was Rulon Tully. Do you know who Tully is?"

"I've read about him."

"Well, Tully hates Marty Taylor."

"Something about a woman," Yuri said.

"That's right. Taylor screwed Tully's wife, and Tully has never forgiven him. So when Tully found out Diller was trying to sell missile technology to the Iranians from a congressman he owns, he passed the information on to the *Daily News*."

"And Tully did this hoping to damage Taylor's company?" Yuri asked.

"Not just to damage his company. He was hoping Taylor would end up in jail. But since Diller has disappeared—an event the FBI thinks you're responsible for, by the way—that's not going to happen."

"So Mr. Tully's plan failed," Yuri said.

"Wrong. Mr. Tully's plan succeeded—but he just doesn't know it. Because of Diller, as I've already explained to you, the FBI is now looking very hard at you and Taylor, and in the end, they'll get Taylor for being your accomplice and they'll get you."

Yuri wasn't smiling now; he was no longer the laid-back playboy he pretended to be. He looked like the guy he really was: a guy that killed people when they became a problem.

"Okay," Yuri said. "What else?"

"Rulon Tully isn't finished with you yet. He'll eventually try something else to hurt Taylor, which, in turn, will hurt your business. So you have two enemies: the United States government and Rulon Tully, and Tully may actually be the bigger threat because he's incredibly rich and doesn't play by the rules."

"I see," Yuri said.

"So I figure that what I've just told you is worth twenty-five thousand. I've told you how Diller was caught and who was responsible, I've told you that you're being investigated by the FBI, and I've promised to keep you informed of the investigation in the future. But I'm going to give you one more thing. Inside Rulon Tully's mansion near Ventura is over six million dollars in artwork. His wine collection is valued at four hundred thousand. He has three classic automobiles, one of them a restored 1937 Pierce-Arrow worth half a million. Jay Leno used to own the car. He also has a big safe in his house and God knows what's in the safe, but I would assume Tully's a man that likes to have a good bit of cash on hand. And then, of course, Tully has money all over the place in various bank accounts and you just need the passwords to access those accounts."

"And your point is?"

"I think you already know my point: if you were to take care of Rulon Tully in the right way, you could pay him back for what he's done, eliminate him as a future threat, and you could turn a pretty good profit by stealing everything in his house."

"Ivan!" Yuri yelled, and Angela jumped in her chair.

The big bodyguard lumbered back into the room.

"Get twelve thousand, five hundred from the safe," Yuri said. Then he said to Angela, "If I find out that you've lied to me . . . well, you know."

"I haven't lied," Angela said.

While they were waiting for Ivan to return with the money, Yuri studied her, then smiled—as if he hadn't just threatened her life—and said, "I was wondering if you might like to have dinner with me tonight."

"What about Heather?" Angela asked.

"She's a lovely girl but sometimes a man likes to be with someone a little more mature—but just as lovely."

Angela smiled. "Yuri, gorgeous as you are, I'm gonna pass. Even though the Bureau isn't watching you yet, it's just not smart to sleep with guys the FBI is going after."

Before Angela left she handed Yuri one of the two cell phones she had in her purse and gave him a post office box number where he was to send her money. She told him the cell phones were untraceable and, if he needed to talk to her, to call only from the phone she'd given him.

Yuri called a lawyer in D.C. The man had assisted him in the past with an immigration problem and he had contacts in the Justice Department. He asked the lawyer to check out Pamela Walker but he really didn't expect that he would learn anything more than what Walker had told him.

He had a late lunch with Heather as he had promised but tuned out her childish chatter and focused instead on the Walker woman. If she was who she claimed she was—a disgruntled employee who needed cash—could he use her to keep him informed of the FBI's progress? Maybe. But could he trust her? Of course not. It also occurred to him that she could be some sort of undercover agent, but if she was an undercover, what she had done didn't make sense. She

had not tried to insert herself in any way into his organization to get
evidence against him, nor had she done anything to get him to admit
that he was doing anything incriminating. And she had taken cash
from him. Giving her money didn't cause him a problem, but it could
cause *her* one. He could always say that she was blackmailing him,
and it would be her word against his, but she was the one who would
have to explain what she was doing with money taken from a criminal
—an alleged criminal. So, if she was an undercover agent, he couldn't
see how their initial meeting could harm him and, if she was legitimate, an association with her could turn out to be useful.

After lunch, Heather, annoyed because he was ignoring her, went
to watch television. He didn't care. It occurred to him that he really
didn't care for Heather's company at all, other than in bed, and Pamela
Walker had reminded him of the pleasure of being with a woman
who was not only beautiful but intelligent.

He made a gin and tonic, took it out to the pool, and sat and
looked out at the bay. He loved the view: the blue water, the magnificent navy ships sailing by, the grandeur of the Coronado Bridge.
And the weather today was perfect, as it almost always was. And the
house he had taken from Martin Taylor was the type of house he
would have designed for himself, and it, too, was perfect. He was,
in fact, living a dream—and he had destroyed it. He was going to
lose it all. He was going to have to leave this perfect place, his perfect life.

Uncle Lev had discussed with him on more than one occasion the
qualities of leadership. A leader had to be decisive. He had to take
care of his people yet be willing to sacrifice those same people for the
overall good of the organization. He had to be merciless when needed
but could never become addicted to the perverse pleasures of cruelty.
And one other thing: a leader had to be objective. That was one of
the most important qualities of leadership: the ability to look at a
situation the way it *really* was, and not the way one wished it was.
And Yuri knew, objectively, that he had made a huge mistake and
was now going pay for it.

When they had arrived in San Diego eight years ago, they did the things that he and Uncle Lev had always done. They forced their way into a few small businesses and stripped them of their assets and profits. One of those businesses was an auto body shop and that became their hub for moving stolen cars and auto parts. They established themselves in prostitution and pornography, and set up routes for moving commodities through Mexico. They discovered that moving people was especially lucrative. They did some business in drugs, but not a large amount, because even though drugs were hugely profitable, there was too much competition and the competition was always lethal. Nothing they did was done on a grand scale and they managed to maintain a low profile that rarely attracted the attention of law enforcement, and all their endeavors generated enough profit to satisfy his uncle, though hardly enough to satisfy Yuri.

But then along came Andy Bollinger, Marty Taylor's perverted CEO.

He never would have gotten involved in Taylor's company had it not been for Bollinger. Taylor & Taylor dealt with technologies that he didn't understand and, from a financial standpoint, was enormously complicated. The company also had a board of directors that oversaw the operation and he had no idea how to control such an entity. But when Yuri taped Bollinger having sex with that Mexican kid—it was standard practice to tape all clients who procured their sex services—and then when he discovered who Bollinger was . . . well, it was gift from God.

At first he simply blackmailed Bollinger. The man was enormously wealthy and he took half a million from him in a six-month period. Then the idea occurred to him that he could use Bollinger to steal money from Taylor's company. It was a brilliant idea, and even his conservative Uncle Lev agreed.

T&T Systems became this enormous cash cow, a cow of such magnitude the earth trembled when it walked. Yuri learned that the company was in bad financial shape but he figured it would be years before it went under—and until it did Bollinger would continue to move money from the company's coffers into Yuri's wallet.

When Marty Taylor discovered what Bollinger was doing, at first Yuri had been inclined to kill Taylor. But then he discovered that Taylor was a cowardly weakling, so he began to take money from Marty-boy as well. And it was all going marvelously until he made the mistake of trying to sell missile technology to the Iranians.

Yuri had known a Russian army officer when he lived in Russia, and the officer had occasionally provided weapons for Yuri and Uncle Lev to sell on the black market. When the officer retired from the Red Army, he moved to Iran and became a military consultant to the Iranians. Yuri had a drink with the man one day when he was visiting LA, and together they hatched the idea of selling T&T's technology to the Iranians. Had they been successful, the profits would have been staggering—but they weren't successful. Although he could not have realistically anticipated that an American spy would attend Diller's meeting in Tehran, he had to admit, in retrospect, that it had been foolhardy to deal with one of America's biggest enemies. It had, in fact, been incredibly stupid.

Now, because of what he had done, and because the whole situation had been exacerbated by the death of that spy, he had placed himself directly in the crosshairs of federal law enforcement. And he wasn't in those crosshairs because he was a thief—the American government could somewhat tolerate a thief, but what it could not tolerate was a thief who helped an Islamic country ruled by a madman.

He had killed the cash cow. It wasn't dead yet, but it soon would be.

Pamela Walker, whether she was an imposter or not, was correct: the FBI would eventually get him. The things he and Bollinger had done were just too complicated; there were too many people involved and there were bound to be incriminating records that the FBI would find. If he didn't want to spend the rest of his life in jail, he was going to have to kill Taylor and Bollinger—the only two people who could testify directly against him—and then he was going to have to leave the country.

And then there was Uncle Lev to consider. He had met Lev when he was a teenager, when he'd been a homeless boy who survived by robbing tourists. The old man took him under his wing, trained him, and later made him his second in command when he saw Yuri was more intelligent than the other brutes in his organization. At the time, Yuri had been enormously grateful to his adopted uncle but after a few years he realized Lev was a man who thought small and always would.

They left Russia because Lev had crossed criminals who were more powerful than him. He thought it would be easier in America but he soon found out that American criminals, particularly the ones in New York, were just as ruthless and well organized as the ones in his homeland. Yuri agreed that the move to San Diego had been necessary and prudent, but once they arrived the old man simply did what he had always done. He did nothing big, nothing to grow the organization, nothing to increase their profits. He and Uncle Lev made money but they didn't make all that much—they were no richer than so-called upper-middle-class Americans—and the people who worked for them couldn't even be categorized as middle-class.

When he first came up with the idea of forcing Bollinger to siphon off money from Taylor's company, Lev had been reluctant. It was too complicated, he had said, too different from what they had always done. But finally Lev relented and the money began to flow—buckets of money, more money than Lev had ever seen in his long life. And as the leader of their organization he took the lion's share of the profits even though Yuri was the one doing the work. After a year, Lev essentially retired, moving into a seaside villa near Puerto Vallarta. Yet, in spite of Yuri's success, he continued to carp at Yuri, warning him to be careful, not to move too quickly, not to become overly ambitious. So as Lev took the money with one hand, his other hand wagged a gnarled finger at Yuri telling him not to overreach.

Well, it looked like the old man was going to have the satisfaction of saying I told you so. Because of this thing with Diller they were going to lose it all. He would still be able to strip Taylor of a lot of money before he had to flee, but very soon he would have to run and when he did he would have to abandon everything in San Diego —the car-theft ring, the porn, the drugs, the illegal alien import business—because if he stayed he would end up in jail.

And he would have to leave Uncle Lev. If Lev were a rational man, he would understand that Yuri had made him enough money to be secure for the rest of his life—but the old man wasn't rational when it came to money. He talked constantly of "rainy days," unable to admit to himself that at his age the number of days, rainy or not, were limited. Nor was he rational when it came to failure, and Yuri had definitely failed. The worst problem, though, was Lev's paranoia: he would be worried that if Yuri was caught he would be, too.

So being objective, Yuri knew that he had to abandon everything, including his uncle, but before he ran he might do as Walker had suggested regarding Rulon Tully. If he did it right, one lightning strike against Tully could net enormous gains.

There was one other thing that appealed to him about Pamela Walker's idea regarding Tully: Tully was at the root of all his problems. It was Tully's fault that Diller's trip to Iran was publicly exposed and the spy was killed. Killing Tully would be, emotionally, very satisfying. He might even do it himself.

"Ivan!"

Ivan, good dog that he was, lumbered out to the pool.

"Tell Heather to go home. Then call Mikhail and tell him to come here immediately."

Chapter 38

———❖———

Angela had been gone for almost four hours and DeMarco was worried.

He knew it hadn't taken her that long to make her pitch to Yuri, and since she wouldn't let him go with her, he didn't even know where Yuri lived. He needed to go out and find her. He had just made up his mind to call Neil and have Neil get Yuri's address when Angela phoned and said she was back in her room.

"Where the hell have you been?" he demanded as soon as he saw her. He sounded like an anxious father whose teenage daughter had stayed out past her curfew.

She ignored him as she took the blonde wig off her head and tossed it onto the bed.

"Well?" he asked. "Where were you? I was worried."

"After I saw Yuri, I had to get together with some guys we have out here watching folks. Then I had to call Langley."

She walked over to the mirror and began to brush out her hair. She seemed to be moving very slowly, as if she could barely lift her arms.

"So how'd it go with Yuri?"

She kept brushing for a moment, then lowered the hairbrush and turned to look at him. Her eyes were oddly bright.

"It went just the way LaFountaine wanted it to go. I suggested to Yuri that he might want to commit a home invasion on Rulon Tully and kill him in the process. I also planted the idea that he might want to kill Marty Taylor, as Taylor might testify against him in the future. For my suggestions, Yuri gave me twelve grand and invited me to sleep with him. I passed on the sex, but the money is in that Nordstrom bag over there by my purse."

"And you're okay with all this?"

She didn't respond.

"How do you think you're going to feel when Yuri shoots his way into Tully's house and ends up killing some cook or a maid or whoever else might get in the way?"

She threw the hairbrush down hard on the makeup table; she had probably wanted to throw it at him. "How the hell do you think I'll feel?" she said. "But how will *you* feel if Tully gets away with what he did? It was his fault Mahata was killed, and you know he killed Acosta. And you also know we'll never get him if we play by the rules."

"So if some innocent schmuck gets whacked, we'll just write that off as collateral damage?"

She started to spit out some hot-tempered retort, but then didn't. She closed her eyes for a moment and when she opened them she said softly, "I want to be part of something that matters, Joe. This is my chance."

"What are you talking about?"

"I'm talking about terrorism. This country is in a war with religious fanatics and it's never going to end, and one of these days, if we don't stop them, they're going to do something that will make 9/11 look like a car crash. I want to be one of the people who keeps that from happening."

"Then tell LaFountaine to transfer you into some division that deals with that stuff."

"That's not the way it works. I told you, when I was a cop I was a glorified meter maid. I was the one they dressed up in a miniskirt when the mayor wanted to get his name in the paper for being all hard-nosed on prostitution. And it's pretty much the same way at the CIA.

I'm still being treated like a meter maid while all the real decisions are being made by a bunch of bureaucratic dinosaurs that have been at Langley for years. Well, this is my chance. I told LaFountaine I'd do what he wanted when it came to Mahata but only if he gave me a bigger role in the agency, one directly involved with terrorism."

"So you're doing this for a *promotion?*" he responded, unable to keep the disdain from his voice.

"No! Goddamnit, I just told you . . . oh, never mind. And I don't need this holier-than-thou shit from you. If you don't have the stomach for this, just walk away. No one's stopping you."

She was right. He could walk away—but he wasn't going to.

"I'm gonna go get a drink," he said. "I'll see you later."

"The drink will have to wait," Angela said. "We need to talk about—"

"Then we can talk in the bar," he said and left the room.

DeMarco took a seat at the bar and ordered a Stoli martini—the only Russian thing he approved of at the moment. As he sat there, he caught sight of his reflection in the mirror behind the bar: Mr. Holier Than Thou.

No one was holy in this thing, including him. Especially him. While Angela was actively executing LaFountaine's plan, he was passively standing by and watching it all happen. If he didn't like what LaFountaine was doing, the right action to take, instead of carping at Angela, would be to blow the whistle. Call somebody—the press or the Bureau—and tell them what was going on. But if he did that, what would happen next?

The answer to that question was that he would definitely lose his job and Angela might lose hers. If she wasn't fired outright any chance for advancement would be over. Nothing would happen to Mahoney and LaFountaine, of course. Those guys were too slick to have anything stick to them. They'd deny they ever gave an order to do anything to Rudman or Tully, and Angela would be accused of being a rogue agent who'd been acting on her own. Yuri and Marty Taylor might eventually be convicted for whatever Yuri was doing with Taylor's company, and Rudman might lose his seat in the House, but certainly nothing would happen to Rulon Tully—a man who had killed at least one person and who was, more than anyone else, responsible for Mahata's death.

Yeah, blowing the whistle was the holy thing to do—but the outcome was all wrong. Yet not blowing it meant that innocent people could get hurt. Maybe there was some way he could stop Yuri before anyone was killed, but he had no idea if he'd get that opportunity. All he knew for sure was that he wasn't walking away. He wasn't going to leave Angela on her own, not when a man like Yuri Markelov might be coming after her.

An annoyed Angela joined him in the bar ten minutes later.

"Let's get a table," she said, and he dutifully followed her to one.

She looked at his martini and he thought for a moment that she might order one, too, but then she ordered her usual Diet Coke. He would have thought that after the stress of meeting with Yuri, and considering it was after five p.m., she might relax her standards a bit. But no.

"Look," DeMarco said, "I'm sorry I—"

"Never mind that," she interrupted. "Tomorrow, we need to meet with Marty Taylor and—"

Her cell phone rang. She looked at the caller ID screen and smiled, and when she said hello her tone of voice was different, like she was really glad—*desperately* glad—to hear from whoever had called. But then after a moment the smile disappeared and she said, "I see," and he watched her lips compress in irritation.

"Why don't you come out here, instead," she said. "I think I'm going to have some free time this weekend. We'll drive up the coast, see the sights. It'll be fun."

See the sights?

She listened for a moment then said, "Yeah, right. Who the hell do you think you're kidding, Brad?" Then she snapped the cell phone closed. She sat there for a minute staring down at the tabletop, then looked up and waved at the nearest barmaid.

"Gimme one of those," she said, pointing at DeMarco's martini.

"Is there a problem?" DeMarco asked.

She didn't answer him, and when her drink arrived she drained half of it in a single swallow.

"My jackass husband is having an affair. He was just calling to tell me that he's flying to Key West for a conference. What he's really doing is taking a little holiday with the bitch he's currently screwing, probably some twenty-four-year-old resident who thinks he's God."

She drank the rest of her martini and ordered another one.

"You might want to slow down on those," DeMarco said, gesturing at the empty glass. "They have a tendency to sneak up on you."

She ignored him.

As they were waiting for her second drink to arrive, she muttered, "What the hell is it with you men?"

"What?" DeMarco said.

"Yuri was with some girl young enough to be his daughter. Marty Taylor dates women who still get carded in bars. And my damn husband is the same way. I mean, do all you bastards . . ."

She suddenly rose from the table, bumping it with her hip as she did, almost spilling DeMarco's drink, and left the bar.

DeMarco sat there, wondering if she was going to come back. He'd known her husband was an asshole the minute he saw the guy.

Fifteen minutes later, she did come back and it looked like she'd bawled her eyes out—and he bet it took a lot to make Angela DeCapria cry. If he ever got the chance, he was going to beat the crap out of her husband.

She picked up her martini and once again chugged it down like it was a tequila shooter. Martinis are not meant to be drunk like that.

"My husband's a heart surgeon," she said. "And you remember what Robert Redford looked like when he was young, when he was in *The Sting*? Well, that's who Brad looks like."

DeMarco didn't bother to mention that he'd seen her husband, and he didn't think the guy was *that* good looking.

"When I married him, my mother got down on her knees and thanked God. She couldn't believe it, her little tomboy daughter married to a doctor, and a handsome one at that. Then she started in on me: You oughta stop working, Angie. You oughta get pregnant, Angie. Have some babies. Stay home and take care of your kids and your husband." Angela said all this in a high-pitched whine that DeMarco assumed was an imitation of her mother's voice.

"And maybe she was right. At first Brad thought it was pretty cool having a wife that worked for the CIA. But then it wasn't so cool because instead of me being there all the time to do whatever he wanted, I had a career. And I learned pretty quickly that Brad's the type who needs a lot of attention. A lot of *adoration,* actually. He's used to having people, especially women, fawn all over him."

"He's an asshole," DeMarco said.

"Shut up! What do you know?"

Oh, boy.

Angela ordered a third martini. DeMarco was thinking he was going to have to carry her back to her room.

"Uh, maybe we oughta get dinner," he said. "Have an appetizer or something."

"Things weren't so bad for the first four years, but the last three have been a living hell. I don't know how many affairs he's had, but he's had a lot. And now he doesn't even pretend he's being faithful. I don't know why he doesn't just leave me."

"Why don't you leave him?" DeMarco asked.

Her eyes flashed and she started to say something, probably to tell him to shut up again, but then she just shook her head.

"Because I love the asshole," she said.

"Okay. Tomorrow we're gonna go talk to Marty Taylor," Angela said.

She was halfway through her fourth martini and DeMarco noticed her eyes were beginning to have a hard time focusing. He could tell because he was only on his third.

"We gotta . . ."

"You know, you might want to talk a little softer," DeMarco said, spinning his head around to see who was sitting near them. Fortunately, no one was.

"We gotta make sure he understands that . . ."

She stopped to take another gulp of her martini.

". . . that he unnerstans . . ."

She stopped to suck the olive off the swizzle stick.

"Understands . . . Shit, I forgot what I was going to say. Oh, yeah. We gotta . . ."

She stopped again and looked at DeMarco, directly into his eyes. "Let's go to bed."

DeMarco felt his heart do a backflip. "Okay," he said.

She kissed him as soon as the elevator doors closed. She fit perfectly. Her body just molded into his.

They reached her room and she had a hard time getting the key card to open the door, but she finally did it. She walked into the room, hips swaying, taking off her shoes as she went, stumbling a bit as she did. She began to unbutton her blouse and then saw that DeMarco was still standing in the doorway.

"What?" she asked.

"I can't let you do this," DeMarco said. "Because if we do this, you'll hate yourself tomorrow and you'll hate me. I don't want that. If you weren't drunk, it'd be different, but . . ."

"What, I'm not your type or something?"

"No, that's not what I'm saying. I'm saying . . ."

"You're just like Brad and that ass-wipe Yuri, aren't you? I mean, I'm almost forty for God's sake. Is that the problem?"

"No! Hell, no. You're beautiful," DeMarco said. "There's no woman on this planet I'd rather go to bed with. But not this way, not tonight."

She walked toward him. He wondered if she was going to kiss him again. If she did, he wouldn't be able to resist.

"Go fuck yourself," she said, and slammed the door in his face.

Chapter 39

Marty Taylor had disappeared.

He wasn't at home or at his office, and he wasn't answering his cell phone—and this was making Yuri quite angry. He was going to hurt Marty when he found him. In fact, he thought he might have Ivan jam Marty's cell phone up his rectum as a way of reminding him to answer his phone in the future.

Yuri told Ivan to take a couple of men and find the fool. He gave him a list of Marty's usual haunts: the marinas where he kept his boats, beaches where he liked to surf, and several bars where he liked to drink and look out at the ocean.

"Does he have a woman?" Ivan asked.

"Not right now," Yuri said. Then he laughed. "Marty isn't the ladies' man he used to be. He's been a bit despondent lately."

DeMarco waited for Angela in the hotel lobby, wondering how she'd act toward him after what had happened last night. Not sleeping with her had been the right thing to do. So why didn't he feel like he'd done the right thing? All he felt was regret for not having gone to bed with the most desirable woman he'd ever met.

And he felt even worse when he saw her get off the elevator, the trim body, the good legs, the long hair hanging to her shoulders. She was wearing sunglasses this morning—probably to hide bloodshot eyes—but the sunglasses just made her seem more glamorous. To use an expression from his teenage days, Angela DeCapria just turned his crank.

"Hey," he said when she reached him.

She ignored him and kept walking—so he followed her to their rental car, regretting with each step having lost an opportunity that he was sure would never come again.

———✦———

They were two blocks from the hotel before she finally spoke.

"Thanks," she said, her voice sounding hoarse.

"For what?" DeMarco asked.

"For not . . . you know."

"Sure," DeMarco said.

"And that's all I'm going to say about last night. I had too much to drink, I said a bunch of things I shouldn't have said, and almost did something stupid. And it'll never happen again."

Oh, man, don't say that.

———✦———

"We're going to save Marty Taylor's life," Angela said.

"I thought LaFountaine was hoping that Yuri would just whack Marty? You know, save the government all the time and trouble of actually having to prove he's guilty."

"He changed his mind. He doesn't want to sit around forever waiting for Yuri to take care of Tully, and it occurred to him yesterday if Marty disappears that'll put pressure on Yuri and maybe make him move quicker against Tully."

"So what are we going to do? Kidnap Taylor?"

"Don't be ridiculous. What we're going to do is convince him that his only option at this point is to be the government's best witness against Yuri and let us hide him until the right time comes. Then, after Yuri takes care of Tully, we'll turn Taylor over to the Bureau and they can nail his ass to the wall."

DeMarco shook his head. "In case you haven't noticed, LaFountaine's plans haven't been working out too well. He figured Tully would take care of Rudman, but that hasn't happened yet. And maybe Yuri will decide that going after Tully is too risky and, thanks to you warning him yesterday, he may just take off."

"I've got my orders."

There was no point going down that road again, so instead DeMarco asked, "What makes you think Taylor's going to be willing to risk his life by agreeing to testify against Yuri, not to mention giving up his reputation without a fight?"

"We're gonna be persuasive," Angela said.

Marty Taylor straddled his surfboard, four hundred yards from the beach, looking over his shoulder at the incoming waves. He'd been sitting there a long time, at least half an hour. The waves weren't great today but he didn't really care. He was content just looking out at the ocean.

He needed to get free of Yuri. His life just couldn't go on the way it was. It was time to stop thinking about it and take some kind of action.

This thing with Diller had been the last straw. The fact that Yuri had killed Diller—and had used him to help—didn't bother him as much as the fact that the Justice Department was coming after him. Right now he didn't see that they had a case, or so the old lawyer, Porter Henry, said—and Marty's own lawyers agreed—but God knows what sort of mistakes Yuri and Diller might have made.

Nor could he stand Yuri running his life any longer. He'd become the man's puppet, a frightened, trembling puppet. He didn't want to die and he didn't want to go to jail and he didn't want to be poor, but he knew that if he didn't do something to help himself, one or all of those things were going to happen. Yet for some reason he just couldn't seem to do *anything*.

Like cashing out his assets. He'd been thinking about contacting a broker to get things started but he hadn't done it yet. He was afraid

Yuri would catch him if he tried to sell his possessions but it was more than that. It was as if he didn't have the energy, much less the will, to do anything. He'd read that's what happened when you were clinically depressed but he didn't know for sure. Until he'd met Yuri, he'd never been depressed.

Then he saw a wave. And he caught it. And for maybe a hundred seconds he forgot about his problems.

"There he is," Angela said.

DeMarco looked out at the beach. There were two dozen people on it: kids running around shrieking when their feet touched the water, mothers watching the kids shrieking, teenagers with surfboards, all of them tanned and in good shape—particularly the girls.

Sitting apart from everyone was a well-built man in his late thirties. He had longish blond hair and baggy swim trunks decorated with cartoon characters, and he was lying on his back, using his elbows to prop himself up on the sand as he looked out at the water. Next to him was a red surfboard.

"How did you know where to find him?" DeMarco asked.

"I've had someone watching him."

Just like that: *I've had someone watching him.*

Angela opened the driver's-side door, swung her legs out, and took off her shoes. Then she stood up, raised her skirt a bit, and pulled down her pantyhose. She was one of the few young women DeMarco knew who still wore pantyhose and he wondered why she did. Knowing her, it was probably a professional dress-code thing. All he knew for sure was that watching her take them off was killing him.

"You might want to take off your shoes and socks," she said. "That sand looks pretty wet."

DeMarco did what she said and rolled up his pant cuffs. The sand felt good squishing between his toes and he wished they were sitting on a blanket, drinking champagne, watching the waves come in.

He wished her husband was dead.

"Mr. Taylor, may we speak with you?" Angela asked.

Taylor turned his head and looked up. He was a good-looking guy, DeMarco thought, but right now he didn't seem like the super-rich, girl-chasing playboy he was supposed to be. He looked like a sad, lost little kid—but maybe that was because of the stupid swim trunks.

"Uh, I guess," Taylor said. "Who are you?"

Angela pulled a badge case from her purse and flipped it open. "Pamela Walker, Department of Justice."

"Aw, Christ," Taylor muttered.

DeMarco noticed that Taylor didn't even look at Angela's badge when she flashed it, which was good since the woman in the ID picture had blonde hair and Angela wasn't wearing her wig.

"What's this about?" Taylor asked. "More questions about Conrad Diller? I've already told you people he wasn't working for me when he went to Iran. I didn't have any idea he was going there."

"We know that, Mr. Taylor," Angela said. "When Diller went to Iran he was working for Yuri Markelov."

Taylor didn't say anything but judging by the expression on his face, the fact that they had linked Yuri to him was a body blow.

"Because of Diller," Angela continued, "we're now investigating you and your company. We don't have proof yet, but we believe that we'll eventually be able to show that Markelov has been using your company to launder money, move stolen goods, and do other illegal things. We also suspect, whether he coerced you or not, that you'll be implicated in his activities, including Diller's trip to Iran. To put it another way, you're going to be convicted as an accomplice to crimes that Yuri Markelov has committed."

"So what do you want? You didn't come here to tell me I'm being investigated."

"We want you to agree to testify against Markelov."

Taylor didn't say anything.

"But the first thing we want to do," Angela said, "is put you in protective custody. The Bureau is moving fast, and it won't be long before Markelov knows that we're going after him, and when he does he'll kill you. He knows you can put him in prison if you testify against him."

"I'm not admitting anything, but what do I get if I testify?"

"Maybe immunity. As a minimum, a reduced sentence, depending on what you've done."

Taylor looked out at the ocean and DeMarco saw what he was looking at. There was a girl standing knee high in the surf. She was wearing a black bikini, was tanned and lithe, and maybe sixteen years old. She was gorgeous but not in a sexy way, more in a pure beauty-of-youth way. And unlike Marty Taylor, she had her whole life ahead of her.

Taylor turned back to face Angela.

"Immunity isn't good enough. I'll give you Yuri; I'll even testify that I saw him murder a man. But what I want in return is all my assets not connected to my company."

"I don't understand," Angela said.

"I'm saying the government can give me a big fine but no jail time, and to pay the fine, you can have my share of the company. But my houses, my cars, my boats, all that stuff, I want the government to sell them and give me the cash. And I want to be put into the witness protection program and relocated to someplace where I can surf. And I want everyone in my family protected from Yuri."

DeMarco could tell that Angela was just as shocked as he was that Taylor was capitulating so easily. She pretended to think about what Taylor had said for a couple of minutes, a frown on her face as if she found his demands unreasonable, then said, "Okay, you got a deal."

Now Taylor looked surprised. "You have the authority to make that deal, right here on the spot?" he asked.

"Yes," Angela said.

What a liar, DeMarco was thinking.

"I want it in writing."

"We'll give it to you in writing. But right now you need to come with us," Angela said. "We need to put you someplace where you're safe from Markelov."

Taylor started to say something but then he looked past Angela, down the beach. "I swear to God, I'm cursed," he said.

DeMarco turned to see what he was looking at and saw three guys coming toward them. The one in the lead was a huge son of a bitch with a goatee.

Angela saw the men at the same moment and muttered, "Shit."

"Have you guys got guns?" Taylor asked.

"No," Angela said, and DeMarco wondered why she was lying. She had her gun in her purse.

"Well, those are Yuri's guys, and they do. And I'm guessing they're here to take me to him. So unless you want to get killed, I'd suggest you boogie on out of here."

"Can you remember a phone number?" Angela asked.

The men were now about fifty yards away.

"Sure," Taylor said. He smiled sadly and added, "I'm a genius."

Angela gave him her cell phone number and Taylor repeated it.

Yuri's men were now twenty yards away and DeMarco noticed that Angela was facing away from them.

Taylor pointed up the beach and said loudly, "You walk that way, maybe half a mile, and you'll see it. They make a great breakfast. The scones are to die for."

"Thanks," Angela said, and immediately started walking in the direction that Taylor had pointed, with DeMarco trailing slightly behind her.

———◆———

DeMarco caught up with Angela.

"Why didn't you just show those guys your badge? They would have backed off. They weren't going to start a gun fight with a federal agent on a beach full of people."

"That one guy, the moose with the goatee? He saw me at Yuri's place yesterday. He might have recognized me even without the wig and I couldn't let that happen. That could screw up what we want Yuri to do."

DeMarco looked back over his shoulder. Taylor and Yuri's three guys were walking back to the parking lot. The big guy had his arm around Taylor's shoulders and Taylor looked small next to him.

"Well, this might be the last time we'll see Marty Taylor alive," DeMarco said.

"Will you just shut up," Angela said.

"Where was he?" Yuri asked Ivan.

"Surfing."

"Marty, haven't I told you before that I always want to be able to reach you?"

"Hey, what can I say? I forgot to charge the battery in my phone. What's the big fuckin' deal here?"

Yuri looked at Ivan—and Ivan kidney punched Marty and he collapsed to the floor.

"If this ever happens again," Yuri said, "I'll put a chain around your neck and connect it to a stake in my backyard. Just the way I chain up my dog when he misbehaves. Do you understand?"

"Yeah," Marty said, barely able to speak through the pain. He was going to be pissing blood for days.

"Good. You're going to stay here in my house for the next couple of days. I want you where I can keep an eye on you. And there's something I need you to do."

Marty couldn't help himself. He just had to say it. "It's not your house; it's *my* house."

Yuri looked at Ivan again, and Ivan kicked Marty in the tailbone.

"What do we do now?" DeMarco asked.

"We wait. We wait to see if Taylor can get away from Yuri. We wait to see if Yuri goes after Rulon Tully. We wait to see if Tully takes care of Rudman."

DeMarco shook his head, thinking that this was classic CIA be-havior. They put all these complicated, devious plans in motion with-out having any idea what the outcome might be or any real control over it. This was how they got in trouble in places like Cuba, Iran, and Nicaragua—and those were just a few of their more well-known fiascos. The only good news was that the CIA operation currently under way in Southern California didn't involve entities with full-fledged armies or nuclear weapons.

"Do you still have people watching Taylor and Yuri?"

"Not anymore," Angela said. "Our job isn't to protect these people. And we don't want to be witnesses to whatever happens."

"So you're going to just let the chips fall where they fall, and in the meantime we sit around doing nothing?"

Angela didn't answer; her lips just thinned into that stubborn line he was becoming used to.

But then, DeMarco thought, maybe sitting around doing noth-ing wasn't a bad thing.

"Are we going to stay here in San Diego?" he said.

"Yeah. Yuri's here and so is Taylor. Tully's at his home near Ventura and we can get there in three hours if we drive, faster than that if I commandeer a chopper."

"So you wanna see the sights while we're waiting?"

"We're not on vacation, DeMarco."

"No, but there's no reason to spend our time sitting in a hotel room, staring at the walls."

She thought about that a moment. "What do you wanna do?" she asked.

"How 'bout we go to Sea World?"

"Sea World! What are you? Twelve years old?"

"Well, then, how 'bout . . ."

"Actually, Sea World might be kinda fun," she said.

And it was.

Chapter 40

The florist had been watching Rulon Tully's estate for three days. He was tired, dirty from lying on the ground, and the sun beating down on his head was giving him a headache. None of these things would have particularly bothered him—he had endured far worse physical discomfort in the past—but what did bother him was that he was wasting his time.

From his research at the library he had learned that Tully had homes and businesses all over the world and could be just about anywhere on the planet. His primary residence, however, was his ocean-side mansion north of Ventura and, since his divorce, he rarely left the place.

The first day, the florist had parked on Highway 101. According to Google Earth, MapQuest, and a detailed contour map he had purchased at a sporting goods store, Rulon Tully's home was one point four miles from the highway, behind a series of low hills. He could have driven directly to Tully's front door—the maps showed an access road off the 101 that would get him there—but he'd decided that wouldn't be prudent.

He had walked quickly but cautiously through the thigh-high brush covering the hills—the type of brush that fueled California's famous, destructive wildfires. After thirty-five minutes he came to the top of a small hill and had his first glimpse of Tully's estate. He dropped onto his belly and raised binoculars to his eyes.

The house was enormous and sat on at least ten acres, maybe twenty. There were two guest cottages, a six-car garage, an immense swimming pool, a tennis court, cascading fish ponds, and countless exotic, blooming plants. The florist couldn't help but admire the flora and the skill of Tully's gardeners.

That first day he had watched until dark and then left to get the supplies he would need to observe the place for several days: night-vision binoculars, water, food he could eat without cooking, a sleeping bag. He needed to confirm that Tully was in the house and, if he was, develop a plan to take him.

The second day of his surveillance he arrived before dawn with the items he had purchased and, while it was still dark, he had dug a small trench with his hands behind two tall bushes. He cut down a couple of other bushes and placed them on the ground to further camouflage his hiding place and lined the trench with his new sleeping bag. Then he had lain there and watched Tully's house all that day, late into the night, and all the next day.

He did confirm that Tully was in the house. The man came outside once to stand on a balcony while he talked on a cell phone—he appeared to be shouting at whoever was at the other end of the line—and one other time to smoke a cigar. As he smoked his cigar, the florist had studied Tully's face through his binoculars and was struck by what an odd-looking little man he was. And judging by the expression on his face he was getting no enjoyment from the cigar, his beautiful gardens, and his magnificent ocean view. He just stood there puffing and scowling, a man who had everything and was pleased by nothing. But other than learning that Tully was in residence, he learned nothing else that would allow him to take the man.

After three days of watching, he decided it was going to be impossible to penetrate Tully's security. His house was a fortress, perched on a cliff overlooking the ocean. It was surrounded by a ten-foot adobe fence and there were cameras everywhere: on the fence, on the eaves of the house, on various trees. It didn't look like there was any place not covered by a camera. On the fence he could see devices, prob-

ably motion detectors, that would alert Tully's security force if anyone tried to scale the wall. The cliff on the west side of the house
was sheer; a skilled climber could ascend it—but he wasn't a skilled
climber, and even an expert would have difficulty ascending the cliff
at night. He also imagined that Tully had some type of electronic
security that monitored the cliff in case anyone tried to breach the
estate from the sea.

There were a total of six security guards, three on each twelve-hour
shift. One guard sat in a small, stone hut by the main gate, and the
florist assumed that within the hut was the monitoring equipment
for the cameras and motion detectors. The other two guards roamed
the estate continuously, in a random pattern. The gates looked strong
enough to stop anything smaller than a tank from crashing through
them, and he imagined if any attempt was made to invade the house,
alarms would sound and a signal would be sent to the nearest police
department. And considering Tully's wealth, the police would respond immediately and in force. To stop the police from being alerted
not only would it be necessary to cut the landlines going to the house,
but he would also have to destroy any cell phone transmission tow-
ers that provided cell phone service for the area. But even that might
not be enough if Tully used radios or a satellite phone for a backup
communication system.

It was time to develop a Plan B. It would take a team of heavily
armed men to breach Tully's security and the team would need technical expertise, not just muscle and firepower. If all he had wanted to
do was kill Tully, it would have been simple. He was an expert marks-
man and he could have killed Tully with a long-range rifle shot the
next time the little man ventured outside. He didn't have a rifle but
getting one wouldn't be a problem. The problem was that he had to
talk to Tully before he killed him.

He turned his attention to the access road leading to Tully's estate. It came off the 101 and was approximately two miles long. Tully's
security was able to see vehicles approaching when they were within
half a mile of the house, but beyond the half mile point the access

road wasn't visible from the house because the road curved and then disappeared from view as it wound through the small hills surrounding the estate.

It might be possible, he thought, to set up an ambush on the access road, but that would be difficult for one man working alone. And as security conscious as Tully appeared to be, he assumed that some of Tully's bodyguards would accompany him whenever he left the house and he might even travel in an armored car.

So. He couldn't breach the house and an ambush on the access road was highly problematic. It appeared the only option he had was to wait until Tully left his home, then follow him and try to catch him alone the way he had done with Jimmy Franco. He'd been lucky with Franco and maybe he'd get lucky with Tully as well—but he didn't like any plan that relied on luck as a primary component.

He picked up the binoculars again to examine the house and just as he did he saw a flash of light off to his right. He turned his head slowly and looked in that direction. There was another small hill to the north of his position and he could see two men on the hill, lying on their bellies, partially hidden by low-growing shrubs. One of the men had binoculars and he appeared to be doing exactly what the florist was doing—studying Tully's house.

Who were these men and why were they watching Tully's house?

Chapter 41

"It's not going to be easy to invade Tully's house," Mikhail told Yuri.

Mikhail Biryukov was ex-KGB. The collapse of the Soviet Union, combined with a new group of bureaucrats in the Russian government, had ended his career. He could have retired, he was old enough, but there was no such thing as a Russian pension plan that provided a living wage. The only pension ex-KGB personnel had was what they managed to steal when they were in power, and Mikhail hadn't stolen enough. So now he worked for Yuri and Uncle Lev.

He and Yuri were sitting in the sunroom of the house in Coronado that Yuri had taken from Marty Taylor. The sunroom was Yuri's favorite room because of the view, and Mikhail loved the view as well. In fact, he loved everything about San Diego. As soon as he had enough money—he was very careful when he stole from Yuri—he would retire here. He didn't want to see snow again for as long as he lived.

Usually, Yuri used him for activities that didn't really make use of his talents. He supervised Yuri's thugs, provided security for some of Yuri's operations, and was always in charge of moving contraband in and out of the country. And if Yuri wanted someone killed, he'd do that, too, although Ivan was usually given those assignments. It was not particularly challenging work but every once in a while a job would come along that required more than muscle and intimidation. This was one of those jobs.

"Rudy and I observed his place for an entire day," Mikhail said. "We can't breach the gates unless we use explosives and if we try to scale the walls, his security people will know it. If they don't kill us coming over the wall, they'll be able to barricade themselves inside the house and hold us off indefinitely. And unless we disable the landline, cut his alarm system, and jam their cell phone transmissions, his security people will be able to call for reinforcements from the local police."

"How many security people does he have?" Yuri asked.

"There are always three armed guards on the estate; they work two twelve-hour shifts. His head of security lives on the property as well. There are other people in the house during the day—gardeners, maids, secretaries, cooks, and so forth—but none of them stay overnight. So he's always protected by at least four people. But, like I said, the problem isn't the number of guards he has. The problem is that I can't find a way to get inside the estate before his guards call the police and barricade themselves inside. And a gun battle with automatic weapons could destroy many of the valuable things he owns."

Yuri lit a cigarette and stared at Mikhail through a veil of smoke. He didn't like what he was hearing and was waiting for Mikhail to say something that he would like.

"The best thing to do," Mikhail said, "is take him when he leaves the house."

He took out a hand-drawn map that showed the access road leading to the estate. The map was drawn to scale because Mikhail believed in doing things right. Taking a pen from his pocket to use as a pointer, he explained, "This road goes from the highway to his house. Do you see this curve? I'll put a vehicle across the road that will force Tully's car to stop, and a second vehicle, something with four-wheel drive, in this gully here. The second vehicle won't be visible at night. Tully's driver will stop when he sees our blocking vehicle, and our second vehicle will come out of the gully and box him in from behind. After we kill the security people Tully has with him in his car, we'll take him back to his house and—"

"Is Tully's vehicle armored?"

"No. When I was researching Tully, I found out that he was in a minor automobile accident two years ago, and the man who was driving at the time was cited by the police and later fired by Tully. Ivan and I paid a visit to the driver. He said Tully normally travels in a Mercedes Benz sedan. It has bulletproof windows and puncture-resistant tires, but it's not armored. But whenever Tully goes anywhere, his head of security is always with him as well as an armed driver."

"Will Tully's ex-driver tell anyone that you visited him?"

"No. Like I said, Ivan accompanied me."

Yuri gestured for Mikhail to continue.

"If we take Tully on the access road, we may have to disable his vehicle and we can't leave it sitting on the road riddled with bullet holes. So I'll use a tow truck to block the access road, and after we have Tully we'll tow his Mercedes back to his house. Then Tully, with my gun pressed against his ribs, will tell his guards that the Mercedes broke down and to open the gates to allow it to be put inside the garage."

"Won't his security people see the bullet holes in the Mercedes?"

"No. Remember, it will be dark and the tow truck will obscure the vehicle it's towing."

"Won't his people wonder why he didn't call back to the estate and tell them to come and pick him up after the Mercedes broke down?"

"Probably, but guards don't question their boss. If Tully tells them to open the gates, they will, and then we'll eliminate the guards."

Yuri lit another cigarette. He looked at the map a bit longer, then closed his eyes and reviewed Mikhail's plan in his mind.

"What's to keep Tully from calling the police when you stop his car on the access road?" he asked.

"I will have to purchase a cell-phone jammer. The one I need will cost about five thousand dollars."

It would actually cost two thousand.

"Is there a radio in Tully's car?"

"No," Mikhail said. "His ex-driver said they only use cell phones to communicate from the car. But there is a problem that I haven't addressed. Tully rarely leaves his house, and in order for this plan to work, we need him to leave at night, at a prearranged time. I can't sit with half a dozen men and a tow truck parked indefinitely on the access road."

Yuri rose from the chair where he'd been sitting, walked over to a window, and stood there for a while looking out at the bay. God, he was going to miss this place.

"I think I can get him to leave his house," he finally said. "Be ready to go tomorrow night."

"Okay," Mikhail said. He could tell that Yuri was expecting him to leave, but he remained seated.

"Is there something else?" Yuri asked.

"You realize that if we do this, we're going to get an enormous amount of attention from the authorities. Does Uncle Lev know what you're planning?"

"Of course," Yuri said. "Do you think I'd do something of this magnitude without consulting him?"

Only if you have a death wish, Mikhail thought.

<hr />

Marty Taylor was locked in a bedroom in Yuri's house—*his* house. He was allowed out for meals and to use the bathroom but otherwise forced to stay in the room. They'd taken his cell phone and there was no landline in the room.

The bedroom was on the second floor. There was a window he could have crawled through, and if he hung by his arms from the window ledge, he probably wouldn't break his legs when he dropped. The problem wasn't breaking a leg, however; the problem with a window escape was that Yuri's rip-your-balls-off pit bull roamed the backyard.

Marty had no idea what Yuri was planning but he was planning something. He'd seen and heard Yuri's thugs coming and going from the house all day. But the most worrisome thing was the task that Yuri had given him: he had been told to write down all his major assets and where they were located.

He had waited too long to sell his stuff.

He was lying on the bed with his eyes closed, trying to remember how much he'd told Yuri about his possessions. Yuri knew, of course, about his yacht, his sailboat, and his other house in San Diego. All of his cars were parked at the San Diego houses, so Yuri knew about them, too. He might even know about the damn racehorse, because Marty thought he remembered bitching to him one time about how the animal was only good for its semen. The good news was that he didn't think he'd ever told Yuri about the house in Maui and the land in Arizona. And something else he might be able to hide was some of the artwork he'd purchased over the years. There was artwork in both San Diego houses, including some really expensive sculptures, but a lot of other pieces were stored in a secure, temperature-controlled warehouse in La Jolla.

If he was lucky, and depending on Yuri's memory, he might be able to hide an old racehorse, a dozen pieces of very valuable art, the land in Arizona, and the house in Maui. He figured the most he'd get from selling those things was, at best, five million—which was not nearly enough for him to live the rest of his life the way he'd been living the last fifteen years. What he had to do was get away from the bastard and call that lady from the Justice Department. And he needed to escape before Yuri sold all of his possessions—and then killed him.

The door to the bedroom opened. His main babysitter was a man named Andrei, a stocky, mean-looking little prick in his fifties. Marty was taller, stronger, and younger than Andrei but none of that mattered because Andrei carried a pistol in a shoulder holster.

"Get up," Andrei said. "The boss wants to talk to you. He said bring the list."

Shit.

Yuri was standing at the bar in the sunroom drinking iced coffee when Marty entered. He directed Marty to take a seat on the couch.

"Let me see," Yuri said, holding out a hand.

Marty passed him the list and Yuri put on his reading glasses to study it.

"I thought you owned a house in Hawaii," Yuri said.

Shit.

"I do, but it's co-owned with a guy I went to Stanford with."

Yuri looked at him for a moment, apparently to see if he was lying, but Marty didn't even blink.

"Where are the deeds for the houses, titles for the cars and boats, provenances for the artwork?"

"My accountant keeps all that stuff."

"Okay," Yuri said. "I want you to call your accountant today and tell him to have the necessary papers delivered here. Andrei will be on the line with you when you make the call, and Andrei's English is excellent."

Shit.

Yuri handed Marty a four-page document and a pen.

"Don't read it, just sign it. That gives me power of attorney."

Marty just looked at the document, then shook his head. He didn't shake his head because he was refusing to do what Yuri wanted—he shook it in disbelief that this was happening to him—but the next thing he knew he was on the floor and his head was ringing. He looked up and saw Andrei standing over him with a pistol in his hand; Marty's blood was on the barrel.

Marty struggled back onto the couch—and signed the power of attorney.

Yuri handed him a business card. "I want you to call that woman and tell her you want to sell your houses in San Diego and you want them sold fast, even if you have to take a loss. Tell her you'll find another agent if the houses aren't sold in a week and she'll lose an enormous commission."

Yuri handed him a second card. "Call that man and tell him to sell your cars, except for the Porsche I'm using. Tell him to send people here and to your other place to pick them up. I want all the vehicles stored in his warehouse in Chula Vista by tomorrow."

The son of bitch had really thought this through.

Yuri handed him a third card. "That woman will take care of the artwork in both houses. Tell her to send people who know how to package things so that they won't get damaged."

Jesus. He *had* to figure out some way to slow this thing down.

Turning to Andrei, Yuri said, "Have Stephan go over to Marty's other house to supervise the movers. You stay and take care of things here."

Andrei grunted acknowledgment of the order.

"When you talk to those agents," Yuri said to Marty, "you'll tell them that I have power of attorney and you've authorized me to act on your behalf regarding all sales. Give them my cell phone number. And when you call, Andrei will be listening and if he hears you tell these people anything other than what I've told you—if, for example, you imply that I'm forcing you to sell—Andrei will put your left hand into the garbage disposal and not remove it until your fingers are gone. You may need your right hand to sign papers in the future."

Marty looked over at Andrei. The thug was standing next to him, at the end of the couch, looking at him dispassionately, probably prepared to smack him in the head again. If he was quick enough, he might be able to pull the gun from Andrei's shoulder holster and blow Yuri's head off. But he knew he wasn't going to try. He had the speed—but he didn't have the guts.

"Is that all?" Marty asked.

"No, there's one more thing. I want you to call Rulon Tully right now. I want you to set up a meeting with him for tomorrow, or the next day at the latest. And I want the meeting to be someplace other than his house and it has to be after nine p.m."

"Tully? He won't talk to me. He hates me."

"Well, if he doesn't talk to you then you're of no use to me, Marty. And I'm not the sort of person who keeps useless things."

———◆———

"That was Marty Taylor," Rulon Tully said as he put down the phone.

As expected, Quinn didn't respond.

"He wants to meet with me," Tully said. "He says he wants to sell me his company."

Quinn looked out the window. There was a hawk circling in the distance, looking for something to kill.

"This doesn't make sense," Tully said. "I mean, I can understand him wanting to dump the company, it's a sinking ship, but why call me? He knows how I feel about him. He said the reason he wants to sell to me is because he figures I can turn things around, and the only reason he cares about that is because he doesn't want to see all his people lose their jobs."

Tully pushed off with his foot against the drafting table and his stool spun around, a weak, single-turn spin.

"Looking out for his people, I can buy that part," Tully said. "He always was a bleeding heart. And I *am* in a good position to save the company, or at least parts of it, but there's at least three other guys I can think of that could do that, too."

Quinn looked at his watch.

Tully screamed, "Well, goddamnit, what do you think he's up to?"

"I have no idea, Mr. Tully. I'm your chief of security, not your financial advisor. I know nothing about running your business."

Tully started to tell the wooden bastard that he just wanted a sounding board, a commonsense assessment of the situation, but what was the point? He rubbed his small chin and thought some more.

"I suppose it could be guilt making him do this. He feels bad for . . . well, you know, and this is his way of making it up to me. Or maybe he thinks if he does this, I'll stop coming after him, which, of course, I won't. Hmm. No, I think I was right the first time. He thinks this is the best way to get out of the business and keep some of his people employed."

Tully spun around on the drafting stool again.

"I think I'll meet him. I want to watch him grovel. And I want to find out how much trouble he's in with the feds."

"When's the meeting?" Quinn asked.

"Tonight at ten."

"Where?"

"A restaurant in Ventura."

Quinn shook his head. "Why not have him come here? That would be better from a security standpoint."

"He said he wanted to meet on neutral ground, like that's gonna make a difference." Before Quinn could say anything else, Tully laughed and said, "Yeah, I'm going to meet with the bastard. I'm going to tell him that I'm never going to stop until I've destroyed him. Then I'm going to spit in his eye."

Chapter 42

———❖———

The florist was parked on Highway 101. Directly across from his position was the entrance to the access road leading to Rulon Tully's estate.

Since he hadn't been able to figure out a way to take Tully from his house, he had decided that he would wait for Tully to leave the estate, follow him, then hope some opportunity presented itself the way it had with Jimmy Franco. The problem with this plan—if you could call it a plan—was he had no idea *when* Tully would leave. He could be waiting for days, if not weeks. But what else could he do?

He realized the answer to that question was obvious: he could simply go back to Virginia and resume his life—but he knew he wasn't going to do that.

He poured another cup of coffee from his thermos, his third cup in the last two hours. He was fighting to stay awake and it was only nine p.m. He thought again about the two men he had seen the day before, the ones spying on Tully's estate at the same time he had been. He had no idea who they were or what they had been doing. One of the men—the older, gray-haired one—looked like he could have been a cop, but his companion—a stocky brute with tattooed arms—looked more like a criminal than a cop. The most likely explanation for their presence was that the two men were robbers casing Tully's house. If they were robbers, and if they had any intelligence at all, they would have quickly concluded that breaking into Tully's place would be nearly impossible. Whoever they were, he could only hope that whatever they were doing didn't interfere with his plans.

There was that word again: *plan*. He had no plan.

He lit a cigarette. He couldn't believe after ten years of not smoking he was smoking again. True, he was under some stress, but he was still disgusted with his lack of willpower. He yawned. He decided he would wait half an hour more, then return to his motel and get some sleep. There was little chance that Tully would be going out at this late hour.

He wondered idly if there was some way he could force Tully to leave his home. The only thing that had occurred to him was to start a brush fire near the estate and hope it would become large enough to force Tully to evacuate. The problem with that idea was the coastal winds were notoriously unpredictable, and a fire was just as likely to destroy other homes in the area, and people and firemen could be killed. He wouldn't do that.

A police car drove by at that moment, and another thought occurred to him: he could impersonate a cop. He could kidnap a cop, take the cop's uniform and his car, drive up to Tully's estate, and force Tully's security people to let him in under some pretext. Once inside, he would take Tully from the estate at gunpoint. The downside with that plan—other than kidnapping a cop—was Tully's people would see his face and with all the surveillance cameras on the estate they would end up with a picture of him. Still, he liked the idea. He would need to figure out a way to get a cop to come to him in some isolated spot, overcome the man, and, because he didn't want to kill a cop, he'd have to find a place to put him for a day or two. But all that could be done. And it was certainly better than sitting indefinitely on the highway waiting for Tully to appear. He wished the idea had occurred to him earlier.

Tomorrow, he would . . .

A tow truck had just stopped in the left-turn lane, the lane that turned onto the access road. He wondered if one of Tully's cars had broken down, but if one had it seemed odd to be calling for a tow truck so late at night. Then a second vehicle, a Range Rover, pulled into the turn lane behind the tow truck, and the florist was almost positive the man in the passenger seat of the Rover was the gray-haired man who had been watching Tully's house. What was going on?

The tow truck, with the Range Rover following, turned onto the access road. The florist hesitated for a moment and then started his car. He gave the other vehicles a two-minute lead and followed them down the access road with his headlights off. He knew where they were going. They were going to the blind curve, the ambush curve. He didn't know why he was so sure of this, but he was. When he was about a hundred yards from the curve he stopped his car on the side of the access road, got out, and began crawling through the low shrubs near the road.

There they were. The tow truck was parked sideways, effectively blocking the road, but he couldn't see the Range Rover. Ah, it had backed down into a shallow gully. Their plan was obvious; it was just what he would have done if he'd had men working with him. If Tully left his estate, the tow truck would block his way in front and the Range Rover would come out of the gully and box him in from behind.

He couldn't imagine, however, that these men planned to stay parked on the access road indefinitely, so he figured they must have information that Tully was planning to leave his house tonight. But *why* were they ambushing him? The most logical answer was they were planning to kidnap him. Tully was enormously wealthy and his company would pay a fortune to ransom him. Or maybe they wanted to murder him; from what the florist had read, Tully had certainly made more than his share of enemies.

Whatever the case, this was the opportunity he had been looking for.

———◆———

Yuri smiled at the young waitress and ordered a second cup of coffee. He was always surprised at the number of beautiful waitresses in

California; he supposed half of them were would-be film stars—or maybe good genes just abounded in this golden state.

He was at a cafe on the 101, and the plan was for him to wait there until Mikhail called and told him he had captured Tully and breached his estate. Once he received the call, it would take him only fifteen minutes to get to Tully's place. He could have gone with Mikhail and the others and directed the operation himself, but he had no desire to be involved in the gunfight that was likely to occur when Mikhail took Tully. That was the reason he employed people like Mikhail: to take the risks—and the bullets.

He was impressed, as always, by Mikhail's attention to detail. All of Mikhail's men would wear masks and gloves. Once they were inside Tully's estate, they would try not to kill his security force immediately; they might need them later to help move Tully's possessions. Two large moving vans were parked at a rest stop ten miles farther down the highway, and the drivers would be called when Mikhail was ready to begin moving things from the house. In the morning, Tully's staff would arrive—the gardeners, the secretaries, his cook, his masseuse—and these people would be allowed inside the gates, then placed in a locked room, except for one of the secretaries who would answer the phones and tell callers that Tully was unavailable.

Yuri planned to complete the operation in less than twenty-four hours. As soon as Mikhail told him everything was under control, he would go to Tully's estate, and while Mikhail's men were moving things from the house into the moving vans, he would force Tully to transfer money to his account in Mexico, where it would be transferred again to another account in Switzerland. By this time tomorrow night, Tully would be dead and his possessions would be on their way to a fence in Los Angeles who had the contacts to sell the sort of exotic things that Tully owned. Yuri hadn't decided if he would kill all of Tully's people when the operation was complete, but once he had killed Tully it wouldn't matter how many other people died because the authorities would react in an overwhelming manner to Tully's death. He would decide when the time came.

The waitress returned with his coffee.

"Thank you," Yuri said. "You're a very pretty girl. Are you an actress?"

———◆———

Xavier Quinn sat in the backseat of the Mercedes with Tully, doing his best to ignore his employer. Tully was as excited as a little kid on his way to the circus—an ugly, spoiled little kid—and the opportunity to meet with Marty Taylor and humiliate him had made him giddy with anticipation. Every once in a while Tully would bark out a laugh and hit the seat next to him with one of his tiny fists. Quinn imagined Tully was thinking about what he would say to Taylor and was laughing about what he expected Taylor's reaction would be.

Rulon Tully was insane.

Quinn decided, at that moment, that he would leave Tully's employment at the end of the month. His initial goal had been to wait until he had banked two million, and he was a man who hated not to meet a goal, but the time had come. Then another thought occurred to him as the maniac on the seat next to him giggled again. He decided he would force Tully to give him the villa he owned near Florence. The villa was small and Tully hadn't used it in years but he would still resent giving it to him. But he would. Quinn had information that could send Tully to prison without ever implicating himself, and Tully knew this. Yes, he liked the idea: Tully's Italian villa would be part of his severance package.

The only thing that concerned him was he had no idea what he would do after he retired. He couldn't just sit in the villa day after day drinking wine and enjoying the view. He supposed he could consult on security problems for wealthy Europeans; they were constantly being kidnapped. He wouldn't have to do it full time, just when he got bored or needed an infusion of cash. And having worked for Tully would impress folks, and he'd ensure that Tully gave him a glowing recommendation. Yes, that might be . . .

"Mr. Quinn," the driver said. "Look."

Quinn stopped daydreaming and looked out the front windshield. There was a large tow truck blocking the road in front of them.

"Stop!" he told the driver.

"What's happening?" Tully asked.

Quinn ignored Tully. "Jack, back up, now! Fast!"

Jack slammed the Mercedes into reverse, spun his head to look behind him, then said, "Oh, shit."

Quinn turned. A Range Rover had come out of a gully on the left side of the road and was now blocking their path.

"Ram it, Jack," Quinn said.

"What's going on?" Tully screamed.

Jack stepped on the gas but the Range Rover was only five feet from the Mercedes's back bumper. Jack hit it hard, but he hadn't been able to get the momentum needed to knock the Rover out of the way.

"Go off the road!" Quinn said. The terrain on the right side of the road was rough and most likely impassable, but they had to try. Then Quinn noticed that two men wearing ski masks had gotten out of the tow truck and were pointing Uzis at them, and before Jack had time to drive off the road both men fired simultaneously and shredded the Mercedes's front tires—and Tully became hysterical.

"Shut up!" Quinn screamed at Tully. He could now see five men, all wearing ski masks. Four of the men held Uzis; the fifth man had his hands down at his side, and Quinn sensed that he was the one in charge. He didn't know how long they had—the bulletproof glass would protect them from the Uzis, but not indefinitely. He pulled out his cell phone to call back to the security force at the estate and speed-dialed the number, but the phone showed he wasn't getting a signal. This was bad.

The leader walked up to the driver's-side door of the Mercedes and Quinn saw that he wasn't unarmed as he'd originally thought. The man tapped on the driver's window with a heavy, long-barreled revolver and, realizing they couldn't hear him inside the Mercedes, made a motion for Jack to roll down the window. The barrel of the revolver was almost nine inches long, and Quinn recognized the weapon. It was a .500 S&W Magnum. The Mercedes had bulletproof glass—which in reality was bullet-*resistant* glass—and it was designed not to shatter when struck by bullets fired from most conventional weapons. The .500 S&W, however, was not a conventional weapon; it was supposedly designed for macho hunters who wanted to use a handgun to go after big game, big game like Kodiak bears.

Tully grabbed Quinn's arm and shrieked, "What's happening?"

Quinn jerked his arm away from Tully's grip. "A kidnapping, I think."

"A kidnapping?"

The man with the Magnum tapped the window again, and again motioned for Jack to open it.

"Yes. So just stay calm," Quinn said to Tully. "They'll take you and ask your company for a ransom and the company will pay it. They're not going to harm you."

"Bullshit!" Tully screamed. "Do something! Get me out of here. That's what I pay you for."

Now the man pointed the revolver at Jack's head, and Quinn yelled, "Jack! Open the door. The glass won't stop that gun."

Tully screamed "No!" but Jack unlocked the doors. The leader stepped back and both Jack and Quinn stepped out of the car, holding their hands up. Quinn knew he was doing the right thing—and the only thing he could do. All he could hope for was that these men were professional kidnappers. They had no reason to kill him and Jack and if they were pros they wouldn't.

The leader told Jack and Quinn to remove their weapons, then opened Tully's door and said, "Mr. Tully, please get out of the car."

"No!" Tully said.

"Ivan," the leader said, and one of his men, a huge brute, reached inside the Mercedes and dragged a screaming, kicking Tully out of the car. The man must have outweighed Tully by almost two hundred pounds, but Tully hit him in the face with one of his small fists, and when he did the big man grabbed him one-handed by the throat, the hand completely encircling Tully's neck, and shook him. "Stop it," he said, and Tully instantly quit struggling. The big man then walked Tully over to the Range Rover, duct-taped his hands behind his back, placed a strip of tape over his mouth, and then shoved him onto the backseat of the Range Rover and closed the door.

"Is this a kidnapping?" Quinn asked calmly.

"No," the leader said—then he nodded to one of his men, and the man pressed down on the trigger of his Uzi and shot Quinn and Jack.

At least two bullets hit Quinn in the chest and he crumpled to the ground. He wasn't in pain but he knew he was dying. He watched helplessly as the man who had shot him walked over and aimed the barrel of the Uzi at his forehead to deliver the coup de grace. Quinn tried to speak but he couldn't.

He wanted to say, *Please kill that little fucker Tully.*

———◆◆◆———

The florist had once been a military man, and he could appreciate what he'd just seen. Tully's abduction had been executed flawlessly—flawlessly but brutally. There had been no reason to kill the driver and Tully's other bodyguard.

The man in charge took off his ski mask, and when he did his men followed. The florist knew from his own experience that ski masks were uncomfortable unless it was very cold. When they removed their masks, he confirmed the leader of the group was indeed the gray-haired man who had been watching Tully's house the other day, and one of the other men present was the man with the tattooed arms.

He heard the leader tell a man called Ivan to put the bodies of the two dead men in the trunk of the Mercedes, and then directed his men to reposition the vehicles and hook the Mercedes up to the tow truck. He noticed the leader spoke English with a Russian accent; he had met a lot of Russians in Iran and he knew a Russian accent when he heard one. He didn't understand why they were hooking Tully's Mercedes up to the tow truck, but while they were doing so, he took advantage of the noise and activity and belly-crawled through the brush until he was lying in the drainage ditch by the side of the road, only ten yards away from the Range Rover that contained Tully.

It took the Russians several minutes to reposition the three vehicles on the narrow access road. When they were finished, the tow truck was pointed toward Tully's estate, Tully's Mercedes was behind the tow truck, and the Range Rover was last in line, also pointed in the direction of the estate. Then the big man called Ivan and two others began to hook the Mercedes to the tow truck, getting in each other's way, cursing, obviously not familiar with the tow truck's controls. While his men worked, the leader took out a cell phone and started to make a call, but then stopped and said to one of his men, "Rudy, shut off the jammer."

Ah, the florist thought: they had a cell phone transmission jammer. Clever.

The leader made his call and the florist heard him say, "Phase One is complete. I'll call you again once we're inside."

The florist realized that this was the best chance he was going to get. The three men connecting the Mercedes to the tow truck had placed their weapons on the ground. Rudy—the man with the tattooed arms—was standing near the Range Rover holding his Uzi loosely with one hand while smoking a cigarette with the other. The gray-haired leader had put the heavy revolver he had been holding on the hood of the Range Rover and was now standing with his arms crossed waiting impatiently for the tow truck operation to be completed.

The florist rushed out of the darkness. He shot Rudy first because he was armed, then the leader, then fired two more shots at the men near the tow truck. He didn't care if he hit the other men; he just wanted to keep them from going after the weapons lying on the ground. He then jumped into the Range Rover containing Rulon Tully, reversed the Rover at full speed up the access road, and disappeared into the night.

He figured it would take the Russians at least ten minutes to come after him. They couldn't make a U-turn on the narrow access road with the Mercedes hooked to the tow truck, so they would have to unhook the Mercedes. The fact that the access road was so narrow had made it ideal for an ambush, but the width of the road now worked completely to the florist's advantage.

He kept the Range Rover in reverse until he reached his rental car, then pulled Tully out of the backseat of the Rover and carried him over to his car. Tully struggled in his arms like an oversized infant, his eyes popping out of his head with fear and rage, and he was attempting to talk even though he had to know he couldn't be understood with the duct tape over his mouth.

The florist dumped Tully into the trunk of his car, and to further delay his pursuers he parked the Range Rover in the middle of the road and threw the keys for the vehicle into the brush.

He was home free—and Rulon Tully was his.

God was with him.

Yuri looked at his watch; it had been thirty minutes since Mikhail had called to tell him Phase One was complete—meaning that he had captured Tully and would soon be proceeding to invade the estate. He knew it would take some time for the men to connect Tully's vehicle to the tow truck, but still, Mikhail should have been inside the estate by now. He wondered if he should drive over and see what was happening, but realized that would be foolish. The fact that he hadn't seen any police cars driving in the direction of Tully's estate with lights flashing and sirens screaming was comforting; if he had seen any, that would have meant Mikhail had failed. But still, why was it taking so long?

His cell phone rang. *Finally,* he thought.

"Yes," he said. He listened for a moment, then screamed, "Son of a bitch!" and his fist slammed down on the table.

The pretty waitress jumped in fright.

Chapter 43

———— ◆◆◆ ————

The florist drove for two hours with Rulon Tully in the trunk of his car. He wanted to find an isolated spot in which to question Tully but he also wanted to put some distance between himself and Tully's estate.

And maybe he also drove for so long because he was delaying what he knew he had to do next.

At two a.m., he stopped at a gas station on a rural road that was closed for the day. He picked the gas station because a single light had been left on at the back, over the restroom doorway. He needed the light because he wanted to see Tully's face when he questioned him.

He pulled his car to the back of the gas station, shut off the headlights, lifted Tully out of the trunk, and propped him up against the restroom door. When he ripped the duct tape from Tully's mouth, the first thing Tully said was, "Tell me how much you want."

Rulon Tully was repugnant. The little man reminded the florist of an evil troll in some dark fairy tale—but not a brave troll. Unlike Jimmy Franco and Benny Mark, the florist didn't have to torture Rulon Tully to get him to talk.

"I don't want money," the florist said. "I want the name of the person who told you about Conrad Diller's trip to Iran."

"What? I don't know what you're talking about," Tully said.

"No. Don't do that. I know a man named Dale Acosta gave the information about Diller to a reporter named Whitmore. I've already killed Whitmore."

Tully's eyes seemed to bug out even farther when he heard this.

"And I know a man named Benny Mark killed Acosta and the man who hired Mark was a man named Franco. I've killed Franco, too. But before he died, Franco told me your chief of security was the one who paid him to have Acosta killed. Which means *you* paid to have Acosta killed, and the reason you killed him was that after Mahata died—"

"Who?"

The florist backhanded Tully sharply across the face. He couldn't believe the man didn't even know her name.

"Mahata Javadi was the CIA agent who died because of Whitmore's story. And you had Acosta killed because you were afraid the CIA would discover that you were behind leaking the information to the press. So don't pretend you don't know what I'm talking about. I've tortured and killed people to get to this point—to get to you. And now you're going to tell me who gave you the information about Diller."

"And if I tell you, then what?" Tully asked.

"Then I won't torture you."

"Look, I'll give you a hundred million dollars to let me go. Did you hear what I said? A *hundred* million. Can you even imagine what you could do with that kind of money?"

The florist smiled at that. "No, the fact is, I can't imagine. I'm a man who was happy selling flowers."

"What?"

The florist took out the .32—Benny Mark's little weapon had served him well—and placed the barrel against Tully's right knee. "Mr. Tully, I'm going to start torturing you now. I'm going to blow out your right kneecap, then your left. It will be extremely painful."

"It was Ray Rudman. Congressman Ray Rudman. He told me about Diller going to Iran and I had Acosta leak the information to a reporter so that traitor Marty Taylor would go to jail. I'm a patriot. I was trying to make sure that Taylor paid for what he was trying to do and that Iran didn't get the technology. I had no idea a spy would get killed."

"Her name was Mahata," the florist said, and he raised the pistol.

"Wait! Why are you doing this?"

"Revenge, Mr. Tully. We're both here because of revenge. You tried to hurt Martin Taylor because you wanted vengeance, not because you're a patriot. And I'm avenging Mahata."

"Two hundred million!" Tully screamed. "I'll give you two hundred million!"

The florist shot Rulon Tully between the eyes.

There was a large stack of old tires at the rear of the gas station and the florist covered Tully's body with some of the tires. He didn't want the body found right away but he was too tired to dig a grave. He figured in a couple of days the body would begin to decay and Tully would be found but, God willing, before then he would have finished with Congressman Rudman.

Before he did anything about Rudman, though, he had to sleep. He hadn't slept in days, not since he started his surveillance of Tully's estate. So he drove to Interstate 5, pulled off at the first exit he saw that advertised lodging, and checked into a Holiday Inn. As soon as he entered his room, and without removing his clothes, he collapsed onto the bed—and then discovered, even as exhausted as he was, that he couldn't sleep.

He should have been a man at peace with himself. He had no reason to feel guilty. He had done only what he had to do, and he should have been content. But the dead—Whitmore and Franco and Tully—and the long dead—his brother and his family—wouldn't allow him to sleep. The dead called out to him, some from hell, some from paradise.

Maybe after he killed Rudman, God would grant him peace.

Chapter 44

Angela was sleeping on her stomach, her face turned away from him, her dark hair fanned out across her bare back. The sheets were pulled down to just past her waist, and at the bottom of the bed, one small, perfect foot was exposed. If DeMarco had been a painter, he would have painted her that way. Since he wasn't one, all he could do was hope his memory would never blur the image. He wanted to remember forever the way she looked at that moment.

He wasn't quite sure how this had happened—but he thanked God it had.

Once he convinced Angela there was no point sitting around and doing nothing while waiting for something to happen with Tully and Yuri, it took a couple of hours for her to stop thinking like a CIA agent and start thinking like a tourist—and when she did, she was a delight to be with. And since neither of them had been to San Diego before, they did the things that tourists do. After Sea World they went to Balboa Park, the Gaslamp Quarter, and the glitzy galleries in La Jolla. They had drinks at the Hotel del Coronado and dinner at a restaurant where they could see the bridge.

He found out that she was a toucher. She'd clutch his forearm to get his attention, tap his chest to make a point, grab his hand as they hurried across a street—and every time she touched him, he felt a little *zing* go through him. She laughed easily and had a sharp, ironic sense of humor, and before long she was teasing DeMarco as if she'd known him for years. She talked about her family—her nagging mother; her depressed, alcoholic father; her perfect, aggravating sister—and the impression DeMarco got was: typical Italian family that fought like cats and dogs, got on each other's nerves, and would do anything for each other. As for her nieces, who were also her godchildren, when she spoke of them she got this look in her eye that said she believed that motherhood would never happen for her and it would be the one thing in her life that she would ultimately regret. He felt achingly sad for her at that moment.

She asked about his family, meaning his dad. He told her he really didn't know what his dad did until he was in his teens and another kid in the neighborhood asked him if his dad kept a bunch of guns in the house. When he asked the kid what the hell he was talking about, the kid said, "Well, he's Carmine Taliaferro's button man, ain't he? He must have a buncha guns." He hit the kid, then went home and asked his mother if what the kid had said was true, and when she wouldn't answer him or look him in the eye, he knew.

"But I never really believed it, not in my heart," he said. "I'm not saying that he wasn't who the papers said he was, but to me he was just my dad. He took me to ball games, he came to *my* ball games, he harped at me about getting an education—just like any other dad on the block. He cooked pancakes every Sunday morning after Mass. I still can't picture him putting a bullet into the back of some guy's head. It broke my heart the day he died."

DeMarco knew by now that he was attracted to a certain type of woman. Physically, he preferred women who looked like his ex-wife, which Angela did: dark hair, dark laughing eyes, trim hips, good legs. His wife had been bustier but Angela's breasts were, as he found out later, perfect. But beyond the physical he was attracted to the kind of bright, aggressive, smart-mouthed Italian Catholic girls he'd grown up with in Queens. The ones that fought with all their brothers when they were young and usually beat them. The ones that went to church every Sunday but swore like sailors when they were pissed. Angela DeCapria was one of those girls.

She wasn't perfect—love wasn't that blind. She had to discuss every item on the menu with the waiter before she ordered and was ridiculously picky about what she ate. She was an annoying, nonstop, backseat driver. She wouldn't admit when she was wrong and had to get the last word in an argument. But he could accept the minor flaws; it was the two major flaws that worried him.

One of those was that when it came to her career she was blindly, dangerously ambitious. For whatever reason, she felt like she had something to prove in the male-dominated world of cops and spies, and she was determined to succeed, no matter what the cost, as evidenced by her current assignment. He knew if she was offered an overseas post in some godforsaken place like the Afghanistan-Pakistan border that was ruled by Taliban gunmen and opium warlords, she'd take the posting without hesitation and DeMarco would just have to live with her decision. And he wasn't sure he could.

The other major flaw was that she was married.

It was most likely a second phone call from her husband, however, that resulted in them going to bed together. The call came when they were eating lunch at Jim Croce's place in the Gaslamp district. DeMarco didn't know what her husband said to her, but all she said was, "Is that right?" and a cold, "Yeah, I'll talk to you later." DeMarco got the impression that ol' Brad had called to let her know he was busy at work but really thinking about her, and it looked like Angela was just weary of all his bullshit. After she hung up, she sat there for a moment, then raised her eyes to DeMarco. "Don't worry," she said. "I'm not going to chug a martini because the jackass called." And then she shook her head, casting out all thoughts of her husband, and said, "So, where are we going next?"

After the phone call she seemed to soften toward him. She became less guarded, looked at him longer, touched him more. He didn't seduce her; she seduced herself. But did she go to bed with him to get back at her husband or did she go to bed with him because she was just glad to be with a man who obviously wanted to be with no one but her? He didn't know—and he didn't care.

It happened on the third day of their mini-vacation, when they were having dinner at a famous, tourist-infested outdoor Mexican restaurant in Old Town San Diego. The place was best known for its gigantic margaritas, and they'd just been served two drinks in glasses the size of goldfish bowls. She reached for her drink then stopped and looked directly into DeMarco's eyes and said, "The other night you wouldn't go to bed with me because I was drunk, and I appreciated that. But I'm not drunk now, although I may be after I finish this drink, so I'm gonna say this before I even take a sip. I've had a great time the last two days, and I've really enjoyed being with you, and when we get back to the hotel you're going to come to my room. Is that okay with you?"

DeMarco had wanted to raise his hand and yell, "Check!" but he knew that wouldn't be cool. So instead he just said, "Yeah, that's okay with me." And when they were in bed, he had that same feeling he'd had the first time they kissed: that she was a perfect fit, designed by an all-knowing God to mold precisely to his body. She was the one made for him.

As he lay next to her he wondered what was going to happen next. Was she going to leave Brad and take up with him? Maybe. Or would she stay married to Brad and see DeMarco on the side? No, that would never happen. She wasn't the sneak-around type—and he was glad she wasn't. Or would she tell DeMarco it had been a wonderful weekend fling but it would never happen again, and it was time to make things work with her husband because she "still loved the asshole." Yeah, that was a very likely possibility—and the worst one of all. So he didn't know what would happen next. All he knew was what he wanted to happen.

He leaned over, kissed her softly between the shoulder blades, and slipped out of bed to take a shower. He forced his mind to dwell only on the present, and not the future.

<hr />

DeMarco walked out of the shower, a towel wrapped around his waist. Angela was awake, sitting up in bed, the sheets covering her lap but nothing else. She reminded him of the Venus de Milo statue, except with arms. He felt the beast stirring beneath the towel but before he could do anything, she said, "Rulon Tully's been kidnapped."

"What?"

Angela turned down the television and, figuring correctly that DeMarco couldn't listen while he was looking at a naked woman, got out of bed and put on a robe. Then she told him what the TV reporters had said.

Last night, at approximately ten p.m., about the time DeMarco was making love to her for the first time, Rulon Tully, accompanied by his driver and his head of security, had left Tully's estate near Ventura. Tully didn't return home that night. The following morning, while on his way to work, Tully's chef found Tully's Mercedes abandoned on the access road leading to the estate with its front tires shredded, and lying near the Mercedes was the body of a man the chef didn't recognize. The police were immediately called to the scene and they found the bodies of Tully's driver and security chief in the trunk of the Mercedes. It was assumed Tully had been kidnapped and the unidentified man at the scene had been killed by Tully's security people, although no ballistic tests had been conducted to confirm this. Tully's chief counsel would appear on television later in the day to make an appeal to the kidnappers.

"I thought Yuri was supposed to rob the guy's house," DeMarco said. He didn't bother to add, *and kill Tully.*

"He was supposed to," Angela said.

Neither of them said anything for a moment. He didn't know what she was thinking but he was wondering how she felt about the fact that two of Tully's people had been killed. He wasn't going to remind her that he'd told her something like this could happen. Now she—and he—would have to live with that. Whatever she was feeling, the only thing she said was, "I need to call Langley and see if they know anything more than what's on the news."

It looked like their vacation was over.

313

Chapter 45

———◆———

Yuri stood next to the doctor, looking down at Mikhail. He was unconscious, his chest was heavily bandaged, and his breathing was labored —and Yuri wanted to take a pillow and suffocate the life out of him.

The doctor's house was located in a run-down neighborhood in National City, California. It was isolated from its neighbors by a towering laurel hedge that didn't appear to have ever been trimmed, and the front windows were obscured by other overgrown, untamed shrubs. The bedroom where Mikhail lay contained a standard hospital bed with side rails and there was an IV stand next to the bed, dripping some sort of clear fluid into Mikhail's veins.

The doctor was an alcoholic and a gambling addict who had lost his license to practice medicine when he was convicted for Medicaid fraud. He now provided his services to gangs in the San Diego area whose members preferred not to go to a hospital when they were injured on the job. Yuri had heard of the man through the criminal grapevine and had used him once before when one of his men had been shot in an argument over a woman.

"Will he live?" Yuri asked.

"Only if you take him to a hospital," the doctor said. "The bullet's in his right lung, and the lung has collapsed. He needs blood and the bullet needs to be removed before infection sets in."

"So remove the bullet."

"I can't do that here; I don't have the proper equipment. He needs to be in a hospital."

"He's not going to a hospital," Yuri said. "But I need to talk to him before he dies."

The doctor shrugged. "If he regains consciousness, I'll let you know."

Yuri went into the doctor's kitchen. He opened the refrigerator hoping to find a bottle of water, but the refrigerator contained nothing but condiments, a greasy carton of Chinese food, and a wedge of cheese that was green with mold. He slammed the door in disgust and then stood at the kitchen sink, looking out at the doctor's untended backyard as he reflected on his misfortune.

The raid on Tully had been a disaster. One of Mikhail's men—a tattooed idiot named Rudy—had been killed, Mikhail had been shot, and Rulon Tully was missing. All Ivan could tell him was that a man had come out of the darkness, fired half a dozen shots, and then took off in the Range Rover containing the billionaire. But everything happened so fast that Ivan didn't see who had attacked them and didn't know if more than one person had been involved. Since Mikhail was still alive, they took him with them when they fled Tully's estate, but they didn't have the good sense to take Rudy's body as well.

Rudy's body was a problem, as it could eventually lead the police to him. Rudy had never been arrested or fingerprinted in America but he had a criminal record in Russia and the tattoos on his arms, and some of his dental work, were distinctly Russian. And because the victim was Rulon Tully, the cops would do everything they could to identify the body, and they would eventually contact Interpol and the Russian police. The only good news was that it would take some time for the Russian authorities, with their notoriously outdated record-keeping systems, to respond to the FBI, but when they did, they would tell the Bureau that Rudy had worked for Yuri and Uncle Lev in Moscow. Then the FBI would come after him for kidnapping Tully—which was ironic, because that was the one crime he hadn't committed.

What a god-awful mess, and all because Mikhail had failed. Now he needed to move even faster to turn Marty Taylor's assets into cash and flee the country. And he would have to hide somewhere with Taylor until all the sales were complete. He felt like smothering Mikhail.

But there was one thing he wanted to do before he fled: he wanted to find Pamela Walker. *Somebody* had interfered with his raid on Tully's estate and the only person he could think of was her. She had given him the original idea, and no one else knew what he was planning regarding Tully except the people in his own organization. She must have decided to wait for him to attack Tully and then, with the aid of at least one male accomplice, she took Tully from him. Walker had not struck him as the sort of person who would get involved in such a violent, high-profile crime, but who else could have taken Tully? She and her accomplice must be planning to ransom Tully or, like he'd been thinking, force Tully to transfer money out of his bank accounts.

At this point, however, he had no intention of taking Tully from Pamela if she had him. Kidnapping a person was relatively easy—but to get the cash in exchange for the kidnapped person was always fraught with danger. And in Tully's case, the exchange would be particularly dangerous because the FBI would be involved. And as for forcing Tully to transfer money out of his account to his kidnappers, by now the FBI was most likely watching those bank accounts and would trace the transfer back to the guilty. No, Tully at this point was of no real use to him—but he still wanted to talk to Walker. He wanted to know why she had taken Tully from him. Maybe she had managed to get Tully to transfer money out of his accounts, and if she had he could take the money from her.

Yes, he wanted to talk to pretty Pamela—finding her, though, might be impossible. If she had Tully, she would certainly be doing everything she could to avoid being found.

Then he realized that he had a way to find her.

"Sir?"

Yuri turned. It was the doctor.

"He's awake. I don't know how long he'll remain that way but you can talk to him now."

<hr />

Mikhail, in a weak, barely audible voice, told Yuri all he knew: a big man with short hair and a heavy mustache shot him and Rudy, and then took Rulon Tully. He had never seen the man before.

"Just one man?" Yuri said, and Mikhail nodded.

Yuri began to rant, screaming how he couldn't understand how a single man had been able to overcome five armed men—so Mikhail groaned in pain and pretended to pass out. Half an hour later, he called out and the doctor came to him. He asked the doctor if Yuri was still in the house. The doctor said no. He then asked about his condition and was informed that the bullet was still inside him, lodged in his right lung, but it didn't appear that the bullet had hit a major artery. If it had, the doctor said, he would have bled to death by now.

"What are you going to do next?" Mikhail asked.

"Well, there's really nothing I can do other than make you comfortable. I don't have the equipment here to operate on you. You need to be in a hospital, but, uh, Yuri said . . ."

"I can imagine what Yuri said."

He could understand why Yuri didn't want him to go to a hospital. A man with a gunshot wound would be questioned by the police and Yuri was afraid that if Mikhail was questioned he'd give Yuri up.

"Bring me a phone," he said to the doctor.

The doctor didn't move; he was obviously more afraid of Yuri than of a man too weak to stand.

"Doctor, I know what you're thinking," Mikhail said. "You're thinking if you don't obey Yuri he'll kill you, and he will. But do you remember the big man with the goatee who carried me in here?"

The doctor nodded.

"He's my friend," Mikhail said. "My best friend. He's not a very smart man but he's extremely loyal, and he'll blame my death on you. He'll strangle you to death. Now bring me a phone."

Actually, Ivan didn't like Mikhail because Mikhail treated him like the brainless oaf he was—but the doctor didn't know that. He brought Mikhail a phone.

Mikhail started to dial a number, and as he did the doctor turned to leave the room. "Wait, doctor," Mikhail said. "I want you to hear this."

Into the phone, Mikhail said, "Uncle, this is Mikhail. I've been shot and I'm seriously wounded." Uncle Lev interrupted to ask questions but Mikhail cut him off. "Not now, Uncle. You need to send an ambulance to Dr. Morrow's house in National City, and have the ambulance take me to a hospital in Mexico. You need to do this very quickly. And you don't want to talk to Yuri until you hear what I have to say. I think Yuri has betrayed you. And one other thing. If I'm dead when the ambulance gets here, can you please tell someone to kill Dr. Morrow."

After he hung up, he said to the doctor, "After I'm gone, I'd suggest you relocate your practice."

───────◆◆◆───────

The teacher was a pudgy man in his forties who was so scared his hands were trembling, but he appeared to know what he was doing.

Pamela Walker had given Yuri a cell phone so they could communicate if they needed to, and he knew from watching television that cell phones could sometimes be used to locate people. He had no idea how this was done, but that didn't matter. One of the advantages of being associated with Marty Taylor's company was Taylor employed people who did have that sort of knowledge. So Yuri had called Bollinger and told him what he needed, but the CEO didn't give him the name of a T&T employee. Instead he gave him the name of a teacher who taught computer science at a junior college. When he had asked Bollinger why the teacher would perform this service for him, Bollinger had hesitated, then said, "He's somebody I know from outside of work." Yuri figured this meant that the teacher was one of Bollinger's pedophile friends. And considering how nervous the teacher was, Bollinger must have told him something about Yuri that made him afraid of Yuri—and this was good.

The room they were in was some sort of lab filled with computer equipment. When Yuri had arrived the teacher had examined the cell phone Pamela Walker had given him and asked if Walker's cell phone was similar in appearance. When Yuri said yes, he looked up some things in a manual he had. He then disassembled Yuri's phone, examined its innards, reassembled it, and typed for a few minutes on a keyboard.

"Okay," he said, "you can make the call now. And try to keep whoever you're calling on the line as long as possible. Please."

Yuri punched in the number Walker had given him but he was surprised when she answered. "Where is he?" he demanded.

"What? Who are you talking about?" she asked.

"You know who I'm talking about. The man on the front page of every paper in the country. Where is he?"

"I thought *you* had him."

While Yuri talked, he watched the screen of the teacher's laptop. He didn't know what the man was doing but he saw a map of San Diego appear. Then the view shifted as the teacher appeared to zoom in on a particular part of the city. He couldn't believe that Walker was still in San Diego.

"I don't have him," Yuri said. "I think you have him. I think you took him from my people."

"You're insane."

"No, I'm not insane. I'm angry. And I would suggest that you tell me the truth."

"I *am* telling you the truth."

"Where are you right now?"

"I'm back in Washington. But I don't have any more to tell you about the FBI's investigation than I told you the other day. You'll have to be patient."

Yuri looked at the monitor. He recognized the area of San Diego known as Harbor Island, a section of the city near the airport, and at that moment the technician gave him a thumbs-up. Yuri nodded, then said into the phone, "You're going to find out what happens when people lie to me, Pamela." He hung up before she could answer.

"Whoever you were talking to is at the Hilton Hotel on Harbor Island," the teacher said.

"Good," Yuri said and patted him on the shoulder.

He wasn't sure what to make of his conversation with Pamela Walker. It sounded as if she didn't have Tully, but that meant nothing. More convincing was the fact that she was staying in a hotel. Certainly she wouldn't be keeping Tully at the Hilton if she had kidnapped him. Whatever the case, he still wanted to question her and find out why she had disrupted his plans with Tully, and why she had lied and said she was in Washington.

As Yuri was leaving the teacher's office, it occurred to him that if Pamela Walker wanted to find him, she could do the same thing he had done and trace him through the cell phone she had given him.

He threw the phone into a trash can as he walked to his car.

"That was Yuri," Angela said. "He accused me of kidnapping Tully. He said I took Tully away from his men."

"Well, if he doesn't have Tully," DeMarco said, "then who does?"

They both stood there silently, thinking about that question.

"It's gotta be the guy who saved me in Myrtle Beach," DeMarco said. "He's the only other player in this thing, and somehow he's traced the leak from Whitmore to Acosta, and now to Tully. Maybe he followed you when you went to see Yuri."

"He didn't."

"Then I don't know how he did it, but he figured out Tully's involvement. And if he's got Tully, I think he's going to kill him, just like he killed Whitmore. Whoever this guy is, he's avenging Mahata's death."

"Yeah, I think you're right."

"And I'll tell you something else. If he's got Tully, he'll go after Congressman Rudman next. And he'll kill Rudman."

"Maybe," she said.

"Bullshit, *maybe*." When she didn't respond, he asked, "So what are we going to do next?"

"There's nothing we can do. The California cops and the FBI are looking for Tully, and we're not going to get in the middle of that. All I can do is call my contact at Langley, tell him Yuri doesn't have Tully, then wait to see what LaFountaine wants me to do. At this point, he may just tell me to come home."

"From your lips to God's ears," DeMarco said.

He just wanted to get back to Washington and get on with his life— a life that would hopefully include Angela.

Chapter 46

Yuri decided that he didn't have time to deal with Pamela Walker himself. He needed to focus on expediting the sale of Marty Taylor's assets and make plans for fleeing the county. And he needed to kill the CEO, Bollinger. It was time to seal up all the loose ends.

He pulled out his cell phone.

"Do you remember that woman who came to my house the other day, the blonde with the glasses? The lawyer from the Justice Department?"

"Yes," Ivan said.

"She's at the Hilton Hotel on Harbor Island. I want you to take someone with you, pick her up, and bring her to me."

"What?" Ivan said.

Yuri hung up. He really wished he had someone brighter than Ivan to deal with Walker. If Mikhail wasn't dying, he'd have been the ideal choice.

Then something occurred to him, somthing he should have thought of earlier. If it could be done, he could make even more money off Marty Taylor.

Marty was sitting in the kitchen with his handler Andrei, waiting for Yuri to return, and he was more depressed—and more desperate—than ever.

A group of Mexicans in greasy coveralls had just driven off with his cars, presumably taking them to the warehouse in Chula Vista that Yuri had mentioned. The expensive artwork had been removed from the house an hour earlier by another group of Mexicans, to be taken to a gallery in La Jolla. And half an hour ago, a real estate agent had called and asked if it would be okay to show the houses to a prospective client tomorrow. Because Andrei was listening in on the phone call, he said yes, and told her to direct any further questions to Yuri.

He had to get away from Andrei before Yuri returned, call that lady from the Justice Department, and stop the sales. He had to.

He looked over at Andrei; the thug was leaning against a counter, sipping coffee, staring at him with his flat, black eyes. He looked like he would welcome another opportunity to smack Marty with his gun.

Then Marty noticed the coffeepot. It was almost full—and Andrei was standing about five feet from the pot. It was time to make his move.

He was going to ask Andrei's permission to get a cup of coffee. If Andrei said yes, he'd casually walk over to the coffeepot and pick it up, but then he'd pretend that he'd forgotten to get a cup. Still holding the pot, he'd walk over to the cupboard to get one, which would put him within arm's reach of Andrei—and then he'd whack the shit out of Andrei with a pot full of hot coffee. He knew he could take the guy if he could keep him from pulling his gun.

"Hey, you mind if I get a cup of coffee?"

Andrei shrugged.

Marty got up from the table, made a show of stretching, then walked toward the counter and picked up the coffeepot —and at that moment, the kitchen door swung open and Yuri walked into the room.

Did God hate him, or what?

With Yuri was another hard-looking guy in his forties with a badly repaired cleft palate. His name was Stephan and Marty had seen him only once before—the day Yuri had killed the accountant at the warehouse.

"I want you to sell all the stock you have in your company. Right now," Yuri said.

"I can't do that," Marty said, and Yuri looked over at Andrei—and Andrei punched him in the mouth. The coffeepot shattered on the floor.

Ivan parked the van in a loading zone near the Hilton. With him was a smart-mouthed kid named Pyotr, whom he didn't like. Pyotr had been in the country for only a couple of years but he'd picked up the language very fast. Yuri used him mostly to move dope, and because Pyotr was so young, he'd hang around college campuses, party with rich kids, and sell them cocaine and pot.

Pyotr also dressed like a college kid. Today he wore a black T-shirt, baggy shorts with multiple pockets, and tennis shoes without socks. On the front of the T-shirt were the words "Dirty White Boy," which Ivan thought might be the name of a rock band but he wasn't sure. Ivan suspected that Pyotr used cocaine himself, and if he did, and if Yuri found out, Ivan was going to have the pleasure of beating the shit out of Pyotr.

But right now his problem wasn't Pyotr. His problem was snatching Pamela Walker. Yuri had told him that she was in the hotel but the hotel was huge and he had no idea how to find her or how to take her when he did. There was one thing he did know, though: he knew he had to succeed. This was a big opportunity for him; it could mean a raise.

He sat for a couple of minutes thinking about the problem, then told Pyotr to wait in the van—and to turn down the damn radio. He entered the hotel, proceeded to the gift shop, and looked for something cheap to buy but everything in the shop was ridiculously expensive—and he knew Yuri wouldn't reimburse him. He finally decided on a pink T-shirt that had the words "San Diego" on it. It cost twenty-two dollars. Outrageous. He asked the woman if she could gift wrap the T-shirt for him. She could, she said, for five dollars. Son of a bitch.

Gift-wrapped package in hand, he approached the front desk. It was at times like this that he hated his size; people tended to remember him.

"I have a gift for Ms. Pamela Walker," he said to the cute black girl at the registration desk. "Can I have her room number please?"

"I'm sorry, sir, but we don't give out the room numbers of our guests."

"Oh," Ivan said. He had never stayed at such a grand hotel. It had never occurred to him that they wouldn't tell him the room number. If she had given him the number, he and Pyotr would have forced their way into Walker's room and taken her from the hotel via one the stairwells.

"Well," he said, "could you ring her room and tell her the package is here."

"Of course," the girl said.

Since Walker had seen him before, he couldn't follow her back to her room when she came for the package—but Pyotr could. She had never seen Pyotr. He reached for his cell phone to call him, but then he noticed the girl frowning at her computer.

"I'm sorry, sir," she said to him, "but there's no Pamela Walker registered here."

"Are you sure?" Ivan asked.

"Yes, sir."

He mumbled something about having made a mistake and quickly left the hotel, hunching over a bit to minimize his height. Now what? And what was he supposed to do with the stupid T-shirt he had bought? It was too small to fit either his wife or his mistress. Twenty-seven bucks down the drain. He squeezed himself back into the van and threw the gift-wrapped box into the back.

"So wuz up?" Pyotr asked.

"Shut up," Ivan said.

"Wait a minute!" Marty screamed, and Yuri raised a hand to stop Andrei from hitting him again.

"Listen to me," Marty said. "I'm the chairman of the board and the biggest shareholder, and if I were to sell all my stock at one time the company would go into a tailspin. So they have rules. I have to notify the board if I'm planning to sell stock, and the SEC has to be notified. And my broker knows this, and he can't legally complete the transaction until he's verified that the board's been notified. And once the board is notified, they can delay the sale—and they will, because if I sold all my shares at once, the price of the stock will drop like a rock and every shareholder we have left will get screwed. So what I'm telling you is that I can't instantly turn my stock into cash. It would take days to do that, maybe weeks."

It didn't sound as if Marty was lying, but Yuri called Bollinger to confirm his story. The CEO said he was telling the truth.

Before he hung up, Yuri told Bollinger that he wanted him to go home and that he would come to his house before the day was over. Bollinger didn't argue; he knew better than to argue with Yuri.

When the call was finished, Yuri stood there looking at Marty. He could kill him now. He had power of attorney, so he didn't really need him to sell the remainder of his possessions. He finally decided, though, that as much as he hated to do it, he should delay the pleasure of killing him. Some issue could arise, something he hadn't thought of, and he still might need the man to complete the sales. But he *wanted* to kill him. He was so angry about how badly everything was going that he wanted to take out all his rage on this weak, pampered shit. To calm himself, he poured a shot of vodka and drank it in one swallow.

With Marty, Andrei, and Stephan all watching him, wondering what he'd do next, he walked over to the window and looked down at his pit bull in the backyard. It was shitting again. He was tired of cleaning up the animal's shit but he was the only one who could because the dog would attack anyone else. He felt like shooting the dog, too.

He had taken almost four million dollars from Bollinger, Taylor, and Taylor's company. But half of that had gone to Uncle Lev, and

20 percent had gone to paying his crew and his other expenses, leaving him with just a little over a million in the bank. If he could sell all of Taylor's possessions, even at fire-sale prices, he'd make about twenty million. But the question was, could he evade being captured by either the FBI or Uncle Lev until the sales were finalized? He had no choice. He couldn't leave the country with only a million. So what he needed to do next was find a place to hide until the agents completed their work. And if he was caught before that happened, so be it.

Gesturing with his head at Marty, he said to Andei, "I want you and Stephan to take this piece of shit to a motel. Take him out of town, someplace within an hour's drive of San Diego, maybe someplace up in the hills, like Julian or Santa Ysabel. Get a place that has little cabins, not adjacent rooms. And don't let anyone see him. I'll call you later and find out where you're staying."

Then he turned to Stephan, the man with the cleft palate. He'd heard rumors that when Stephan was in prison in Russia he'd enjoyed sodomizing the other prisoners, particularly the young, pretty ones. That sort of behavior made Yuri sick to his stomach, but then who was he to judge? He'd never spent any time in prison.

"Stephan," he said, "I don't want Marty killed and I don't want his face disfigured in case I need him later. But if you become bored while you're with him and want to amuse yourself in some way that doesn't show, I won't object."

Marty immediately went pale and asked, "Hey, what are you talking about?"

Yuri ignored him and asked Stephan, "Do you understand?"

Stephan's face remained expressionless and he merely nodded— but Yuri saw the wet gleam in his eyes.

Stephan took Marty by the arm and led him from the kitchen. Andrei started to follow but Yuri called him back and whispered to him to take from the garage any tools they might need to dispose of a body. Plastic sheets, shovels, maybe a pick. The usual stuff. Andrei nodded; he'd disposed of bodies before.

When everyone was gone from the kitchen, Yuri reviewed the situation.

Mikhail was at the doctor's house and would soon be dead—which was probably for the best at this point.

Ivan and Pyotr were hunting for Pamela Walker but he didn't have any real expectation that they'd be able to take her.

Most important, the agents were busy selling Marty's assets.

His next task was to pay a visit to Mr. Bollinger.

———◆———

Angela was pacing the hotel room like a caged cat.

She had called LaFountaine to find out what he wanted her to do next but he hadn't returned her call. It was always possible, being the director of the CIA, that he had other things on his mind but DeMarco wondered if LaFountaine was ducking Angela's call for some reason.

He hinted, subtly, that crawling into bed with him might relieve some of her tension but he could tell that sex was the last thing on her mind. Consequently, he spent his time in the most productive manner he could think of: watching a baseball game on TV with the sound muted. The Padres were playing Pittsburgh and both teams sucked, but since he was a fan of the worst team in the league, the Washington Nationals, he couldn't be too critical.

"I'm going for a run," Angela said. "I'm going nuts just sitting here. You wanna go?"

"Jogging?"

"Yeah," she said.

He wanted to say, *I'd like to go jogging about as much as I'd like to get a hip replacement.* But he didn't; he didn't want to come off as a slug who didn't like to exercise. Instead he said, "I'd love to but I jogged for about ten years and it destroyed my knees." And this was actually true. His right knee *was* a mess: he could hear the little bones or cartilage or whatever it was grinding together every time he flexed the joint. "Now I just lift weights and work out on the heavy bag," he added.

"Well, okay," she said. Then, being Angela, she just had to add, "You probably couldn't keep up anyway."

She changed into shorts, a T-shirt, and jogging shoes that had these weird-looking heels with little air-bubble pockets in them, then clipped her cell phone to the waistband of the shorts. She was about to leave when he said, "I'll go down with you. I want to get a paper, see if there's anything on Tully that wasn't reported on TV. And maybe take a walk around the block."

"You're going to walk *all* the way around the block?" she said. Sheesh.

Ivan did not want to call Yuri and tell him he didn't have any idea what to do next, but what else could he do? He supposed they could just park near the hotel for a couple of hours and hope Pamela Walker would appear, but what were the odds of that happening if she wasn't staying at the hotel? Then it occurred to him that maybe she was staying with someone or using a different name. Okay, that was possible, but how did that help him?

Maybe what he should do was have Pyotr start a fire in the basement of the hotel then pull the fire alarm. If Walker was in the hotel, she would have to go outside when the alarm sounded and maybe he could get her then—assuming he could spot her in the crowd of people that would be streaming out of the hotel. And it was a big hotel.

He sat there for a moment stroking his goatee. He wasn't used to thinking this hard; he was actually getting a headache. Maybe he should . . .

Wait a minute. A man and woman had just come out of the hotel. He'd noticed the woman because she was wearing shorts and had good legs, although she was a bit skinnier than he preferred. Then he realized he'd seen the man before. Where had he seen him? The beach! He saw him and the woman talking to Marty Taylor on the beach!

"Give me the binoculars," he said. "In the glove compartment. Quick!"

Pyotr handed him the binoculars and he focused on the woman. It was Pamela Walker. She had blonde hair when she came to Yuri's house and now she was a brunette, but it was definitely her. She was too pretty to forget.

The woman was doing stretching exercises; it looked like she might be going for a run. The man with her, though, wasn't dressed for running; he was just talking to her, watching her as she stretched. She gave the man a little wave and started running.

This was good.

He could wait until she reached some fairly isolated place and snatch her, but he had no idea where she was going. Right now she was jogging on the sidewalk of a busy street and she just might stay on busy streets for her entire run. He looked around. There weren't many pedestrians that he could see, but cars were streaming by. It would be almost impossible to grab her and not have someone see them. On the other hand, they were driving an unremarkable white van. It had been stolen months ago, and they had replaced the original license plates with plates they took from another vehicle. And if they showed Walker a weapon, they might be able to get her into the van without her making a fuss. Yes, that's what he would do: tell Pyotr to show her his gun, threaten to kill her if she screamed, and order her into the van.

"You see that woman, the one running?" he said to Pyotr.

"The good-looking one with the nice ass?"

"Yes. I want you to get in the back and open the sliding door. Don't open it all the way, just unlatch it. I'm going to drive up next to her and you're going to jump out when I stop, show her your gun, and tell her to get in the van. If she screams or tries to run, hit her and throw her in."

"You don't think it's a little too busy here to be doing that?"

"Just do what I tell you."

The kid shrugged, raised the "Dirty White Boy" T-shirt, and pulled out his gun.

———◆◆◆———

DeMarco pulled a newspaper from the machine, then looked up and down the block for a place to get a cup of coffee and read. There had to be a Starbucks somewhere nearby; you couldn't walk a block in most cities without seeing one. He looked across the street to see if maybe there was a coffee shop over there, and as he did a white van passed in front of him, blocking his view.

The driver. It was that huge son of a bitch with the goatee he'd seen on the beach when they'd talked to Marty Taylor. He noticed then that the van was moving slowly—a lot slower than the other cars. And it was going in the same direction that Angela had gone. He looked up the street. She was less than a block away. She wasn't *that* fast.

He yelled, "Angela!" but she didn't hear him. He slapped his belt where his cell phone was supposed to be—and slapped nothing but belt. He'd left his phone in the room. He was always forgetting the damn phone! He took off sprinting.

"Angela!" he shouted again, as loud as he could, but at that moment a plane flew overhead and again she didn't hear him.

———◆◆◆———

Angela saw the young guy jump out of the van, and then he stepped right into her path. Without even thinking about it, she started to dodge around him but he grabbed her arm and pulled her close to him and she felt the gun barrel jammed into her side.

"Get into the van or I'll kill you."

There was no way Angela was getting into the van. She was dead if she got into the van. She also figured the kid wasn't going to shoot her. This guy had been ordered to snatch her, not kill her. If he'd been sent to kill her he would have just shot from the van as it drove

331

past. So even though the kid had the gun jammed into her side, she pulled away from him, breaking his grip on her arm.

But the kid was quick. Before she could run away, he reached out and grabbed her by the front of her T-shirt and pulled her to him. At that moment, she heard the driver yell, "Get her in the damn van."

She recognized the driver. He was the big bodyguard at Yuri's house, the one Yuri called Ivan.

She was not getting in the van. She slammed her forehead into the kid's nose and he let go of her T-shirt—and hit her on the top of her head with his gun.

———◆———

DeMarco saw the van stop and watched in alarm as a skinny kid in long shorts jumped out and grabbed Angela. When she pulled away from him, DeMarco saw the gun in the kid's hand. Son of a bitch.

He was less than fifty yards from the van at that point, running faster than he'd ever run in his life. He didn't know what he was going to do when he reached the van—but he kept running.

He saw the kid grab Angela by the front of her T-shirt and he watched in amazement as Angela head-butted him—and then the kid hit her in the head with his gun. DeMarco was going to kill him.

He was twenty yards from the van now. Angela was on the ground, and the kid—his nose bleeding, holding his gun in one hand—was dragging Angela by one arm over to the open side door of the van—and that's when he became aware of DeMarco running at him. The kid loosed his grip on Angela, turned toward DeMarco, and raised the gun to shoot him but at that moment DeMarco was flying through the air. He heard the gun fire while he was in the air but didn't feel any pain and figured the bullet had missed him, and then he hit the kid like a defensive tackle taking down a quarterback. He slammed into the little bastard so hard he knocked the breath out of him. The kid was now on the ground, too stunned to bring his weapon to bear, and DeMarco was on top of him.

DeMarco hit him in the jaw with the best right cross he'd ever thrown.

He glanced at Angela: she was still on the ground, out cold. Then he heard the driver's-side door of the van open. The driver, that huge bastard, was coming to help the kid. DeMarco grabbed the kid's gun and just as the driver lumbered around the front of the van DeMarco pointed it at him.

"You take one more step, I'm gonna blow your head off."

The big guy stopped and raised his hands.

DeMarco got off the kid and stood up.

He looked over at Angela, saw the blood trickling from her head, and it took all his willpower not to kick the kid.

The kid got to his feet, groggy from DeMarco's blow, and leaned back against the van. The big guy with the goatee just stood there, hands still in the air, obviously not sure what to do next.

DeMarco needed to get Angela to a doctor. He didn't know how badly she was hurt. He moved toward her, intending to get her cell phone and call the cops and the medics, but then it crossed his mind that getting the cops involved in this whole CIA mess might not be a good idea.

"Get out of here," he said to the big guy. "I know who you are and who you work for, and if she's not okay I'll be coming after you. Now get out of here before I shoot you both."

The big guy didn't hesitate. He walked around the van and opened the driver's-side door and got in. The kid, moving slower because he still hadn't completely recovered from DeMarco's punch, opened the passenger-side door but before he could get into the van DeMarco said, "Hey." The kid turned to look at him and DeMarco hit him in the mouth with the butt of the gun hard enough to break his teeth.

"That was for hitting her," he said.

The kid staggered into the van, now bleeding from his nose *and* his mouth, and the van took off.

DeMarco dropped to his knees next to Angela. He touched her face gently and she opened her eyes. Thank God.

"Angela," he said softly, "don't move. I'm going to call an ambulance."

She shook her head and winced when she did.

"No," she said. "I'm all right. Just help me up."

"You could have a concussion."

"Quit arguing with me. Just get me back to the room."

Chapter 47

The hospital was in Tijuana and Mikhail shared a room with an old Mexican man who appeared to have an infinite number of concerned relatives. Right now he was being visited by two fat teenage girls and a woman in her eighties. They had brought him flowers and fruit and magazines to read, and the girls were hovering over him, holding his hands, whispering to him. The old lady was fingering a string of rosary beads. The Mexican, who was recovering from surgery just as Mikhail was, lay there with his eyes closed, obviously in pain, but his relatives didn't have the good sense to leave him alone.

Mikhail, too, was in pain. He had a drainage tube coming out the right side of his chest, a catheter inserted into his dick, and his back hurt from lying so long in the same position. But he was alive. The surgeon had told him the bullet had been removed and that he should recover completely. Not once did anyone at the hospital ask him how he'd been shot.

As he lay there listening to the Mexican women babble to the old man, he thought about his future. He was sixty-two years old; it was time to retire. He could no longer work for someone like Yuri, where getting shot was a fairly common on-the-job injury. His plan had always been to buy a small house in San Diego and then ensure that he had a steady if not spectacular monthly income. He had managed to save over a hundred thousand dollars, but better than that, he had found a man, a veteran confined to a wheelchair, who received a handsome disability benefit from the army, and another man, only sixty-six, who received Social Security benefits. Both of these men were childless widowers and it had taken Mikhail almost two years to find them. He still had a few details to work out but when he retired, the men would disappear and he would assume their identities—and their pensions.

But to buy and maintain a house in San Diego was just too expensive; his money would not go far at all. Now, lying in a Tijuana hospital, he was beginning to think that Mexico might be ideal. The weather in Mexico was just as good as in San Diego and he could buy the house he wanted for a fraction of what he would pay in California. And the cost of labor was ridiculously low; he'd be able to afford a woman to clean his house and cook his food.

Yes. That's what he would do: retire to Mexico. Now the only thing he had to do was find a way to leave Uncle Lev and Yuri, and he suspected that, once he talked to Lev about Yuri, Yuri wasn't going to be an issue.

He must have fallen asleep because the next sensation he had was someone gently squeezing the big toe on his right foot. He opened his eyes. It was Uncle Lev.

He had no idea how old Lev was. He might be seventy or maybe eighty, but then he could be in his sixties. Men who lived the way Lev had lived had a tendency to age badly.

Lev was only five foot seven but the bulk and the muscles of his youth were still evident. He was wearing a polo shirt and the tattoos on his arms were visible, but the blue and red ink was so faded by time that it was almost impossible to make out the symbols. His head was completely bald, his nose had obviously been broken several times, and the tip of it was dark and a small piece was missing due to frostbite. Mikhail had once taken a steam bath with Lev and knew that he had several more scars on his torso, all made by crude homemade knives, and three of his toes were also missing due to frostbite.

Lev had spent twenty years in the gulags. To survive ten years in the gulags was unusual; to survive twenty was a miracle and this made Lev something more—or less—than human.

Lev smiled. He had beautiful teeth—they were false.

"So," he said. "You have something to tell me about Yuri."

———◆◆◆———

Yuri looked at the body of Andrew Bollinger slumped in the chair behind his desk. A .38 automatic was lying on the floor below Bollinger's right hand.

It appeared as if the degenerate had shot himself.

An hour earlier, he had come to the CEO's house and convinced him to transfer funds from his savings accounts to Yuri's account in Mexico. He had been surprised to find that Bollinger had only eighty-five thousand in cash but Bollinger had explained, like Yuri was a child, that cash in a savings account didn't earn anything and all his money was in stocks, bonds, and real estate. He wanted to pistol whip the pedantic pervert but what would be the point?

So he killed him.

His cell phone rang as he was leaving Bollinger's house. He looked at the caller ID, and saw it was Ivan. He answered the phone and as he listened his jaw clenched with anger. The gorilla had failed to get Pamela Walker. She had someone with her, a tough bastard who beat the hell out of Pyotr and drove them off. He asked Ivan if the man had a mustache and Ivan said no. But that still didn't mean that he wasn't the one who had taken Tully away from Mikhail; mustaches could be shaved.

"What do you want me to do?" Ivan asked.

"I want you to shut up and let me think."

He could have Ivan stake out the hotel where Walker had been staying but he doubted she would remain there. And now that she knew he was trying to get her, she would be prepared if Ivan tried again. And the man with her, the man he suspected had shot Mikhail and killed Rudy, was obviously good and would be difficult to handle.

As much as he hated to do it, it looked like he was going to have to give up on Pamela Walker. Nothing was going right these days.

He told Ivan not to go home, that the police could be looking for him because of what had happened with Tully. He instructed him to check into a motel, and said he would call him later. When Ivan started to say he didn't have the money for a motel, he hung up.

It occurred to him that he should check on the status of Mikhail. Hopefully, he was dead by now. If he wasn't, he would have to kill him; he couldn't afford to have Mikhail fall into the hands of the police—or, even worse, talk to Uncle Lev. He called the doctor's home, but no one answered. Did that mean Mikhail was dead? The doctor certainly wouldn't have left his house if Mikhail was still alive. Still, he needed to be sure.

He drove to the doctor's but no one answered when he rang the bell. Where the hell was he? The man was an alcoholic; maybe he had passed out. He walked to the back of the house to look in through a window, but the curtains were drawn. Infuriated, he broke the window on the back door and entered the house. He found a pile of bloody bandages in the room where Mikhail had been but Mikhail was gone and so was the doctor. He didn't understand what was going on.

His cell phone rang again. He thought it must be that idiot Ivan calling back to ask for more instructions. Then he looked at the caller ID.

It was Uncle Lev.

He didn't answer the phone.

Chapter 48

———◆———

Angela was lying on the bed, still dressed in her jogging clothes, pressing a plastic bag filled with ice against her head.

"We need to get you to a hospital and get your noggin looked at," DeMarco said.

"I'm all right," she snapped.

"You were *unconscious*. You could have a skull fracture."

"I wasn't unconscious. I was just stunned."

This was the third time they had had this discussion. The woman was unbelievably stubborn.

"I wonder how Yuri found out I was here," she said.

"I don't know, but if he could find you once he can probably find you again. And next time he might not send two morons. We need to get out of this hotel and you need to call your boss and have him send in some reinforcements."

At that moment, Angela's cell phone rang. She answered, said "yes, sir," then got off the bed and almost stood at attention. DeMarco figured it was LaFountaine calling—and it was.

He heard only Angela's side of the conversation, as she told LaFountaine that they didn't know anything more about Tully than what had been reported on the news but she was positive that Yuri didn't have Tully. She also told him Yuri's men had tried to kidnap her but DeMarco had managed to drive them off. She concluded by saying that Tully had most likely been kidnapped by the same man who had killed Sandra Whitmore, and then she listened as LaFountaine spoke for a long time. She concluded the phone call with another, "Yes, sir."

"Well?" DeMarco prompted.

"Ray Rudman is back in his district, in Anaheim, and the director wants us to stake him out."

"He thinks the mystery man is going to go after Rudman next, doesn't he?"

"Yeah."

"And he wants just the two of us to protect him? Is he fucking nuts?"

"No. He's going to send a team out to relieve us."

"Well, thank God for that." Then another thought occurred to him. "This guy, whoever he is, has killed Whitmore and kidnapped Tully, and he's good enough that he's been able to stay one step ahead of the cops and the CIA the whole time. So let me ask you this. Just how exactly are we going to be able to stop him from killing Rudman when we don't even know what he looks like?"

"I don't know. We'll cross that bridge when we come to it."

There you go, DeMarco thought. *The CIA motto.*

DeMarco shook his head. "This is wrong. LaFountaine needs to put Rudman under protective custody, and he needs to do it now."

"He doesn't want to do that. At least not yet."

"Yeah, and I'll tell you why. He *wants* this guy to kill Rudman."

Angela didn't say anything, which meant that she knew that he was right.

The florist slowly opened his eyes and for a moment wasn't sure where he was. Then he remembered: the Holiday Inn. He looked at his watch; he had slept almost fourteen hours.

It was time to complete his mission.

He supposed that Rudman was in Washington, D.C., which meant another long plane ride across the country, but he called the congressman's office to verify this. He told Rudman's secretary he was a constituent who was going to be in Washington tomorrow and he wanted to shake the congressman's hand and thank him for all his good work. The secretary informed him that Rudman was back in his district and would be working out of his Anaheim office all week.

He thanked the woman and hung up.

Chapter 49

Mahoney felt like he was gonna die. In fact, he was *sure* he was gonna die.

Last night, he'd gone to a function by himself because Mary Pat couldn't go and he always drank more when his wife wasn't there giving him the evil eye every time he refilled his glass. He was half in the bag before dinner was even served.

The event had been hosted by some tree-hugger group who wanted to reduce carbon emissions to zero—yeah, like he was ever gonna drive a friggin' Prius—but he attended because they donated money to him every two years when he ran for reelection. He would have left right after the dinner, but then he started talking to some gal—one of the tree huggers—who had a rack on her like Dolly Parton.

He remembered sitting with her by a fireplace, trying to look down her dress whenever she reached for her glass, but wondering the whole time if there was any way he could get someone this young and good-looking into the sack. After that, though, the evening was pretty much a blank. In the morning he found himself lying on the couch in the living room of his condo—somehow he'd managed to get home—and he was still wearing the suit he'd worn to the party, including the jacket. He woke up when his wife poked him, handed him the phone, and told him it was the deputy national security advisor calling. Then she gave him that look she always gave him when he drank so much he passed out before he could get undressed. She wouldn't speak to him for the next two days.

He winced when he was told to be at the White House in forty-five minutes. He staggered to his feet and thought he was going to throw up but managed to suppress the feeling. After a shower and a shave, he brushed his tongue for about ten minutes but still couldn't get rid of that nasty, a-duck-shat-in-my-mouth taste. An hour later he was sitting in the White House situation room, his head throbbing, knowing that all the bourbon he'd drunk the night before was *seeping* out of his pores and everyone in the room could probably smell it.

There was a gaggle of people in the room. The majority and minority leaders from both houses; four White House staff weenies; the chairman of the joint chiefs; and four other military guys: two generals, an admiral, and for some reason a mere major. They were all waiting for the president to show up to tell them why they were sitting there. Mahoney guessed, with all the military guys in the room, that the president was planning to bomb someone.

While they sat there, the generals started whining to the politicians about how they needed more money. That's what they always did when they had a captive bunch of legislators. Mahoney ignored the pleading and just sat there with his head in his hands, praying for the pain in his skull to abate. Five minutes later, the president, LaFountaine, and the president's national security advisor entered the room. The national security advisor was a woman named Edna Clouter. She was in her fifties and was one of the homeliest women that Mahoney had ever seen—she made Eleanor Roosevelt look like a beauty queen —but Clouter was also a stone-cold genius.

The president took his seat at the head of the table. LaFountaine and Clouter occupied seats on either side of him.

"Okay," the president said. "Jake, tell 'em what we've got."

LaFountaine looked directly at Mahoney and said, "Mr. President, is there some reason we need members of Congress here for this meeting?"

Before Mahoney could respond, the president said, "I like to keep Congress in the loop on things like this."

"Sir," LaFountaine said, "I believe it would be best if we limit this to people with a need to know. And to people we can be sure will keep the information to themselves."

Mahoney, in spite of the pain in his head, rose partially from his chair. "Why you son of a—"

The president raised a hand to silence Mahoney and said, "Jake, get on with it."

"Yes, sir," LaFountaine said, satisfied he'd made his point. He cleared his throat and said, "We have information that the Iranian government is sending half a dozen rockets to a Hezbollah splinter group in Lebanon. This group plans to hit several high-value targets in Israel the next time the Israelis give them the slightest pretext for doing so, and the rockets the Iranians are sending are more accurate and more powerful than those Hezbollah has used in the past. These aren't bottle rockets; they can do real damage."

"So tell the Israelis," one of the generals said with an indifferent shrug. "Let them take care of the problem."

"We'll tell the Israelis eventually," LaFountaine said, "but we want these rockets to reach Lebanon before any action is taken."

"I'm confused," the lone admiral at the table said. "Do we know where the rockets are right now?"

"Yes," LaFountaine said, "and we know the route they're taking to Lebanon."

"Then why don't we just destroy these things before they get there?"

"We can't do it that way," LaFountaine said. "We want the missiles to reach their destination, and after that someone in Lebanon will tell the Lebanese government and the Israelis about the rockets. That way it will appear that the leak came from a mole inside Hezbollah, and not from somebody in Iran. Then we'll demand the Lebanese destroy the rockets, and if they don't . . . well, then the Israelis can do whatever they want."

Jesus, Mahoney thought. *Typical CIA: wheels within wheels.* Just trying to follow LaFountaine's serpentine logic was making his head hurt more than it already did.

"I still don't understand," the stubborn admiral said. "What difference does it make if the intelligence can be traced back to Iran or not?"

"Trust me, Admiral, it makes a difference," LaFountaine said.

When LaFountaine said "trust me," Mahoney snorted and LaFountaine's face turned red.

Looking at the chairman of the joint chiefs, the president said, "The reason you're here, General, is I want the military to work with Director LaFountaine's people and develop a backup plan to take out the rockets if we have to."

"Yes, sir," the chairman of the joint chiefs responded.

Charge of the Light Brigade, Mahoney thought. *Theirs not to reason why.*

Senator Clyde Rackman spoke up at this point. "Mr. President," he said, "I deeply resent Mr. LaFountaine's implication that Congress can't be trusted with national security information, but I'm not sure that I understand why we're here. You don't need authorization from Congress to do what you're proposing."

The president smiled. "Clyde, if Jake's plan backfires, a bunch of Israelis are going to get killed. And then they'll rain down bombs on Lebanon and probably invade the damn country again, and then whatever shaky peace we have over there will completely evaporate. I'm sharing this with you because if you have any objections, now's the time to say something."

In other words, Mahoney thought, the president wasn't going to be standing at the podium in the White House press room saying he'd acted unilaterally if his plan failed. His friends in Congress were going to share the blame. The president was a big believer in blame spreading, and rarely did any of it stick to him.

"Yeah, but you're asking us to buy a pig in a poke," Mahoney said. He directed this statement at LaFountaine rather than at the president, that being the more politically correct thing to do. "We don't know the source of the intelligence and we don't know why you want the rockets to reach Lebanon, but you're asking us to go along with this thing anyway."

Edna Clouter spoke for the first time during the meeting. "Mr. Speaker, I've seen the intelligence package and I agree with Director LaFountaine's approach."

At that point, Mahoney gave up. He didn't trust LaFountaine, and he and all the military guys in the room considered the president to be a lightweight when it came to military matters, but *everyone* trusted Edna Clouter. If she said that what LaFountaine was doing made sense, you could take that to the bank.

"Okay, ladies and gentlemen," the president said. "Thank you for coming."

As Mahoney was leaving the room, he realized he'd just heard something important, but he couldn't put his finger on it. Whatever it was, he'd have to figure it out later. Right now he had to get back to his office and lie down and die like the hungover dog he was.

Chapter 50

With Stephan watching, Marty Taylor packed a bag with a change of clothes and then they joined Andrei in a Subaru station wagon. Stephan motioned for him to sit in the back, and as soon as he was inside Andrei hit the button to lock all the doors even though Marty could tell that they weren't the least bit worried he'd try to escape. And why should they be worried? There were two of them and they were both armed.

As they drove, Andrei and Stephan chatted in Russian, so Marty had no idea what they were talking about. At one point he thought he heard his name, and both men glanced back at him and laughed. Forty minutes later, they were on a paved two-lane road, gaining in elevation, and Marty saw a sign that said they were twenty miles from the town of Julian. Julian was in the Laguna Mountains and had been a gold-mining town back in the nineteenth century. Now it was best known for its apple pies. There were two deer grazing near the sign and as Marty turned his head to look at them, he noticed for the first time what was in the storage area behind the backseat.

There were two shovels lying there, and a pick.

Oh, fuck.

Problem: What do you do when you're in a moving vehicle and you have to get away from two armed thugs who make their living killing people?

Marty figured he had two advantages. Neither Andrei nor Stephan was physically imposing; he suspected he could have beaten either man easily in a fair fight—although there wasn't going to be a fair fight. The other advantage he had was that these guys thought he was a pussy and didn't expect him to resist in any way. That gave him a little bit of an edge, but not much of one. Maybe the best thing would be to wait until they got to the motel because at some point one of them would go out for booze and food, and that would leave only one guy watching him.

But the shovels made him wonder if they were really going to a motel. Maybe Yuri had just said that so Marty wouldn't resist getting in the car and they were really taking him out into the boondocks to kill him. He had thought that Yuri would keep him alive until all the sales were complete but since Yuri had power of attorney, he didn't really need him alive.

He didn't know. He didn't know if he was going to a motel or to a shallow grave in the mountains. All he knew for sure was that he had to get away from these goons and he had to do it *before* Yuri sold all of his possessions. The Justice gal had said that she'd get him into the witness protection program and agreed to let him keep the proceeds from the sale of his assets, but if he waited too long, there wouldn't be any proceeds and he'd be starting his new life as a virtual pauper. He just couldn't let that happen. He'd been rich for so long he couldn't even remember what it was like being poor, and he didn't intend to find out now.

He casually reached over the back of the seat. He could touch the handle of one of the shovels. But so what? He couldn't swing the shovel within the confines of the car. He could, however, take the shovel, hold it like a spear, and jab Andrei in the head. But what good would that do? Even if he could get any force behind the jab, which was unlikely inside the car, the most that would do was maybe cause a wreck—which could kill him, too. Then another question occurred to him: What difference did it make if he was killed in a car wreck or killed by Stephan and Andrei later?

They were driving through a forest at this point, a road cut along the side of a hill, and the ground dropped off steeply on the left side of the car. He glanced at the men in the front seat; they were still talking and ignoring him. He noticed for the first time that Stephan wasn't wearing his seat belt—which made him snug the one he was wearing even tighter across his chest.

He knew that what he was about to do was dangerous but didn't see that he had a choice. And he had one thing working in his favor: people tended to survive car wrecks these days, with seat belts and airbags and all that crash testing they did. So he figured he had a good chance of surviving a wreck, and since he knew it was coming, maybe he'd be able to get away in the confusion after it happened.

Or maybe he'd get killed.

He waited until they were approaching a curve where Andrei would have to turn the steering wheel hard to the right to negotiate the road. He looked to the left again and saw that the ground on that side of the car dropped off like a ski slope and was covered with trees. It was going to be a hell of a ride. He reached back, grasped the shovel, and when the car was halfway into the curve he thrust the handle through the spokes of the steering wheel. Andrei screamed out a curse but he couldn't turn the wheel, and the Subaru crossed the yellow line and went airborne as it left the roadway.

For a moment the car seemed to be suspended in the air—and then it crashed and rolled. He heard windows in the car exploding when the car rolled the first time, but the roof didn't flatten and crush him. He heard airbags inflating. He heard Andrei and Stephan screaming. His left cheek bounced hard off the door frame as the car rolled two more times, and then it slammed into a tree. The seat belt across his chest felt like it was going to cut him in half.

When the car finally stopped moving it took him a moment to get over the shock of the accident and assess the situation. The good news was that the car had ended up on its wheels. Then he saw more good news: the driver's-side door was resting against the last tree the Subaru had hit and Andrei couldn't get out of the car. And Stephan looked like he was either unconscious or dead. That'll teach you not to wear your seat belt, you fuckin' dummy.

Andrei was cursing in Russian, trying to get the airbag out of his way, and at the same time he was trying to open his door. It took him a few seconds to realize that because the door was blocked by the tree, the only way out of the car was for him to push Stephan out the passenger-side door.

Marty couldn't open the back doors of the station wagon because they were locked, but that wasn't a problem because the windows were gone. He unhooked his seat belt and scrambled toward the rear passenger-side window, and when he did he saw Andrei reach for the gun in his shoulder holster. Andrei was going to shoot him to keep him from getting away. Marty stopped long enough to punch Andrei in the head and then, because it felt so good, he punched him again before crawling out the window. He was ten yards from the car when Andrei fired at him five or six times. Fortunately, trapped in the car and having to shoot over the seat, Andrei couldn't aim very well—or maybe he was just a shitty shot. Whatever the case, the bullets whipped through the foliage as Marty ran, scaring the hell out of him, making him run even faster.

As he ran, he developed a plan. He was going to head for the road they'd been on before the crash and just keep running until he found a phone. The first thing he'd do was call all the agents to stop the sales, then he'd call that gal from Justice and tell her to come and get him.

But right now what he had to do was outrun Andrei—and he was damn sure he could do that.

Chapter 51

The florist called Congressman Rudman's Anaheim office and was informed that Rudman wouldn't be available to see constituents until the following day.

His next stop was an Internet cafe to do a little research on Rudman. He didn't know where the man lived, or for that matter what he looked like. The congressman's Web site provided his biography and a photo. His address was available in the White Pages directory.

Just as the florist pulled into a parking space near Rudman's house, a car pulled into Rudman's driveway and a woman in her early thirties got out with two young boys. The woman rang the bell and the congressman came to the door. He tried to hug the boys but they squirted past him and ran into the house. The congressman then hugged the woman and she entered the house. Fifteen minutes later, the woman left by herself.

He wondered if the boys were Rudman's grandsons—the congressman seemed too old to have sons that age—and if the woman was Rudman's daughter or daughter-in-law and had dropped the kids off for a visit. Whatever the case, he wasn't going to take Rudman with two young children in the house. He just wouldn't do that.

He decided he needed to find a place from which to watch Rudman's house for an extended period. He couldn't remain where he was, parked so close to the place, because someone was liable to notice him if he was there for very long and might call the police. He looked around for a different vantage point and noticed the house directly across from Rudman's was for sale. It appeared that the house was empty: there were no curtains or blinds on the windows or any furniture that he could see in the living room. Nor was there an Open House sign on the lawn.

He exited his car, walked to the alley behind the house that was for sale, and stepped through an unlocked back gate. After making sure no one was watching, he broke a window in the backdoor and reached in and opened it. No alarm sounded. He would be able to sit on the floor in the living room of the vacant home and watch Rudman's house across the street; if a real estate agent or the home owners should happen to drop by, he would simply leave by the backdoor.

He was hoping that at some point Rudman would leave by himself, and if he did he would take him. But he wouldn't wait forever for the opportunity to get Rudman alone. If he had to, as soon as the children left, he'd force his way into Rudman's house and take him there. From reading Rudman's bio he knew the man had a wife, and he expected that she was in the house with him, but that couldn't be helped. He would wear a ski mask so she wouldn't be able to identify him, and he'd restrain her so she couldn't call the police right away, but that was the best he could do. She would simply have to bear the trauma of seeing her husband kidnapped.

DeMarco sat alone in the car watching Ray Rudman through binoculars.

The congressman lived in a modest, ranch-style home and he was in his backyard barbecuing hamburgers on a Weber grill, a blue apron stretched over his considerable gut. Two little boys who appeared to be about six or seven were running around the yard and knocking each other to the ground in what appeared to be a game of full-contact tag. DeMarco remembered from Rudman's file that he had two grandkids and he assumed that's who the boys were. Rudman's wife—a plump, gray-haired woman—was hustling back and forth from the house to a picnic table, bearing Kool-Aid, potato salad, and bottles of ketchup and relish, stopping periodically to pull the boys apart.

Rudman's house sat on a corner lot at the bottom of a street with a fairly steep grade. If it ever snowed in Anaheim the street would have been perfect for sledding. DeMarco and Angela had parked their car at the top of the hill and from that position could see Rudman's front porch, a portion of his backyard, and his driveway. But as Rudman's house was on a corner, it could be watched from four different directions and, consequently, someone else could be watching Rudman, and DeMarco and Angela wouldn't be able to see this person. Because of this, Angela would periodically leave DeMarco sitting alone in the car and walk around the neighborhood looking for lurking strangers. She wouldn't allow DeMarco to go with her because the mystery man had seen DeMarco in Myrtle Beach. When she took these walks, she'd change her appearance as best she could: she'd wear her hair up or down, put on a baseball cap and sunglasses. Sometimes she'd wear a light Windbreaker, sometimes not. DeMarco figured she was following some sort of Spy 101 tradecraft that she'd been taught at Langley; he also figured she was wasting her time. The man they were looking for wouldn't be easy to fool and would be hard to spot.

As DeMarco watched Rudman take the hamburgers off the grill, he couldn't help but think how *ordinary* Rudman seemed. He looked just like any other middle-aged man barbecuing for his grandkids— grandkids that he most likely loved and cherished. Yet this same man, for completely self-serving reasons, had caused the death of a dedicated American intelligence agent. It was hard for DeMarco to understand how Ray Rudman could be both of these people.

Angela opened the door and entered the car, tossing her baseball cap disguise onto the rear seat.

"Well?" DeMarco prompted. "Did you see anybody skulking about?"

"I got a call while I was out," she said.

The way her voice sounded, DeMarco turned and looked directly at her.

"They found Tully. He's dead."

DeMarco wasn't surprised that Tully was dead but it was still shocking to hear the news. More than anything else, though, he was worried about what he and Angela were doing. The mystery man had killed Whitmore. And based on what Yuri had told Angela, he had taken Tully away from Yuri's men. The guy was good, and he was brutal. He was a killing machine—and it was pretty unlikely that he and Angela working alone would be able to keep him from killing Rudman.

"Where the hell's this team that LaFountaine was supposed to send in to relieve us?" he asked.

The team LaFountaine had promised should have been there hours ago. And since they'd been watching Rudman, Angela had called Langley twice and asked to speak to LaFountaine but was told he wasn't available. So she had called that guy with the cane, Foley, but he wasn't available, either.

"I don't know," she said. "Maybe they were delayed for some reason."

"Bullshit," DeMarco said. "There is no team. And that's why LaFountaine is ducking your calls. We're on our own here."

She didn't answer.

"I'm telling you, Angela, LaFountaine wants Rudman dead and our only reason for being here is to identify the guy who kills him."

She still didn't answer.

The front door to Rudman's house opened and the two boys burst out. They had a Frisbee and they began tossing it to each other. The boys were dark haired and wiry and filled with energy—and they reminded the florist so much of his own sons. He even remembered his boys playing with a Frisbee once, bouncing it off a window, and their mother yelling at them. The memory almost broke his heart.

Was that the same woman walking past Rudman's house? Two hours ago he'd seen a woman walking by with long dark hair. This woman looked similar, but she was wearing a baseball cap and sunglasses and he couldn't see her hair. He should have paid more attention to the first woman—noted the way she walked, studied her face—but he hadn't. Now he couldn't tell if it was the same woman or not. He was getting sloppy.

DeMarco was about ready to go out of his mind.

They had been watching Rudman's house for hours and he wasn't sure how much more he could take. He had always figured that to be a good stake-out guy a lobotomy was required.

He finally asked the question he'd been thinking about the whole time they'd been sitting there.

"What about us?"

She looked at him for a long time before she answered, and he was dreading that she was going to say the words he didn't want to hear. But she didn't.

"I don't know," she said. "I just . . . Look, I don't know. When this is over . . ." And she let the words trail off.

And before he could say anything else, her phone rang and he heard her say, "Yes. Where are you?" Then there was a long pause as she listened to the caller and she said, "Just stay there; someone will pick you up."

"Who was that?" DeMarco asked when Angela finished the call.

"Marty Taylor. He got away from Yuri and he's hiding in a motel near Julian. He still thinks I'm Pamela Walker, his savior from the Justice Department, and he wants me to come and get him."

"So what are you going to do?"

She sat there for a moment, then said, "I'm going to call Ryan Schommer, the FBI agent who told us about Yuri and Taylor in the first place. I'm going to tell him that Marty's ready to roll over on Yuri and he should send some guys to pick him up."

"You're not going to check with LaFountaine first?"

"No."

Well, good for you, DeMarco thought.
But what about us?

———◆◆◆———

It was getting dark. The florist hoped that the boys weren't planning to spend the night with the congressman. He had plenty to drink because the water in the house had not been shut off but there was no food in the place and he hadn't brought any with him. He hadn't been expecting a prolonged surveillance.

Rudman's garage door opened and a car backed down the driveway. Rudman was driving. He was alone. Thank God.

The florist made no attempt to be stealthy. He walked out the front door of the vacant house and went quickly to his car, which was parked only fifty yards away. When he started the engine, Rudman was less than half a block ahead of him.

———◆◆◆———

"I'm gonna take another walk around the block," Angela said.

DeMarco didn't like the idea of her walking around by herself in the dark. He started to tell her that he was going with her, and the subject wasn't open to debate, when he noticed Rudman's car backing out of the garage.

"Hey," he said. "Rudman's leaving."

"Follow him. But don't get too close."

"Yes, ma'am."

———◆◆◆———

The florist glanced into the rearview mirror as he followed Rudman. He could see a car behind him containing two people, but the car was too far back for him to make out the occupants' faces. He wondered if they could be following him or Rudman, but that seemed unlikely.

Rudman switched his left-turn signal on and a moment later turned into the parking lot of a supermarket called Ralph's. The florist didn't follow Rudman into the parking lot. He parked on the street about half a block away from the entrance to the store. Because he had to concentrate on parallel parking his car, he didn't notice the car that had been behind him followed Rudman into the store parking lot.

He sat for a moment, then took Benny Mark's little .32 from the glove compartment and exited the car.

———◆◆◆———

DeMarco and Angela followed Rudman into the supermarket parking lot.

"Can you believe that guy?" DeMarco said.

"What?" she responded.

"He parked in a handicapped space."

Angela shrugged. "He's got a sticker; he's not doing anything illegal."

"He's not handicapped; he's just fat and too lazy to walk."

They parked and watched as Rudman entered the store.

"I'm going inside with him," Angela said.

"Why? He'll buy whatever he's buying and come back."

"I just want to keep him in sight," she said. "Wait here and keep the engine running."

As Angela entered the store, DeMarco barely noticed the big guy with short hair and a heavy mustache walk in behind her.

———◆◆◆———

Rudman walked directly to the frozen food aisle and Angela followed him. When he stopped to look at the ice cream, she walked past him, stopped at the end of the aisle, and pretended to look at the frozen pizzas. She glanced back at Rudman and he was standing there with the freezer doors open, apparently trying to decide which kind of ice cream to buy.

She noticed another man at the opposite end of the aisle, a big guy with a mustache. He was just standing there and he appeared to be watching Rudman, too, then he walked down the aisle, stood next to him, and placed his mouth close to Rudman's ear as he spoke. She wondered if the man might be a constituent who had recognized Rudman and decided to exercise his democratic right to bitch to his elected representative about the job he was doing. But then she saw the look on Rudman's face. He wasn't saying a word and he looked scared. He slowly put the ice-cream carton he'd been holding back into the freezer and walked away with the mustached man. She noticed then that the man was keeping one hand in the pocket of the jacket he was wearing.

Rudman was being kidnapped; she was sure of it. And the mustached man was the mystery man, the killer. She reached into her purse for her gun, then stopped. She could draw her gun and tell the man taking Rudman to stop, but she didn't want to do that in a store crowded with people. The man had killed before, he was certainly armed now, and he might start shooting—and she wouldn't be able to shoot back because she might hit Rudman or another shopper. And there was another thing: if she apprehended the man in the store, the cops were sure to get involved, and then she'd have to explain why she, a CIA agent, had been watching Rudman. The best thing to do would be to get the guy when he was alone with Rudman.

━━━━◆◆◆━━━━

DeMarco saw Rudman exit the store. With him was the guy that had followed Angela into the store—the big guy with the mustache. DeMarco expected Rudman to split away from the other man and walk to his car but that didn't happen. Instead, Rudman and the other man both got into Rudman's car and, because Rudman had parked in the handicapped space closest to the door, they were in Rudman's car seconds after exiting the store.

Angela walked out of the store immediately after Rudman. She must have seen Rudman and the other man leave the store, and she must know that the man with Rudman was probably kidnapping Rudman, but she walked right past Rudman's car and joined DeMarco.

"That's the guy," she said. "He's kidnapping Rudman."

"I can see that," DeMarco said. "We need to—"

Rudman's car was now leaving the parking lot.

"Follow them!" Angela said. "We can't lose them."

"We need to call the cops, Angela," DeMarco said. "This guy's going to kill Rudman."

"Follow them!"

"Angela, call the damn cops, for Christ's sake!"

"We can't call the cops. We can't get them involved in this."

"Yes, we can. It's time to end this thing."

"Just follow them!"

Rather than continue to argue with her, DeMarco followed Rudman's car out of the parking lot—then he reached for his cell phone. If she wouldn't call the cops, he would. But then Angela took out her cell phone and punched in a number—whoever she was calling, though, didn't answer. She made another call. This time DeMarco heard her say, "Foley, goddamn you, why haven't you returned my calls? The guy who killed Whitmore and Tully has Rudman. We're following them right now. Where the hell's this team that LaFountaine said he was sending?" DeMarco didn't know what Foley said to her, but he heard her say, "That's bullshit, Foley, and you know it. You tell LaFountaine to call me. You *make* him call me. I want to know what he wants me to do."

———◆———

"Do you want money?" Rudman asked, the sweat rolling down his round face.

"Just drive," the florist said.

"You have to know something. I'm a United States congressman. You really don't want to hurt me."

"I know who you are, Mr. Rudman. Now be quiet and drive."

359

DeMarco wondered where the guy was taking Rudman. He didn't appear to be headed toward the freeway; he was just winding his way through Anaheim in a seemingly random pattern. DeMarco stayed a couple of car lengths back from Rudman's car, making no attempt to hide the fact that he was following. He didn't want to lose Rudman and, for that matter, if the killer knew someone was tailing him he might not kill him.

Rudman turned onto a street that contained a large Goodwill store. The store was closed for the day and there was nobody walking on the street, nor were there any other cars driving on the street except for DeMarco's and Rudman's. DeMarco was certain the man with Rudman would realize at any second that he was being followed.

This had gone on long enough. DeMarco reached for his cell phone to call 911—and just at that moment Rudman abruptly turned into an alley that ran alongside the Goodwill store. It was the alley folks drove down when they were dropping things off at the store.

DeMarco could think of only one reason why they had driven into the alley: the man had been looking for an isolated spot in which to kill Rudman and he'd found it. He drove past the mouth of the alley, saw Rudman's car stopped about thirty yards away, and he immediately pulled over to the curb and parked.

"He's going to kill Rudman," DeMarco said. "He's going to kill him now."

He reached past Angela, opened the glove compartment, and grabbed the gun he'd taken from the Russian kid wearing the "Dirty White Boy" T-shirt. As he exited the car, he said, "Call the cops."

"Joe, wait!" she said—but he didn't.

DeMarco ran into the alley. Rudman was on his knees near his car. The kidnapper was standing behind him, pointing a gun at his head.

"This is the way she died," the florist said. "On her knees, terrified, waiting for the bullet that would end her life. She was only twenty-eight when she died. And you killed her."

"Please! You need to let me explain," Rudman said.

DeMarco stopped, spread his legs, and holding his gun in a two-handed grip aimed at the kidnapper. DeMarco had fired a pistol only a couple of times in his life, he was a lousy shot, and he knew that his chances of hitting a man standing thirty yards away were practically nil.

"Put down the gun!" DeMarco yelled.

Rudman's assassin spun toward DeMarco, obviously surprised to see him, and pointed his gun at DeMarco. DeMarco should have fired then, but he didn't. Fortunately, neither did the other man.

"Put down the gun!" DeMarco said again.

The man didn't do anything for a moment, and then he did something completely unexpected. He smiled sadly at DeMarco and said, "I'm sorry, but I can't do that."

Then he turned as if DeMarco wasn't there and aimed his gun again at Rudman's head.

Three shots were fired almost simultaneously. DeMarco fired at the killer, the killer fired at Rudman, and Angela fired the third shot. Instead of calling the cops, she had followed DeMarco into the alley. DeMarco had no idea whose bullet hit the kidnapper—his or hers—but he guessed it was most likely hers.

DeMarco ran down the alley. The kidnapper was on the ground with a wound in his right side. His eyes were closed and he was bleeding heavily but he was alive. He had dropped his gun when he hit the ground and it was a couple of feet from his outstretched hand. DeMarco kicked the gun a few more feet down the alley.

"Is Rudman dead?" the man asked without opening his eyes.

DeMarco didn't answer, but Rudman wasn't dead. He was still on his knees, panting like he'd run a marathon. There was no way the killer should have missed Rudman standing as close to him as he'd been. Angela's or DeMarco's bullet must have hit him just before he fired, throwing off his aim.

"Are you all right, Congressman?" DeMarco asked.

Rudman said, "I'm, I think . . . then Rudman grabbed his left shoulder and toppled over. Aw, Jesus, the son of a bitch was having a heart attack.

"Call an ambulance," DeMarco said to Angela, and for once she didn't argue.

He knelt down next to Rudman. "Hang in there, Congressman. An ambulance is on the way." Rudman's eyes were shut tightly. He was taking rapid, shallow breaths and was obviously in a lot of pain. And then his eyes popped open as if in surprise or shock and he gasped and stopped breathing.

"Ah, shit!" DeMarco said.

He started to perform CPR on Rudman but after a couple of minutes he stopped. Rudman was dead.

DeMarco turned and looked behind him. Angela had her gun in one hand and was watching the killer as she talked to someone on her phone. The killer was just lying with his eyes closed, seeming oddly content. He didn't plead for help or complain about his pain, and DeMarco got the impression that he didn't care if he lived or died.

Angela closed her cell phone. "Is Rudman dead?" she asked.

DeMarco nodded, too out of breath from performing CPR to talk.

"A city ambulance is on the way but we need to take this guy and get out of here. I know a place to take him and a doctor will meet us there."

DeMarco thought about what she had said. He didn't really care if the killer died, and Rudman was already dead, so there was no point in staying and waiting for the ambulance. If they waited, the cops would ask questions that they'd refuse to answer and inevitably the media would find out what had happened and would begin to speculate in print as to why a CIA agent, a congressional lawyer, and a gunshot man were in an alley with the body of a dead congressman. He didn't need any of that, particularly anything that got his name in the paper or his picture on the news.

DeMarco picked up the killer's gun and then he and Angela carried the man over to DeMarco's rental car and laid him down on the backseat. He didn't resist in any way.

DeMarco looked over at Rudman's body and, for some reason, thought about how bad his grandkids would feel when they heard he was dead. He also thought that when the cops arrived on the scene, they were going to ask themselves a lot of questions. They were going to wonder why Rudman, instead of going to the market to buy ice cream, had ended up having a heart attack in an alley miles away from the store. They were also going to find a fresh pool of blood that didn't belong to Rudman and three shell casings from three different weapons. The only good news was an autopsy would show a fat man had died of a heart attack, and that was all that really mattered.

"Where are we taking this guy?" DeMarco asked.

"A veterinarian's clinic," Angela said.

"You don't think an emergency room for humans might be smarter?"

Angela didn't answer.

The man in the backseat groaned and DeMarco turned and looked at him.

"Who are you?" DeMarco asked.

The man's lips twitched briefly in that same sad smile DeMarco had seen before he tried to kill Rudman.

"I'm a florist," he said.

Chapter 52

Ivan sat at the kitchen table in his mistress's apartment in Escondido, bouncing his son on his knee. The little tyke seemed almost fully recovered from the horrible cough he'd had.

Yuri had told him to go to a motel but he had decided that he wasn't going to waste the money. How would the police know about his mistress, anyway? Until Yuri called and gave him another assignment, he would just enjoy his children.

His cell phone rang. He looked at the caller ID and didn't recognize the number but the only people who had his number were people in Yuri's organization.

"Hello?" he said.

"Ivan, this is your Uncle Lev. There's something you need to do for me."

Marty Taylor thought that maybe, just maybe, everything was going to turn out all right.

He had run about three miles after he got away from Stephan and Andrei, then was able to wave down a ride from an old coot driving a Jeep. He had the guy drop him off at the first motel he saw and checked in using cash and a phony name.

The first thing he did was call the agents who were selling his stuff.

He told them to stop the sales immediately and if they didn't he was going to sue their asses off. Fortunately, the houses and land in Arizona hadn't been sold yet. Some of the artwork had, and a couple of his cars were gone, but he still had almost everything else. After that had been taken care of, he had called the good-looking lady from the Justice Department and told her where he was.

The more he thought about it, the more he liked the idea of going into witness protection. He'd be safe from Yuri, and if he testified against him, he wouldn't have to worry about getting tossed in jail for what Diller or Yuri had done. But it was more than that. He just wanted to start over. He was tired of his company and he didn't want to work anymore. He was tired of being Marty Taylor. He just wanted to sit on a beach some place and surf. He wouldn't be as rich as he was now, but with the twenty or thirty million he got from selling his possessions . . . well, he'd be just fine.

There was a knock on the door. He pulled back a curtain and peeked out the window: two serious-looking guys in suits. One of the men knocked again and said, "Mr. Taylor. FBI. Please open the door."

Marty flung open the door and said, "Thank God, you're finally here. I was getting kinda worried. I called Walker hours ago."

"Walker?" the FBI agent said.

"Yeah, Pamela Walker. That's why you're here isn't it?"

"Sir, all we've been told is that you're willing to testify against Yuri Markelov for crimes he's committed. Is that correct?"

"Yeah, as long as you hold up your end of the deal."

"Deal?"

"Yeah. The deal Walker agreed to. You're taking me to the witness protection guys, right?"

"Mr. Taylor, I have no idea what you're talking about and I don't know a Pamela Walker. We were just told to take you into custody."

"No, no. You need to call Walker."

"Mr. Taylor, we're not calling anyone. We're taking you to the federal prosecutor in San Diego. You may want to call your lawyer when we get there."

Benny Mark was crying. His wife was, too.

In about five minutes they were going to wheel him into an operating room and whack off his foot and part of his leg.

The gunshot wound in his foot had stopped bleeding by the time he got to the fishing resort in Canada and he had figured that with time his foot would heal completely. Betty Ann kept bugging him to go to a doctor but he had ignored her.

Then his foot got all puffy and streaks of red appeared up his leg. Then his foot turned kinda purple—but he figured it was just bruising from all the trauma.

Then his foot began to turn black and it started to stink.

It didn't seem fair. As far as he knew, all the people he had killed had been criminals and the world wasn't going to miss them at all. Well, there had been that one guy in St. Louis—the guy he'd shot by mistake because he had the same name as the target—but hell, everybody makes mistakes.

Whatever the case, fair or not, it looked like his days as a hit man were over. Who was going to hire a killer with an artificial foot?

But then he thought: a guy with a plastic foot and maybe a cane? They'd never see him coming.

Porter Henry tossed a ham and cheese sandwich and a yellow legal pad into his battered briefcase.

In half an hour, Marty Taylor was going to be interrogated by a federal prosecutor regarding his role in Conrad Diller's attempt to sell classified technology to Iran. More importantly, Taylor had been dumb enough to say he was willing to testify against Yuri Markelov if he got some sort of deal from the feds. He hoped the fool hadn't talked too much about Yuri.

Marty Taylor's chief counsel had called Henry an hour earlier and asked him to attend the meeting and sit second chair if the case went to trial. He said he wanted Henry's help because he knew the background on Diller and had dealt with the prosecutor before. But Porter Henry figured the real reason Marty's lawyer had called him was because he was a partner in a white-shoe law firm that dealt mostly with financial matters and had little experience representing criminals.

He wasn't worried about getting Marty off regarding Diller. The feds had no evidence that Marty had been involved in Diller's trip to Iran, and with Diller missing and Andy Bollinger dead, they wouldn't get any. More worrisome was Marty's ties to other crimes Yuri might have committed. Even if Yuri had forced Marty to cooperate in his illegal schemes, the fact still remained that he should have called the authorities and told them what Yuri was doing. And Marty's stockholders—they would be screaming for Marty's blood if it turned out Yuri had been stealing money from the company and that Marty had done nothing to stop him.

So he didn't know how things were going to turn out for Marty, but there was one thing he did know: this was going to be his last case. He would charge young Mr. Taylor an outrageous amount of money to defend him, get his money up front, and if he could get him off that would be nice.

And if he couldn't, who cared?

———◆◆◆———

After he had received the call from Uncle Lev—the call that he hadn't answered—Yuri hadn't been quite sure what to do.

He had to assume that Mikhail had talked to Lev, and that Mikhail had told him everything—about how the FBI was pursuing him because of Diller and the dead spy, and the bungled raid on Rulon Tully. So Lev would be angry. Dangerously angry.

But he had thought, *Maybe the situation is still salvageable.* He could tell Lev he was selling Marty Taylor's possessions and that the sale would gross millions, which he would, of course, share with his uncle. He called Andrei to see where they had taken Taylor, and Andrei informed him that Taylor had escaped and Stephan was dead. He called the sales agents next and they all told him the same thing: that

Taylor had stopped the sales and they wouldn't proceed even if Yuri did have power of attorney.

He knew then the only option he had was to run.

He checked into a hotel so he would be off the street in case either the cops or Lev was looking for him. Tomorrow, after he'd gotten some sleep, he would drive to Canada. He was afraid to fly because airport security might already have his picture and be looking for him. But if he could get across the border, there was a man he knew in Vancouver who could smuggle him onto a cargo ship, and then he would . . . hell, he didn't know what he would do. All he knew was that it was time to leave San Diego and get as far away from Lev as he could.

Then he got very drunk.

The next morning, he walked out to his car hungover, tired, and depressed. He keyed the remote to open the car door and at that moment heard a foot scrape on the concrete behind him. He turned. It was Ivan.

"What are you doing here?" he asked. Then he thought of another question. "How did you know where to find me?"

Ivan walked toward him, a smile on his broad face. "Uncle Lev said something about a device you have on your car. A LoJack? Something like that. I really don't understand how it works."

The Porsche he had been driving belonged to Marty Taylor. It had never occurred to him that it might have a LoJack system installed.

"So why are you here?" Yuri asked again, but as he spoke he moved his hand slowly toward the gun that was shoved into his belt at the back of his pants.

Ivan's hands shot out. One hand grabbed his arm to keep him from reaching the gun. His other huge hand encircled Yuri's neck.

As Ivan began to squeeze, Yuri heard him say, "Uncle Lev said to tell you he's going to miss you."

Chapter 53

The doctor—presumably on retainer for the CIA—came out of the operating room, stripping latex gloves off his hands as he walked.

DeMarco had seen the operating room when he and Angela carried the killer into the veterinary clinic. There was an electric hoist over the operating table and the table looked big enough to accommodate major-sized mammals.

"He'll be okay," the doctor said. "Whoever owns this clinic has better equipment than I have at the hospital where I work. Anyway, I got both bullets and he'll recover."

"Both bullets?" DeMarco said. It looked like both he and Angela had shot the guy.

"Is he conscious?" Angela asked.

"Yeah, but he's drowsy," the doctor said. "I gave him some pain medication. I hope that was okay."

DeMarco shook his head. He guessed the doctor meant, *I hope it was okay to relieve his pain and that you didn't want him suffering so he'd be more likely to talk.* CIA physicians took a different sort of Hippocratic oath.

"As long as he's lucid," Angela said.

It turned out that there was no need to withhold the man's pain medication to get him to talk. He was more than happy to tell them his story and he obviously didn't care about the punishment he would face for killing Sandra Whitmore and Rulon Tully. Whether he'd killed Ray Rudman was debatable, and at this point irrelevant.

He said his name was Parviz Kharazi—and that he was Mahata's uncle.

"You're lying. Mahata's family is all dead," Angela said.

Kharazi shook his head. "All but me," he said. And then told his story.

In 1979, the shah of Iran, Mohammad Reza Pahlavi, was driven from the country and Iran became a theocracy led by the Muslim cleric Ayatollah Khomeini. At the time, Parviz Kharazi was just a young man who couldn't find a job. He wasn't religious and he wasn't the least bit political—he was just broke. So when an old family friend came to him and offered him employment with the organization that eventually became known as the MOIS, the Ministry for Intelligence and Security, he took it.

When the shah was in power, there was an organization called SAVAK, which was the shah's secret police. It's function, among other things, was to kill or imprison anyone trying to overthrow the shah. The mullahs, regardless of their religious leanings, soon found need for a similar organization, and thus the MOIS was formed. The organization's first mission had been to hunt down the shah's old supporters and dispose of them—even people who had fled the country. Once that task had been accomplished, the MOIS set about doing essentially what SAVAK had done: making sure the population toed the party line.

Young Parviz Kharazi was a mere foot soldier in all of this. He was told to arrest people, and he did. He was told to torture people to get information, and he did. He was told, upon occasion, to kill people and he did this, too. He wasn't a sociopath or a psychopath, so when he did these things he convinced himself that he was on the right side of God and politics, and that his was an honorable job.

When he saw Angela look at him with distaste, he said, "I served my country in the same way that American CIA and FBI agents serve their country. I worked for my government and I followed the laws of the land. I was a patriot."

He rose through the ranks, advanced to a middle management position—and he prospered. He married. He had two sons. He owned a modest home in Tehran but he kept his money in a Swiss bank. He may have been a loyal Iranian but he knew better than to trust the national banks. Had it not been for his brother, he would still be in Iran today and, very likely, a senior member of his former service.

His brother, Mohsen, had been the fly in the ointment. Mohsen was ten years younger than him, the beloved baby of the family, and everyone doted on him including Kharazi. And thanks to Kharazi, his brother received a good education, including some schooling abroad, and he eventually became a professor at a prestigious university. Maybe Kharazi's downfall occurred because of Mohsen's exposure to Western culture, or maybe it happened just because Mohsen was an intellectual surrounded by other intellectuals. Whatever the reason, it seemed as if all Mohsen and his friends did was drink coffee and talk about things like human rights, women's rights, and religious freedom—and all the other nonsense that had nothing to do with the way the world really worked. Kharazi tried to tell him he was going to get in trouble if he didn't quit shooting off his mouth, but every time he tried, his smart little brother bombarded him with high-toned rhetoric that Kharazi couldn't even understand, much less counter.

Eventually, his boss came to him—the man that had originally enlisted him in the MOIS—and told him he had to control Mohsen. He knew the only reason his brother was still alive or not in jail was because of his position, but his boss said Mohsen had gone too far and had to be stopped—one way or another.

After that meeting, Kharazi pleaded with Mohsen. He begged him to stop what he was doing. But his brother—his handsome, brilliant, passionate brother—just spouted more nonsense about the need for people to stand up for their rights, to fight corruption, to . . . Kharazi had slapped him. He slapped him so hard he knocked him to the ground. "They're going to kill you!" he screamed. "Don't you understand that?"

But Mohsen didn't understand.

His boss came to him one morning and said, not unkindly, that Mohsen was going to be arrested. And then Kharazi made a mistake. He said, "No one better hurt him." It was okay if his brother had to go to jail for a while—maybe the experience would be good for him, make him grow up—but he didn't want him to be tortured and certainly not killed. But the way he said it, it came out as a threat. And his boss was not a man you threatened. And his boss knew him. He knew that the man who had just threatened him was a very competent killer.

He begged his boss for one more chance. He told him Mohsen was coming to his house for dinner that night and if he couldn't convince him to stop what he was doing, he would arrest Mohsen himself. His boss looked at him for a long time, and he thought he saw sadness or maybe regret in his boss's eyes, but eventually he agreed.

Mohsen came to his house that night. Reluctantly, petulantly, arrogantly, but he came. Mohsen's wife came with him, but not his daughter. Little Mahata had a cold and they had left her with a kindly neighbor. They sat down at the dinner table—Kharazi's wife and his two sons, Mohsen and his wife. His plan was to try and have a pleasant family dinner then talk privately to his brother afterward. Kharazi wasn't going to let him leave until he convinced him to stop his dissident ways—or he was going to arrest him that night.

The thing that saved him was the refrigerator door. They started to eat but his wife had forgotten to put the cheese on the table. Since he was closest to the kitchen, he got up and went to the refrigerator, and when he was bent over, head inside the fridge, reaching for the cheese, he heard glass breaking, then an enormous blast.

Shrapnel flew through the house and the dining room became an inferno. The refrigerator that had shielded him from the shrapnel and the initial fireball was blown into a wall, almost crushing him. The roof partially collapsed and the houses on either side of his also caught fire. He pushed the refrigerator off him and saw that the dining room was an incinerator and he knew immediately that everyone inside the room was dead. There was no way they could have survived.

He determined later that it had been a satchel bomb filled with explosives, metal—nails, screws, and bolts—and some type of flammable liquid. He also figured out that the bomber must have been standing across the street from his house and had seen the family sit down for dinner, and as the bomber was sneaking up to the window to fling his deadly package, that was when he had left the table to retrieve the cheese from the refrigerator.

He never knew if his boss had ordered them to kill his entire family but he knew his boss had issued the order for him and his brother to die, and he understood why his boss wanted him dead: the man knew that he would avenge his brother's death. But did he intend for Kharazi's wife and sons to be killed with him? Maybe. Maybe his boss was afraid that one day Kharazi's sons would try to avenge their father's death. Or maybe his boss just said to kill him and Mohsen, but didn't make it clear it should be done in such a way that others would not be killed. He didn't know what his boss had intended and, afterward, his intentions didn't matter. One thing he was sure of: his boss had never considered the possibility that he would survive.

Mohsen's friends arranged for little Mahata to be sent to London. A year later, she was adopted by an Iranian American couple, the Javadis, who were living in London at the time. She was such a beautiful, bright little girl that it was easy to understand why a childless couple would welcome her into their home.

Parviz Kharazi spent the year Mahata was in London avenging his family. He killed the man who made the bomb, the man who threw the bomb, three of his boss's bodyguards, and finally his boss. After Kharazi killed the bomb maker, his boss must have known that he had somehow survived the explosion, and the man did his best to protect himself, but Kharazi—the man he had recruited and trained— was just too good a killer to be stopped.

Ironically, it was his brother's idealistic friends who helped him flee Iran, and it was a network of those same friends who helped him get false papers and eventually immigrate to America. And because his money was in a Swiss bank, he had money when he arrived in the United States and he bought his flower shop about a year after his arrival. And his luck continued. He was always so damn lucky. His flower shop provided a good living.

By then Mahata had been with her adopted family for over two years and was living in America. He considered approaching her and telling her that he was alive. He even considered kidnapping her from her adopted family and raising her himself. But he did neither of these things. He could see she had a good home, was being raised by people who loved her, and was better off with them than she would ever be with him. The other reason he didn't try to take her from her adopted parents was that he knew his old organization was still trying to find him, and if they ever did they would kill him—and then Mahata would be an orphan again.

He watched her grow up from afar. He attended her soccer games and he watched with pride as she played the violin in her high school band. He was in the audience when she graduated from high school and from college. He knew she had been hired by the CIA. One of the things he did occasionally was follow her to a coffee shop near her apartment. The last time she had seen him she had been four, and he wasn't worried that she would recognize him. He just liked to sit near her, listen to her and her roommate talk, and he heard her tell her roommate she had been hired by the agency as a translator. That had made him smile—that a daughter of Iran was now working for the American government. Then she disappeared—and for six agonizing years he had no idea where she was—until he read about her death in the paper.

He concluded with, "I never remarried. She was the only person left on this earth that I loved."

Angela asked him how he had killed Whitmore and Tully, and how he had found out that Rudman was the one who leaked the story.

He told them, and DeMarco was, of course, embarrassed. It had happened just as Angela had said—Kharazi had started following him the day he visited Whitmore at the federal lockup in Manhattan. He and Angela were both surprised, though, when he told them how he had captured and tortured Acosta's killer, which led him to Jimmy Franco, which in turn led him to Rulon Tully.

"And Tully told you about Rudman before you killed him?" Angela said.

"Yes."

Just *yes*. No remorse. No attempt to rationalize what he had done.

Looking at Angela, Kharazi said, "I know Mr. DeMarco works for Congress, but may I ask who you are?"

"I'm a federal agent," Angela said.

That was true, but DeMarco noticed she didn't say that the federal agency she worked for was the CIA. But Kharazi seemed satisfied by her answer.

"And so what happens now?" he asked. "Will I be placed under arrest and stand trial for my crimes or do you have something else in mind for me?"

Instead of answering his question, Angela said, "Don't make any attempt to escape from this clinic. It will go badly for you if you do."

Kharazi was recovering from two gunshot wounds and his right ankle was handcuffed to the bed, but DeMarco was thinking he would have liked it better if they had a few more people watching the man. The only ones in the clinic were him, Angela, and the indifferent surgeon who had tended to Kharazi's injuries—and what they really needed for Kharazi were a couple of heavyweights with machine guns.

But in response to Angela's threat, all Kharazi said was, "I'm not going to try to escape. I've done what I needed to do, and now you people can do what you need to do."

Then he closed his eyes and fell asleep, a man at peace with himself.

DeMarco knew that there was no way in hell the CIA was going to turn Parviz Kharazi over to the cops. If he were to stand trial, the CIA would have to explain how they had caught him, which would open up a very smelly can of worms as to exactly what the CIA had been doing in regard to everything Mr. Kharazi had done.

For that matter, DeMarco had no desire to explain his role in Kharazi's capture, either, nor would Mahoney want him doing that. On the other hand, they couldn't just let Kharazi go. The police were still investigating the deaths of Whitmore, Tully, and Rudman, and at some point the trail might lead to Kharazi—and if it did . . . well, they were back to that smelly can of worms again. One possibility was that Kharazi could just disappear into that murky world where detained terrorists were sent. Kharazi had snuck into the United States under a false passport and he had worked for the MOIS. Per the Patriot Act, as interpreted by some in the government, those facts alone were sufficient justification to whisk him off to some place like Guantánamo and hold him incommunicado indefinitely.

Angela must have been having similar thoughts because she said, "I need to talk to my boss."

"Yeah, me, too," DeMarco said.

DeMarco left the clinic and went to stand outside on the porch. As he punched in Mahoney's number, he looked up at the stars, surprised so many were visible through California's famous smog. He'd always wanted to take a class that would teach him which stars were which; the only constellation he could identify was the Big Dipper. He was getting old enough that maybe it was time to quit putting off all the things he wanted to do "some day."

DeMarco told Mahoney all that had happened, concluding with the fact that the man who had killed Whitmore and Tully was handcuffed to a nearby bed and happy to confess his crimes to anyone who wanted to listen. Mahoney's response was predictable. He was shocked by what Kharazi had done, and even more shocked that DeMarco had captured him, but his nimble mind immediately leaped to the potential political consequences of Kharazi talking. He told DeMarco to keep Kharazi away from a phone, the cops, and the press until he could talk to LaFountaine.

DeMarco was about to hang up when Mahoney said, "There's something else." But then he didn't say anything for a while, as if he was reluctant to speak. Finally, he said, "What I'm about to tell you is classified so high that they don't even have a name for the classification level." Then Mahoney told him about the meeting he'd attended in the White House situation room. DeMarco didn't understand why Mahoney was telling him about rockets and some Hezbollah splinter group—so Mahoney explained.

"Aw, Jesus," DeMarco said. "Are you sure?"

"Hell no, I'm not sure. But my gut tells me I'm right."

"So what are you gonna do about all this?" DeMarco asked.

DeMarco knew what *he* wanted to do: he wanted to get on a plane back to Washington and leave Parviz Kharazi and this whole mess for the CIA to deal with.

"I told you," Mahoney said. "I don't know what I wanna do. But before I do anything, I'm going to talk to that bastard LaFountaine."

Chapter 54

In Potomac Park, a short distance from the grand World War II Memorial on the National Mall, is the less grand memorial to John Paul Jones, America's first naval hero. Jones's statue is cast in bronze, is ten feet tall, and rests on a magnificent marble pylon. Chiseled into the stone are Jones's famous words: "Surrender? I have not yet begun to fight." This statement was supposedly uttered by him when the captain of a British frigate, apparently thinking he had Jones defeated, had asked the American to strike the *Bonhomme Richard*'s flag.

Mahoney had always thought that somebody had made up the quote. A guy engaged in an old-time naval battle—with grapeshot flying across the deck, blowing the masts off his ship, cutting his men to ribbons—probably wouldn't think to say something like, "I have not yet begun to fight." A more likely response would have been, "Fuck you. You surrender."

Mahoney saw LaFountaine's car pull to the curb and watched as LaFountaine slowly walked down the sidewalk to where he was standing. He could tell that LaFountaine had no desire for this meeting. When LaFountaine was next to him, Mahoney jerked his big chin at Jones's statue and said, "Do you think he really said 'I have not yet begun to fight'?"

"No," LaFountaine said. "He probably said something like kiss my ass. That's what I would have said."

It was a shame, Mahoney thought, but in a different universe he and LaFountaine might have been friends.

"So what are you gonna do with Kharazi?" Mahoney asked.

"I'm gonna use him," LaFountaine said.

Mahoney hadn't thought of that, but he wasn't surprised. "How?"

"I'm going to stick him back in Iran. New face, new identity. He could be a big help to us if we ever need someone over there to . . . well, you know."

"Yeah," Mahoney said. What LaFountaine meant, but wouldn't say out loud, was that if they ever needed somebody in Iran taken off the board, this guy Kharazi had the skills to do the job.

"What makes you think he'll take the deal?"

"I'm going to give him a choice: he can either work for us or spend the rest of his life in a cell. And I'll sweeten the pot. I'll give him the name of the guy who was in charge of Mahata's interrogation. Of course, he could say that he'll take the deal and then just disappear once we insert him back in Iran, and if that happens, I guess that's okay, too. But I think he'll take the deal."

Mahoney nodded.

"Tell me something, Jake. Are you going to tell him that you're the one who was really responsible for Mahata getting killed?"

LaFountaine, to his credit, didn't pretend to be offended and say, *What in the hell do you mean by that?* He just looked away from Mahoney, unable to hide the shame he must have felt.

When LaFountaine didn't respond, Mahoney said, "You have another spy over there in Iran, someone more important than Mahata. Don't you? I figured it out the other day at the White House when you said you didn't want the source for the intelligence on those rockets traced back to Iran. So I think Mahata was a red herring of some kind and that you leaked that story about Diller intentionally. You *wanted* it leaked. But then something went wrong, and somehow that girl got killed."

LaFountaine shook his head. "Mahata wasn't a red herring. Everything I told you about her was true," he said. "And she gave us some good stuff when she was there, but she was a woman, and in that society, no matter who she was sleeping with, no matter what kind of job she got, she was only going to hear so much and rise so high. She was just never going to have access to the really important things. But you're right. We've got another guy over there, someone we turned fifteen, sixteen years ago, and he had finally worked his way up to *almost* the inner circle. But he needed something to get him into the circle, and we figured if he was the one that exposed Mahata as an American agent, not only would that be a major coup for him but, on top of that, we'd get rid of Mahata's lover, because he had the bad judgment to be shacking up with a spy.

"So when I talked to the committee about Diller's trip to Iran, I was planning on the story getting out, but I didn't expect that Ray-fucking-Rudman, God rest his soul, would tell Tully and that Tully would leak it to the press. We had a different plan."

"What plan?"

"You don't need to know that," LaFountaine said.

"Jake, right now I need to know everything. And if you don't tell me I'm going to drag your ass into a hearing room and make you testify to this whole mess in front of a hundred cameras. And politics be damned."

Mahoney expected an argument from LaFountaine, but LaFountaine just nodded his head. The wind seemed to have gone out of his sails.

"Glenda Petty was supposed to tell an Iranian agent about my testimony to that committee," LaFountaine said.

"What!" Mahoney shrieked. "Glenda's working for you?"

LaFountaine nodded.

"You mean the whole time she's been acting like she hates the CIA, she's been faking it?"

LaFountaine laughed. "Glenda hasn't been faking anything. She really does hate us." LaFountaine paused as a couple of Japanese tourists walked by, then continued. "About three years ago, Glenda was at her gym working out and this handsome guy takes an interest in her."

"What handsome guy would be interested in Glenda? She's got a face like a hammerhead shark."

"Yeah, but she's not built that bad for a gal her age. Anyway, the guy's charming as all hell. He says his name is René Picard and he's a Canadian trade representative from Quebec, and his ID matches his name. To explain his accent, he claims his first language is French, and he's actually fluent in French. Well, his real name is Nasser Moghadam and he's an Iranian. He's been in this country for about five years and we knew who he was the day he got here and we've been watching him ever since he arrived. He hangs out around Capitol Hill, gets invited to parties, and schmoozes with folks hoping to pick up something useful to send back home. Until Glenda came along, almost everything he told his boss back in Iran was stuff he saw on CNN."

"Why the hell didn't you arrest or deport the guy?"

"We didn't want him deported. We were monitoring what he was doing and everything he said. He communicates with Iran via an encrypted e-mail program that took the NSA about fifteen seconds to crack. By letting him operate we've been able to find other Iranians that are in the country illegally and some al-Qaeda types. The FBI actually stopped a terrorist attack in Chicago eighteen months ago because we saw Nasser passing cash to some guys.

"Anyway, like I was starting to say, Nasser meets Glenda at the gym, comes on to her, and she falls for it. When she goes to bed with him, he takes videos of them in the sack and he tells her that if she doesn't start passing him information she picks up in committee meetings, he's going to send the videos to her husband and broadcast them on YouTube. Ol' Nasser thought he'd hit the jackpot.

"Well, unbeknown to both Nasser and Glenda, we were recording them every time they got together. So I sat down with her one day and explained the facts of life to her: that from this point forward she was going to pass things on to Nasser but only things we wanted passed. Things that would confuse the Iranians, things that would make them think we knew more than we really knew, information that would make them do things so we could learn more about them."

Mahoney was almost too stunned to be angry. Almost. "You rotten son of a bitch. You've been forcing a United States congresswoman to be a double agent?"

"Yeah, but we never tried to control her vote. Just look at her record and you'll see I'm not lying about that. And a year ago, we donated twenty grand to her campaign to help her keep her seat in the House.

"Anyway," LaFountaine said before Mahoney could interrupt him again, "our original plan was to have Glenda tell Nasser that the CIA knew about Diller's meeting in Iran. We wanted the information to go from Nasser to Nasser's boss. Then our other spy in Iran, who works with Nasser's boss, would have started quietly investigating everyone who had attended the meeting with Diller to figure out which Iranian had told the CIA about the meeting. After a whole bunch of clever detective work, our guy—because we told him where to look—would find clues pointing directly to Mahata. And then he was supposed to *almost* catch Mahata just before she fled from Iran. But when Whitmore's article was published, the whole operation turned into a cluster fuck."

"Why didn't you just get her out when the article first appeared?" Mahoney asked.

"If we had done that, it would have been obvious to everyone over there that she was our agent and our other spy wouldn't have gotten the credit for figuring it out. We could have even delayed the *Daily News* from publishing the story, but we didn't because we thought we could still manage the situation. But then things went to hell. Our other spy didn't move fast enough. He had to talk to certain people and one of them was out of town. He had to find the clues, but he had to make it look real, and that took time. And because of the article, other folks started investigating, too, and one of them identi-

fied one of the people in Mahata's network. It all just went to shit."
LaFountaine shook his head. "She still could have gotten away but then
something happened with a car she was supposed to use to escape, something that should never have happened, and she was caught."

"Jesus," Mahoney said. He couldn't even imagine how LaFountaine
must have felt.

"Yeah, but in the end, it worked out the way we wanted. Our other
agent got a big promotion and Mahata's lover got a bullet in the back
of the head. And Mahata getting killed actually worked to our advantage. It allowed me to make a big deal publicly about how important she was, and that made our other spy in Iran even more of a
superstar for figuring out that she was an American agent."

"So this big vendetta of yours, going after Rudman and Tully, that
was all for show," Mahoney said.

"No! It wasn't for show! I meant every damn word I said to you. I
couldn't stand the fact that a guy like Tully would leak the story to
the media just because Taylor nailed his wife. I wanted Rudman and
Tully to pay for what they did.

"And there's something else: I wanted everyone at Langley to know
that as long as I'm the guy in charge, I won't tolerate American citizens, no matter who they are, jeopardizing our agents."

"Yeah," Mahoney said, "but your people never knew you exposed
her intentionally."

"Five people knew about the operation but everyone else thinks
she died because of that article in the *News*. And I couldn't let that
stand."

"What about the story you gave me the other day, that Jean
Negroni made you tell Congress about Diller? Was that a lie, too?"

"Yeah. I had to tell you something because you kept bugging me
about why I ever told the committee about Diller in the first place."

"But all I had to do was call up Negroni to see if you were lying."
LaFountaine smiled. "But you didn't."

"And what about that scheme for modifying Taylor's hardware so
we could control Iranian missiles?"

"We actually did think about that—for about five seconds. We knew right away it wouldn't work."

Mahoney just shook his head; he couldn't believe the way he'd let LaFountaine bluff him. He was trying to figure out what to say next when LaFountaine said, "So, yeah, I lied to you, John. More importantly, I fucked up, me and a guy named Carson who was responsible for Mahata's escape. And I'll have to live with that for the rest of my life. But you know something? If I had to do it again, I'd still do it, because it was so important for us to get somebody in a position over there where we could get real-time, firsthand dope on what those crazy bastards are doing. The thing with those rockets going to Lebanon that you heard about at the White House the other day? Well, that's nothing compared to some of the shit they're planning."

LaFountaine was silent for a moment. "A beautiful, brave young woman died because my people and I didn't do our job right. Those are the stakes in this game. At the same time, three people who had no loyalty to this country are dead, and that doesn't bother me a bit. So what are you going to do, Mahoney? Tell the president? Tell your buddies on the Hill? Tell the press?"

Mahoney thought about that for a moment, then said, "No, I'll keep all this to myself. You, in turn, will get your hooks out of Glenda Petty and destroy the tapes of her screwing this Iranian spy. I don't like Glenda but I won't let you use her in that way any longer."

"Deal," LaFountaine said.

"That's not all, Jake. You crossed the line with Glenda. And you crossed a lot of other lines, too. You gotta go."

LaFountaine didn't say anything for a long time, and Mahoney had no idea what he was thinking. Mahoney imagined he might be thinking that he could get away with everything he'd done—but that if they forced Glenda Petty to testify against him, his ass would be cooked.

"All right," he finally said. "I don't need to spend the next year sitting in hearings. That wouldn't be good for the Company." Then it was his turn to jerk his blunt chin toward the statue. "Unlike John

Paul, I know when it's time to quit." He smiled then, a bitter smile but nonetheless a smile. "I was thinking about getting out when the president's first term was done anyway. Harvard said they'd like to have me and I was thinking that maybe I'd teach a course called Ethics in Government."

Mahoney didn't laugh at LaFountaine's lame joke. He looked at the monument again and said, "I wonder if it was . . . I don't know, *cleaner* back in his day or if they pulled the same kind of stuff we do."

"It was no different," LaFountaine said. "You know they had some bastards just like us back then, guys that did things they didn't ever want included in the history books. But if those guys hadn't done those things, this country wouldn't be what it is today."

Mahoney wasn't so sure about that.

Chapter 55

———◆———

Angela got off the phone and turned to face DeMarco. "There's a team coming out here from Langley. For real, this time. They'll be here this afternoon and they'll take over for us."

"What's going to happen to Kharazi?"

"I can't tell you. But I can tell you that Mahoney knows what we're doing and he can live with it."

DeMarco felt like saying there were a lot of things John Mahoney could live with that he couldn't, but he didn't see the point. Mahoney would tell him later about whatever agreement he had reached with LaFountaine.

"And what about us?" he said.

She looked at him for a long time before she answered. "I don't know. I'm going to divorce Brad; that's long overdue. Then I'm going to sit down and think about you and me. I like you. I like being with you. But I'm not sure you're going to be able to accept what I do. LaFountaine's going to give me the job he promised, and I'm going to stay at Langley, but later on, if they offer me an overseas posting, I'm going to take it. Can you live with that?"

DeMarco didn't say anything for a moment, then he smiled.

"Why don't we cross that bridge when we come to it."

Author's Note

It is a fact that three journalists, including Judith Miller of the *New York Times,* were jailed for contempt in the Valerie Plame leak case, just as Sandra Whitmore was jailed for contempt in *House Justice.* However, I don't actually know if press shield laws have been revised since 2003 to provide additional legal protection for journalists attempting to protect the identity of their sources. A recent article I read indicated that the laws are pretty much the same as they were in 2003.

The idea for Marty Taylor's company came from a short article I saw on the Internet about a big defense contractor who makes missiles and missile-guidance systems entering into a research agreement with a small company that makes computer-gaming peripherals like wireless mouses (or is that *mice?*).

There is no Glendon Hills Golf Course in Myrtle Beach, South Carolina. The golf course described in *House Justice* is a combination of a place where I play—badly—in Washington and a golf course I played on in Myrtle Beach.

While a .500 S&W Magnum will penetrate some bulletproof glass, I'm sure it will not penetrate all bulletproof glass. I just liked the idea of Mikhail having a great big handgun, and when I saw a picture of the .500 S&W and read that some suicidal fools actually buy these pistols for hunting bear, I said: *That's the one.*

There was an article in the *Washington Post* in 2005 saying there were over thirty-four thousand registered lobbyists in D.C. I have no idea if the article is accurate or if there are that many lobbyists there today. I do know that whatever the number is, it's a whopping big number.

I also know many Iranians today are struggling to improve democracy and human rights in that country and they do not support terrorism and would never condone torturing people, spies, or otherwise, as I have depicted in *House Justice*.

Lastly, history books be damned, I'm sure John Paul Jones never said, "*I have not yet begun to fight.*" I'm convinced it was something akin to "kiss my ass" as Jake LaFountaine says in the book.

Mike Lawson